ALTERNATE
HISTORY

What are you doing? Enlisting? Or going on a date?

Well-raised boy that he is, Strand walks her the rest of the way home, but the only conversation takes place between voices in Rio's own head. She has just upended her entire life based on a diner conversation with her best friend and an awkward exchange with a boy she barely knows.

Now, right *now*, here at her front door where she must say good evening, is the time to take it all back.

But I do want to go to a movie with him. I do want to.

"Good night, Strand."

"I'll come by at seven, if that's all right with you."

"That would be perfect."

Rio rushes inside, closes the door behind her, and leans against it.

She is going on a date.

And also, going to war.

ALSO BY MICHAEL GRANT

Gone

Hunger

Lies

Plague

Fear

Light

Messenger of Fear

The Snake: A Messenger of Fear Story

The Tattooed Heart: A Messenger of Fear Novel

Silver Stars

FRONT LINES

MICHAEL GRANT

KATHERINE TEGEN BOOKS
An Imprint of HarperCollins Publishers

Library of Congress Control Number: 2015939082
ISBN 978-0-06-234216-4

Typography by Joel Tippie
16 17 18 19 20 PC/LSCH 10 9 8 7 6 5 4 3 2 1
❖
First paperback edition, 2017

I dedicate this book to the magnificent
Kurdish women soldiers of Kobani.
How could I not?

And to my equally magnificent
if slightly less deadly wife,
Katherine (K.A.) Applegate,
our son, Jake, and daughter, Julia.

1942

War rages in Europe, China, Southeast Asia, and Northern Africa. Millions have died. Much of London has been bombed to rubble. In the Atlantic, German submarines sink more than a thousand ships. The western Soviet Union has been conquered by the German army, the Wehrmacht, and in their wake come the SS death squads. Throughout conquered Europe the Nazis have begun the systematic extermination that will come to be known as the Holocaust. And in Amsterdam, on her thirteenth birthday, a girl named Anne Frank receives a diary.

Never in human history has a more terrible evil arisen to test the courage of good people. The fate of the world rests on a knife's edge.

Among the great nations only the United States has stayed out of the fight. But in the dying days of 1941, Germany's ally Japan attacks Pearl Harbor and brings America into the war.

Adolf Hitler is said to be dismissive of the Americans as a self-indulgent, mongrelized people unwilling and unable to fight.

He is mistaken.

FLASH: "In a surprise ruling with major ramifications, the United States Supreme Court handed down a decision in the case of Becker vs. Minneapolis Draft Board for Josiah Becker, who had sued claiming the recently passed Selective Training and Service Act unfairly singles out males. The decision extends the draft to all US citizens age eighteen or older regardless of gender."
—United Press International—Washington, DC, January 13, 1940

"We interrupt this broadcast to take you to the NBC news room. From the NBC news room in New York: President Roosevelt said in a statement today that the Japanese have attacked Pearl Harbor, Hawaii, from the air."
—NBC Radio News, December 7, 1941

"Lastly, if you will forgive me for saying it, to me the best tidings of all is that the United States, united as never before, have drawn the sword for freedom and cast away the scabbard."

—British Prime Minister Winston Churchill to the US Congress, December 26, 1941

Prologue

107TH EVAC HOSPITAL, WÜRZBURG, GERMANY—APRIL 1945

I'm not going to tell you my name, not right away.

I'm in this story, and you'll see plenty of me. But I don't want to tell you this story in a way that makes it about me. I don't expect you'll understand that, Gentle Reader, so let me try to explain it like this: I'm not the hero of this tale; I'm just alive to tell it.

As I type this I'm sitting here safe in this hospital waiting on the official announcement that we have won this war. I'm here alongside a bunch of other women and girls hurt as bad or worse than me, some a hell of a lot worse. All around me are women with stumps of arms or legs wrapped up tight in white bandages or casts; women with half their bodies covered in gauze; women who can't hear or can't see or who are glad they can't see so they don't have to look at themselves in a mirror. Some are on their cots, some are in wheelchairs, some are just standing, staring out of the tall, dirty windows. We play cards sometimes. We listen to the radio. We talk about home, about boys and husbands.

We wait.

It's funny that they keep the men and women separate here, because we sure weren't separate up on the front line. But they're just across the hall now, the guys. The people running this place tell us we aren't to fraternize, but we are all of us done taking orders. So we stumble or shuffle or roll ourselves over there after evening chow because they've got a piano and some of the boys can play and some of the girls can sing. No smoking, no drinking, no fraternizing with the opposite sex, those are the rules. So naturally we smoke, drink, and fraternize most evenings.

At night we cry sometimes, and if you think that just applies to the females then you have never been in combat, because everyone cries sooner or later. Everyone cries.

We are the first generation of female soldiers in the American army. Lucky us.

My sisters-in-arms are still out there right now, flushing out the last German strongholds, and more of us will die. This war isn't over yet, but my part of it is.

Anyway, I've had this feeling nagging at me, this feeling that once they declare the end of the war, all my memories of it will start to leak away, to fade and become lost. Will you understand, Gentle Reader, if I tell you that this is something I both long for and dread?

There's a typewriter here, and I've taught myself to be pretty quick on it. There isn't much else to do, and I want to get it all down on paper before the end.

The snap of the keys striking the page soothes me. Is that because the sounds are something like the noise of gunfire? That'd be something, wouldn't it? For the rest of my life am I going to hear a typewriter and be back on some beach or in some freezing hole?

Well, let's not get too deep. How about I just tell the story?

I'm going to be just as honest as I can about each of the people in it. I know these women and men. I sat many a long hour in troop ships and foxholes and on leave drinking beer and swapping stories. There isn't much about them I don't know, and what I don't know, well, I'll make up. But it'll be as close to true as any war story can be.

I'm in a fever to tell it all, right now before it fades, before I start to rewrite the truth and make it more acceptable to myself and you. See, Gentle Reader, I know the rules of war stories. I know I'm supposed to present a tale of patriotism, of high-minded motives and brave deeds, hardships endured with a stiff upper lip and a wry grin. I'm supposed to tell you about the brotherhood—and now sisterhood—of soldiers. But there's one thing I cannot do as I pound these typewriter keys, and that is lie.

My body is damaged, my mind is too full, my soul too raw. The things that I saw and did are too real. If you're looking for the kind of story that will puff you up with an easy reflected pride, I am not your girl. If as you read this you come to admire these soldiers, I want it to be because you know them with all their weaknesses as well as their strengths.

You may imagine that any war story must be all about righteous hatred of the enemy. And yes, you'll hear some of that. I was at the camps. I was there. I saw. So, hate? Sure, I'll show you some hate.

There will be hate.

But I suspect over time the hate will fade, and it will be the love that lingers: the love of the woman or man standing next to you in a hole; the desperate love of a home that seems farther away with each squeeze of the trigger; the fragile love for the person you hope—or hoped—to spend the rest of your life with.

A moment ago I reached the end of a page and ripped it from the machine, and in trying to insert the next sheet I made a mess of it. My fingers shook a little. I feel jacked up, high and wild, a twanging nerve, a guitar string tightened and tightened until it's got to break, till you kind of wish it would just break. I'm sweating, and it isn't hot. But as long as I keep hitting these keys, as long as I don't stop, maybe that will all pass. I don't know.

We are the first generation of young American women to fight in a great world war. "Warrior Women" is what the newspapers like to say. But when it all began three years ago, we were not any kind of women; we were girls mostly. And with the wry mockery that comes so easily to men and women at war, we made up our own headline and called ourselves not warrior women but soldier girls.

As I sit here pounding feverishly on these keys, I feel as if I am all of them, every soldier girl who carried a rifle, dug a hole, slogged through mud, steamed or froze, prayed or cursed, raged or feared, ran away or ran toward.

I am Rio Richlin. I am Frangie Marr. I am Rainy Schulterman and Jenou Castain and Cat Preeling. As long as I'm pounding these keys I'm all of them.

This is the story of what happened to a few of us who ended up on the front lines of the greatest war in human history.

PART I

VOLUNTEERS
AND DRAFTEES

1

RIO RICHLIN—GEDWELL FALLS, CALIFORNIA, USA

1942.

Remember 1942? It's been a long three and a half years since then, hasn't it? In 1942 the Japs were unchecked, rampaging freely across Asia. The Germans had taken all of Europe and some of Africa before running into trouble in the Soviet Union. Our British allies had been hit hard, very hard.

And we Americans?

Well, we were just getting into it. Still with plenty of time to worry about the little things . . .

"Rio Richlin, stay out of the sugar. Heavens, girl, the ration for the family is thirty-two ounces a week, and I'm saving for your sister's birthday cake."

"I just used a teaspoonful for my coffee, Mother."

"Yes, well, a teaspoon here, a teaspoon there, it adds up. Who knows what Rachel is getting to eat?" Mrs.

Richlin says. She has deep and dark suspicions when it comes to navy rations.

Rio is sixteen and pretty; not a beauty, but pretty enough. Tall for a girl, and with the strong shoulders and calloused hands of a farmer's daughter. *Rangy*, that's one word. If she'd been a boy, she'd have played ball and you'd expect her to be able to throw from center field to home without much trouble.

Her complexion is cream in the mild Northern California winter and light-brown sugar during the long days of summer, with faint freckles and brown hair pulled back into a practical ponytail.

"I guess the navy is feeding her; wouldn't make much sense to starve your own sailors," Rio points out.

"Well, I don't suppose her captain is making her a nineteenth birthday cake. Do you?"

Mrs. Richlin emphasizes what she sees as her conclusive statement by taking the ration book with its multicolored stamps and fanning it out on the table in front of Rio. "You see the situation. Thank goodness for the cows. I trade my milk to Emily Smith for her coffee ration, otherwise your father and you would have nothing to drink."

"There's always beer." This from Rio's father, Tam, who rushes through the kitchen on his way to the feed store he owns. "But not for you, young lady," he adds quickly, pointing at Rio then winking.

It's a spacious kitchen with green-painted oak cupboards on most of one wall, a battered and well-used white-enameled stove and oven, a long porcelain sink, and a deeper tin sink beside it. There's a bare wood counter so long-used that dips are worn into the edge where three generations of Richlin women have kneaded bread dough and chopped carrots and parsnips and sliced tomatoes fresh from the garden.

In the center of the room stands a round table—antique, quarter-sawn oak—surrounded by five chairs, only two of which match and all of which squeak and complain when used.

The house is old, having passed down from her father's great-grandfather, the Richlin who settled in Gedwell Falls after coming two thousand miles in an ox-drawn wagon. Rio has never doubted that she will spend the rest of her youth in this place, going to school, doing her chores, and spending time with her best friend, Jenou.

She's also never doubted that she'll marry, have children, and keep house. When they discuss these matters, as they often do, Jenou always emphasizes to Rio the importance of marrying someone prosperous. "Money and looks, Rio," she always says. "Money and looks."

"What about kindness, generosity of spirit, and a sense of humor?"

To which Jenou invariably responds with a despairing shake of her head and a slow repetition. "Money and looks. In that order."

Rio assumes, has always assumed, that she will be like her mother, who is like her grandmother. For the most part Rio accepts that. But there is a small voice in her mind and heart that senses something off about it all. Not bad, just off. Like she's trying on an outfit that will never fit, and isn't her color.

This dissatisfaction is vague, unformed, but real. The problem is, being dissatisfied does not mean she has any better goal. Or any goal at all, really, except of course to get through her final year of high school with grades that don't disgrace her and the family.

Rio sweeps her math work sheet into her brown leather book bag, slings it over her shoulder, kisses her mother on the cheek, and follows her father toward the front door.

Her father is stopped there, framed in the doorway against the early sunlight of the street beyond. He's a tall man with a face carved to leanness by the hard years of the Great Depression, when he kept a roof over his family's heads by taking on any work he could find, often going straight from his shop to mucking out cesspools or painting barns.

In the teasing voice that is their common currency, Rio says, "Come on, Dad, some of us have places to . . ."

Rio focuses past him and sees a uniformed telegram delivery boy.

Rio's heart misses two beats. Her steps falter. She tries to swallow and can't, tries to breathe but there's a weight pressing down on her chest. She moves closer. Her father notices her and says, "It's probably nothing."

"Is this the Richlin residence?" the delivery boy asks. He mispronounces it with a soft "ch" instead of the correct "ck" sound.

He should be in school, that boy. He can't be much older than twelve. Maybe this is an early delivery before heading off to school. Maybe . . .

Tam Richlin takes the envelope. It's buff-colored, thin paper. He hesitates, turning the envelope as if he can't find the right way around. He licks his lips, and Rio's unease deepens.

"What is it?" Her voice wobbles.

"Thank you," Mr. Richlin says. The delivery boy touches the brim of his cap and speeds back to his bicycle, relief showing in the quickness of his step.

"What is it?" Rio asks again.

He licks his lips again, takes a deep breath. Suddenly urgent, he tears the envelope open and draws out the sheet. He stares at it. Just that, just stares, and Rio knows.

After a terrible long silence in which the world stops turning and the birds stop singing and the breeze does not blow, she reaches for it and takes it from his nerveless fingers. The words are all in capital letters.

THE NAVY DEPARTMENT DEEPLY REGRETS TO INFORM YOU THAT YOUR DAUGHTER RACHEL RICHLIN . . .

Rio makes a small, whimpering sound. She looks at her father. He sags against the door jamb, head bowed. She sees him in profile only, a dark outline of a man looking at nothing.

. . . YOUR DAUGHTER RACHEL RICHLIN WAS KILLED IN ACTION IN THE PERFORMANCE OF HER DUTY AND IN THE SERVICE OF HER COUNTRY.

"Tam? Rio?"

Rio turns guilty eyes already glittering wet to her mother. Her mother sees the telegram and the expression on her husband's face and the way he slumps there like every ounce of strength is gone from him. She falls to her knees, falls like she's been shot, like the muscles in her legs have just quit all at once.

"No, it's . . . ," she says. "No, it's, no. No. No. No, no, no, no. Not my baby, not my baby, not my baby, please no,

8

please no." It starts off denial, ends up pleading.

Rio runs to her mother, kneels beside her, puts her arms around her mother's shoulders—though what she wants is for her mother to comfort her, tell her that it's a joke or a mistake or a simple impossibility. Her mother is shaking. Saying *No, no, not my baby, please, please*, over and over again, as if saying it will make it true, as if it's a magic spell to ward off the wave of pain coming her way.

Tam Richlin leans there with head bowed and says nothing. His fists clench then relax as if he simply lacks the strength to go on. But he says nothing. Nothing, no sound, as his wife howls in plain misery, howls into the hollow of her surviving daughter's neck.

Tam Richlin says, "I best go open the shop." And with that he is gone.

Rio moves her mother to the sofa, literally physically having to take her mother's heaving shoulders and lift. Rio goes to the kitchen to make tea, because isn't that what people do at moments like this? Don't they make tea? As the water heats, she sets out the good silver tea service, focusing for as long as she can on the placement of the elements: the pot, the sugar bowl, the little, slightly mismatched cream pitcher, all of it clattering because her fingers are clumsy. It feels right, somehow, using the good silver, the silver that only comes out for Christmas, baptisms, rare occasions when some important person

9

comes calling, and when sisters die. The person you used to gossip with, quarrel with, share clothing with, learn from. . . . The person you wanted to be like when you grew up. This day could not be marked with tea from a chipped old china teapot.

"I just see her in that cold, gray water," Millie Richlin says. Tears spill from her eyes, and she makes no attempt to wipe them away. "I just want to . . ." Her arms reach for what is no longer there and close around air. "But she's with Jesus now. She's in the loving arms of Jesus."

Where was Jesus when the Japanese bombs fell straight and true?

Rio is not ready for the comfort of religion. Anger fills her. "Dirty Japs," she mutters. "Rotten, dirty Japs. Rachel wasn't even on a battleship, it was a . . ." She realizes she doesn't know what kind of ship Rachel was on; the censors forbade that kind of information. All she knows is that Rachel reassured her she was in no danger. *I'm just on a big old tub no one would waste a torpedo on.* "Dirty Japs. Dirty Japs, why did they start this war? Why did . . ."

"She was always so . . ."

"I'd kill them myself if I could, the dirty . . ."

". . . good with the chores and so helpful, and so . . ."

". . . Japs. Them and the Krauts both."

". . . cheerful. She must have . . ." She grabbed Rio's

arm. "Why did she go? Why did she enlist?"

"Because she's brave," Rio snaps. Now the tears come fast. "She's brave, and she wants to do her part." She will not use past tense for her sister. Rachel is brave, not was. Is.

Her mother looks at her in alarm. "No, Rio, no."

"Rachel did her part, and now she's . . ."

Not that word. Not yet.

"I sit here with my stupid algebra homework." Rio kicks at the leg of the coffee table. The tea set rattles.

"You stop that right now, Rio. I've lost . . . I won't . . . I couldn't stand it. I would lose my mind. And your father . . ." Desperation in that voice, hopelessness, fear, and it all feeds Rio's anger.

Rio glances at the door through which her father disappeared. No one has closed it. The street outside is cruelly bright, a gorgeous Northern California morning with palms riding high and lavender flowers threatening to cover the sidewalk.

Rio's father will have reached the feed store by now. He will have unlocked the door and turned the Closed sign around to Open. Being a man, that's what he's doing, being a man who does not cry because men do not cry. Crying is reserved for women.

Rio's gaze goes to the small vertical window beside the door where the service flag hangs, a red-and-white rectangle with a single blue star sewn onto the side facing the street. There are those flags all up and down the block. All over Gedwell Falls. All over California, and all over America. They show that the family has a member in service. Some houses bear flags with two or three such stars.

At the beginning of the war there were only blue stars, and it was an honor, a matter of pride, but now in many towns around the country some of those blue stars are being removed and replaced by gold ones.

A gold star hanging in your window means a family member has made the ultimate sacrifice. That's the phrase, the approved phrase, *ultimate sacrifice*. Rachel's gold star will be the first in Gedwell Falls.

Rio wonders how it is done. Who switches the blue star for gold? Does the government send you a new flag? How very kind of them. Will her mother have to do the sewing herself? Will she have to go to the sewing store to get the star herself, God forbid, to get the right color thread and to ask the clerk . . .

If Rio is drafted the flag will bear a gold star and a blue.

Don't think of how scared Rachel must have been. Don't think of the water smothering her as . . .

"I'm not of legal age yet," Rio says, placating her mother with a touch on her arm. "I won't be eighteen for more than a year."

But her mother is no longer listening. She has withdrawn into silence. Rio sits with her in that silence until, after a few more hours, the news spreads and friends and relatives begin to arrive with covered dishes and condolences.

The sad and somber rituals of war have arrived in Gedwell Falls.

2

RIO RICHLIN—GEDWELL FALLS, CALIFORNIA, USA

"This town is so boring. So, so, so boring." Jenou Castain lolls her head back and forth with each "so" before dropping forward on the "boring." This has the effect of causing her voluminous blond hair to sway very attractively and earns her appreciative looks from the booth full of boys at the far end of the diner. A fact that Jenou is, of course, quite aware of.

"You always say that," Rio points out. She is vaguely annoyed at Jenou for pulling the hair routine. Rio has been sneaking peeks at a boy named Strand Braxton, who has been glancing back from time to time. Once they even make eye contact, which causes both to blush and quickly focus attention elsewhere. But Rio has been hoping for a second such accidental meeting of ever-so-casual glances, and Jenou, forever playing the blond seductress, has diverted Strand's attention.

"I always say it because it's always true. Let me ask you something, Rio . . . and don't bother making eyes at

Strand, I heard he's taking Hillary to the dance. Is that a shocked look? Rio, if you're going to suddenly discover the human male you're going to need to also discover gossip. Now, where was I?"

Hillary? And Strand?

"You were telling me how boring everything is," Rio says. "Which is kind of boring by itself, you know? Saying the same thing over and over."

"No, I remember." Jenou snaps her fingers. "I was going to ask you if there is a single square foot of this town that you don't know by heart."

The waitress appears at that point, and Jenou says, "I'll have a cheeseburger."

"Not today you won't," the waitress said. "No cheese."

"No cheese?"

"Dontcha know there's a war on?" the waitress asks wearily. "Deliveries are all fouled up." She's in a faded pink uniform and a food-stained apron and the kind of white shoes that nurses wear.

Jenou, exasperated, smacks the table with her palm. "That does it, now the war is getting serious." Then she winces and says, "Oh, honey. Sorry. Sometimes my mouth . . ." She shrugs.

"Hey, it's okay," Rio says.

The waitress looks quizzical, and Jenou explains, "Her sister."

"Oh, I heard about that," the waitress says, losing the

wise-guy attitude. "Condolences, sweetie. She's in a better place. Dirty Japs."

I'm that girl now. The one everyone has to pity, Rio thinks. It's been weeks since Rachel's death, but the Richlin home is still the only one with a gold star hanging in the window. Life goes on for everyone, almost as if there was no war, until they notice Rio. Then comes the mask of pity, the low voices of sympathy, the threats, the tough talk.

Rio wants to forget it too, the way they all do with such apparent ease. She wants to be normal for a while, to gossip and tease and laugh.

"Hamburger," Rio says, trying to avoid the tears that have stalked her since the coming of the telegram, coming suddenly without warning, prompted by some familiar sight, some gold-hued memory. She wants to shoot the breeze with Jenou and flirt with Strand and not have death and tragedy and her father's stony silence and her mother's drawn and defeated face hanging over it all.

"Two hamburgers and two milk shakes," Jenou says. "What flavors?"

"Well, we have vanilla, and then we have vanilla."

"I see: no chocolate because there's a war on." Jenou reaches across the table and pats Rio's hand.

They sit in comfortable silence until the hamburgers come. It doesn't take long; the patties aren't much thicker than a sheet of construction paper and cook up quickly on the long steel grill behind the counter.

They take a few bites, and Rio says, "I found a journal she kept. Rachel, I mean. Up in her room, hidden under her mattress. I was in there to . . ." She shakes her head to ward off the tears and takes a big bite of burger, swallowing it past the lump in her throat.

Breathe. Breathe. Okay.

"I was in there to snoop," Rio admits. "Anyway, I found her old journal. I wondered if maybe she'd kept one like it on the ship."

Jenou nods cautiously.

"If she was a soldier, maybe we'd get her things, you know? What they call her effects. But it's all on the bottom of the Pacific, I guess, and we won't ever know."

"I guess not," Jenou says. "What did she write about?"

Rio shrugs. "I don't know. I haven't had the . . . I haven't read it. Her secret crushes, I guess. But if I read it . . . I mean, what if she just complains about her annoying little sister?" She tries to force a smile, and it doesn't quite work.

"You know you don't have to be funny and lighthearted with me."

"It's not for you, Jenou. I heard someone say, I don't know who, some wise man, or some snake oil salesman, whoever, anyway . . . I heard somewhere that you make a choice in life between tragedy and comedy."

"It's a choice?"

"Well, you can't choose what happens. You can't even really choose how you're going to feel about it, I guess. But you can choose how to cope with it."

Jenou nods her head. "You're becoming deep, Rio."

"Am I?"

"Very deep."

Rio raises a skeptical eyebrow. "It just seems that way because I've always been so shallow."

"Nonsense. I'm the shallow one. I insist that I am more shallow than you."

"Rachel was not shallow. She was always different, not like me. Rachel had ambition and goals and . . . ideas." She shrugs again. "She was so definite. Do you know what I mean? I feel . . . I mean, I never had to think about—"

She's interrupted by the loud crash of a dropped glass behind the counter. Strand looks up at the sound, sees Rio, and smiles.

"Never had to think about what?" Jenou prompts.

"Oh, I don't know. About the future. Life. You know. I mean, who am I, anyway? I'm just some silly girl. I was Rachel's little sister, and your less-pretty friend. But—"

"You are not less pretty," Jenou says, reaching over to pat her hand. "You're just less sexy." She whispers the last word, earning one of Rio's slow-build grins, which in turn causes Jenou to giggle, which causes the boys to turn around, their eyes and bodies all eagerness and energy.

"See? That was a sexy giggle," Jenou says. "Shall I teach it to you?"

Rio throws a small french fry at Jenou.

Thank God for Jenou.

"I guess if I was ever to enlist it would be in the army," Jenou says. There's a false note to her nonchalance that pricks Rio's interest.

"You enlist? They'll have to draft you, Jen, and then hunt you down with a net."

Jenou does not immediately laugh. Rio sets down her burger and leans forward. "Jen?"

"Did I mention that this town is really boring?"

"Jenou Castain, what are you thinking?"

"Well, everyone knows sooner or later this war goes to France, which means Paris. Haven't you always wanted to see Paris? City of lights? City of love? City of lovers? City of my rich and handsome future husband? You know, I come from French stock."

"Yes, you've mentioned it a hundred times, but, Jen, are you serious?" Jenou has always craved travel, especially to romantic France. She has always—well, since age twelve anyway—insisted on the French pronunciation of her name. Not a solid American *j* sound like *jump*, but a soft *zh*. Zhenou. Or Zhen for short. Jenou.

Jenou looks up from her burger with the slyly defiant expression Rio has seen on many occasions, most often occasions that end with Jenou on the wrong end of a stern lecture from parents or from the pastor or even, on one occasion, from the chief of police.

"You haven't thought of it?" Jenou asks.

"Me? I've got months before I'm of legal age and—"

"Oh, do you really think you couldn't get around that?" Jenou puts on her most worldly-wise face. "Where there's a will there's an eraser and a typewriter. Easiest thing in the world."

"My mother would lock me in the barn with her cows." Rio makes a joke of it, forcing an unsteady laugh. But she doesn't shut the conversation down. She feels like a trout must feel after realizing there's a hook inside that tasty worm.

But then Strand looks over at her, and it's more than an arguably accidental glance this time—it's a *look*. Which Rio returns as boldly as she is able.

"I guess she would," Jenou allows. "But your little cutie-pie Strand?"

"He's not my cutie-pie!"

"*He* got his notice. He ships out next week."

"What?"

"Drafted. As in, *Greetings: You are hereby ordered for induction into the Armed Forces of the United States.*"

Strand suddenly looks different in light of this development. He's a good-looking boy, a serious boy with dark hair and skin only lightly afflicted by adolescent pimples. Now he looks at once younger and older. Too young at barely eighteen, and yet old enough legally. Too old for school books, too young for a rifle and a helmet.

She pictures him in an olive drab or khaki uniform. She imagines polished brass buttons and a hat with the brim riding low over his eyes. Yes, he would look pretty sharp in that uniform. He has the shoulders for it, and the narrow waist. But Jenou is still talking, so Rio has to break off contemplation of just what else Strand would look good in.

"If you enlist, they say you get to choose what you do. You know, like are you a typist in an office somewhere, or are you getting shot at. If you wait to get drafted, it's straight to the front with *bang-bang* and *boom-boom*. You know I can't stand loud noises."

Rio has heard this before, everyone has, it's common knowledge, though Rio's father bitterly dismisses it as nonsense. "I was in the last war," he said. "Believe me, the army sends you wherever they want you, and if you think you're arguing about it, then you don't know the army."

"I guess if I was to be drafted, I'd *want* to go to the front," Rio says. She wants to sound bold, to match Jenou and Strand, and Rachel too. Is Jenou serious? Surely not.

But Strand doesn't have the option of being unserious, does he? Not if he's gotten his notice.

"What? Oh, you think you'd kill some Jap for what he did to Rachel?" Jenou nods knowingly and pops a fry into her mouth.

"Maybe," Rio says, defiant. But it troubles her to think that revenge would be her motivation. It isn't really true either. Sure, she would like to find a way to somehow deal with her sister's death, but she really has no desire to kill anyone, not even a filthy, cowardly Jap.

No, if she were drafted then she'd want to do her part. That's it: a desire to do her part.

Her *part*.

Her part.

The entire conversation is now making Rio uneasy. It feels almost as if Jenou is tempting her. It wouldn't be the first time, and now she's remembering that time at the gravel quarry, she and Jenou walking along the edge high above eerily green water of uncertain depth. Jenou had jokingly suggested jumping, and Rio had been seized by a sudden desire to do it. She hadn't, but for a few seconds she had wanted to.

It bothered her at the time; it bothers her now as she recalls the emotion, that "what the heck?" feeling. A sense of reckless liberation, of breaking away. The freedom of foolishness. Had Jenou jumped in herself, Rio would have followed.

Now Jenou is considering jumping. And Rio feels the pull again.

Everyone would be amazed.

Who? Rio? Rio Richlin enlisted? Why, I never!

"It seems to me," Rio says, not really even talking to Jenou anymore, "it seems to me that this being the first war where they let girls fight, we ought to make a good account of ourselves."

Rio enjoys the way Jenou's exquisitely shaped eyebrows rise.

"They *let* us fight? Let? Funny how I never even knew I was deprived, not going off to war."

Rio nods slightly, discreetly, to indicate Strand, who is behind Jenou but who Jenou can still somehow see with that all-around, three-hundred-sixty-degree boy-awareness Jenou possesses. "Why should he maybe get hurt and not me?"

Jenou shrugs. "It's how it's always been, up until now. But you don't have to sell me, honey. I can see all the advantages in being far from home and surrounded by healthy young males. That's why I'm enlisting."

It's Jenou's first definite statement, and even though she's been talking about it for the last five minutes, Rio is still caught off guard. She hadn't quite believed it.

Jenou really is jumping. Rio sees it in her eyes: defiance,

anxiety, a little sadness. But excitement as well.

It's that hint of excitement that tempts Rio.

"Look," Jenou says, spreading her fingers palm-down on the table and leaning in. "First of all, they're not going to send women to the front lines to get involved in all of that. They'll have us typing forms, answering telephones, and driving trucks. I figure the war's on for another six months or a year at most. So I spend the first part of it checking out the available stock of masculine animals, and the last part closing the deal."

Rio shakes her head in mock despair. "For you even a war is just another excuse for being boy crazy."

"What can I say, honey? I'm an optimist."

And you can't stand this town, can you, Jen? And neither can I, without Rachel and without you.

Rio and Jenou pay and leave and walk together as far as the town square. It's spring, and the day lingers. The town square is a leafy, green space with a mix of elm trees and the occasional palm tree. This is Northern California, land of sunshine plus quite a bit of fog and just enough rain to keep the grape vines heavy with fruit.

The square is the heart of Gedwell Falls. Here are the newsstand, the telegraph office, the five-and-ten-cent store, the barber shop, a hat store, the fabric store, and one of the two full-service grocery stores. Cars and trucks, ranging from newish '38 models to dusty old pickup trucks dating to back before the Depression, are parked angled-in in front of the businesses.

At one corner of the square is a raised, circular covered bandstand. In spring and summer an oompah-pah band sometimes plays marches and classics for folks in folding chairs set up on the grass. It's the venue for beauty contests, the awarding of prizes in flower shows, and speeches by campaigning politicians.

Rio leaves Jenou and heads across the square alone. A warm wind blows across her neck. She's wearing a pink sweater and a faded-blue frock that frets a little in the chilly breeze.

There comes the sound of footsteps behind her. She glances back and sees Strand Braxton gaining on her. He looks very focused, and Rio wonders where he's rushing to.

It seems he's rushing to catch up to her since he slows upon seeing that he's been noticed. Then, as if forcing himself to go on, he gains speed again, looking very determined, even grim. Rio stops and waits, mystified. Strand is somewhat out of breath when he reaches Rio, who now waits at the foot of the bandstand steps and tries very hard to appear nonchalant. She leans casually against a railing that's too low to lean casually against.

The sun is setting, orange fingers reaching through the clouds, and as she turns to face him, Strand Braxton is silhouetted against that sunset. It is such an absurdly cinematic moment that Rio almost laughs. But her appreciation of the perfectly artistic framing is undercut by a rush of anxiety.

I have nothing clever to say to him.

"Hello there, Rio," Strand says.

"Hello, Strand."

With that out of the way they stare awkwardly at each other for a few moments until the tension becomes too great for Strand and he finally says, "So, I guess you know I got called up. Oh, and I never said how sorry I am about . . . you know."

"About Rachel."

"Precisely," he says, and digs his hands into his pockets.

"Thank you."

A new silence threatens, and already Strand looks slightly panicky.

Taking pity, Rio says, "Are you worried? About going away, I mean?"

"Worried?" He makes an incredulous face, like nothing could be further from his thinking. But then he rethinks his reaction. He blinks, looks down at the ground, and when he raises his face again a wry look has replaced the phony nonchalance. "I suppose I am. Worried, I mean, a little, anyway. They say most fellows from Gedwell Falls get sent somewhere south to train, and I've never been fifty miles from this spot."

"Maybe I'll see you there," she says, striving for a nonchalant tone of her own.

That makes him draw back in confusion. "Pardon me?"

"I'm enlisting," Rio says.

What?

What?

Why did I say that?

She is on the point of laughing and saying it was all a joke. But she can't. She doesn't really want to take it back.

"But . . . why?"

"I guess because this is the biggest thing that will ever happen in my life," Rio says, the words coming just ahead of the thoughts. "Any of our lifetimes. I guess . . . I guess I just want to do my part."

There's a rushing sound in her head and a panic clutch in her throat as she realizes the enormity of what she's just committed herself to.

Strand is talking, but she hasn't heard him. "I'm sorry, Strand, what did you say?"

Strand smiles sheepishly. "I said, well, that throws everything out."

"What does it throw out?"

They are physically closer without either having consciously decided to be. She has to tilt her head just a little to make eye contact; she's tall, but he still has a few inches on her. Strand has lashes any girl would die for. She notices that, notices the fineness of his nose, focuses on random details as her heart beats fast for him, and faster still from panic.

Why did I do that?

"It throws out . . . Well, here's the thing. I've been talking to some of the guys who are getting called up or enlisting, and almost all of them say they'll write home to some girl. But I don't really have a girl to write to."

"You won't be writing to Hillary?"

"Hillary?" A confused frown. "Her? No, she and I . . . I mean, we had one date. But she's seeing someone else. And anyway, we were always just friends."

So much for Jenou's gossip.

"I see." What she saw was a boy even more handsome up close than at a distance, which she thinks must be unusual—didn't most people look better from a distance? And didn't most people think about enlisting in a war rather than just blurting it out like a ninny?

He's panicked her, that's what it is. He and Jenou. The fear of being left behind. Nonsense, all of it—a whirl of motivations, none of which can be pulled into the light of day and examined in any reasonable way as long as she's looking at the line of his chin, and the sculpted look of his lips, and just the general large and strong and yet gentle feeling of . . .

Take it back, Rio. You have to take it back.

Is he seeing her up close now and noticing her nose is too small? She fights the urge to touch her dark hair, which is probably sticking up in some unattractive way. Why didn't she check her hair in the bathroom mirror of the diner?

She feels she might faint. It's all too much, way, way too fast. She's confused, her thoughts zooming like rockets, leaving random trails of sparks and smoke and . . .

"So, anyway," Strand goes on, struggling with every word, "I know we don't really know each other all that well. But I was wondering whether you might go see a movie with me tomorrow night. Then I could write to you when I'm away. But now if you're going away as well, so . . ." He looks exhausted suddenly, as if he's used up the last of his courage getting the conversation this far.

"I imagine soldiers can write to each other," Rio says, sounding chirpy and false to herself. "I mean, wherever you are, and wherever I am, we could still write letters back and forth. Couldn't we?"

What are you doing? Enlisting? Or going on a date?

But she can hear Jenou's voice in her head, and that voice says, "Oh come on now, honey; you know exactly what you're doing."

Rio's suggestion gives Strand an infusion of energy,

perhaps a little too much energy, as he practically shouts, "Yes! Yes, we could, couldn't we? After all, it's not as if you'll be off in the trenches somewhere. They'll keep the girls here in the States. Or perhaps send some to England, but in any case, you'll be able to write." He claps his hands, then seems surprised by those very hands, stares at them for a second in confusion, sticks them into his pockets, and goes on. "We could compare notes on . . . on army life. Of course we could. Why not?"

"And it would make sense for us to know each other a little better before embarking on this correspondence," Rio says.

Embarking on this correspondence?

That sends his eyebrows up.

"Yes, that was an interesting phrase," Rio admits rue-fully. "I meant, a movie, like you said, we could go to a movie."

"Yes! That's it, of course, because I did mention a movie, didn't I? Tomorrow night. That's what you meant, wasn't it?"

"Of course!" she says, and it comes out as a squeak.

Well-raised boy that he is, Strand walks her the rest of the way home, but the only conversation takes place between voices in Rio's own head. She has just upended her entire life based on a diner conversation with her best friend and an awkward exchange with a boy she barely knows.

Now, right *now*, here at her front door where she must say good evening, is the time to take it all back.

But I do want to go to a movie with him. I do want to.

"Good night, Strand."

"I'll come by at seven, if that's all right with you."

"That would be perfect."

Rio rushes inside, closes the door behind her, and leans against it.

She is going on a date.

And also, going to war.

3

FRANGIE MARR—TULSA, OKLAHOMA, USA

"I don't want you to go, baby."

Dorothy Marr tugs at the fabric, lines it up, glances at the spool of thread, presses the pedal, and *ree-ree-ree-ree-ree-ree*.

"I know that, Mother," Frangie Marr says. "But you can't pay the bills on your own. We'll end up in the street if I don't."

Just about eighteen hundred miles east and a little south of Gedwell Falls, seventeen-year-old Frangie Marr sits with her mother on the screened porch where her mother hauls her battered sewing machine on hot, humid nights like this.

The screens have been torn and patched and torn again, and the mosquitoes have memorized every last one of the holes. Unseasonably warm weather has released the insects from their slumber, and Frangie slaps one that lands on her arm, leaving a spot of her own blood that she flicks away.

She's a tiny thing, Frangie Marr, that's what people always say about her and have since she was twelve. Her adolescent growth spurt came late and petered out early. Until age fourteen she'd been just four foot ten. Now she is five foot one—if she cheats a bit and sort of lifts herself up in her shoes.

Her mother presses the pedal on the sewing machine and runs a dozen stitches. The rabbity sound of the machine has always been part of Frangie's life, though it used to be slower before they had electricity and the machine was foot powered.

"You should get some sleep, Mother." Frangie is tired of this conversation; she's had it before. Each time her mother tells her she doesn't have to go, and each time Frangie says she does. It feels like her mother is pushing off the responsibility, like she wants to be able to say, *"I told her not to go."* Maybe Frangie's being unfair thinking that, but she feels what she feels.

"Can't sleep, sweetie, you know I have to get this dress done for tomorrow morning. You know Miss Ellie."

"Oh, I know Miss Ellie," Frangie says. "That is one complaining white woman." This is safer territory for conversation. Frangie complains about her mother's customers, and her mother in turn says things like, *"Oh, she's not so bad,"* or *"Well, she has her ways."*

Sure enough: "She's all right," Dorothy Marr says with a tolerant smile. "At least she pays on time. And she had that ham sent around for Easter."

Yes, she pays on time, and when Frangie was younger Miss Ellie would rub her head and say, "Need me some pickaninny juju."

Frangie despised that and despised the woman. If she'd actually had any juju she'd have used it for her family or for herself, not transferred it to a skinny, mouse-haired, flint-eyed white woman. When Miss Ellie wasn't rubbing Frangie's head for luck she was making remarks like, *"I reckon I could scour my pans bright with that brushy Nigra hair of yours."*

At times like that Frangie's mother would press her lips tight into something that was not quite a smile, but not a readable expression of disapproval either. One did not talk back to white folk or object to words like *pickaninny* or *Nigra*, no, not even when it was your own daughter being referred to with casual condescension and unearned familiarity.

Maybe it'll be different in the army.

Frangie raises her glass of barely sweet tea and says, "To getting paid."

Her mother winces. "I always wanted you to finish school, Frangie. I saw you maybe going to college. Maybe being a doctor. That's what you've been saying since you were four years old."

"Aren't a lot of colored doctors around." Frangie has to say it to show she's not some silly dreamer. She dreams all right, but she can't set herself up to look foolish when she fails. That particular dream is for her, just for her, not even for her mother.

"Used to be before the trouble. Used to be black doctors, black lawyers, even that old professor."

"And what happened?" Frangie asks rhetorically. "White folks rioted and burned everything down. All those doctors and lawyers and such left Oklahoma for good."

"More than twenty years ago," her mother says. "You weren't even born."

"You were though." Frangie isn't sure whether or not she should just drop it. She's overheard whispers at times about what her mother, then just fifteen years old, endured at the hands of the mob.

"You don't know nothing about that," her mother said, shutting down the conversation.

A moth beats itself against the screen, not as clever as the little mosquitoes. Survival by adaptation, that's what they said in the science books that her school did not allow. Frangie figures in a few thousand years moths will all have died off in the face of the screened-porch challenge, but mosquitoes? They have already adapted.

"Things are changing, maybe," Dorothy Marr says, uncomfortable with her daughter's silence. "There are plenty of colored folks being called up to this war, that's going to mean something." Then, as if realizing what she is saying, she stops herself and says, "But that doesn't mean—"

Frangie laughs. She has a musical laugh that always brings smiles to the faces of even her sternest teachers. "I won't be enlisting for the sake of colored folk, Mother. I'll be enlisting because Daddy can't work. Let's be practical."

"Please don't ever say that to him." Her mother glances meaningfully toward the interior where Frangie's father sits listening to a radio program, some horror story judging by the wobbling organ music being played between bits of dialogue. Her father loves radio plays, the more gruesome the better.

"I would never," Frangie says.

"His pride . . ."

"His pride. He gets his hip crushed on the job, and the city gives him a severance that's half what a white man would get. Doesn't even cover the cost of whiskey to dull the pain."

"It ought to be your brother going," Dorothy says, whispering the last word. Frangie's brother, Harder, is much older, nearly twenty-one now, but he is no longer welcome in the home, and never to be spoken of within her father's hearing.

Harder is with the union, and he's a communist, a revolutionary, at least he talks like one. Communists are levelers who want everyone to have the same—no rich, no poor, no bosses, and no differences between races. All that might be okay, but commies are also atheists, who reject Jesus and most likely other folks' religions, too, all of them, not just some, and that's unacceptable, intolerable to Frangie's father.

"Well, it isn't him, is it?" Frangie snaps. Then she laughs to take the edge off the sound of bitterness. A little thing with a great laugh, that's Frangie Marr. Occasionally she would also be called cute, but that's because no one ever calls her pretty. Cute she is, with hair still wild and natural—getting it straightened costs a half dollar and only lasts a couple weeks—and a lower lip that sticks out just a bit farther than its mate and gives her a pugnacious air. The feature that makes people look at her twice, sometimes with suspicious glances, is her eyes. They are too large, wide-set, slanted a bit. And they judge, those eyes do, they watch and they take note and they judge all that they see, and lots of folks do not like that much.

To the innocent, her eyes are arresting. To a person with something on his conscience, they seem too knowing.

Her mother sews another few dozen stitches, the machine making its crazed sound. "Life is hard."

"Pay for a private is fifty dollars a month, and they have it set up where you can send almost all of that home. They call it an allotment. Well, I guess forty dollars a month would help a lot around here, especially with one less mouth to feed."

Her mother can't answer that and stares down at her work. The sewing machine bulb creates a sphere of light illuminating calloused, nimble fingers, a seamed, worried face, and the gleaming steel of the rapidly stabbing needle.

Of course the money will help. It will be the difference between scraping by and ending up on the street begging relatives to take them in.

"If only your father was well, he could get on at the bomber factory once it gets running," Dorothy says.

Just then Frangie's little brother, Obal, comes tearing out onto the porch to report breathlessly on his doings with friends and how his best friend, Calvin, found a broken-down bike in the dump. He thought maybe they could get it fixed up well enough for him to deliver papers, or maybe even telegrams, which pays better.

"I would help him whenever he couldn't do the work. I could make a quarter maybe, fifty cents sometimes."

Down the street toward central Greenwood the juke

joint is warming up as the night ever so slowly cools. The ramshackle building with its single, blinking red florescent letter, *R* for Regent's Club, vibrates with the sound of drums and trumpet.

"Diz is playing," Frangie says wistfully. "I'd give just about anything to be able to play a horn like that."

"Jazz," Dorothy says dismissively. "Devil's music." But there isn't a lot of intensity behind that judgment, and Frangie notices her mother has a tendency to move in her chair in response to the rhythm coming down the street.

"I'm going to do it," Frangie says, as if waiting for an argument.

Her mother does not argue, and Frangie thinks, *My God, I am actually going to do this*. There's something familiar in the sense of abandonment that wells up within her, and then she remembers the day when her mother first dropped her off at school. She turned and walked away while little Francine—as she was called then—bawled her eyes out and got a smack on the butt from her teacher. "Well, maybe it will be no worse than school," she tells herself.

"I'm going for a walk," Frangie says. "Can I bring you back anything?"

"No, sweetheart."

There is something final about that word coming from her mother. *Sweetheart*. It's a word she uses when comforting Frangie. She used it when her grandmother, Meemaw, died. *"People die, sweetheart, even the ones we love."*

Frangie passes her father, asleep now in front of the ancient radio that only gets two of the four available stations. The program has shifted to a mystery.

Frangie goes first to her "hospital" in the backyard. It's not much—a sort of doghouse constructed out of bits of this and that. It has a chicken-wire "yard" in front with a dish of water and one of food scraps. At present there are two patients—a cat recovering from burns and a pigeon with a broken wing.

Neither patient is happy about the presence of the other. But they are separated by some chicken wire on sticks.

"How are you doing, Cleo?" Frangie kneels and reaches in to pet the understandably jittery cat. "I am going to get you both out of here if I'm going away."

She fishes around in the small toolbox that is her medical kit—lard for salve, rags for bandages, half a bottle of iodine—which the cat really does not enjoy, no, not even a little—Popsicle stick splints and a carefully wrapped needle-and-thread kit for stitches. She takes the lard, picks a bit up on two fingers, and soothes it over the cat's exposed skin.

"There you go. Now do not lick that off! And do not

eat Mooch. Mooch, you squawk if Cleo bothers you."

Frangie wipes her hands, checks the chicken wire to make sure her charges are safe, and sets off toward Greenwood Street. There half a dozen two-story brick buildings have replaced a segment of what was destroyed in the riot but which give way on all sides to vacant lots, fire-scarred derelicts, low bungalows, and intermittent sections of storefronts featuring a malt shop, pawn shops, dress shops, drinking establishments, a pool hall, and a church.

It's always busy out on Thursday nights when maids who work for the rich white folk get their traditional night off. Busier even than usual with this muggy weather that threatens tornadoes. Frangie wears a faded-green floral-print sundress and walks barefoot. The riot and the Depression both linger on in Tulsa, especially in Greenwood. Frangie owns a pair of shoes, but they're a size too small and reserved for church, school, and bad weather. She figures she will put on her shoes when she goes to enlist, and the army will give her a good pair of boots. They'll probably take getting used to, the boots, after so long running around barefoot or else wearing her size-too-small hand-me-down pumps.

Frangie lets herself be drawn like a fly to honey by the music throbbing from the Regent's Club, a ramshackle affair built of wood siding and nailed-on sheets of tin. The street is dark at 9:00 p.m., but lively with maids and washerwomen, gardeners and butlers, all dressed to the limit of their pocketbooks.

"Hey, pretty girl." This from a man in a zoot suit with its draping, high-belted trousers and absurdly long, padded-shoulder jacket.

"You're too old for me, Grandpa," Frangie says breezily.

The man laughs and mimes a knife going into his heart. "Oh, little sister, why you want to hurt a man like that?"

Frangie walks on by, pleased with herself. She slows her pace as she passes the club. There's a clarinet playing now; a wild, thrilling sound backed by what some people called "jungle" rhythms.

Frangie sings softly to herself, mimicking the instruments. "Bada da da, dada dada . . . bum bum bumbum bum bumbum bum badum bum." Cool clarinet now, and drums and stand-up bass, all urgent and relentless.

Frangie would love to go inside, but that costs a dime except on Ladies' Nights, and Frangie does not have a dime. But there's no law against lurking on the street outside, swaying to the music, feeling it speak to something inside her.

Devil jazz. It seems to Frangie that devils have good taste in music.

"Frangie? Is that you?"

The voice belongs to an old schoolmate of hers, Doon

Acey. He was a year ahead of her, but unlike many upper classmen he'd always been decent enough to her.

He moved away, she thought, up to Memphis; anyway she hasn't seen him around lately. And she's certainly never seen him like this: he's wearing an Army Class A uniform, dark green, with a single yellow chevron on his shoulder and a rakishly tilted cap on his head.

"Doon? Well, look at you."

Doon grins with far more confidence than he'd ever shown when she knew him as one of the less conceited athletes at school.

"You like the monkey suit?" Doon asks. He points at the stripe. "Private first class. But you can just call me PFC Acey."

"Looks like I'll have one for myself soon," Frangie says. "A uniform, anyway, maybe not such a fine stripe."

The grin drops from Doon's face. "You got drafted? But you're not even eighteen yet, are you?"

Frangie shrugs, feeling a little strange talking about her decision. "I'll be eighteen soon enough, and I'm not waiting around for some draft board. I'm enlisting."

"Enlisting?" Doon looks at her as if she might be crazy. "Why would you do a foolish thing like that?" He takes her arm and guides her a few yards away to where the crowd is less thick and the music not so urgent. "Frangie, I don't know what you think is going on in this war, but it's not what folks think it is, at least not for *us*."

The laugh-a-minute Doon is gone suddenly, replaced by an earnest young man. Frangie is almost alarmed by the change.

"So tell me," Frangie says.

"First of all, nothing changes between black and white. We have white officers—only white officers, no Negro officers. Most of the NCOs are colored, but it doesn't help because we're still doing the same old shit—sorry, I shouldn't use that word. The same old stuff. I'm in the artillery." He points to a small badge on his collar, two ancient cannons, crossed. "See those cannons? That's just about how old our equipment is. The white regiments get the new stuff; we get what's too old or broken . . . I mean, don't start thinking things are different for us just because we're fighting for the same country."

"My pop's too hurt to work."

"I heard about that."

"And we need the money."

Doon nods, accepting that, but he is still concerned. Frangie figures it's not the first time he's heard a similar story. "My mama talks about me going to college but can't pay the grocer."

"College girl, huh?" Doon brings back that wide smile of his, and she likes him for that. Too many people still didn't believe females belong in college, let alone colored ones. "What would you study, little Frangie, if you were to go to college?"

"I guess I wouldn't mind being a doctor," Frangie says shyly.

"You get to be a doctor and I'll break my arm just to give you something to fix up."

She doesn't know how to answer that, so she just looks down and suddenly realizes how young she must look, a short girl with no shoes. Probably looks thirteen.

"You know, you can put in to be a medic," Doon says, snapping his fingers. "Yeah, why not if you want to be a doctor?"

"They taking us for that?"

"Medics? Sure. What do you think, some white doctor is going to tend to a Nigra that gets shot?"

Frangie has already thought along the same lines, but she is glad to have the confirmation from Doon. A medic. Has to be better than cleaning toilets or cooking stew, although her stomach rumbles a bit at the thought of stew. Dinner was beans and corn bread and not too much of either.

They stand for a while, listening to the music. The band is blistering but still somehow cool and in control.

"That man can play," Frangie says after a while.

"Don't you know who that is? That's Benny Goodman. I heard a couple of his own boys are down with the grippe and he had to cancel their own gig downtown with his big band, so he came down here to play with Diz."

"A white man playing at the Regent?"

Doon smiles. "Jazzmen don't care a damn—sorry— for what color you are, it's just can you play or not. And that particular white man can play some clarinet."

"Well, I guess I have to get back or my mother will fret," Frangie says. "Take care of yourself, Doon."

"Send my regards to your mom and pop. I don't forget your dad speaking up for me that time, getting me that work. So if there's anything I can do. You know?"

"I do." Frangie starts to walk away, turns, now walking backward, and says, "Just don't stick your head in the wrong end of any of those old cannons. I still remember you and that car muffler you thought you could spit into."

Doon laughs. "I'd say I'm smarter now, but look at me." He waves his hands elegantly to indicate his uniform. "How smart am I?"

4

RIO RICHLIN—GEDWELL FALLS, CALIFORNIA, USA

Rio Richlin sits far more stiffly than she intends, in the sixth row, center left at the Jubilee Movie House with a small bag of popcorn on her lap, a soda on the floor by her feet, and sweat on the palms of her hands.

There is something strangely rushed about this date. One minute she'd been idly glancing at Strand—a boy she'd more or less known all of her life, or at least known to nod politely to—and now they are at a movie together. A romantic movie at that.

Rio has heard people talking about how the war seems to accelerate the pace of daily life, how it seems to bring sudden change. As sudden as losing Rachel.

She is acutely conscious of Strand, which is strange in itself. Strand has always been there, a year ahead in one class or another, school or Sunday school, a presence, a boy among many possible boys she might see at a baseball game or wait behind in line at the grocery store. It would be wrong to compare him to a familiar lamppost or stop sign, but in some ways that's what he's been: a part of the landscape.

And suddenly, just a few days ago, she began to actually see him. And then to see him in detail. And then to see him to the exclusion of other boys.

He's touching me!

His arm and hers share an armrest. There are four layers of fabric between them—her blouse, her sweater, Strand's shirt, and Strand's sports coat—and yet they are touching. It feels very awkward to Rio, but she definitely does not want to break off contact. She wonders what he is feeling—does he particularly enjoy the contact between their respective sleeves? Is he as aware, as she certainly is, of the body heat that crosses those fabric barriers? Is he feeling the muscle in her arm as she is his, and if so, is he thinking that she's too muscular?

She does a lot of physical work, and she likes it mostly. Maybe it's not how she would choose to spend her whole life, hauling hay bales and milking cows and stacking bags of fertilizer at her father's store, but she has never disliked hard labor.

Well, if Strand thinks she's unfeminine, well . . . Well, then that's that. Maybe she isn't Jenou, maybe she's not the most girly girl, maybe her skin is too tan, but she is . . . well, again, she is what she is. Who she is.

Whatever that is.

Neither of them has spoken in a while, and Rio wonders if he feels as awkward as she does.

"That's a great dress," Strand says. He sounds as if he's spent quite some time preparing the compliment.

"Thank you, Strand."

"I . . ."

"Yes?"

"It's starting," he says with obvious relief.

The house lights go down, and the audience waits for the newsreel. First, though, comes the sales pitch for war bonds, followed by Daffy Duck taking on Adolf Hitler.

Rio wonders whether—or maybe when—Strand will try to take her hand. Assuming he's not actually disgusted by her and regretting this date. And she wonders how many sets of prying eyes will mark the event. Then again, what if he never does take her hand? Those same ever-observant eyes will note that fact as well. The news bulletin around the school will be "Strand and Rio!" Or, alternately, whispered reports, accompanied by head-shaking, that Strand is not really interested in Rio. Poor Rio.

They'll say it's a pity date because of Rachel.

"How strange," Rio whispers, not really intending to be overheard.

"What's strange?"

"Oh, nothing. Just . . . Just that life goes on, doesn't it? Even with a war on."

As if reading her mind, Strand nods in the direction of Jasmine Burling, a high school junior who could have a great future in journalism, if her love of the very latest gossip is any indicator. Jasmine is three rows down and off to the right, whispering to her irritating milquetoast boyfriend while quite clearly looking at Rio and her definitely-not-boyfriend Strand. Jasmine's boyfriend turns and looks, his face such a mask of boredom and despair that Rio laughs.

"What's funny?"

"Nothing," Rio says, then amends, "People. Sometimes people are funny."

The newsreel starts in with the usual dramatic music followed by a stentorian voice narrating the footage. In this case it shows marines on some blasted, godforsaken island fighting the Japanese. The narrator uses terms like "hard-fought," "slogging," "slug match," and "desperate."

"That was depressing," Strand whispers.

"It said we were on the march," Rio counters. "That's good, isn't it?"

The newsreel moves on to a story about a movie star, then a story about a very fast horse, concluding with a silly piece about two babies switched at the hospital even though one is white and one colored.

Rio looks carefully at the little black baby. She's never seen a black person in Gedwell Falls, only in movies—maids or butlers or comical tap dancers. It looks almost exactly like the white baby except for being darker.

A second cartoon starts and lightens the mood enough that Strand feels free to dip into Rio's popcorn, and she retaliates by stealing a chocolate-covered almond from him.

She risks a glance at him. He is quite handsome in profile. He has a good, strong chin, a straight nose, and the sort of lips Jenou describes as "kissable," which for Jenou covers a lot of ground.

They settle in finally for the main feature, announced with a blare of trumpets and pounding drums. It's a love story with Tyrone Power and Joan Fontaine, a love story but a war story as well. It's hard to get away from the war.

No wonder I feel swept up.

Just around the part where Tyrone regains his sight, Strand takes Rio's hand.

He's holding my hand!

He looks at her as if to ask permission, and Rio, with her heart pounding so hard she is surprised anyone can hear the last scene of the movie, smiles queasily and squeezes his strong fingers and wonders whether he can feel her callouses and whether he is shocked and whether his heart is pounding too.

He walks her home after the movie. They take their time, not wanting the night to end. Rio learns that Strand enjoys taking photographs. He learns that she likes riding horses. He has his pilot's license and wants to grow up to fly, maybe for the post office carrying air mail, after the war. She admits she hasn't really thought much about her future.

No vows are spoken. No promises are made. He does not kiss her, but had he tried she'd have let him. And that fact, too, joins so many other facts in making her wonder whether something very profound has changed in the world around her.

They hold hands as they walk and talk and Rio's feet never touch the ground.

"So?" her mother asks as Rio literally twirls in through the front door. "I suppose you had a good time?"

"I suppose I did," Rio says, smiling and making no effort to hide her very, very good mood. She glances at the phone on the little table at the bottom of the stairs and considers calling Jenou. But of course Jenou will demand details—every last detail—and there is no privacy to be had talking in the hallway. Jenou can wait. Besides, Rio wants to make sense of her feelings on her own for now.

She climbs the stairs to her room, falls back on her bed, bounces once, and pulls her ancient stuffed bear—Barely

Bear, or BB for short—to her chest. BB was a fifth birth-day present given to Rio by Rachel.

"BB, it's possible I'm in love," Rio says in a whisper. "What's that, you say? It's only a first date? Don't be such a prude. You're a bear, what do you know?"

The bear does not argue the point. Nor does it object to Rio tracing a small heart onto its furry chest with her finger as her eyes close and she hovers between sleep and waking, between dreams and imagination.

Rio is not sure whether she is awake or asleep when she hears a woman's cry.

She sits up, tosses BB aside, and listens, waiting for a second cry to reveal the source. Nothing. She gets up and opens the door to the hallway, sticks her head out, and listens intently. Nothing. She withdraws back to her room and raises the sash window. Still nothing to be heard but a breeze in the trees and a distant truck engine. She is about to shrug it all off when she notices a glow, an orange glow, that at first glance seems like a single candle in the darkness.

She blinks, then squints, trying to get some sense of scale in a tableau only faintly touched by moonlight. Not a candle: fire.

Fire!

Rio throws on a robe and slippers and rushes out into the hallway intending to rouse her parents, but their door is closed and no light shows through the cracks. So, as quickly as she can without making noise, Rio descends the stairs, lifts the phone from its cradle, and dials the operator.

"Operator, I believe there's a fire over on Fitch Street. Please alert the fire department, won't you?"

This is the extent of her civic obligation, but Rio is fully awake now and it's a moderately warm night, and the streets of Gedwell Falls are safe, even for an unaccompanied girl at night. So she dons a pair of dungarees under her robe and sneaks out into the night.

She has never been out in the street this late at night—or this early in the morning—and there is something wrong and yet thrilling about it. She knows every house, but the deep, silent darkness of the time beyond midnight turns the familiar strange and even sinister. Windows become staring eyes, doors are astonished mouths, and trees seem too active and alert to be merely ruffling passively.

From ground level she cannot see the fire at first, but as she walks she begins to catch glimpses in the gaps between homes. Then, coming around the corner, there it is.

It is a very old wood-frame house, two stories behind a weed-grown garden, and Rio recognizes it immediately. It is the Stamp Man's House.

The Stamp Man's House—it is always referred to that way—is the most often stared at, most often shunned house in Gedwell Falls. No one has ever seen the Stamp Man, at least not that Rio has ever heard. There are rumors, and there are tall tales. There are even ghost stories told 'round campfires at church camp. But there are no firsthand sightings that Rio knows of.

The Stamp Man lives with his sister, a middle-aged woman with wild gray hair and a face etched by suffering, leading naturally to suggestions by the more imaginative children that she is some sort of witch. Rio has seen her in town, nodded in a neighborly way, but never spoken with her. Rio knows—everyone in the small town knows— that the sister makes a weekly sortie to the post office to pick up the mail that comes to the Stamp Man, mail from strange, exotic locales bearing the brightly colored stamps he is believed to collect.

It is she, the Stamp Man's sister, who now stands barefoot in a threadbare nightgown on the sidewalk in front of the house, hand over her mouth, staring in helpless horror at a window flickering orange.

The sister notices Rio and cries, "Help him! Help him!" Her eyes glow with reflected firelight.

"What's . . . What is . . . ," Rio stammers, no longer enjoying this forbidden excursion.

"It's Peter! He won't come out!"

For a moment Rio is confused, not connecting the name Peter with the Stamp Man. "Is he awake?" she asks.

"It's the fireplace in my room, I told him we needed to have the chimney swept, but he . . . I have to . . ." She makes a tentative move toward the porch but doesn't get far. There is something indecisive, a conflict of some sort. "I shouldn't have burned coal. I should have . . . but wood is so . . . and I can't . . ." This is all accompanied by weak, fluttering hand gestures.

An upper-floor window's glass pane cracks, and seconds later the glass bursts outward, shards clattering on the porch roof and sliding down the shingles to smash on the walkway. A tongue of fire licks upward, touching the eaves. The smell of smoke is acrid and deeply disturbing, not the comfortable smell of burning firewood or leaves, but the more complex smell of burning paint and wallpaper paste, of pillow feathers and Bakelite and tar.

"Peter!" the sister screams. "Peter!"

A sound comes from within the house. It might be human, must be human, but it is not a sound Rio has ever heard come from a human throat. It is not a scream but a cry, a warning, but with words slurred to incomprehensibility, a guttural, throat-clearing, strangled sound. Whatever the meaning of this cry, the sister seems to understand it.

"No, Peter! You must come out!"

She says it, shouts it, but again Rio detects a doubt, an ambiguity in her tone.

Rio looks around frantically, hoping for someone, anyone to come along and do . . . something. Something, she doesn't know what, but something that will take the burden off of her own shoulders, for she sees pleading in the sister's eyes, a mute neediness. Despair.

Rio takes tentative steps toward the porch, willing the volunteer fire department to bestir themselves and come to the rescue quickly. But if the volunteers are on their way there is no sign of them.

"Help him! Peter! Peter!"

Rio climbs the three wooden steps to the front door, which is closed but surely not locked since the sister must have come out this way. She touches the doorknob. It is not hot to the touch. She peers through the narrow vertical slits of lace-curtained windows beside the door and sees a stairwell inside, and no sign of fire on the lower level.

Taking a deep breath, she opens the door and reels back from the stench of smoke that has crept down the stairway and now billows out through the door and passes above Rio's head to rise into the night sky.

"What do you think you're doing?" Rio asks herself.

And just then Tam Richlin comes rushing up and asks the identical question, "What do you think you're doing?"

Rio has never been so glad to see her father. "The Stamp Man is upstairs. He won't come down."

Tam Richlin hears this and nods, showing no surprise but a grim understanding. "He may not care, but this fire could spread to other homes."

"I called the operator and told her to call the fire department."

"Good girl. But it'll take them a half hour this time of night," Tam says.

"Can we save him?"

"Nothing can save him," Tam says darkly. "He died a long while ago." But then, ignoring his own cryptic assessment, he says, "I'll give it a try."

He races to a garden hose, turns on the spigot, and drenches himself in water. He tears the sleeve from his pajamas, soaks the cloth, and ties it around his head, covering his mouth and nose.

"Be careful. Don't get hurt!" Rio cries as her father plunges through the door and pounds up the steps.

Rio hesitates, feeling useless as the sister weeps openly, and now other doors on the street are opening and other lights are coming on, and at last she hears the distant wail of a siren. But something feels very wrong about standing there and doing nothing. Her decision is not thought out but instinctive: she follows her father's example, tears away the pocket of her chenille robe, and wets it. Holding the rag over her mouth, she rushes into the strange house and up the stairs.

As soon as her head rises above the level of the upper floor she gags on smoke, and that's when she hears the unmistakable sharp, unbearably loud sound of a gunshot. The sound sends her rushing up, taking steps two at a time. Three rooms, one with an open door, are bright with fire that crackles and roars on fresh breezes from the broken window. A second door is closed. A third is open and lit only by candlelight. Rio hears her father's voice and peers cautiously around the corner.

The room is stuffed, stuffed almost to the exclusion of furniture, with cardboard boxes spilling reams of paper: old newspapers, age-curled magazines, and thousands of envelopes with the stamps neatly cut away. One entire wall is bookshelves loaded with stamp albums in a dozen different sizes and covers.

In the center of the room, against the far wall, is a bed. It's a mahogany sleigh bed like those to be found at many a home in Gedwell Falls.

Tam Richlin stands before that bed with his back to Rio. And beyond him, propped against a stack of pillows, lies a monster.

Rio stifles a scream. The creature in the bed must once have been a man, but now he is a nightmare in a sleeveless white T-shirt, revealing a frail, parchment-flesh left arm and a shocking stump where the right arm would once have been. He has only half a face, half an old man's face, slack and sickly. But the right side of that face is gone. There is a deep crater, as though that half of his face was bitten off by a wild beast. The mouth is a twisted grin on its intact side, but from there the lips seem to melt away, revealing teeth all the way back to the upper molars. The lower molars are mostly gone as the jawbone simply ends, absent, leaving a gaping hole in sagging flesh.

She can look—must look, cannot look away—at the Stamp Man's throat, a gulping, spasming pink tube revealed through those absent teeth and jaw.

The Stamp Man's right eye is gone as well, but this is blessedly covered by an eye patch.

He is holding a pistol, aimed at Tam Richlin.

"We have to get you out of here, Captain," Tam says.

The Stamp Man shakes his head vigorously, a gruesome sight.

"You don't want to burn to death, Captain. That's no way to go."

The Stamp Man shakes the gun as if to say, "I won't wait to burn." Then he waves the gun around the room, not threatening, just indicating all of it. He makes sounds, a wet, slurry mimicry of human speech. Rio can see his tongue trying to form sounds, see his throat contracting and releasing, all of it creating no intelligible word, only a cry, a plea, a wail of despair.

Tam for the first time notices Rio behind him. "What

the hell are you doing up here?" he snaps.

"I just . . . I thought I could help." She cannot look at him because she cannot will herself to look away from the man in the bed, the Stamp Man, who her father calls "Captain."

"Get out of here, Rio." And when Rio doesn't move, Tam grabs her bicep and shoves her hard. "Now! Go!"

Rio flees the room and stumbles down the stairs, gagging on smoke that has thickened to near opacity as the fire builds, sending waves of searing heat and choking smoke to pursue her until she escapes through the front door and almost collapses on the sidewalk.

"Is he dead?" It's the sister. She is no longer crying. Her eyes have gone dull.

"No, he's—"

And a single shot rings out.

Terrible, fearful moments later Tam Richlin emerges, choking, his face darkened by soot and by something liquid that slides down his cheek leaving a red smear.

The fire truck comes rattling down the block, and even before it comes to a complete stop men in asbestos coveralls and iconic fireman's helmets pile off, unlimbering a thick canvas hose. Axes and hoses and portable fire extinguishers in hand, the firemen race to the porch, but Tam knows the fire chief and grabs his arm.

Rio does not hear their conversation, but she sees the

fire chief's face go from determined and a little excited to grim. He nods, and with a few words to his crew, sets them to directing their hoses toward the siding and roof of the adjoining home.

No fireman enters the burning house.

The sister says nothing, does not urge them on, but sinks down to sit, legs splayed gracelessly across the concrete sidewalk.

"Let's get out of here," Tam says, and takes his daughter's arm. There is no arguing with the sad finality in his voice.

They walk in silence, ignoring shouted inquiries as half the town is now out in the street. Just before they reach home, Tam stops. He hangs his head for a moment, silent. Then he says, "I was about to say I'm sorry you had to see that, but I suppose it's a good thing."

"What was that? The Stamp Man wasn't burned, what . . ."

"Captain Peter McFall, US Marines. He was at Belleau Woods in the last war. They had a bad time of it. And he had a very bad time of it."

Rio remains silent, seeing the conflict in her father's eyes. Tam Richlin is a quiet man, not one for long speeches, or even short ones. She waits.

"I guess the fire was the last straw for him. I guess he's been waiting for death since that day. Year after year like

62

that. The pain . . . Never able to go out into the world . . . The fire was taking all he cared about, all his stamps, all his . . . what little he had left."

"Did he shoot himself?"

Tam was silent for so long Rio thought he hadn't heard. Finally, in a single long sigh he said, "He wanted to. But suicide is an unforgivable sin in his faith. You see, it leaves you no chance to repent and atone." Then, under his breath, bitterly, "As if he had not already paid for the right to sit straight and proud at God's table."

Rio was forming the next question, thinking the words, *but I heard a shot*, when she realized the truth.

Captain Peter McFall, retired, would not have been able to repent of suicide. But Tam Richlin had time enough to seek forgiveness.

5

RAINY SCHULTERMAN—NEW YORK CITY, NEW YORK, USA

"Du bist nisht mayn tokhter! Mayn tokhter shist nisht keyn mentshn. Afile natsis!" This pronouncement comes with a side order of two hands chopping the air for emphasis and a head thrown back as if to implore God to bear witness.

The speaker is Elisheva "Rainy" Schulterman's mother. The language is Yiddish. In English it means, *You are not my daughter! My daughter does not shoot people. Even Nazis!*

It is a very dramatic statement, rendered somewhat less convincing by the fact that in her eighteen years of life, all in this same fourth-floor apartment, Rainy has heard that she is not her mother's daughter on literally hundreds of occasions, including when she took up piano instead of violin, when she first went out in public with her head uncovered, and when she added ketchup to scrambled eggs.

"Mother, I doubt very much I'll be shooting anyone. I've qualified on the M-1 carbine, but only just barely. Anyway, I've been assigned to the army intelligence training school."

"This is good," her father says from behind his newspaper, which, he has made clear, he will put down once all the food is served. "The army sees she is intelligent."

Rainy's mother, who has been hovering around and bringing new dishes to the table, stalks over, rudely pulls down the newspaper, sticks her face just inches from her husband's, and says, "Intelligence, old man. *Nyet* intelligent, intelligence! Learn to speaking English like American, hokay? And no newspaper at my table!"

Rainy's older brother, Aryeh, who, like her, is in uniform, winks at her. Rainy rolls her eyes in response.

They are at the dinner table, which is loaded with mismatched serving dishes full of noodles, chicken, pickled beets, bread, and spinach that has been cooked to a gray-green paste. Steam rises into the light of the shaded bulb hanging from the ceiling.

Also at the table are the elderly couple from upstairs who are nodding along in noncommittal agreement. To be fair, they also nod along with Rainy. They're there for the free food.

"Do they give you gun?" Rainy's mother demands. "Aryeh, eat some spinach, is good for you blood. If they give you gun it is for shoot, no? Hokay. It is for shoot."

"They gave me a gun too," Aryeh says, hiding a smile. "They give them to all marines. It's something they kind of insist on."

"Hah!" Rainy laughs, which is a mistake, because this launches a five-minute-long diatribe in a patois of English, Yiddish, Polish, German, and some words that are invented on the spot, all of which culminate in the pronouncement that sons are not daughters, and daughters are not sons, and only a woman can give birth, painful birth, lasting hours, while the man is in some tavern drinking.

"The chicken is good," Rainy's father observes once this storm has blown itself out.

"A woman's place is in the home, respecting and obeying her fool of a husband!" Rainy's mother cries.

"Yes, Rainy," her father says in a tone of weary irony. "Why can't you learn from your mother to be respectful and obedient to men?"

"Very tender, the chicken," one of the neighbors says.

With dinner completed, Rainy helps clear the table, moving swiftly between the narrow but elegant dining room and the tiny kitchen so as not to be caught alone with her mother.

It's her father who corners her, drawing her down the hallway to a discreet distance.

"Rainy," he says.

"Dad?"

He sighs, scratches his head, makes a face like maybe what he's about to say is a bad idea. Then he shrugs and says, "Listen, *bubala*, you know your cousin Esther?"

"Not really. Do I have a cousin Esther?"

"She's your grandmother's sister's daughter. They live in Krakow. In Poland."

"Yes, Father, I know where Krakow is." She doesn't mean to sound like a sarcastic teenager and softens it by prompting, "So, what about Cousin Esther?"

"Well, she writes letters to everyone, every branch of the family. Your mother gets a letter three, sometimes four times a year."

Rainy waits, sensing a revelation, which comes after a dramatic pause.

"Nothing. Nothing for a year now," her father says. "One letter missed, two even . . ." He shrugs.

"Well, there is a war on."

"True, very true. I heard something about that on the radio, I think." Her father is capable of his own sarcasm. "But when I talk to people at temple, it's the same thing. No one hears from Poland, no one hears from Ukraine . . . I'm just saying, you're going to do intelligence work, no? You might hear something . . ." He lets it hang.

Rainy draws back, unconsciously putting distance

between them. "Father. Dad. I can't talk to you about my work. Those are the rules."

He shrugs and dips his head and squints in a gesture that eloquently conveys his understanding, but also his expectation that rules are not always to be followed blindly. "I understand, and I will never ask you to break a rule, Rainy. I'm just saying you have a responsibility to the army, to this country that we love. But you also have an obligation to our people. Maybe you keep your eyes open. Maybe you see things, maybe you hear things . . ."

"I better finish clearing the table," Rainy says, bringing the conversation to a halt.

With that awkward exchange and the clearing of dishes concluded, Rainy goes to her favorite place, the roof of the five-story building. The roof is flat tarpaper, with some of the tar still liquid from the day's heat. Blackened pipes stick up in a seemingly random pattern. Beyond Rainy's perch is a mile of roofs just like her own, and beyond that, in the distance, the skyscrapers that to most people's minds defined New York City. The skyline is mostly dark for fear of the German submarines lurking just offshore that use city lights to silhouette vulnerable cargo ships plying the coastal route.

Aryeh joins her, bringing up two cups of hot tea.

"Had to get out of there, huh?" he asks.

His sister is a young woman with black hair, which

unbound is so wild that it must be obsessively pinned down. She's cut it for the army, but even short it struggles to get free. She has an olive complexion untroubled by blemishes. Her face in repose is alert, smart, skeptical, and thoughtful. Her mouth is wide, with full lips. Her eyes are large, dark, and quite beautiful.

"You handled that well," her brother says. "I saw you about to explode a few times, but you didn't." He clinks his cup against hers. "Very mature of you."

They are more than brother and sister; they are best friends and have been since a seven-year-old Rainy lost patience with her brother's incessant teasing and broke his nose with a loaf of very stale rye bread.

His nose healed but not perfectly, and the slight crook that twists it gives a touch of character to his movie star looks. Rainy doesn't mean to idolize him, it's not normally her way, but she can't help it.

"I've just spent thirteen weeks being shouted at by people with stripes on their shoulders," she says. "I've had to learn to—"

"Accept criticism?" Aryeh offers lightly.

"Who's criticizing me?" Rainy snaps before realizing he's playing with her. "You think I'm crazy too, don't you?"

"A little bit," he admits. "But not crazy enough to be a marine."

Rainy laughs and affectionately messes his unmessably short hair. Then she's serious. "I can't sit this out, Ary. I have to be part of it."

"They're scared is all, Mom and Dad."

"They want grandchildren."

"I think they want a daughter," he says softly. "You know you're their favorite. You got the brains in the family, and that's what they care about." He doesn't mean to sound resentful.

"And all you got is the looks? Poor baby."

They sip their tea and look out across the city they both love.

"So how long does this intelligence school last?"

"Eight weeks," she says.

"Spy stuff?"

"Cloak and dagger," she jokes. "They picked me because I speak German."

"You speak everything."

"Not true. Just German. And some Italian. A little French. Yiddish, of course."

"Are there other languages?" He likes playing dumb with his brilliant little sister.

"One or two. I don't speak Japanese, though, so I guess we won't be running into each other out there." She waves a hand, meaning to encompass the world, not just New York.

"Nope. Looks like we marines'll be killing Japs on our own, no army help needed."

This is too much for her. Far away the Japanese are having similar conversations, full of bold talk about slaughtering American marines.

"Stop," he says, seeing the worry in her eyes. "I'll be fine. You know me. Aren't I always fine?"

But tears are welling up now, and when she looks at him her eyes glisten. "If you get hurt, I'll kill you."

"I'm supposed to meet up with some buddies. We're going to go down to the USO club, see if there are any girls who want to dance with big, bad, bold marines. Why don't you come?"

"Right, that's what you need before you ship out: your little sister tagging along."

He doesn't argue; he knows she'll say no.

"I wish you hadn't joined the marines," she says after a long silence. "There are safer jobs in the army."

"I don't think anyone wanted me for intelligence work," he says, making a joke of it.

"Do you know where they're sending you?"

"To California by train, then a nice little boat trip to Hawaii where I will lie on the beach and soak up the sun."

"And then?"

"Come on, Rainy, don't do that."

She puts her arms around him and squeezes him tightly.

He strokes her head and says "come on" again. And then again.

Then she pushes him away and wipes the tears from her cheeks. There are small wet marks on the chest of his uniform.

"This tea is terrible."

"Hey, I made it myself," Aryeh protests.

"That, I could guess."

"Listen . . ." He sighs. "I lied a little. Not about making the tea. I'm not going to the club to meet girls. I mean, I am going to the club with some buddies. But I'm not meeting girls. Just a girl."

This is news, and Rainy's eyebrows rise. "A girl? Singular? Just one girl? You?"

"I kind of like her. Jane. But not plain Jane, very pretty Jane." His tone is light and carefree and doesn't fool Rainy for a minute.

"Are you in love? I'm amazed. Have you actually fallen for someone?"

He blows out a long breath. "I may have asked her to marry me."

That freezes Rainy solid for a full minute. "There's a problem, isn't there?"

"See, that's exactly why you'll be good at the spying game. Right away you glom onto—"

"Don't try to distract me with flattery, Ary." She

searches his face intently, as if he's written the answer there. And maybe he has, because she begins to sense the reason for his caution. "What's her last name? Her family name."

"Jane? Oh, it's Jane Meehan."

"Meehan?" She sees guilt in the averted gaze. "Meehan? That doesn't sound like a Jewish name." His silence is confirmation. "Good lord. Good lord, Ary. Are you serious? You want to marry a shiksa?"

"Don't you start in with that."

"Look at me, Ary. Do you think I'm the one you need to worry about? Have you told Mother and Father? No, of course not, I would have heard the explosion. The whole city would have heard the explosion! The building would be flattened!"

"I thought maybe you could help me find a way to explain it to them."

Her eyebrows achieve their maximum height. "Explain it? Explain to our parents that their grandchildren will not be Jewish? I could more easily explain the general theory of relativity!"

"General who?"

She puts her hands against the side of her face and looks at him, amazed, and, she has to admit, with disapproval. "You can't marry outside. What are you thinking?"

He shrugs. "I guess I'm thinking I love her, and I don't

see where it's so all-fired important whether she believes in a single God or a God with a Son."

"If you say that to Mother or Father, I won't have to worry about a Jap killing you. They'll do the job."

"Which is why I need your help. Because, see, I'm going to marry her before I ship out. So she'll have the insurance if . . . And so that . . . Um . . . Well, it should have a name."

And now the full weight of the truth comes crashing down. "No. Don't tell me she's pregnant, this girl."

Aryeh fidgets and suddenly looks panicky. He's been hiding this earth-shattering truth.

"I'm not leaving her in the lurch," he says. And now the tears are threatening to fill his eyes, and that, Rainy knows, will humiliate him. But his humiliation can wait. First . . .

She slaps him hard on the cheek. It makes a satisfyingly loud crack, so she does it again.

"I thought you would—"

"You thought? You didn't think. Or at least you thought with the wrong part of your body!" The fact that Rainy's tone is an almost perfect reflection of her mother's voice is not lost on Rainy, but she pushes past that moment of realization.

Aryeh's miserable but defiant as well. "I love her, Rainy. I mean, it's the real thing, and she's pregnant, and I'm

going off to . . . to maybe. . . . And she'll be all alone."
And then adds, "And broke."

"Ah. Here it comes. The final shoe."

"We're getting married tomorrow. I can give her my allotment, but it won't be enough, not in this city. She'll need more."

"You want me to help."

"It's a lot to ask."

"It can't be a lot because I don't have a lot. A PFC stationed overseas earns $597.60 a year."

"You'll be a corporal in no time," he says with a winning grin.

"Like hell," Rainy snaps. "I'll be a sergeant in no time." She shakes her head in a show of disappointment, but of course she's already decided to help, and her brother knows it.

"You're the best, Sis. Just don't tell . . . you know."

"So you want money and discretion. Swell. Anything else?"

"You'll help."

"Of course I'll help. You're my brother. How can I not help?"

"Lots of sisters wouldn't," he says.

She goes on shaking her head woefully, face grim, sending him the message that this is serious, sending him the message that he had better not screw up anymore. But he's Aryeh, so most likely he will.

"If it's a girl we'll name it after you."

"I'm going to slap you again."

"I have it coming," Aryeh says.

6

FRANGIE MARR—TULSA, OKLAHOMA, USA

"So, tell me: what is on your mind, Frangie girl?"

The question comes from Pastor John M'Dale, the spiritual leader of Frangie's family. He's a middle-aged man, a serious man, a thoughtful man, a scholar even, cursed (or blessed) with a round, cherubic face. His office is all dark wood, books, dust, a big globe on a three-legged stand, a small stuffed pheasant, and various symbols of his faith and position. The chair Frangie occupies is cracked leather and feels vast. She resists the urge to swivel it back and forth.

"I'm signing up, I guess," Frangie says. "So I wanted to tell you I won't be singing in the choir anymore for a while."

M'Dale sits back and takes a long, deep breath, nodding and looking closely at Frangie. "Your daddy still out of work?"

"Don't imagine he'll be working ever again, Pastor M."

He nods. It's not the first time he's heard a story like this. "You think you want to fight in this war of white men killing Japanese or else killing other white men?"

"I don't aim to kill anyone. I aim to try out for medic."

"Well, that is honorable work, Frangie. But even if all you're doing is patching up hurt boys, you'd still be part of it all."

"Yes, sir."

She gives in to the urge to swing the chair left to right and back, just a small motion but comforting. She looks down, finding his gaze too challenging. There's a small feather, like a crow's pinfeather, on the rug, and it's drifting in the breeze of her chair's motion.

"I can tell you what the Bible says about that." He's forming a tent out of his fingers, sticking the tips up under his ample chin. "First, love. You know that, you know that if you pay attention during my sermons." He winks at her. "You do pay attention now, don't you?"

She welcomes his bantering tone. "I memorize every word, Pastor M."

He laughs. When he laughs, he shakes, and that makes Frangie smile.

"First, love. Love above all. Love for the ones who love you, love for the ones who hate you. That's pretty hard to follow if you're in a war."

"Were you ever?"

The question takes M'Dale by surprise. He sits farther back still and drops his hands to his lap. "No, young Miss Marr, I have not. But I have counseled many men who did go to the last war."

"Yes, sir," Frangie prompts.

"Well, they talk about the horrors. But they do also talk about the brotherhood with other black soldiers. I've only ever spoken with one who acknowledges taking a life. He says it was either shoot that other man, or be shot himself."

"I guess that's what war is," Frangie says. "But it's also patching a fellow up after he's been shot."

"Our friends of the Jewish faith say that he who saves a single life saves the world entire," M'Dale says. "I may not have that quotation quite right, but the sense of it is there. That's not from scripture, but I believe our Lord would agree with the sentiment. But real life can be more complicated than that. You heal a soldier in a war, and he goes off next thing to take a man's life. How then do you avoid responsibility for that death?"

"Sometimes you have to fight," Frangie says.

"Sometimes you do. Sadly, yes, sometimes you do. And what would you be fighting for, Frangie Marr?"

"Fighting *for*?"

The question overwhelms her and she has to think about it, and as she thinks she looks down at the feather, more like down, really, it's so light. Its little feathery fate rests on the next breeze.

"Should I not go, Pastor?" It will be easier if he forbids it. If he forbids it then she'll have to find some other way to support her mother and father. Some other way to make her own life better than her mother's life.

"I can't tell you go or don't go," M'Dale says at last. "I can tell you what the scriptures say. They say to love and not to harm. They say to turn the other cheek. But each of us faces a path with many forks and turns, and that which guides us on that path must be our own conscience, as reflecting the light of Jesus."

Frangie makes a shaky sigh. She's just gotten permission, however reluctant.

I am not a feather. I will not be blown this way or that. Not from now on.

M'Dale sees all this. "You pray on it, little Frangie. You're a good girl. You're a faithful daughter to your parents and to this church. You pray on it, and if your conscience says go, then you go, and take with you the love and prayers of this congregation."

Now tears fill Frangie's eyes, and she cannot speak.

M'Dale waits until she has mastered her emotions.

"Will you add me to the prayers, Pastor?"

He gets up from his seat and comes around to her. He opens his arms and she stands, and he practically absorbs her in his large frame. "Little girl, we will pray for you at every service until you come home safe to us."

Frangie spills tears onto his collar and knows these are not the first tears to stain his coat, and won't be the last.

He pushes her away, holds her at arm's length, and says, "When you're ready you let me know, and I'll send a couple of my deacons with you. Some of the white folk don't much like our kind enlisting. You'd do best to have company."

She nods, wipes away the tears, and says, "Then I guess you best send for them."

It's an eight-block walk to the nearest enlistment center, eight blocks during which humanity around her grows steadily lighter in color. At first Frangie and the two solemn, elderly deacons are just part of the passing scenery, but whites had begun to encroach on what had been an all-black neighborhood before the riots, and the abandoned Mason Hall that has been made over as an induction center is now in a fringe area.

A line of black recruits—mostly male—extends from the propped-open doorway out onto the sidewalk. The line seems to be moving, though slowly. But a white crowd has gathered, young men in school letter jackets or blazers, others in white T-shirts and jeans. They smoke cigarettes and make loud, braying laughs, and amuse themselves by flicking lighted matches at those waiting.

A white cop at the end of the street looks on tolerantly, ready—perhaps—to step in if any of the white folks turn nasty. Ready—very definitely—to step in if any of the colored folks object to being mocked.

So boys and men and some women who will soon be at war dodge flying matches and hold their dignity tight to them as the insults fly.

Frangie hesitates. The two deacons slow as she slows, following her lead. Perhaps if she comes back later the line will be shorter and she can go right inside. Or perhaps the crowd of white trash will grow bored and find something better to do.

"We can't start trouble with them white boys," one of the deacons advises her.

"Yes, sir, I know that," she says.

They have come to a stop half a block away. It will be Frangie's decision whether to go ahead. Bile rises in her throat, a barely suppressed rage at being put in this position. She doesn't even want to do this. She's only doing it to help her family. Why would these crackers feel they need to make it all still worse?

She's angry too at the deacons, though she knows it's unfair. Pastor M'Dale insisted they keep her company, but what good are they? Old black men, old men who were here when the buildings burned and black women were raped and the Tulsa police—the police!—flew a rickety plane over Greenwood throwing gasoline bombs on black businesses and homes.

Helpless then, helpless now.

"I made it here," Frangie says, her voice tight and low in her throat. "You did your duties. Go tell Pastor M that I made it safely."

"Now, Miss Frangie—"

"No. You know what happens if the three of us go stand in that line. I'm just a little thing, they won't start trouble, not too much trouble, anyway. But if I have body-guards . . ."

The deacons did not take too much convincing. They knew she was right, and they knew they were weak and useless in her eyes, as they were in their own.

Frangie walked the last half block. The crowd of whites noticed her immediately.

"Well, look at this, boys. It's a sweet little colored girl come to sign up to shoot Japs."

"Nigra bint lookin' for a government check, more like."

"Now I know we're going to lose if that pickaninny is who's fighting."

She joins the line behind a young man who stands so stiff she wonders how he breathes. He ignores her, focus-ing on his own self-control.

"Hey, want a light?" One of the white men flicks a

match at her. It spins, hits her shoulder, and falls extinguished. She does not look at him. Will not look at him.

"Must want to be raped by some of them Japs, yeah, that's what she wants."

Frangie hears it, but she's heard that and worse. Still, it churns her insides.

"You think Japs ever tasted brown sugar?"

"Hell, Dwayne, that's the only kind of pussy you've ever had."

This remark is not taken well, and a scuffle breaks out between two of the white men that provides distraction until Frangie is safely inside.

An hour later she is Recruit Frangie Marr, of the army of the United States of America. She is to report to the bus station the following morning.

She has forgotten to pray for guidance, and now it's too late. She has followed life's path lit only by her own conscience, without consulting either scripture or the God that inspired it.

Her own conscience . . . and the promise of a paycheck to keep the lights on at home.

She had arrived at the enlistment center in her painful church shoes. She walks home barefoot, with her shoes in one hand. The new army boots she'd been hoping for won't be hers until she arrives at the aptly titled "boot camp."

She is determined not to let her parents see her fears and doubts, so just before she gets home she forces a smile and quickens her pace, bounding up the sagging steps.

Her mother is at her machine again and looks up, her face like a jittering filmstrip shifting rapidly from one emotion to the next, before settling on a resigned sadness, seeing the morning's events in her daughter's eyes. This is life: choices, mostly between bad and worse.

Frangie's false and overbright grin fades to one of wry acceptance.

"When?" Dorothy Marr asks.

"Tomorrow," Frangie says.

"Then I best get your wash done."

7

RIO RICHLIN—GEDWELL FALLS, CALIFORNIA, USA

Am I really doing this?

Rio and Jenou beg a ride from Toby Perkins, who has the use of his father's 1936 Chevy pickup truck and can drive them the thirty-seven miles down to Petaluma, a larger town, almost a small city. Toby has been sweet on Jenou since they were both in third grade, a fact that Jenou has exploited ruthlessly over the years, never giving Toby so much as a dance but asking him for a favor whenever she needs one.

The three of them drive squeezed in together in the truck, Rio in the center beside Toby, much to Toby's regret. She angles her legs away from the gear shift, and Toby is painfully careful to avoid making contact as he moves through the gears.

"You girls sure you want to—" Toby begins.

"Why, Toby? Do you think we can't hack it?" Jenou asks in a dangerously sugary voice.

"No, I never said that," Toby retreats quickly. "Just ain't right is all."

Rio feels a little sorry for Toby, but mostly she is occupied with a case of nerves. Her stomach is in knots. Her mouth is as dry as the hills around them, and she would have traded her most prized possession—an autographed photo of Van Johnson—for a glass of lemonade.

"What if they don't believe I'm eighteen?" Rio asks, not for the first time.

"No one's going to run off and tell your mother. Goodness, Rio, you do worry. Anyway, you look eighteen, don't you?" Jenou appraises her with mocking eyes. "Well, except for . . . But don't worry, you'll come into your bosoms eventually."

Toby swallows his tongue, and Rio blushes red.

"Very funny, Jen," Rio mutters, and elbows her friend.

"Toby here thinks we're just weak little girls," Jenou says.

"Despite your impressive bosoms?" Rio's still annoyed at Jenou, but teasing Toby is too much fun for her not to get in on it.

"Rio's strong, Toby. She can crack a walnut with her fingers," Jenou says. "Did you know that? I've seen her do it. She's a dangerous young woman."

Rio smiles. "No walnut is safe from me. Just let some Jap or Nazi come at me with a walnut. You'll see."

They've both dressed for the occasion, Jenou in a white flannel skirt and tight-fitting, blue-striped blouse, and matching high heels; Rio, significantly less fashionable, in a plaid skirt and too-large white blouse handed down from her sister, and flats. Both wear their hair up, wanting to acknowledge the importance of the occasion and to look older and more sophisticated.

As Rio climbs from the truck she spots a familiar face: Strand is among those standing in line.

Rio notices Jenou smirking at her. "What?" she demands irritably.

"He's pretty tall. You'd have to stretch all the way up on your tiptoes to kiss him."

"Who said anything about any of that?" She feels a blush prickle her neck. Jenou is being particularly irritating.

"Oh, nothing. Nothing but the way you touch your hair and blush and lick your lips," Jenou says. "Little things like that."

Rio has not told Jenou about her date with Strand, or the terrible fire afterward, mostly because Jenou was out of town on an overnight visit to her aunt in the city, and also because Rio has yet to come to grips with either part of it, the date or the fire.

Two images are married in her mind now: Strand's

handsome face lit by the movie projector's flickering beam and the Stamp Man. And both are colored somehow by the memory of her father's grim expression following that single gunshot.

What a terrible life the Stamp Man's sister must have had during the interminable twenty-three years she spent caring for her brother.

Rio imagines caring for Rachel, similarly hurt. Or Strand, if she were his wife. She would stand by him, of course, any wife would or at least should. But what complete abnegation would be required, a total abandonment of any life other than as a nurse to a ruined man.

Only at the furthest reaches of her imagination does the thought come that if she is really doing this, if she is really enlisting in the army, the shattered, dependent patient in need of constant care might be Rio herself. But immediately behind that chilling thought comes a reassuring sense that no, of course not, that would never happen. Not to her.

But Strand?

There is no avoiding Strand. Now Rio and Jenou straighten their clothing, lock arms, and advance on the induction center. Rio feels her face burning, a pink so obvious that Strand can hardly help but misinterpret things. Or perhaps not so much misinterpret as see feelings she doesn't want him seeing.

Yet.

"Hi, Jenou," Strand says. Then, his voice subtly lower, says, "Hi, Rio. Come to see me off?"

"Us?" Rio feels suddenly guilty. She's involving Strand in a deception, after all. "We're just . . ."

"Signing up, the two of us," Jenou supplies. "Rio Richlin, Jenou Castain, ready to go off and wipe out the Japs and the Krauts too."

Strand smiles. "All by yourselves?"

"Well, I guess you can help too, if you want," Jenou says.

"So I thought for a minute you girls might be here to see me off." He's feeling his way forward in the conversation, casting glances at Rio, searching for clues, not sure what she's told Jenou about their date. "Today's the day. I came down here because my mother was threatening to show up and argue my case. Loudly. Figured it'd be best to take the bus down here and do it quiet. And why are you two here and not back up in Gedwell Falls?"

"Similar." Rio stumbles over the word. "Similar problems. My folks don't want me to enlist either."

"I guess they wouldn't," Strand says cautiously. "I guess I was relieved to get my notice. Means I don't have to go right up against my folks. I'm an only child, see, since the polio took my sister."

"You two have so much in common," Jenou says

breezily. "You should probably ask Rio out, Strand."

"Jen!" Rio cries. She is beginning to suspect that Jenou knows something.

Strand lowers his eyes to the ground, desperately confused but trying to play along with whatever game Rio is playing. "I think I might be punching above my weight, asking a girl like Rio out."

Jenou does a comic double take and says, "You think she's too good for you? I love her like a sister, Strand, but she's *not* too good for you."

At this Rio is left speechless, having no idea what she can possibly say.

"Rumor is we're shipping out pretty quick," Strand says. "Otherwise I sure would ask Rio out. She wouldn't have to say yes. I would understand."

"She would absolutely—"

"I suppose I might say yes," Rio blurts. "If you weren't shipping out." She makes "thank you" eyes at him, hoping she'll have a chance to explain her rather silly deception.

"Well, maybe after the war's over," Strand says.

"All right," Rio says. "I hope we . . . I hope you . . ."

"We're going in now," Jenou says, rolling her eyes in disbelief at the awkwardness of the conversation. "Good-bye, Strand."

Rio and Jenou plow through the door to the relative safety inside.

"Don't say anything," Rio warns her friend.

"You two will make such beautiful babies together."

"Certainly not that."

"Or you two could just take in a movie together," Jenou says. "Maybe share some popcorn and chocolate almonds. Then, about halfway through the movie, he could hold your hand. Then afterward you could talk and talk and talk and not even a good night kiss."

Rio stares daggers at Jenou, who laughs gaily and says, "My goodness, Rio, did you really think I wouldn't hear about it? Me? I've heard three different accounts, all from reliable sources."

"You mean gossips."

"Only the most reliable gossips." She play-slaps Rio's arm. "I cannot believe you are holding out on me. On me! Me, your best friend! I demand details. Later, not now, but you owe me the complete skinny."

"And you wonder why I didn't tell you. We're quite busy ruining our lives here; the gossip can wait."

"For now I just have one question: have you written your name and his surrounded by a heart in your journal?"

Rio has done exactly this. And she has written *Rio Braxton* several times as well.

"No, I wrote *Jenou Castain* with snakes crawling all around."

They're in a crowded hallway where a harassed-looking woman with a clipboard directs traffic.

"Where do we go to sign up?" Jenou asks.

They are directed to a side room that still has a sign reading Postmaster above the open, glass-paneled door. The furnishings inside are minimal: three stiff-backed chairs, a metal filing cabinet, a hatstand, and a wooden desk, behind which sits a doleful-looking man in a crisp khaki uniform. There are four stripes on his shoulders, but for the life of her Rio cannot remember what they signify.

"I'm Sergeant Tell. Can I help you girls?"

"We're here to enlist," both say at once, though one voice sounds cocksure and the other tentative.

Rio stands at a sort of civilian's version of attention and sidles close to Jenou, who slouches nonchalantly.

The sergeant shakes his head slowly, side to side. "I never thought I'd see the day."

"Sir?" Rio asks.

"Girls in the army. Never thought I'd see . . ." He shrugs it off and in a stern tone says, "Look, ladies, it's not sir. Sir is for officers. I work for a living. You call me sergeant."

"Yes, sir, Sergeant," Rio says.

The sergeant seems unsure of whether she's being a smart-aleck, but it's getting on toward lunchtime and there will be many other NCOs down the line to instruct these two in military etiquette. He sighs and produces two flimsy sheets and one pen. "You both eighteen or over as of this date? Fill in your names and addresses. Read it, sign it."

He has not even paused for them to answer. Rio is relieved but also a bit disappointed—she has a whole convoluted lie worked out about her age.

They sign, first Jenou then Rio. The sergeant has a stamp that he pounds first on the ink pad and then *bam, bam*, on each sheet.

"Through that door," he says.

"Through that door" brings them together with the draftees who'd been processed in a different queue. Rio glances around nervously and sees to her great relief that Strand is far toward the back of the line. She is all out of conversation with Strand, and she's terrified of being revealed as a shallow, empty-headed ninny with nothing to say.

Stop thinking about how big his hand was.

There were four tables, each manned by a corporal or sergeant and each apparently required to produce a piece of paper and bang a stamp down onto it.

Paper: *bang!* Paper: *bang!* Paper: *bang!*

Stop thinking about that single gunshot.

Then, "Are you now or have you ever been a member of

any organization devoted to the overthrow of the American government?"

"What?"

"I'll take that as a no." Paper: *bang!*

Thus far Rio is certain that not one of the soldiers has actually made eye contact with her. That changes at the last stop where yet another aged, bored-looking sergeant does not at first look up as he says, "Do you like girls?"

"They're all right," Jenou says. "But I quite prefer boys."

At that the sergeant looks up. "Ah. Sorry. Not yet used to the female of the um . . . Ahem. Do you like boys?"

"I guess so," Rio answers. "Some. Well . . . one. But it's—"

"Do you have any diseases that might affect your ability to perform your duties?"

Two "no" answers.

Bam. Bam.

"Take your papers through that door for your physical."

They head for the obvious door, the one marked Physicals.

"Not that door!" the sergeant yells. "Can't you see the sign that says Ladies?" The door before them is not labeled Gentlemen or Men Only. But Rio hears distinctly masculine voices from within.

Jenou freezes with her hand on the door. "Uh-uh. No, Jenou. No, you cannot go in there," Rio says. Rio drags her to the properly marked door.

Beyond the properly marked door is a small number of almost entirely naked people, all of them female.

"Strip down, all the way down to your bra and panties, stack your clothing in a box, and step into the line." The sergeant in this case is a woman, not as old as some of the men outside, but every bit as bored and indifferent. It's been just over five years since the courts decided that women *may* serve, and just over a year since deciding that women *must* serve. At this point then, any woman ranked above private was a volunteer who had most likely gotten in before the war even started.

Rio has never undressed in front of anyone except the family doctor. "I didn't realize that we . . . you know." They are the only two girls; the others are all women. Adult women.

I look like a stick figure.

"Come on, honey, no time for false modesty," Jenou says.

"There's nothing false about my modesty. This is perfectly genuine modesty." Rio begins to strip, stacking her clothing carefully in the box.

She feels extraordinarily exposed. And since it is a brisk day and the building is not heated she also feels cold, especially her now-bare feet on the linoleum floor.

She joins the line along with Jenou, who, to Rio's quiet satisfaction, finally seems just a little abashed and uncertain.

The line shuffles forward until they reach a man in a white coat. The fact that he, too, seems bored strikes Rio as funny.

"Lots of men might enjoy this job," she whispers to Jenou.

"Maybe he doesn't like girls."

"What do you mean?"

Jenou looks at her, seems to see something in her eyes, and shakes her head in wonder. "You really are so sweet, Rio. Remind me someday when we're as bored as he is and I'll tell you all about the birds and the bees, and also the bees and the bees and the birds and the birds."

"Step up!" the doctor snaps. "You, brunette. Have you had any disease that might affect your ability to perform your duties?"

"The other man already—"

"Yes or no?"

"No," Rio said.

"Do you have any form of venereal disease?"

"Pardon me?"

"That's a no. Pregnant?"

"I'm not married, as you can see!" She holds up an empty ring finger.

"Cough."

"What?"

"Cough. Cough, cough, cough. Are you going to make me repeat every question and instruction? Cough!"

Rio coughs.

"Turn your head left. Now right. Now look at the chart on the wall behind me, cover your left eye, and read the top line."

"E, G, R—"

"Now the other eye."

"E, G, R, Q—"

"Quiet." He holds a cold stethoscope to her chest. "Now prop your leg up on this stool."

Rio does, and the doctor snaps a triangular rubber mallet against her knee, causing her leg to twitch.

"Well," the doctor says, "at least you two are big, strapping country girls."

"Excuse me?" Jenou demands archly.

"The Depression took a toll on the size and health of recruits. If this were 1922 instead of 1942, there wouldn't be many females up to par. But a lot of males are undersized and understrength. If you only knew how many young men I have to reject for lack of sufficient teeth, or bowed legs, or . . ." He realizes he's complaining to a pair of recruits, stops himself, and quickly stamps their papers.

Then it's time to retrieve their boxes of clothing, dress, and proceed through one more door, where they merge again with the men and boys.

And there a final corporal stands waiting. As soon as twenty recruits have filled the room, he yells, "Attention!"

All twenty people in the room execute something that vaguely resembles the sort of attention they've seen in movies.

An officer strides into the room, barely glances up, and reads from a wrinkled and coffee-stained piece of paper.

"I, state your name."

"I, Rio Richlin" melts into a sea of voices pronouncing names.

The oath is dry and formal but has the effect of silencing the last whispers and titters in the room.

It's happening. Right now, it's happening.

"Do solemnly swear or affirm that I will support and defend the Constitution of the United States of America against all enemies, foreign and domestic; that I will bear true faith and allegiance to the same; and that I will obey the orders of the President and the orders of the officers appointed over me, according to regulations and the Uniform Code of Military Justice. So help me God."

The captain shoves the paper back into his shirt pocket and says, "Congratulations. You are all now members of the US Army."

Rio turns slowly to meet Jenou's unusually serious face.

"Just like that," Jenou says. "We're soldiers now."

Rio looks past her friend and finds an even more serious expression on Strand's face. He is at the far end of the room and has forgotten to lower his hand after taking the oath.

Then he spots her, realizes his hand is still up, lowers it, and smiles a sheepish smile.

Rio thinks, *We're soldiers now.*

8

RAINY SCHULTERMAN—NEW YORK CITY, NEW YORK, USA

"Women soldiers are an abomination!"

Rainy turns to look at the source. There is a group of perhaps twenty people, mostly women, holding signs reading *Eve is not Adam!!!* and *1 Timothy 2:12. Suffer not a woman to teach, nor to usurp authority over the man, but to be in silence!!!*

She doubts even the Christian Bible comes with that many exclamation points, and she toys with the idea of offering her own favorite verse from the Torah, Judges 4:21: *"But Jael the wife of Heber took a tent peg, and took a hammer in her hand, and went softly to him and drove the peg into his temple, till it went down into the ground . . ."* But she thinks better of it. A future in military intelligence does not begin with picking fights in train stations.

On the platform she tries to hear the garbled announcements from the public address, but it's as noisy as a fair, with farewells all around her and the hissing of steam engines and the shouts of false gaiety from nervous and excited soldiers.

She can hardly bear to look around her. So much sadness and worry from so many little family groups, so many mothers with tears, and so many fathers struggling not to reveal any emotion at all. It's a sea of olive drab and khaki, white handkerchiefs held to red noses, pink ribbons tied around newspaper-wrapped food parcels, coral lipstick on the lips of girlfriends; but these sprinkles of color only seem to accentuate the grayness of it all, the gray coats and shabby graying dresses, and gray-green fedoras pulled low, and gray abashed faces of men who are seeing off girlfriends for the first time in history.

Girl and women soldiers are going off to war, wearing pants and boots, shouldering heavy packs and duffels. Some are at the end of their leave after basic training, heading off to deployments in places whose names will be excised from their letters home by the censors. Some are home on leave from Britain or Australia.

It can't ever have been easy, Rainy thinks, not any war. But the rituals are different now. It has always been that the men went off and the women wept and waved. There is no blueprint for what is happening now. There is no easy reference point. People don't know quite how to behave, and it's worse for the men in the station who are staying behind and feel conspicuous and ashamed.

She sees belligerent, defensive looks even as men hug their uniformed sweethearts. She sees looks of dark suspicion aimed at male soldiers when they acknowledge their fellow female soldiers with a grin or a handshake or a clap on the back.

It is all worth noticing, worth considering, Rainy believes. It is all a part of this war. It's all a small part of something unimaginably huge. Millions are dead already, millions more will die; she is grimly certain of that. She has never really accepted the notion that the arrival of the Americans will end things in a few months. Rainy can read a map, and she has seen how much of the world now lies beneath the flag with the swastika.

Rainy has insisted on coming alone to the station, fearing the flood of parental emotion that would weaken her determination. She'd already been through that when she first enlisted, and when she went off to basic training, and now she's heading to this intelligence school for still more training, after which . . .

Well, after which no one knew for sure. Everyone says America is ready, finally, to go up against the Germans. Marines are already fighting the Japanese, but despite the special rage and hatred people felt for the Japanese, Rainy knows the Germans are the greater danger.

Aryeh can kill Japanese; Rainy wants to kill Nazis.

They are the great enemies of humanity; they are the cancer on civilization. The German armed forces—the Wehrmacht—has already destroyed vast armies, conquered millions of square miles. They have deliberately starved hundreds of thousands at Leningrad. The German air force—the Luftwaffe—has slaughtered tens of thousands of civilians in Poland and in England. The German navy and its vicious submarine wolf packs have littered the ocean floor with ships and the bones of sailors.

It is the Germans, the Nazis, who have enslaved millions of French, Dutch, Poles, Czechs, Danes, Belgians, Ukrainians, and others.

It is the Nazis who force Jewish children into camps in Poland and Russia.

Why hasn't Cousin Esther written? Why has no one gotten a letter from any Jew in Nazi-occupied territory?

Rainy does not expect to fire a weapon in anything but training, but intelligence work can be as deadly to her foe, and the Nazis are her foe, her personal foe. She will remember—she has ordered herself to remember—that each day she performs her duties well will contribute to destroying that enemy.

And saving the world.

That thought coaxes a small smile from her. *All by yourself, Rainy?* She mocks herself. *Will you destroy Hitler and his empire of hate?*

"If I get the chance," she whispers.

Finally she hears her train being called, snatches up her bag, and pushes her way through the crowd. It's a long train behind two huffing black engines leaking clouds of steam, and it takes her a while to find her assigned compartment. She's the second to get there, behind a civilian woman with a vast handbag stuffed with salamis and wilting flowers.

"Ma'am," Rainy says respectfully, and takes a window seat. The woman glares at her and pulls her bag closer, as if fearing Rainy will take something.

Three young male soldiers pile in—the compartment can hold eight if no one breathes too deeply. They're either drunk very early or drunk very late, depending on whether they've gone to bed.

"Hey, it's a girl!" one of them says, and flops fragrantly beside her. They're all privates; no insignia of rank yet adorns their uniforms.

"You sure that's a girl? Don't look like no girl. Looks like a . . ." And there his verbal abilities fail him, and he trains unfocused eyes on Rainy before slumping back, unconscious.

A conductor is pushing his way down the jammed and noisy corridor, leading a male officer. He reaches the door to the compartment, holds it open, accepts a tip, and, as he closes the compartment door, slides down the roll-up blind.

Rainy watches the officer, a first lieutenant. The lieutenant watches her right back, takes in the three drunks and the civilian woman, and sits opposite Rainy.

The two more-conscious soldiers immediately attempt to straighten themselves up, adjusting caps and in one case making a valiant but doomed attempt to align buttons with their proper holes.

It is unusual, to say the least, to have an officer sitting here in the cheap seats. Maybe the train is overloaded. But no, this officer was guided here.

"Lieutenant," Rainy says, and nods. Protocol does not call for saluting in this situation.

The lieutenant makes a show of reading the name tag on her uniform. "Schulterman, is it?"

"PFC Rainy Schulterman, sir," Rainy acknowledges.

He smiles. It's not a leer, nor is it a friendly smile. It's a practiced smile. He's carrying only a briefcase, no duffel. His boots are shined; his uniform is crisp. He's perhaps twenty-five, with watery-blue eyes behind glasses, blond hair, scrubbed pink skin, thin lips and shoulders. He's a crease-checker, one of those men who reach compulsively to pinch the crease in his trousers, making sure it stays straight, that it stands tall above the thigh before being flattened by the pressure of the kneecap.

"Where you headed, PFC?"

"South, sir."

"Just south?" Again, the practiced smile. "That covers a lot of ground."

"Yes, sir."

He considers this, and the train jerks as the big steel wheels engage. The platform and its waving, weeping population slide away, made to look like a dreamscape by the wreaths of steam.

"Girl like you, I guess you're headed to Fort Ritchie, right?" He waits a beat for an answer and gets nothing. "It's all right, Private, we're on the same side." He laughs confidentially. "I swear I won't tell a soul." He makes the sign of the cross over his heart.

"Is that where you're heading, Lieutenant?"

He pretends not to hear.

The passed-out drunk is sliding as the train moves, feet beneath the seat, knees extending, back slipping; he'll be on the floor as soon as they hit a turn.

The officer pulls a pack of cigarettes from his chest pocket. He taps one halfway out and offers it to Rainy.

"No thank you, sir."

"Don't smoke?"

"It seems a bit . . . close . . . in here," Rainy ventures.

"Do you mind if I . . ." He holds a cigarette hovering near his lips.

"Not at all, sir," she says. She does mind, but she's not going to chide a military intelligence officer. That is of

107

course what he is, she has no doubt of that, despite the lack of any revealing insignia.

He lights his cigarette and blows a blue cloud. "What do you think of all this, if you don't mind my asking, Private?"

"All what, sir?"

He shrugs and waves the cigarette in an arc encompassing the compartment and perhaps more. "Must be strange, being a girl and all."

"No, sir. I've been a girl my whole life."

It's the kind of response that walks right up to the line of being a smart-ass answer. The lieutenant's grin is quick and genuine this time. "Yeah, I guess it's not so bad for some girls. You might meet a nice fellow."

Rainy doesn't answer.

"You're not so talkative, are you, Private?"

Rainy manages a tight smile, and this seems to encourage him. "Well, maybe I haven't introduced myself properly. Lieutenant Janus. Heading to Pittsburg myself. I'm in supply and logistics there."

Sure you are.

"Pleasure to meet you, sir."

The sharp, jerking movement comes as they clear the station and accelerate, and sure enough the passed-out drunk slides toward the floor. Rainy leans forward and lays a hard tap with the edge of her hand on his knee. He jerks awake just long enough to curl himself sideways and avoid sliding all the way.

The civilian woman does not approve of any of this. The other two privates are leaning into each other, having the kind of very intense conversations men sometimes have when inebriated. The topic appears to be a friend who's been rated unfit for service, 4F, and whether or not he's a wolf who will be going after their girls ten seconds after the train is out of the station. Also, beer. And something to do with some jackass sergeant who . . .

They suddenly recall that there's an officer present and fall silent.

"May I ask what attracted you to supply and logistics, sir?" And again the question is absolutely respectful and cheeky at the same time.

"Mostly the logistics," he says solemnly. He's beginning to suspect she's playing with him.

"Yes, sir. I've never been entirely clear on what that involves."

He does not offer to enlighten her. "You from here in New York City?"

"Well, that's where I caught this train, sir."

"Family?"

"Yes, sir."

"Mother? Father?"

"One of each, sir."

"I don't suppose they're happy seeing you dragged into this stupid, pointless war, eh?"

"I wasn't aware that the war was stupid. Or pointless."

A long drag on the cigarette. A crease check. "Well, it's not our war, is it? Why should we be fighting to save Britain from the Germans? Let alone the Russians, those Bolshevik, Commie bastards. Tell me, Private: why should we be fighting for a dying colonial empire and a dangerous totalitarian state?"

Rainy takes a moment to consider the correct answer. "Because that's what the chain of command has ordered us to do, sir."

Check. And mate.

He sees it now. He sighs. "I'm going to see if I can get some fresh air. You're right, it's rather close in here. Join me, PFC Schulterman."

It's not a request. Rainy stands up and follows him into the still-jammed corridor. She spots the Full sign the conductor has hung on their not-really-full compartment. The lieutenant leads her to the end of the car, just a few feet, and onto a rickety, noisy gallery between rattling cars. The platform is not two feet deep. It's cold out, and a whole lot colder with the forty-mile-an-hour wind generated by the train's increasing speed.

"You can cut the crap now, PFC." He has to raise his voice over the clatter of steel wheels and steel coupling.

"Sir. One of two things must happen now, respectfully."

He tilts his head. "Oh?"

"Sir, either you show me identification stating that you are with army intelligence, or I will have no choice but to report you to the first officer I find. You're asking a lot of questions."

"Ha!" He's both delighted with, and abashed by, her answer. "How long did it take you?"

"Sir, your ID, please."

His mouth hangs open for a second, then with a genuine grin that takes five years off his face so he looks like an adolescent playing dress-up, he reaches inside his tunic and hands her a cardboard identity card.

His name is not Lieutenant Janus, it's Captain Jon Herkemeier. And he is army intelligence.

"Well done, PFC Schulterman." He puts the ID away and reveals that in addition to being a crease-checker, he's a lapel tugger. Fidgety and fastidious. "And now answer my question: how long did it take?"

"No time at all, sir."

"Ah."

"You're an officer in enlisted country. The conductor brought you to that specific compartment. You ignored the others and focused on me. You have no luggage. The conductor hung a Full sign as soon as you came in. So, if I may speak freely . . ."

He waves his cigarette by way of permission.

"You were either a very indifferent masher, or you were FBI or army intelligence checking me out."

He nods, sticks the smoke into his mouth, and extends his hand. She shakes it formally.

"You know how to keep your mouth shut," he says. "That's good." One last drag and he flicks the butt out over the track. "That's very good."

"Thank you, sir."

"So, the military intelligence school for you, eh?"

"Sir, either you know where I'm heading, or you don't."

"Huh. All right then, PFC Schulterman. Carry on."

He leaves her there, and by the time she makes it back to the compartment the Full sign is gone and her seat has been lost to fresh bodies.

Rainy is irritated at losing her seat. And sinfully proud of having successfully run this gantlet.

I'm going to like this game.

The next day, showered, her hair as under control as it ever is, her uniform as neat as she can make it, Rainy joins the first class of recruits in the history of the Military Intelligence Training School to number females among its complement. Twenty-seven males and fourteen females jump from their steel chairs as a gaggle of officers enter and take the stage.

Rainy is not surprised to see the erstwhile Lieutenant

Janus—Captain Herkemeier—standing behind and to one side of the colonel who commands the school.

For about two minutes Rainy feels the pride of standing alongside other enlisted personnel chosen for their intelligence, discretion, judgment, and skill at languages. Colonel Derry, a small man with a thin mustache and thick glasses, throws a very big bucket of cold water on that emotion.

"The Supreme Court, in its infinite wisdom, has decreed that we must . . ." Here Colonel Derry searches for the right word and ends up spitting it out like a piece of bad meat. ". . . *accept* . . . Has decreed that we must *accept* females into this training facility." Maybe he is naturally pop-eyed, or maybe the lenses of his spectacles make his eyes appear ready to pop like overfilled water balloons, but most likely, Rainy believes, he is actually enraged. His voice is certainly tense and high-strung. And he bounces on the balls of his feet with each word he emphasizes. It creates an odd sort of show since his choices of emphasis seem almost random.

"I have been *ordered* to thus *accept* females, and I carry out my orders. But as long as *I* am in *command* of this facility, I will exercise my discretion to the *maximum*, to ensure that the natural *order of the sexes*"—that phrase comes with three rapid bounces—"a natural order that has *decreed* that woman shall bear children and *tend* the hearth, while *men* shoulder the harsher burdens of life's *vicissitudes. . . .*" He loses his way for a moment, but finds it quickly enough. "Females will be accorded all the *courtesies* of their rank, and *woe* to any male who treats them ill. But woe as well to any *female* who forgets her place or fails to exhibit the *virtues* of her *sex*!"

Throughout this Captain Jon Herkemeier stares straight ahead, neither nodding nor shaking his head.

There are suppressed snickers from some of the male soldiers. Rainy can hardly blame them. *Virtues of her sex* is a phrase almost designed for deliberate misinterpretation.

Rainy doesn't look around—one does not look around when a colonel is speaking—but within her peripheral vision are two other females, neither looking pleased.

"In short," Colonel Derry concludes, "I expect each of you to pay the closest attention to your instructors. I expect your fullest devotion to the *task* at hand. This is no easy course of study, and if any of you male soldiers think you're going to avoid service overseas, I can tell you that *you are likely* to be disappointed. The ladies will surely stay safe, but for you men, your lives and the lives of other soldiers may well depend on the techniques *and* skills you learn *here*."

In one five-minute speech, Colonel Derry crushes any hope Rainy has that she will be treated fairly.

Is there any point in this? No doubt there are useful assignments here in the States, but that's not the image that's been in Rainy's mind, the image that's motivated her to push through the pain and humiliation of basic training. She did not learn to qualify on rifles, machine guns, rifle grenades, and mortars in order to sit at a desk in some swampy hole somewhere safe. She did not drag her exhausted body up and down hills, through obstacle courses and live fire drills, only to end up typing and answering telephones in Arizona or some other godforsaken hole.

She cannot, will not, spend the war in a swivel chair. Not while Aryeh is chasing Japs across the Pacific Ocean.

But open defiance will get her cut from the program. Complaining up the chain of command will get her cut from the program. Trying to recruit support from male soldiers will make her look weak and cause her to be cut from the program.

There is only one way to prevail. That is to outwork, outthink, outperform every soldier in the school.

Rainy Schulterman is ready for that challenge.

9

RIO RICHLIN—CAMP MARON, SMIDVILLE, GEORGIA, USA

"Atten-HUT!"

Rio, Jenou, and two dozen other new recruits, more male than female, stand more or less straight, in rows that are more or less straight. They have just piled off a bus from the train station following a sixteen-hour trip, and they are tired, frazzled, and a bit nervous. They stretch and shake out their arms and yawn at the deep-blue sky.

In Rio's estimation, they are in the middle of nowhere. The last town they passed had a gas station, a hardware store, a feed store even smaller than the one Rio's father owns, a diner, and a shack that might have been a tavern. And that was pretty much the beginning, middle, and end of the town of Smidville, Georgia, a town that made Gedwell Falls look like Chicago by comparison.

The camp, which they've been told is named Camp Maron, consists of a series of long wooden barracks that, judging by the smell of pinewood and paint, have been slapped together within just the last few days.

But this new construction is mirrored by an older, more run-down version of itself called Camp Szekely, which is just across a sluggish, green, reed-choked stream. No bridge crosses the stream, so to move from Camp Maron to Camp Szekely you have to leave by the front gate of one, drive half a mile down an orange clay road, and enter the other camp. It's a mile away by road, but you could throw a rock from one camp to the other.

The colors here are green, gray, and orange. Green trees—hemlock, beech, and oak, but more shaggy, unsteady-looking pine than anything else. Some of the hardwoods are hung with Spanish moss, a sort of gray garland that gives everything an aged and mournful look.

The cleared areas are startlingly orange. Wet red clay holds shapes well, so the roads and bare fields are patterned by the big tires of deuce-and-a-half trucks, jeeps, graders, tractors, and, most basically, boots.

The first mosquito appears within twenty seconds of Rio climbing from the bus.

"Parade rest. That means you widen your stance and link your hands behind your backs. NO! Not with the soldier next to you, goddammit! Your own hands! Now, listen up, men," the sergeant says in a perturbed but not-unfriendly voice. "You will pick up your gear and fall out to the barracks you see on your . . . Not now, you fugging ninnies, you fall out when I give the order! Sweet suffering Jesus in a chicken basket!"

The few who went running to their bags and shabby suitcases piled up outside the steaming bus quickly hop back in line.

"You will fall out to the quartermaster to be issued your uniforms and gear. Then you will proceed to your assigned barracks. And there you will find your new home. One barracks—and only one—will be shared by male and female recruits; we do not have the luxury of separate facilities. So there is a curtain that will be drawn across to separate you. Women bunk on the north side, men bunk on the south side of that line. Get squared away and be ready in one hour. Atten-HUT! Dismissed!"

Rio and Jenou trot back to search for their bags— they've been told to bring nothing but a few small personal items and a change of clothing. One of the men offers to carry Jenou's bag for her, and Rio can see that she's just about to consent.

"She can carry her own bag," Rio says. "Thanks just the same."

Jenou gives her a wry look, but Rio has an instinct born of the long train ride and the bus ride with male recruits. Her instinct tells her that the way to survive here is to take nothing from anyone.

The quartermaster occupies a long, low wooden

structure with trucks parked in back and jeeps in front. Inside, the sexes are sent in different directions, women following a tacked-up piece of paper that says "Ladies." Rio wonders if the quotation marks are meant to be a smart-aleck commentary.

A female corporal with a clipboard repeats, "Strip to your panties, put your things in a box, label the box using the grease pencils, advance."

They file mostly naked into the hallway, which has blessedly been blocked by a hastily attached curtain. But they must pass a window en route, and a pair of soldiers are leering in at them, pointing and making inaudible comments.

Rio's face burns red, and she clutches the box to her chest protectively, while Jenou winks at the soldiers and half-lowers her box teasingly before sticking out her tongue.

They advance to a waist-high counter. A female private behind the counter looks Rio up and down with the quick professional glance of a woman who was, until three months ago, a clerk at Carson, Pirie, Scott department store in Chicago. "Twenty-four waist, thirty-four length, and a medium blouse." She reaches into the cut-down cardboard boxes behind her and produces two olive drab uniforms and a set of fatigues. These she slaps on the counter.

Rio starts to move on.

"Wait." The clerk produces three undershirts, three pairs of men's boxer shorts, three pairs of socks. "Shoe size, cup size?"

"My pumps are size six, but—"

"Size seven." Boots appear.

"Cup? Come on, honey, you've bought a bra before, haven't you?"

"Thirty-two B."

"Sure, if you say so." The private reaches into a box clearly labeled Brassiere, OD, Size: A Cup. "The strap's adjustable. You'll get used to it. Move along."

Rio is on the point of arguing, but there isn't much a person can say standing there in panties. So she piles her new clothing up, slides her arms beneath the pile, and staggers back to the converted closet where women and girls chat noisily and begin a process that will not end before the war itself: complaining about the army.

"What are these things supposed to be?" A woman holds up her new olive drab bra with far more buckles and straps than usual.

"These socks itch like crazy."

"This is definitely not my size. Who sewed this blouse? Just look at this stitching."

Rio dresses and waits for Jenou to catch up. Both breathe a sigh of relief when they are fully covered, though nothing fits quite right.

It's the boots that feel strangest. They are undeniably masculine, brown leather, laced up to above the ankles. They are heavy and solid and the leather squeaks as Rio walks in them, trying them out.

For the first time, Rio and Jenou step out into the world wearing a uniform. These are not their first trousers—Gedwell Falls girls generally do some sort of physical labor at some point that requires overalls or dungarees—but it is the first time either of them by their dress have announced themselves as belonging to something. *Being* something other than just two high school girls.

They walk, terribly self-conscious, to the barracks.

The barracks is a very simple affair, one long room with metal frame cots in rows on each side, near but not precisely aligned with tall windows, eighteen bunks on each side, for a total of thirty-six soldiers. At the foot of each cot is an OD-painted wooden locker. Against the wall is a rack with four wooden hangers and a rickety shelf above. The floor is polished linoleum, cream and maroon squares. The walls are tan-painted wood paneling. Artificial light comes from eight bare lightbulbs hanging down from the ceiling on cords. At the south end of the barracks is a large latrine area. A stenciled sign reads Male.

The heat and humidity inside the barracks are enough to steam rice.

At the north end is a separate room the size of a small bedroom, with a stenciled plaque that reads Sgt. Mackie. Across from this lone bit of personal territory is a smaller latrine labeled Female.

"So, this is home," Jenou says.

"I guess so, for the next thirteen weeks." Rio feels at once excited and lost. The hurried good-bye with her parents did not go well. There were tense, angry words and threats, in particular a threat to march Rio down to the intake center and tell them that she was not yet of legal age.

"It's no good, Father," Rio said after several heated exchanges. "It's either now or when you can't stop me. But if I go now I may be able to stay together with Jenou. I'd rather have a friend with me; we can look out for each other. But one way or the other, I'm going."

Jenou's parents did not bother to show up at all, but Jenou's family is not as tight-knit as Rio's. In fact, if Jenou is to be believed—and Rio does believe her—it's barely a family at all. It was irritating being cross-examined by her tearful parents, but Rio preferred it to the cold indifference that sent Jenou off to join the army.

"What do you think, Jen?"

"I think this is my cot. You take that one."

Rio looks around, wondering why this particular cot has attracted Jenou. Then she sees that the curtain separating the men from the women will be drawn right next to Jenou's cot.

"I'm not sure your mind is completely focused on protecting and defending the Constitution of the United States of America," Rio says.

Jenou grins. "I swore to protect and defend the Constitution of the US of A from all enemies, Rio. They didn't say I couldn't have fun while I was at it."

"Listen up." The voice is not loud, but it is authoritative, and to Rio's surprise it belongs to a woman. Rio's first impression is that Sergeant Mackie looks a bit like Rio herself. The sergeant is tall and has that hard-to-define quality that is the mark of a life spent largely out of doors. Her black hair is cut short, almost as short as a man's. Her eyes are blue like Rio's but a great deal more intimidating. She wears no makeup of any kind. The creases in her uniform are so sharp she could carve a roast beef with them. There are four gold stripes on her shoulders, three up-pointing darts and one smile-like arc beneath, and a handful of tiny, colorful rectangles on her chest. Her boots could almost be patent leather they're so shiny.

Sergeant Mackie is trim, fit, vibrating with physical energy, and shows no trace of emotion, fellow-feeling, or sympathy. She stands at rest, feet planted wide, and there seems to be around her a sort of invisible fence that makes the very thought of being close to her, let alone of touching her, an impossibility. She is a person who, deprived of uniform and dressed in a church-day frock, would still look like a soldier.

Sergeant Mackie has the effect of making Rio feel deeply, profoundly inadequate—inadequate, soft, weak, silly, and hopelessly inferior. All this before Mackie has spoken more than two words.

"When you are called to attention you will stand at the end of your cot on the right-hand corner, by which I mean that your left hand should point directly down at the edge of the frame. Atten-HUT!"

Men and women alike do their best to comply, but not without confusion accompanied by a certain amount of horseplay and wry looks and winks, especially from some of the younger males.

Sergeant Mackie seems at first not to notice the mirth. Then she walks—strides, really—in measured steps, her mirror-polished boots so steady and slow as to be almost sinister, to a tall, beefy male of maybe nineteen or twenty years who is among those laughing. He's got buzz-cut light-red hair, a forehead that wants to crush the dark eyes beneath, and a determined, angry mouth, though at the moment he's still stifling a giggle as he stands at an insolent, unimpressed attention. Mackie squares off before him. He is taller than she by a head, so she has to tilt her head back to look him in the eyes with an expression that is mystified, as if she can't quite make out just what she's seeing.

"What's your name, Private?"

"Me? I'm Luther. Luther Geer."

"Well, Private Geer, do you know how to do a push-up?"

"I reckon I do."

"Then drop and give me twenty-five."

"What?"

"Drop. To the floor. And execute twenty-five stiff-backed, stiff-legged push-ups."

"I—"

"NOW!"

It's as if her voice has the power to seize direct control of his body, because Private Geer drops to the floor and begins to do push-ups. It clearly surprises even Private Geer.

"Are you telling me you consider that a push-up?" Sergeant Mackie demands after Geer has done three. She shakes her head in sincere disgust. "Eyes on me."

This last is an entirely unnecessary instruction since thirty-six pairs of eyes are already glued to Mackie. Well, thirty-five, since Luther Geer is staring at the floor and laboring to perform his fourth push-up.

"You," she says, jerking her chin at Rio. "Count them off."

The sergeant falls to the floor in a single swift motion,

lands on her palms, and, stiff as an ironing board, begins to perform push-ups as Rio says, "One! Two! Three!"

Now Geer is challenged so he tries harder, but Mackie is at ten before he reaches six, and at twenty-five when he's gasping and shaking to make it to fifteen.

At eighteen he tries to give up. Sergeant Mackie is not having it.

"Give me one more, Geer. Nineteen. One more. Come on, one more. Push, push, push . . . twenty."

They go on like that until Private Geer is as pink as cotton candy, sweat drenched, and trembling like a man with fever chills.

When done he stands at attention, sweat stains spreading from his armpits, and he is no longer smirking.

Rio expects Mackie to berate the boy, but Mackie is smarter than that. "Don't you worry about it, son, by the time we're done with you you'll be doing twenty-five without even breathing hard. Because *you*"—she takes a beat on that word, making it specific—"are going to be a soldier." She pushes his shoulders back, with the heel of her hand positions his head, and with her boot kicks his feet into proper alignment.

She steps back smartly to where the entire barracks can see her without craning their necks and can witness the fact that she has not a hair out of place or so much as a bead of sweat on her olive skin.

"I won't lie to you, people. This is going to be the hardest thirteen weeks of your life up to this point. But in the end, if I am not forced to spit you out, you will be soldiers. Answer 'Yes, Sergeant.'"

"Yes, Sergeant!"

"Ninety percent of what you will say over the next thirteen weeks will be those two words: *yes* and *sergeant*."

Rio has no confidence that she can do three push-ups, let alone twenty-five. And that is nothing compared to what might come next. She has thus far focused all her thoughts on the job of enlisting without giving a lot of thought to the question of whether she can get through training. And as much as she is worried about her own abilities, she worries still more about Jenou. Jenou, despite her curves, is built on a strong enough frame, but she is no athlete, and unlike Rio she has never slung a bale of hay or hauled a sack of fertilizer.

"Your lives are now under army control," Mackie says. It isn't a threat, just a statement of fact. "You will fall out at 0600 every morning. Not 0615. Not 0610. Not 0601. You will dress in fatigues, stand ready, and be marched outside for PT at 0615. There the other NCOs and I will endeavor to train your bodies for the hard work ahead. Do you comprehend?"

"Yes, Sergeant!"

"After PT you will shower and shave and stand ready

to be marched to chow at 0730. At 0800 you will begin the day's assignments. You will learn drill, weapons handling, small unit tactics, and battlefield first aid. PT will get tougher with each day. Training will become more difficult with each day. Do you comprehend?"

"Yes, Sergeant!" There's a slightly desperate sound to that affirmation.

"Lights out will be at 2100 hours. That's nine o'clock p.m. for those of you who don't do so well at math. From 2100 hours until 0600, you will not smoke, talk, read, or move from your bunk except to use the latrine, which you will do one at a time during the night. Do you comprehend?"

"Yes, Sergeant!"

"If you are still awake at 2200 hours I will have no choice but to feel ashamed. I will be ashamed because it will mean that I have not worked you hard enough. That may happen once. I assure you it will not happen twice."

She walks now in that measured, deliberate way, that pace that evokes radio plays of supernatural terror.

"The curtain separating male and female will be drawn one hour before lights out. Anyone crossing that line will be guilty of a court-martial offense. Anyone harassing a fellow soldier will be guilty of a court-martial offense. Anyone fraternizing in an improper way with a fellow soldier will be guilty of a court-martial offense. Do you comprehend?"

"Yes, Sergeant!"

"But before you have a chance to whine and beg for mercy in front of a court-martial, you will have to deal . . . with me."

She stops in front of Private Timoteo "Tilo" Suarez, a dark-haired, sly-faced, sensuous-eyed city boy. She pivots so her face is within six inches of his and says, "Do you comprehend, Private Suarez?"

"Yes, Sergeant!"

Then she walks back to Jenou, and with her face so close to Jenou's they are breathing the same air, she says, "Do you comprehend, Private Castain?"

"Yes, Sergeant!"

Sergeant Mackie has unerringly picked out the two most likely offenders, one from each gender. Jenou has already been eyeing Tilo Suarez, and he has returned that attention. Rio has to grit her teeth to suppress the grin that's struggling to break out.

"All right." Mackie relaxes her posture a few degrees and softens her voice. "For a lot of you this is your first time away from home. Some of you are old enough to know how to handle yourselves, but a lot of you are young. Some of you very young." Her eyes flick toward Rio.

She knows!

"So here's what you need to do. First off, listen to the NCOs. An NCO is any sergeant, corporal, or private first class. If you see stripes on a shoulder, that's an NCO, also known as a noncom. One stripe is a PFC, two stripes is a corporal, three stripes is a buck sergeant, four stripes, well, that's a staff sergeant and that's me. Beyond that you don't need to know except that should you ever happen to glimpse six stripes with a star in the center, then you have laid eyes upon the sergeant major, which is to say God's holy avenging angel on earth. And woe unto you if you embarrass me in front of the sergeant major."

She's berating, she's threatening, but, Rio realizes, she's also teaching.

"Second, help each other out. Pay attention to your training, because in a very few weeks you may be the target lined up perfectly in an enemy's sights. You're going to want to know what to do in that situation so as not to end up dead. The army is a team, a team belonging to the government of this great nation, the greatest nation on earth. Am I correct about that?"

"Yes, Sergeant!"

"You are GIs. Government issue. You are all on the GI team. That team extends from President Franklin Delano Roosevelt down through the chiefs of staff, down through the generals and the junior officers, all the way down through the noncoms, and finally, to you. You." At that moment she seems to be looking at each of them, one by one, which isn't possible, but it's how Rio feels. "One team. One purpose. What's your name, Private?"

She has come to stand in front of a young man with intelligent eyes and a widow's peak.

"Private Dain Sticklin, Sergeant."

"What is the purpose of an American soldier, Private Dain Sticklin?"

"To kill the enemy," he says.

For a fleeting moment an actual human expression threatens to appear on Mackie's face. "Not the worst answer, Private Sticklin. But your purpose is to obey the orders of your superiors. Obedience to orders. Obedience to orders. Obedience. To. Orders. Do you all comprehend?"

"Yes, Sergeant!"

"You will follow orders. You will learn. You will do many different jobs in my army, Privates, but before each of you leaves my care, you will have learned to obey orders. And . . ." She nods at Private Sticklin. ". . . you'll also have learned how to kill the enemy. Chow in thirty minutes; get your gear squared away. Dismissed."

There is a collective breath, a collective sagging of shoulders, a few low whistles.

"She knows you're boy crazy," Rio says to Jenou.

"That's ridiculous," Jenou says with a wink. "No one in the army is really a *boy*. They're men, Rio. I'm *man* crazy."

"I quite like our sergeant," a young man who couldn't

131

have been much older than Rio says in a distinctly non-American accent. "Friendly lass."

The man with the accent is two bunks down from Jenou. He's thin, tall, has ginger hair, blue eyes, and radiates an unmistakable sense of charm and fun. Rio knows Jenou will like him—she likes smart-alecks.

Sure enough. "And who might you be?" Jenou asks.

"I might be the prime minister of Great Britain, but sadly I'm just plain Jack Stafford. Private John Lloyd Merriwether Stafford, officially, but you can call me Jack."

He sticks out a hand, and Jenou and Rio take turns shaking it—Jenou taking a bit longer with the motion. Because she's Jenou.

"What's with the accent?" Jenou asks.

"I might ask you the same thing," Jack replies. "But I suppose you are remarking on the fact that I speak English as it was meant to be spoken."

"What are you doing in our army?" Dain Sticklin asks, not confrontational, just curious. "Shouldn't you be in the British army?"

"Mmm, yes. Probably should. But this seems to be the only way for me to get back there." In a less cheeky tone, he explains. "I was evacuated to America, me and my little sister, along with a lot of other kids, back when the bombing started. I was just sixteen at the time, and the King's army doesn't take you until you're eighteen. I've been living with an aunt in Hagerstown since then. Now that I'm old enough, well, no way to get back home."

"Can't your parents . . ." Rio senses the misstep before the words are all the way out of her mouth.

"Afraid not," he says, pushing past a wobble in his voice and a small, involuntary tightening of his jaw. "German bomb took them."

"Well, we'll go kill us some Germans together, right? Get some payback." Tilo Suarez grins at Rio and says, "Tilo Suarez. But you can call me handsome."

"But then you'd have to be handsome," Rio says, deadpan. "Otherwise it would be like I was mocking you."

There's a sharp laugh from Stafford and a stiffening from Tilo. Dain Sticklin suppresses a grin.

"Quick," Jack says, consoling Tilo by patting him on the back. "The woman is quick."

"Women in the army. It's a mistake," Tilo says with a sneer, but he glances warily in the direction Sergeant Mackie has taken.

"And yet, here they are," Jack says. "As are we all."

"If I could find a girl to take my place, I'd sure go for it," another young man says. He's a strong-looking boy with reddish hair, a round face, and an easygoing manner. "Kerwin Cassel, from Teays, West Virginia," he says, and there follows still more hand-shaking.

"Well, new chums and teammates and all of that,"

Jack says. "Shall we go in to dinner?"

Tilo Suarez is not happy to be lumped in as a chum or a teammate, but in the end he can't think of a way to decline. And Kerwin Cassel seems genuinely pleased to have found anyone to talk to. Sticklin starts to move away.

Jack calls to him, saying, "Come on then, old boy, you and I are doomed to be mates, right? Jack and Stick? Or Stick and Jack, if you prefer."

A slow smile spreads over Sticklin's serious face. "I was trying to leave that nickname behind me, but I guess there's no avoiding it."

"Is this the popular kids, or the social outcasts?" The question comes from another woman soldier. She's as tall as Rio, but broader, with a solidity of form that suggests that like Rio she's carried heavy objects at some point in her life. The sturdy shape is belied a bit by a strange, down-turned smile that shows only her upper teeth. She has strawberry hair and dark eyes that shine with humor and skepticism.

Jenou says, "Any gang I'm in is the cool kids. Who are you?"

"Cat Preeling."

"What's Cat short for?" Tilo asks. She makes him nervous, most likely because she looks at him the way a scientist looks at germs under a microscope.

"It's short for Cat, slick."

Rio lags a little behind as the seven of them blunder their way to the chow hall—it's hidden behind the quartermaster's building. Rio, Jenou, Cat, Stick, Jack, Tilo, and Kerwin. Rio thinks, *Only one normal name among them, and he's an Englishman.*

She wonders idly who Jenou will target. Stick is not her type, too serious. Tilo is the obvious choice—he's the sort who will dance and drink and flirt—but maybe that makes him too obvious? Plus he's just about an inch shorter than Jenou, and she's never liked short boys. Kerwin? No, the hillbilly accent will put Jenou off.

No, Rio suspects that Jenou will go for the charming redheaded foreigner with the charm.

Anyway, that's who Rio would go for.

10

RAINY SCHULTERMAN—MILITARY INTELLIGENCE SCHOOL, CAMP RITCHIE, PENNSYLVANIA, USA

Rainy stands before Colonel Derry in his office. She is at attention. He leaves her at attention while he makes a show of looking over her file.

Rainy has a pretty good idea what he's seeing there: of the forty student soldiers in Rainy's class, she is first in German fluency, second in her command of Italian and French, fifth in the math skills that are particularly useful in deciphering coded messages, consistently scores well in her comprehension of the handbooks and lessons, and reads a map reasonably well. She seems to have an intuitive grasp of aerial photography.

On the downside—or what Colonel Derry will no doubt see as the upside—the report from basic training indicates that she can't shoot worth a damn, can barely raise the heavy M-1 to aim, and is of no use whatsoever in hand-to-hand combat.

Rainy's instructors—even the "sensible" older hands who, like Colonel Derry, believe that women have no business even being here—give her high marks for leadership. And neither the censors nor her fellow soldiers nor her NCOs nor her officers have ever gotten an indiscreet word out of her.

She can, in short, keep a secret, a fact she's inordinately proud of.

Colonel Derry is not a subtle man, and his motives are not hard for Rainy to grasp: he had obviously been hoping to wash out all the females. This is no longer basic training—basic training is almost impossible to wash out of since the army is quite keen to fill uniforms. But this is an elite school, and eliminating the weak is a legitimate part of its role. In fact, as Rainy knows very well, of the initial forty in the school, three women and five men have already been reassigned.

Rainy approves of every one of those reassignments so far. She shares the desire to graduate only the most capable. And when it comes to capable, Rainy Schulterman stands out, trading first place back and forth with Sergeant Andy Sprinter—Andy Sprinter who stands six feet three inches tall and could toss Rainy Schulterman in the air like a drum major's baton.

Rainy holds her attention stance. Colonel Derry is *willing* her to break attention. He is *willing* her to speak out of turn. But she stands there with her arms at her side, back stiff, chin up, eyes level, barely breathing.

I can stand here all day if that's the game you want to play, Colonel.

"At ease."

The change from full attention to at ease is slight. Proper but minimal. She will not show relief.

"Private First Class Schulterman, what do you *think* of this school?"

"I think it makes a vital contribution to the war effort, sir." The smart, safe answer. "Sir" is replaced with "you jackass," but only in her mind.

"And are you *content* with the course of study?" He's seated so he can't bounce on the balls of his feet, but he can jerk his head forward for emphasis.

A fractional hesitation. Then, "Sir, my opinion is that I must trust in the wisdom and integrity of my superiors and assume that this school is the very best facility of its kind anywhere, sir."

Rainy thinks, *He despises me.*

"PFC Schulterman, your *scores* are . . . acceptable. This does not alter my opinion that your *proper* role is at home working in a defense industry and raising children."

You forgot baking cakes, you ancient, irrelevant windbag.

"And to be perfectly frank, your people are not known for their warrior spirit. Oh, I'll give you your Maccabees, but what has the Jew done since those ancient times? Your people are tailors and fruit sellers, lawyers and accountants. I daresay you cannot think of a single Jew military hero."

"Brevet Brigadier General Frederick Knefler, sir, promoted for conspicuous courage in leading the charge on Missionary Ridge in the Battle of Chattanooga, sir."

That was probably too much, Rainy realizes as soon as the words are out of her mouth. It is seldom a good idea to appear to be better informed or more intelligent than one's superior officer.

But Colonel Derry just curls his lip and says, "Brevet only. It is a temporary rank, no doubt assigned in the heat of emotion following a battle. It was an emotional age."

Rainy is just wise enough to nod and say, "As you say, Colonel."

Derry blows out a great sigh and with obvious reluctance says, "However, according to the regulations, you are entitled to that which I am giving you today."

"Sir?"

He takes off his spectacles, lays them on the desk, shakes his head slightly side to side, and in a mournful tone says, "You are hereby promoted to the rank of sergeant."

He would have shown no greater regret if he'd been announcing that the war was lost.

"Thank you, sir," Rainy says, and manages, just barely, to suppress a grin. She's been one of the lowest-ranking soldiers in the school, and now she is a peer. A sergeant.

"Is that all you have to say, *Sergeant* Schulterman?"

"Sir, I will do my best to honor the uniform, the stripes, my unit, and my commander. Sir."

Rainy maintains a straight face until she nears the female quarters she shares with seven of the remaining women. The room is mostly empty—the colonel has deliberately scheduled the encounter during noon chow so as to deprive her of a meal—but Sergeant Amalia Peterson is there, polishing her boots.

Rainy drops to her bunk, kicks her feet up on the adjoining bench, and says, "I don't suppose you've got any spare stripes and a needle and thread?"

Peterson looks up from her work, sighs mournfully, and says, "Now you'll really be hard to take, Schulterman."

"Yes, I will," Rainy says, feeling quite pleased.

Peterson is in her late twenties, a grown woman with a husband she's divorcing, a college degree in anthropology, and the most luscious auburn hair Rainy has ever seen, though it is cut short. Peterson was offered a commission upon enlisting, owing to her college education, but she declined on the grounds that her father had been an enlisted man, his father had been an enlisted man, his father in turn had been an enlisted man who died in the Civil War after someone shot him in the eye, and unless and until her father dies, she was not going to dishonor the family by becoming an officer.

Amalia jerks her head. "Foot locker. Second layer, wrapped up in a sock."

Rainy rouses out the stripes and the needle and thread and gets to work on a clean uniform blouse.

"Did the colonel suffer a stroke when he informed you?"

"The colonel's attitude is not for me to discuss," Rainy says in a tone that leaves very little doubt as to her true opinion of Colonel Derry.

"Uh-huh," Amalia drawls. She is a westerner who grew up in a house that was still partly made of sod on the outskirts of Omaha, Nebraska. Her husband had sunk progressively into drunkenness, which had escalated to slaps and then to punches during the years of their unhappy marriage. War is Amalia's escape from that unwise marriage, and she has Rainy's same determination to make it, though her motives are very different.

Two other women enter laughing, see what Rainy's doing, and retreat sullenly to the far end of the room, which is not very far. The female quarters hold five double bunk beds, not all in use.

Each soldier is allowed to place one photograph on the wall by her bunk. That is the one personal touch allowed. Most of the women have pictures of boyfriends or parents. Rainy feels that is indiscreet and has simply tacked up a *TIME* magazine cover showing General Dwight D. Eisenhower framed by US and UK flags.

No sooner has Rainy finished sewing and changed into her newly admirable uniform than they have to rush to make afternoon class, which is in aerial photography, a complicated, painstaking, detail-oriented grind that Rainy enjoys. They are shown a series of photographs of an unidentified airfield somewhere in Occupied France—the same field at four different times. Rainy notes the planes on the ground, notes changes from one shot to the next, and correctly posits that a double rank of German dive bombers are actually plywood dummies placed there to fool prying eyes and draw the attentions of Allied bombers away from actual targets.

After class she is called to Captain Herkemeier's office.

"Sergeant Schulterman, reporting as ordered."

Herkemeier comes around the desk to shake her hand. "Congratulations on the stripes, Schulterman."

"Sir, I have a suspicion that I owe these to you."

"You have a suspicious mind, Sergeant," he says. "Take a seat."

She does, and in unconscious imitation of him, tugs

at the crease in her uniform pants to keep it straight and sharp.

"I'll get right to it. There's a critical need for German translators in the field."

"In what field, sir?"

He doesn't answer directly. "We've spent the last year in America training, preparing, manufacturing. We've killed a few Japs, but we haven't so much as laid a finger on the Krauts. That's about to end."

Rainy's smile is slow and predatory. "I'm pleased to hear it, sir."

Herkemeier nods. "Schulterman, you're a damned good student. Should you complete this course, you'll graduate either first or second, and at that point there will be two options open to you: you can either attend officer candidate school and be commissioned a second lieutenant, probably find yourself as an S2 at the battalion level in a stateside or rear unit that doesn't need a damned S2, and by the end of the war be wearing captain's bars. Or you can remain in enlisted rank and most likely end up staying stateside in a vital staff job. Or maybe teaching others like yourself."

"Sir, I sense the suggestion of a third option."

He nods and looks dubious. "Yes. As I said, the need for translators is acute. You could ship out at your present rank to a line company and—"

"I'll take that road, sir."

"Would you mind very much if I finished what I was saying?"

"No, sir."

"Those would be your options, all other things being equal. But frankly there's a problem with you going to officer school. A troubling fact has come to my attention. It is of no concern to me, and I have not forwarded this piece of information up the chain of command. But it could, if it became more widely known, abort your career in army intelligence."

Rainy is baffled. She frowns, searching her memory, trying to figure out what Herkemeier can possibly be referring to.

"Rainy, what does your father do for a living?"

"My father, sir? He delivers milk in New York City."

"Yes, he does," Herkemeier says. "He is also a numbers runner for the Genovese crime organization."

Rainy stares. And while she stares, her mind frantically shifts through all she has seen and heard from her father about his life, his work. A numbers runner? Gambling is illegal, though many people indulge. A numbers runner is a person who takes bets on slips of paper, collects them, and brings them to the central booking office, which tracks winners and losers. He collects from the losers and pays the winners.

Her father? A numbers runner?

Milk delivery. Door to door. A perfect cover for a numbers runner.

In her mind she compares what she knows of the family's finances against what she believes she knows of the likely income of even a successful and industrious delivery man. Her memory illuminates photos of the annual family vacation, the necklace her mother wears on special occasions, the one her father dismisses as "nothing but paste, really," but that glitters like real diamonds. She considers the lessons the family has always been willing to pay for—violin, piano, languages. The books. The food.

Rainy feels honor compels her to protest. But honor is not analysis.

"Sir, I was not aware."

"You don't dispute it?"

"I neither endorse nor dispute, Captain. I don't know. But I believe it is possible, and I do not believe you would have confronted me unless you felt the evidence was compelling."

"You are not cleared to see the actual evidence," he says. Then he lifts a sheet of paper from his desk, forms it into a funnel, takes a lighter from his pocket, and sets the paper afire.

They watch it burn, and when it is almost entirely

consumed, Herkemeier drops the last of it in his metal trash can.

"The FBI of course has a copy, and in time it may surface. If you were stationed here in the States, that might spell trouble. You might be busted out of MI and sent to a different duty. You might end up a clerk in some backwater. I think that would be a hell of a waste of a damned good mind, an army intelligence mind."

"Sir." She can't manage another word just then because her throat is a lump and her heart is pounding and her mind is filling with black anger.

"Half the people here, and more than half of the women, want a nice soft billet far from the shooting. Now, you? I think you want to cause damage to this country's enemies. Am I mistaken?"

"Sir, you are not," Rainy says tersely.

Herkemeier straightens his tie, straightens the collar, and leans forward. "I don't think we win this war with protocols, Rainy. I think we win this war by ruthlessly applying a single unifying principal: killing Germans by any and all means necessary. So I don't really give much of a damn what sex you are, or whether your father is a petty crook."

That phrase, "petty crook," feels too harsh, too final. She loves her father; he is and will always be a great man to her, but that's not the issue now—that is for another time.

"Let me kill Germans, sir."

Herkemeier grins. "I had a premonition you might say that. You are hereby ordered to present yourself to the transport clerk where you will show him these orders. . . ." He raises a manila envelope and hands it to her. "Whereupon he will arrange your earliest possible departure. Once you're in theater, no one will give a hoot in hell about your background. It will be up to you to make the most of that."

He stands, and Rainy does as well, though her legs are weak and her mind is still swimming with dark thoughts and far too much emotion.

"Sir, I . . ." She is brought up short by the realization that tears are forming in her eyes. She manages to say, "Thank you, sir."

Herkemeier shakes her hand and says, "Now, you go get 'em, Rainy Schulterman."

"By any and all means necessary, sir."

11

RIO RICHLIN—CAMP MARON, SMIDVILLE, GEORGIA, USA

"Jumping jacks, twenty-five and sound off. HUT!"

Rio doesn't recall this particular sergeant's name, but she resents his being this awake and fit and energetic at an hour when sunrise is still a long way off.

Forty mostly young, but not all young, recruits begin. Feet thrown to the side, arms over the head, recover. All across the base are identical formations of identically bleary and sore soldiers, all shouting along to the rhythm of their own PT leader.

Voices, some male, some female, yell, "One! Two! Three!"

"Why can't we eat first, that's all I want to know," Kerwin Cassel mutters under his breath.

"Four! Five! Six!"

"Because that would make too much sense," Jenou mutters back.

In just a few short weeks they've already perfected the

art of speaking without moving lips, between beats, and pitching it so only those nearest can hear. They are evolving the fine art of military grumbling.

"Hands laced behind your necks, deep-knee bends, twenty-five and . . . HUT!"

"One! Two! Three!"

"I hate this one," Rio says.

"I hate them all," Jenou shoots back.

"Quiet in the ranks!" the sergeant yells.

"Four! Five!"

"Plenty fun if you have my view," Tilo says, managing a leering sound in between gulps of air. He's behind Rio and Jenou.

"It's fine for me, Suarez. You look at us, and we don't have to look at your skinny butt," Jenou says.

"That's a win-win," Rio chimes in.

"Nine! Ten! Eleven!"

Week three. Friendships have formed; dislikes as well. There are still lewd remarks and many passes made and the occasional grab or clutch, but word has come down to the NCOs in no uncertain terms that they are not to tolerate any nonsense. Many of the male soldiers have made peace with the idea of the women being here. Some, like Jack Stafford, the cheeky Englishman, took a chivalric approach and shut down the more obnoxious of the men.

Others were nowhere close to accepting females, and that number includes officers and NCOs as well. And the hard truth is that despite the army's reluctance to send anyone home who might carry a rifle, females are washing out at a higher rate than the males. Many of the girls and women simply lack the physical strength and endurance. The females still left tend to be taller and stronger than average, many from farms or ranches. Even Jenou is solidly built beneath the feminine curves, and her jumping jacks have the requisite snap and precision. As for Cat, she could probably best some of the men in a fist fight.

The integration of men and women is far from easy or settled, but is still more advanced than the integration of the races. Rio has learned that the camp across the river is for colored soldiers only. From time to time she glimpses them over there, doing much the same things that the whites on this side of the river are doing, but always over there, and never over here.

Rio is curious about that other camp and the colored soldiers over there, but she seems almost alone in her curiosity. They are seldom spoken of, those others. Only Jack has remarked on the irony that America is going to war against a white supremacist enemy with a segregated American army. And when he made that remark he was hooted down, especially by GIs from the south, male and female alike.

They jump, squat, sit up, and perform a complicated move called the Army Stomp, until each of them is sweating and shaking with exhaustion. But there is no doubt that they are already stronger and fitter than when they had first arrived. The fact that they are able to complain is evidence of that, since in the early days they'd all been busy gasping for breath. No, although they complain more, the pain is far less, and pride in her own physical strength has begun to bubble up within Rio Richlin.

"Push-ups! Twenty-five! HUT!"

I can do this.

"One! Two! Three!"

This is the one exercise that always left the women behind. The men can all do it—all twenty-five push-ups. But none of the women has gone past seventeen.

"Twelve! Thirteen! Come on, Castain, push it! Fifteen!"

Rio is strong to fifteen, but then comes the lethargy, the burn, the inability to control her breathing.

No, I won't stop.

"Seventeen! Eighteen!"

Rio's shoulders and stomach muscles tremble from the exertion, like she has fever chills, all the small muscles shaking while the big muscles burn.

"Nineteen! Twenty!"

Jenou collapses, facedown on the matted grass.

Sergeant Mackie joins the noncom who is leading calisthenics. Rio catches a sweat-blurred view of her and feels Mackie's eye on her. Mackie takes over the count.

"Twenty-one!"

Impossible. Just lie down.

"Twenty-five!"

The women were all either facedown or climbing stiffly to their feet. The last male is done. Rio is on twenty-two.

"Give up, Richlin!" Tilo heckles.

Twenty-three. Two more.

It's as if she's trying to push up with a tractor on her back. Rio's muscles just do not want to obey. Just . . . do . . . not.

Twenty-four! A shaky, sloppy twenty-four, but a twenty-four just the same.

Down. Collapsed. Finished. Done in.

No.

The twenty-fifth push-up takes what feels like five full minutes. Rio's teeth grit. Her face is beet red. She makes a sound like an animal in distress.

Twenty-five!

Applause breaks out from some of the men and some of the women.

"Twenty-five," Rio says as she rises to her feet.

"Congratulations, you can count," Tilo mutters.

From Mackie there is just the very slightest nod of

acknowledgment. More than enough to cause Rio's heart to swell. She almost staggers from dizziness, but she manages to maintain her place in the line.

Rio Richlin is someone now, someone in Sergeant Mackie's eyes, at least. She is the girl who's done all twenty-five. The only female so far. The first.

That's right: Rio Richlin. Twenty-five!

"Chow in thirty minutes. Atten-HUT. Dismissed."

Rio walks to the barracks with the half-crippled gait of an exceedingly sore back. She grabs her towel and ditty bag from her foot locker, hurrying because even if you get there early hot water is never a certainty, and if you're last in line it's guaranteed to be freezing. Jenou falls in beside her, but already other women have gotten a lead on them.

"Great work," Jenou teases. "Now Mackie's going to expect us all to do that."

"I doubt I'll ever manage it again," Rio says, but she's confident that she will. "It was Suarez that motivated me. I had to show that little . . ."

"That's you all over, honey. Any time someone tells you you can't do something it excites your inner mule."

"My inner mule?"

"Hey, sweetie, why don't you come shower with me? You could scrub my back."

Rio freezes. The voice is male and familiar: Luther Geer. She doesn't want to turn and face him, and now she feels foolish and conspicuous just freezing like this, with her towel and her shower bag in her hand.

She starts walking again, and now the voice is even more suggestive.

"Or you could scrub something else," Luther says with an unabashed leer in his voice. "Right, boys?"

"Feeling threatened, boys?" Jenou snaps.

Rio, her face reddening, feels tears begin to fill her eyes. She is humiliated by the suggestion, and even more humiliated that Jenou feels the need to defend her. She knows she should spin around and give this rude young man a piece of her mind, but the right words do not come quickly and that hesitation becomes yet another cause of embarrassment.

She walks away on stiff legs, pursued by more than one wolf whistle and derisive chuckles.

"Scrub a dub, baby, scrub a dub," Luther calls after her and makes a loud kissing sound. "I got something dirty that needs cleaning."

In the crowded, hectic women's latrine Jenou says, "We should tell Sergeant Mackie."

"No," Rio snaps.

"But she's the—"

Rio turns a face now gone white with rage on Jenou. "No."

Jenou sighs. "No, you're right. We'll have to find a way to—"

"*We* don't have to do anything, Jen. I have to deal with Private Geer." She looks at herself in the mirror and consciously changes her expression until she achieves a look of resolve rather than rage. "It has to be me."

"Boys will be boys," said Carlita Swan, an older woman of twenty-nine who is wasting her limited time plucking her eyebrows over the sink. "Don't let it get to you, kid."

"I won't," Rio mutters.

But it has already gotten to her. Weren't they all in this together, the males and the females? Weren't they all soldiers?

She feels furious and cowardly and even more furious for being cowardly, the one feeding on the other. Her moment of triumph has been turned into resentment.

Enough.

The rage is gone. All emotion in Rio Richlin has gone cold, and something else, something grimly practical, has taken hold.

"Rio? What are you thinking?" Jenou asks, nervous at the expression on her friend's face. This is a different look, unfamiliar to Jenou in a lifetime of gauging Rio's inner feelings. There is something almost . . . predatory.

"Let it go, kid," Carlita says.

"I've let it go and let it go and I'm done with it," Rio says. She sets her shower bag down carefully and does an about-face. She marches out of the women's latrine, past

Mackie's closed door, and along the hundred feet of polished tile to the other end of the barracks.

She takes a single deep breath before striding directly into the men's latrine.

The shrieks and cries have a strangely nonmasculine sound. Naked men twist away or cover themselves with whatever comes easily to hand, sometimes pulling a still-clothed buddy in front of them in a soapy, steamy panic.

"Where is Private Geer?" Rio demands. "I am here for his apology."

A dozen pairs of appalled, scandalized, and frankly frightened eyes turn toward the far end of the room, silently betraying an oblivious Geer singing in the shower.

It's not the cries but the sudden silence that alerts Geer, who sticks his face into the shower jet, rinses soap from his hair and forehead, and says, "What's going . . ." His eyes widen, a rivulet of soap runs down into his left eye, which blinks madly all on its own. His mouth opens and moves, but no sound comes out. He looks like a large, pink catfish that has just landed in the bottom of a fisherman's cooler.

"I would like your apology," Rio says, pleased that her voice is at least somewhat steady and holds her gaze rigidly on Geer's face.

Geer does not answer. He reaches with a fumbling hand for his towel and holds it in front of himself. He swallows convulsively and his eyes inscribe a panicky circuit from left to right, looking for salvation.

An older man, maybe as old as some of Rio's teachers, and blessedly still wearing at least the most vital parts of his clothing, says in a laconic voice, "I think maybe you'd best apologize to Private Richlin, Geer, so all these boys can breathe again."

Luther says, "Ksh . . . Mf . . . Shuh . . ." and various other monosyllables before finally discovering his voice and vocabulary. "I didn't mean . . . anything. I was just . . . But I apologize."

"I accept," Rio says.

She executes a military about-face, only slightly spoiled by the fact that on the wet tile she over-rotates a little, and marches back out of the room.

Jenou followed her in and now follows her out.

"Well, that was an education," Jenou says.

"Much to think about," Rio agrees solemnly.

Halfway back to the women's bathroom stands Sergeant Mackie.

"Richlin. Castain. The men's latrine is off-limits. Report to the mess sergeant for KP."

KP—kitchen patrol—involves peeling a great many potatoes, brewing vats of coffee, and washing pots and pans. It's a lot of work for two tired, sore girls.

But it's less work when Cat comes sauntering in. "I am

in the mood to peel me some taters," she says in an exaggeratedly rustic accent.

This is perhaps not too great a surprise, though Cat is the only female to join in. Then Jack appears in the doorway. "Hot, soapy water, just my cup of tea. Stick has other duty or he'd be here."

And then the appearance that stops them all in mid-laugh: Tilo Suarez.

Tilo shrugs irritably. "What? All the pretty girls are here. I'm not leaving them to this foreigner." Jack tosses him a towel.

Upon returning to barracks they find a somewhat changed atmosphere. For one thing, people have come up with several names for Rio's stunt. It is now Private Richlin's Raid. Or Richlin's Surprise Inspection. Or more crudely the Rio Richlin Short-Arm Showdown. Even Private Richlin's Willie Hunt.

And Rio herself is treated differently. About half the men find the whole thing entertaining and grudgingly admire her courage. The other half (most of whom were in the showers at the time) are not at all amused. Not at all. Some are angry. Some seem almost wounded.

In a single day, with twenty-five push-ups and a brief foray into the men's latrine, Rio goes from being a sort of appendage to the more outgoing Jenou to being an object of curiosity, admiration, fear, and resentment.

The same array of attitudes is evident among the other women, some of whom see her as a champion, while others are annoyed at her sudden elevation in status.

She begins a letter to Strand, thinking she will tell him all about it, but then, after contemplating various descriptive passages, decides not to. How on earth is she supposed to tell him that she's gone storming into the men's latrine?

Even the push-ups . . . What if Strand *can't* do twenty-five? Does she want to seem to be bragging? Does she want him to think of her as some muscle-bound girl? Men don't like muscular girls, everyone knows that. No man likes a girl who is stronger or bolder than he is.

No, best not to talk about it with Strand. But Jack—who was not in the shower at the historic moment—cannot stop grinning. So maybe Strand will find it funny too. Someday.

"Lights out in five," Sergeant Mackie calls from her room.

Jenou is already in her bunk. She's tugging her hair forward to look at split ends. "I think I may get a Mackie cut," she said.

"Cut your hair that short?"

"I'll still have all of this." Jenou waves a languid hand, indicating her body. "And honestly, when we dry-fired our rifles I lost a hairpin and my hair ended up getting in the way."

"How short?"

Jenou holds up two fingers like scissors and pretends to cut at about the three-inch mark.

"You'll look cute," Rio says.

"Cute? How dare you? I'll look stunning," Jenou corrects her.

Rio rolls onto her side and pushes closer, lessening the gap between them so she can lower her voice. Jenou mirrors her movement.

"Am I becoming mannish?" Rio asks.

Jenou barks a short laugh, then puts a hand over her mouth. "Mannish?"

"I was just thinking of writing to Strand."

"Oh, I get it. You're wondering if he'll still like you when you can beat him up."

"Yes, that, what you said, aside from the beating-up part."

Jenou shrugs. "I have given this some thought."

"I was sure you would have."

"And what I've decided is: tough shit."

Rio waits, looking into her friend's luminous eyes, but there is no more, so she prompts, "Tough shit?"

"Look, honey, we are in the army now. We have to do what we have to do to make it through. Right?"

"Right," Rio agrees tentatively.

"So we have no choice anymore. This is it. We have PT

160

before sunrise, and we have marches, and we have runs, and we have drills, and we have no choice in the matter anymore. And if Strand, or any other boy, doesn't like it, tough shit."

"Tough shit?"

"Tough shit."

"Okay. Tough shit."

"I can't believe you said that out loud, Rio," Jenou says with a mischievous smile. "You never used to curse. I think you're becoming mannish."

Rio would throw something if not for the fact that her bunk is perfectly squared away.

The lights go out with an audible snap of the switch. Rio pulls the rough wool blanket over her. Almost instantly sleep comes, leaving her only time enough for two thoughts.

The first is: *But I still want him to like me.*

The second is: *Tough shit if he doesn't.*

Dear Mother and Father,

I only have time for a quick note to let you know that I am well. Jenou and I are settling in. The barracks is fine, there's a heavy curtain separating the ~~girls~~ women from the men. I find the strangest thing is not so much being with the males as the fact that some of the battalion are quite a bit older. The people I spend time with tend to be younger. There's a fellow named Tilo who is twenty, I think. He thinks he's God's gift to the fairer sex, but he's harmless. And Dain Sticklin is twenty-one, but Jack Stafford is just seventeen, barely older than me, and I think Kerwin Cassel isn't much older, either. There are people here in their late twenties, even thirties!

But they're really a swell bunch.

How is everything at home? Did Clarabell have her calf? And is it a bull as we thought?

Your loving daughter, Rio

Dear Strand,

I hope you were sincere when you asked me to write you, because I'm doing it, as you can see.

I have arrived at Camp ███████, *which is just a few miles from* ███████, *which is basically the middle of nowhere.*

The barracks is . . . well, I suppose you're in your own barracks, and I'd guess they're about the same. I was going to add that our sergeant is pretty tough, but I suppose all drill sergeants are. The only difference being that ours is ███████.

I suppose I don't really have anything very clever to say, except that I really enjoyed our date. I especially enjoyed talking with you afterward. I'm enclosing a copy of a photograph my father took of me in my uniform. It's the only picture I have to send right now, but I hope to be able to send you a picture that is a bit less GI. I do still remember what it's like to wear a dress, though it may be some time before I have the opportunity. Still, if you'd like a more girly picture of me, I can ask my folks to try and find one in the photo album. And I would ~~love~~ certainly enjoy a picture of you as well.

I hope you are well, can you tell me . . . ?

Affectionately,

Rio

Hi, Mom and Dad and you too Obal,

Well, I'm here at basic training. I wish I could tell you it's fun, but mostly it's a lot of standing at attention and saluting and making sure your uniform is just so.

We have not fired any guns yet or driven around in tanks, Obal, sorry. Our NCOs—who are all black—are trying hard I think to train us as best they can with ███████████████████████████ and ███████ ████████████████████████████ But the officers ███████████████████████████████ ███████████████████ and ███████████████ so we don't really ████████████ much.

I have told my sergeant I want to apply for ████████ school, but that has to go through ██████████ , who doesn't seem to think colored soldiers will be needing any ████████ because he doesn't think they'll let us fight ever. I suppose that's fine with me, but I still really want to be a ████████ . All I can do is keep trying, I guess . . .

Love, Frangie

Dear Mother and Father,

I am safely ensconced in a place I shall not name for fear of the censors leaving big black marks on this page. But I am well. I am doing my best, and the lessons are challenging. There are obstacles I shall not describe nor name, but I expect to overcome them. And I believe my circumstances will change substantially very soon.

I am getting plenty to eat, and while I have not been able to keep kosher, I have managed to avoid the bacon. I am required to be present at Christian chapel on Sundays, but I am of course not required to participate other than to sit respectfully. I won't say that being a Jew does not present some difficulties, but they pale compared to the obstacles presented by those who disapprove of my ▮▮▮▮▮▮.

But you know me: I am not easily discouraged . . .
Sincerely, Rainy

Dear Ary,
I hope you're half as bored and safe as I am. I hope you're sitting out in the sun on the deck of some big gray ship or better yet on the beach at ▮▮▮▮▮▮ ▮▮▮▮▮. I can't allow myself to think too much about the danger you might be in. But that doesn't mean you shouldn't tell me, because you should. Maybe not Mom and Dad, but you can tell me. At least as much as you can with the censorship.

Sadly, I can tell you nothing. It's unfair and unequal, I suppose, but that's the way it is.

I've arranged for twenty-five dollars to come out of

my monthly pay and go to your "friend." It's probably for the best: it keeps me away from the poker games . . .

Your loving sister, Rainy

Mother and Father,
It's me, your little soldier girl Jenou. I am so tired and can barely move. I'm so sore my fingernails hurt. My hair hurts. My eyeballs actually hurt.

But at least I'm out of Gedwell Falls and out from under your feet, right?

I don't know how much I'll write. Sergeant ▉▉▉▉▉▉ orders us to write, and I am doing so because she scares me. But I don't think you care if I write, and I know I don't. I expect if things go the way I hope they do that I will never have to return to the Falls, and I'm pretty sure that would leave both of you feeling relieved.

There you go, just like the sergeant ordered.
Private Jenou Castain

12

My rifle.

It is 43.5 inches long, measuring from the butt plate to the muzzle. It weighs 9.5 pounds and fires a 30.06 cartridge.

The slug itself is no bigger in circumference than a toddler's little finger, but that slug flies from the muzzle at 2,800 feet per second.

Rio has her rifle in hand. She's seated cross-legged like all of them, with the rifle butt on the grass and the muzzle pointed at the sky.

"Ladies and gentlemen, this is why we have brought you here and given you those snazzy uniforms." Captain Jessep raises a rifle in the air, two-handed. He holds that pose for a moment so the dozens of men and women seated on the grass can see.

"This is the M1 Garand rifle. It is the finest rifle ever to be entrusted to an infantryman. Many of you will never fire a rifle in anger, but each of you will learn how to do so. There may come a time when even the cooks and the clerks and the ladies will be required to shoulder a rifle and fire it at the enemy."

"The ladies," Cat whispers derisively, just loud enough for the captain to hear, though he doesn't react. "Ladies with rifles."

Rio envies Cat's sense of freedom and fun. There's a wildness and energy to Cat, like maybe she'd stick a tack on Sergeant Mackie's chair or spike the coffee with rum. And Cat has no tolerance for being treated like a second-class citizen, unlike some of the women in the company. That's a position Rio finds herself increasingly drawn to.

"A dollar says I outshoot you, Suarez," Cat whispers.

Tilo only half hears. "Did you just threaten to shoot me?"

"Only if you really annoy me," Cat says.

"Crazy bitch," Tilo mutters.

"And there you go," Cat says in her good-natured way. "I'll make sure it's just a flesh wound." Is she winking as she says it? It's hard to tell, but the strange down-turned smile flashes.

The mood of the crowd is somewhere between anticipatory and solemn. The words and the tone incline toward solemn, but the greater fact is that finally they are going to learn how to shoot the rifles they now hold. Their rifles.

My rifle, Rio thinks.

"Therefore you will listen carefully to your instructor. You will listen and learn as though your life depends on it. It does. Lieutenant."

The captain departs, leaving the lieutenant instructor, a bland-looking, high-voiced fellow in khaki. This is the same officer who first showed them how to attach the strap, how to wrap the strap around their left arms, how to insert a clip, how to hold the weapon in each of the major firing positions, and how to dry-fire.

"Okay," the lieutenant begins. "So they give you the best rifle in the world. Me, I'm sick of monkeying around. When do we get to shoot this thing?" He grins. He's given this speech before, probably many times, but he's still enthusiastic. "I heard a man in this company say that very thing yesterday. So I will answer the question now. You'll start shooting the M-1 when you're ready."

That sets off a murmur.

"Lookin' like that may be never," Kerwin says under his breath.

The lieutenant is on a one-foot-tall platform and has a standing chalkboard to one side. His service cap is jauntily cocked to one side.

"Men . . . and ladies . . . your brains are about to get a

workout. This is a skull session, because today I'll teach you elevation and windage."

This is met with blank stares from most and a knowing nod from some.

"Brain work, that leaves me out," Jenou mutters.

"I will teach you how to raise or lower your rear sights to account for the natural drop of the bullet. And how to adjust your sights left or right to account for the effect of the wind."

What follows is a solid hour that sounds a great deal like Rio's math classes back in school. There are even equations scrawled enthusiastically on the chalkboard.

Rio pays close attention, but not so close that she does not spare a sideways glance at Jack. She had a dream about Jack, and though she does not remember any specifics, she woke with a nagging feeling that something improper had occurred—in the dream.

She resists the urge to draw Strand's picture from her inner pocket and tells herself that dreams are just dreams, they don't mean anything. If she could recall specifics they would probably be completely proper and innocuous; yes, almost certainly. No, certainly.

You're working yourself up over nothing.

Rio refocuses, and after listening and watching for a while, she has a fair idea how to manage it. A bullet drops twenty inches in three hundred yards. To adjust for that you click the elevation knob so you're forced to point the muzzle upward while sighting the target.

"In this way, the bullet actually leaves the muzzle heading over the head of the Jap or Kraut you're aiming at. But if you've calculated your range, and you've adjusted your sights properly, that bullet will drop naturally until it hits the bull's-eye."

A man's chest. Or neck. Or face.

The math is not complicated, though predictably Jenou struggles with it. The concept is familiar to anyone who has ever thrown a ball: you throw high in order to reach the catcher.

Windage is more complex, and many heads are scratched.

"There are some simple tricks to help you judge windage," the enthusiastic instructor goes on. "Take something light enough to be blown by the wind, say some dirt or a blade of grass. While standing, toss it into the air and watch where it falls. Point at the place where it lands. Then estimate the angle between your arm and your body. Let's say the angle is forty degrees. Now then, the rule is that you divide the angle under your arm by four—by *four*—in order to get the speed of the wind in miles per hour."

He asks a GI up to act it out on the platform. The crowd loves audience participation and watches avidly, hoping to see embarrassing failure, as the soldier estimates that the wind is moving at about seven miles an hour.

Milking. They'd been milking one of the cows. That was the dream. The ginger Englishman had been sitting on a stool milking one of the cows while Rio laughed and giggled. There! Just as harmless as she'd suspected, nothing at all concerning. And yet the image doesn't feel right. She has the feeling that if she talks about it to Jenou, Jenou will cast a troubling light on it.

Rio shifts position and tries to exclude Jack from her peripheral vision.

"An even simpler way is to raise your arm to level, which is ninety degrees. Then divide that into five segments. Imagine a clock hand jumping from minute to minute. *Click. Click. Click. Click. Click.* Each click, each segment, is five miles per hour.

"With this bit of information you can set the windage screw on the rear sight, so that even as you continue to aim the sights straight at your target, the muzzle will actually be aimed to the left or right of the Jap or Kraut. Then the wind will simply blow your bullet sideways until it hits."

A chest. A neck. A face.

After an hour of this, and an hour of rehearsing the four firing positions—prone, seated, kneeling, and standing—they pile aboard trucks for the three-mile trip to the firing range.

"I'm amazed they don't have us run there," Jack says. "This is luxury!"

"We are truly being treated like movie stars," Jenou agrees wryly, waving a hand around the open truck as it bounces with bone-jarring force over some dried-mud tire tracks.

They are split into two groups. One will stand in the deep trench beneath the targets and mark hits and misses while the other shoots. Then they'll switch.

Additional instructors await, one for every three shooters, acting as spotters and offering helpful tips.

On command, Rio loads her rifle. Eight long brass cartridges lined up two-by-two in the metal clip, which she thumbs into the chamber.

"Check safeties!"

There follows some clicking and sheepish looks and everything is checked by the range instructors, who buzz around like capable bees, often physically manipulating soldiers into the right grip, the right stance.

Rio gathers a small handful of dirt as there are no handy blades of grass. She lets it fall and watches where the lightest bits land. Feeling ridiculous and self-conscious, she points with her whole arm to the spot. Rio does a rough calculation and decides on three clicks left windage.

"Take a prone position!"

This they have practiced many times. Rio lies flat,

with her legs spread medium-wide and cocked to the left, making her body into a lazy L. The front sight has three elements: a left and right side, each about half an inch high and curved outward, a bit like goat horns. Between them is a simple square post half as tall as the sides.

The rear sight is a stubby steel cylinder with a hole in the center. It is this hole that must be adjusted for altitude and windage. *Click, click, click.*

Two hundred yards, that's the range. But they've been taught to take a ranging shot first and see where the bullet strikes before adjusting for altitude on the range.

"Ready. Aim. Fire when ready."

Rio lines the sights up. The target bull's-eye appears to sit just on top of the center post of the front sight as seen through the hole in the rear sight.

Don't jerk, squeeze.

BANG!

The rifle punches her shoulder and almost tears loose of her grip.

Shots ring out to her left and right, much louder than she'd imagined. Painfully loud. There's a ringing in her right ear, and her left ear's not much better off.

The target is lowered. A minute later it rises back into view again, and a black disc is placed over the spot where the bullet struck. It was low, almost off the paper, and to one side.

Rio adjusts her sight. She backs off a click on windage and raises the rear sight by four clicks.

Her second shot is just above the bull's-eye. One click less altitude.

BANG!

The third round clips the edge of the bull's-eye. The fourth does as well.

"Not bad," an instructor says. "You're jerking the trigger just a little. And firm up your firing position." He lifts her legs by the ankles and shifts them left. "Get that strap seated just right around your arm, and I think we better loosen it just a notch and give you more play."

Round six hit the black target.

Rounds seven and eight do as well.

"Keep it up, we'll get you a marksman badge, Private. You'll be able to keep your boyfriend in line."

Jenou has a great deal more trouble, as does Kerwin, who still does not understand the underlying concepts.

The seated firing position is with legs extended, knees raised just a bit, body leaned forward, and elbows braced on knees. Rio does moderately well, but not as well as she had done prone. Kneeling is worse still. The position is wobbly, which is why the army discourages it. And standing she scores only 50 percent.

"You see now," the lieutenant instructor says when they switch places with the target-handlers, "the importance of your firing position. Good position most often equals good shooting. There is no purpose in just firing away, people. Do that and your rifle is just a noisemaker. Make every shot count, and remember this: every time you miss, you've given that Jap monkey or Kraut soldier a chance to take a shot at you or your buddy. Shoot him before he shoots you, because sure as hell you won't be able to shoot him afterward."

Jack, joking, says, "Do you suppose the Germans will helpfully point out where we've missed?"

An NCO, an older man in his fifties standing nearby, says, "You'll know if you hit one."

"How's that, Sarge?" Rio asks.

The sergeant spits a stream of tobacco juice in the dirt. He gives Rio a skeptical, disapproving up-and-down then says, "A lot of ways. You may see blood spray. You may see them fall over. You may hear them cry out for their mother. *Mutter, mutter!* That's German for 'mother, mother.' I don't know if Japs have mothers. Do you want to see that, Private? Do you want to see the blood and hear them cry for their mothers?"

Rio, stunned by the sudden hostility in his voice, can't answer.

He shakes his head. "And that's why women should not be soldiers, little girl, because you have to *want* that. You have to hate that man over there enough to take away everything he is or ever will be." He shakes his head again. "I don't think you girls have that hate inside you. Truth be told, I hope you don't. But good shooting just the same, Richlin."

Hate. The word alone makes Rio queasy. How do you hate someone you've never met? Weren't Germans and even Japanese just soldiers doing what they'd been ordered to do?

"I don't want to hate them," she admits softly.

"Then stay the hell out of combat, sweetheart, because you'll either hate or you'll be dead."

More time is spent that day and on subsequent days teaching them to fire the M1 Garand and the blessedly lighter M1 carbine, as well as the shoulder-punishing grenade launcher and the hard-to-control submachine gun and the falsely named light machine gun, the Browning automatic rifle, or BAR.

"I don't know if I can do it," Jenou says at chow that evening. They are seated in the noisy chow hall, staring with resignation at the evening's meal.

"What, you can't eat that creamed beef on toast?" Rio asks, though she guesses what Jenou means. "You have to: it's your patriotic duty. We are weapons in the service of our government, and we must be strong."

Kerwin playfully throws a squeezed ball of bread at Rio.

"I do not know that I can shoot someone," Jenou

admits. "I mean, what if he's good-looking? That would run counter to all my beliefs in the importance of handsome men."

"Yes, we are important," Tilo says, holding up a spoon like a mirror to preen.

"Oh, I can shoot you, Suarez," Jenou jokes. "No problem there."

Tilo throws up his hands. "What is it with girls threatening to shoot me today?"

"I suppose it's usually their fathers threatening to shoot you," Stick says, and winks at Cat. Tilo kind of likes this; it feeds the myth of his sexual prowess he's been laboring to construct.

Jack catches Jenou's seriousness. "It must be a hell of a thing."

"What?" Rio asks between mouthfuls of the pasty gray substance on her tray.

"Killing a man."

"Not a man, an enemy." Luther Geer has invited himself to join the conversation though he's at another table, his back just behind Rio's.

When no one responds, Luther turns around, lifts his leg over his bench and then over their bench, thus transferring himself to their table. For some reason no one understands, Luther has taken to keeping a calico kitten with him, despite the fact that he runs the risk of being disciplined. The kitten, peeking out from Geer's collar, has a belligerent look that mirrors its owner's. "Why the hell do you think we're here? The army isn't paying us to do push-ups and learn the obstacle course, they're making us over as killers. Look at me. I sell shoes back in civilian life, I don't go around killing people. But you show me some yellow Jap monkey and I'll damned sure shoot him and smile while I'm doing it."

"Crudely put," Jack says, "but I suppose I agree. That is what we're being trained to do."

Rio shrugs. "I enjoyed shooting at targets. I didn't think I would, but I did. At targets."

"Deadeye Richlin," Jenou teases.

"I'll shoot a Jap or a German," Tilo says. "I hope I don't have to shoot any Italians. My mother's Italian. She hates that Mussolini and his crowd, but regular old Italians aren't all big fans of his either. Not like it is with the Germans. You ever see them in those rallies? They love Hitler. They want to take over the world. Italians don't want to take over a damned thing. They want to eat some noodles and drink some wine and make love to a beautiful, blond-haired private."

He bats his long-lashed eyes at Jenou, and she is not entirely dismissive.

"Best if we get sent to kill Japs," Luther says. "That's like shooting a dog."

"Forgive me, but is shooting dogs a form of sport in America?" Jack, of course.

Kerwin says, "Naw, not sport. Geer shoots dogs for dinner."

That earns enough laughter that Luther switches back to his own table, taking his kitten with him.

"I don't know," Rio says. "I don't know if I can do it. I don't want to do it, I know that much. I just want to drive a truck or maybe a jeep."

"She's a surprisingly good driver," Jenou confirms. "I don't believe she's killed more than three, maybe four garbage cans with her driving. And a few mailboxes. But no people. So far."

"Stop picking on me or I'll eat your creamed crap on toast."

Jenou shoves her tray toward Rio. "That's not so much a threat as it is a kind offer."

Rio casts her mind back to the day's training. In her mind's eye she tries to envision the paper target as a man. Tries to imagine herself actually taking aim and killing an actual man. Tries to imagine what the bullet would . . . and then she stops herself and her thoughts swerve elsewhere, to Strand, who seems with each passing day to become more distant, more of an old photograph in her mind instead of the boy who had held her hand in the movie theater.

Rio goes blank and daydreamy and only after a while realizes that in her funk she has let her gaze settle on Jack Stafford.

She blinks and looks away, feeling warmth rise up her neck and into her cheeks.

Conversation turns to other things, but while Rio laughs and jokes, she can still feel the wooden stock in her hands, the butt plate kicking against her shoulder, and the thrill of seeing that little hole drilled in the distant target.

She does not want to shoot at a human being, not even a Jap, not even as payback for what they had done to Rachel. But she is disciplined when it came to firing position, she has twenty-twenty vision and a steady hand, she hits what she shoots at, and the simple truth is, that feels good.

Before she is done with Camp Maron she will earn a Marksman rating with the M1 rifle, and then a Sharpshooter rating, only falling short of the coveted Expert rank.

She is a decent driver, despite Jenou's teasing. A *decent* driver.

But a hell of a shot.

13

FRANGIE MARR—CAMP SZEKELY, SMIDVILLE, GEORGIA, USA

"Some of you actually volunteered to join this great patriotic endeavor to kill the Japanese and the Italian and the German for Uncle Sam." Sergeant Morton Kirkland is a man who does not share the common taste for derogatory nicknames for enemies. Frangie has never heard him refer to a Jap or a Kraut. "But most of you are draftees, here against your will. Many of you would like to go home."

Some of those who enlisted would like to go home, too, Frangie thinks. But neither she nor any of the several dozen men and half-dozen women speaks up to say so. Sergeant Kirkland isn't a bad fellow, but he's a yeller, an old-school drill instructor, complete with an inventive list of insults and insulting nicknames for various recruits: Flounder, Cheesedick, Pustule, Stumbles, and for Frangie, Okaninny, a word combining her home state, Oklahoma, with either "ninny" or "pickaninny"—he hasn't made that clear.

While Sergeant Kirkland won't refer to the enemy as Japs, he will refer to recruits as bedbugs.

They are in a field of red Georgia clay, a large swath of which is garlanded with barbed wire. The wire is stretched across wooden stakes set about eighteen inches above the ground. It looks like a crude device meant to trip an enemy, like something left over from the last war. In places the carefully stretched wire is crossed by random snakes of coiled wire, so the whole thing taken together is nearly impenetrable. The course is the better part of an acre, bounded on one side by a log-and-dirt berm that rises about two feet high.

Frangie's company has not been told what they are to do here—Sergeant Kirkland plays things close to the vest and has a flair for the dramatic. But Frangie cannot help but notice a corporal and a PFC unloading boxes of what looks like ammunition from a wagon-wheeled caisson.

"Well, you bedbugs, those of you who want out of the army, today is the day!"

The closest thing Frangie has to a friend in the company is Clara Moore, a stooped and rather dull girl from Enid, Oklahoma, and thus a fellow Okie. Sergeant Kirkland calls her Moo Cow. It's not the nicest name, but it's not the most insulting either. Clara raises her hand, which causes the sergeant to freeze in midword and stare at her with a look that could melt a tank.

Clara slowly lowers her hand.

"What is it, Private Cow?" Kirkland demands.

"Nothing, Sergeant."

"Then I'd like to go on explaining, if that's all right with you." It is. "As I was saying, for those of you who want out of the army, this is your lucky day. Because all it will take . . . is standing up." He grins, apparently believing he's made a joke. "In fact, all you gotta do is raise your head up. Just a few inches. Just a little bit." He's still grinning, but now his voice turns flinty. "Because today is live fire, bedbugs, live fire. *Bang, bang, bang!*"

Frangie puts it all together in a flash of insight: the barbed wire, the berm, and, now that she looks more closely at the field beyond her amused sergeant, the machine guns placed along that berm.

"Raise your heads even an inch above that wire, and a thirty-caliber machine gun round will drill a hole through your helmet, through your skull, through your brain, and then blast its way right on out the other side. Those machine guns are locked in so they fire just an inch or two above the wire. The bullets are real." He's not joking, teasing, or even insulting now. "You've been trained in how to advance on elbows and knees keeping your rifle clear. Elbows and knees and keep your heads down below the wire. Failing that you may choose to roll over on your back and kick your way along. Are you hearing me, men? And women?"

"Yes, Sergeant!"

The sergeant sounds concerned for their safety, even their lives. This is very different from the way he's sounded when they were practicing hand-to-hand combat (at which Frangie performed pitifully), and bayonet practice (also pitiful), and the regular obstacle course (where she did surprisingly well, being fast on her feet and having a slight frame that is easier to haul over a wooden wall).

They are lined up in rows of twelve. Sixty seconds will be counted off between each group. Frangie is in the third row.

"All right, test fire!" a noncom over behind the machine guns yells. There is the sinister metallic throat-clearing of six machine guns being cocked, and then . . .

It is the loudest thing Frangie has ever heard. These are not the machine gun sound effects she's heard in movies; these are the real thing—six bulky, water-cooled models from the last war. They fire 450 rounds a minute, and each round is like a ball peen hammer against Frangie's eardrums.

The test burst is just a few rounds, but it is more than enough to wipe away the last grin on the last face.

"First row. Go!" Sergeant Kirkland yells.

The machine guns fire, not all at once, but a couple at a time, firing two-second bursts, which is approximately fifteen rounds each.

The first row drops down into the mud. They cradle their rifles by resting them in the crooks of their elbows and crawl like scared babies. The barbed wire plucks at their backs and scrapes along their helmets. The machine guns open up, two-second bursts with a few seconds between.

"Second row, go!"

From the far end of the course a corporal is yelling encouragement. "Move it, you slugs! Keep your damned head down, Matthews! Jesus H.! My baby sister is faster than you people!"

It doesn't look hard. It really doesn't. Until Kirkland yells, "Row three, go!"

Frangie drops quickly to her stomach, cradles her carbine—she's too small to manage the rifle that is both longer and heavier—and slips her head beneath the first row of barbed wire.

She quickly realizes that there is no dignified way to do this. To stay below the stream of bullets she has to press her entire body right down on the mud, splay her knees out, and push with feet and knees while pulling with elbows. But the drag of her body on the mud makes forward movement nearly impossible. Clods of moist clay push their way into her shirt and accumulate on her belt. The urge to rise just enough to gain some leverage is strong, but not strong enough to make her forget the bullets. She has never been close to a bullet in flight before and had not realized that they make a sound that is distinct from the shattering noise of exploding powder. It's a *flit-flit-flit* sound, with the pitch subtly different depending on how close they fly. She is convinced she can tell when they are a safe eight inches away or a terrifying two inches.

She digs her elbows into the mud, keeping her carbine clear of the ground, which forces her facedown practically onto the bolt. Each spasmodic movement threatens to knock her front teeth into steel. Still, she's doing it. She's doing it! From time to time the wire will scrape the top of her helmet, but her back is clear and at least she's not falling behind.

Sometimes, Frangie reflects, being small is a good thing.

She glances left and spots Clara lying still, unmoving. The voice of the corporal can be heard in snatches between eruptions from the guns. It reminds her of listening to the radio during a thunderstorm when the lightning static would punctuate and interrupt the music.

BAM-BAM-BAM-BAM-BAM!

Flit! Flit! FLIT!

"Move your—"

BAM-BAM-BAM-BAM!

Flit! Flit!

"Damn your bones, you—"

BAM-BAM-BAM-BAM!

Frangie looks again and sees that now Clara is definitely falling behind. She can see the other girl's face from this angle. Clara is sweating. Her mouth is gulping for air, like a trout just landed in the bottom of the fisherman's boat. Squinting to see better, Frangie sees that Clara's hands are trembling. In fact, her whole body is shaking.

"Come on, Clara, you can do this!"

The sergeant and the corporal are both yelling now, and the machine guns seem to be firing even more steadily. Clara is doing worse than trembling now; her whole body is quivering like a cornered animal about to make a desperate run for it.

Frangie has a terrible feeling, a sinking in her stomach, a knowledge born of small clues that add up to an awful certainty: Clara is on the edge of panic.

There's a soldier behind Clara, trying now to get past her, and hesitation has let someone from the fourth row close in on Frangie as well.

"Clara! No!" Frangie yells, but if Clara hears, it does not stop her. She pushes up off the ground.

"Stop shooting!" Frangie yells. "Stop shooting!" She shoves her carbine aside and tries to scramble to Clara. "Get down, Clara, get—"

Clara is looking in Frangie's direction when the bullet

hits Clara's helmet with a dull metallic *clang*, spinning Clara's head, and spraying blood and sharp little shards of metal onto Frangie's face.

"Man down! Man down! Cease fire! Cease fire!" the sergeant shouts, and the firing stops. Frangie fights her way to her feet, pushing through the wire, tangling in a coil that won't let go of her boot, and stumbling to drop beside Clara. She tosses Clara's helmet aside and at first sees only a smear of blood covering the side of Clara's face.

Clara says, "What happened? What happened?"

"Let me look at it, don't move!" Frangie yells.

Clara's fighting her, limbs thrashing, so Frangie straddles her, using her small weight to hold the panicky girl down, twisting her head to see the injury.

"It's just your ear," Frangie says. "It's nothing."

It's not nothing. Clara's ear is almost entirely gone, and what's left is hamburger that will have to be cut away. But Frangie does not see any deeper damage. Clara will not die. She'll want to wear her hair long for the rest of her life, but she will not die.

It is no easy task for Frangie and Sergeant Kirkland to extricate Clara from the barbed wire and then manhandle her back to the starting line where they drop her, none too gently, on the ground. Frangie kneels beside her and, in an unusually authoritative voice, demands water.

She is handed a canteen, which she pours over the wound.

"Yeah, it's just your ear, Clara. Another inch and it would have been curtains. Anyone got a handkerchief?"

No one has a handkerchief, but someone produces a clean OD T-shirt that Frangie folds quickly and presses down over the wound. The shirt turns red, but the blood is only seeping, not pumping.

It takes half an hour for an ambulance to arrive with two stretcher bearers to take Clara away to the surgery that will leave her disfigured—but in no danger—and out of the army.

"Like I said, that's one way to get out of the army," Sergeant Kirkland says. "You handled that well, Private Marr."

It is almost the first time he has referred to her by name rather than as Okaninny.

That evening, after chow, Sergeant Kirkland calls her from the barracks. "Captain wants to see you."

This is not happy news. Privates are not called to see the captain. Ever. She searches the sergeant's face for a clue, but he's already done an about-face and Frangie rushes to catch up to him.

"What's up, Sarge?"

"Captain wants to see you."

"I know, but why?"

"The ways of officers are not for mere enlisted men to

question," Sergeant Kirkland says, then in a less pompous voice adds, "and sure as hell the orders of a white West Point captain are not for colored noncoms to question."

Captain Dan Oberdorfer is in his forties, with crew-cut red hair and a fireplug build that causes his uniform to fit like a sausage casing. Many rumors surround Oberdorfer: that he had carnal knowledge of a general's daughter, that he once punched a visiting foreign observer, that he is a drunk or a homosexual or even an escaped lunatic. The rumors are all by way of explaining how a seemingly competent white officer ended up training colored troops.

The sergeant and Frangie snap salutes as they enter his office and stand five feet from the front edge of his battered old gray steel desk. The captain returns the salute properly, then says, "What the hell are you here for, Kirkland?"

"Sir, you ordered me to present Private Marr."

"Ah. So I did. At ease." He has a heavy accent of a type that Frangie cannot identify. He looks at Frangie and lifts a folder from his desk. "I see here, Private Marr, that you are the worst goddamn soldier on this post."

"Sir?"

"You can't shoot, you can't throw a grenade far enough to avoid blowing yourself up, you can't manage five miles in a pack without falling out from heat exhaustion, you got marked down on the last inspection for your bunk, your foot locker, your uniform, and your weapon. In short, you are one piss-poor soldier, even for a coon. Even for a woman coon. What are you, four feet tall? You're a goddamn midget with not enough strength to level a goddamned rifle, and yet it says here you enlisted."

"Yes, sir." The words are automatic. She feels as if she's falling, as if she just stepped off the edge of a cliff. Sergeant Kirkland has yelled at her, as have other sergeants, but this attack is categorical and brutal.

She feels Sergeant Kirkland stiffen beside her. "Captain, Private Marr is—"

"Do not interrupt me, boy. Don't let those goddamned stripes fool you, Sergeant. You are still just a Nigra talking to a white man!" The captain has gone from placid to red-faced furious in about ten seconds.

The sergeant's "Yes, sir" takes several long and tense moments to arrive.

"Now, let me make one thing perfectly clear. I am attempting to follow orders here and turn a bunch of 'yassuh, nosuh,' toe-pickin' field Nigras into soldiers, but Jesus H., this is bullshit. Not just Nigras, women Nigras, and now this little pickaninny, goddamn, that's three strikes right there."

"Captain, I am raising a formal objection to your—"

"Shut the fug up, Kirkland."

"No, sir."

The blustery, bullying, hate-filled air turns still and cold now, a dangerous stillness.

Captain Oberdorfer stands, places his fists on his desk, and leans toward them. "Are you back-talking me? Are you telling me how I can talk about this sin-marked child of Ham? Have you never had anyone read the Bible to you, boy? It was Ham who humiliated Noah, and because of that Noah called him Canaan and said his descendants forever would be servants to the white man."

When this is met with stony silence, Oberdorfer adds, "That ain't my law, that's God's law, and God's law is above all other law."

"God's law says 'thou shalt not take the name of the Lord thy God in vain.'" The words are out of Frangie's mouth before she can stop them. She barely has the presence of mind to add a belated, "Sir."

The captain stares at Frangie like he's just been insulted by a dog. He's torn between amazement and rage. Rage wins out.

"Do not quote scripture at me, you dirty little—"

"Sir!" Sergeant Kirkland says sharply. "I request that Private Marr be allowed to return to quarters."

"The hell I—"

"Sir, I have something to say that I would rather—and you would rather—Private Marr not overhear."

That stops Oberdorfer in midword. He glares at

Kirkland, shoots a murderous stare at Frangie, turns back to Sergeant Kirkland, and says, "You are dismissed, Private."

Frangie snaps a salute that the captain refuses to return. She has no choice but to hold the pose until Kirkland says, "Wait outside, Marr."

She does an about-face and flees the room. Outside in the humid night air she gasps for breath, doubled over, hands on her knees. She is shaking, shaking worse than she did in the live-fire exercise.

After a few minutes a seething Sergeant Kirkland arrives.

"I'm sorry, Sarge," Frangie says.

"Shut up, Marr," he snaps. Then, regaining his composure, says, "It's not your fault that Cajun cracker bastard . . ."

"You don't have to stand up for me, Sarge; you'll lose your stripes."

"Fug my stripes, and I ain't standing up for you, Marr. I'm standing up for the rest of the men. He's not wrong that you don't belong. No power on earth is ever going to make a soldier of you."

Frangie, numb with disbelief, nods, then stops herself. She starts to say something but is overwhelmed by emotions that pull her in different directions. She would like nothing better than to be sent home as unfit for duty.

But there is still the matter of her family's finances. And, too, the captain has tapped a reservoir of rebellious anger deep within her.

"I'm getting you through basic; I have no choice now," Kirkland says bitterly. "I'm getting you through this and hope to hell you don't get sent anywhere there's bullets flying."

Then he pauses, tilts his head, thinking, then snaps his fingers. "Aren't you the one who put in for medic?"

She doesn't trust herself to speak without choking, so she nods.

"Well, then, goddammit, I'll see to it," Kirkland says. The last of his anger ebbs with sighs and shakes of the head.

"I would like that, Sarge," Frangie says tightly.

"You'll most likely be lousy at that too," he says, but without malice.

"Sarge. Can I ask . . . ?"

"What I said to Oberdorfer?" He laughs. "Nothing much. Just mentioned that the cathouse he visits is off-limits and the steaks and chops he brings them as payment are stolen army property."

It takes Frangie a few beats to tease out what the word *cathouse* means. Then she says, "Oh."

"That's how it's done if you're a colored man in a white man's army," he says. "Gotta know something. So I make sure to stay well informed. But you will not repeat that, Marr, or I will come down on you like the true wrath of Jehovah."

"Right, Sarge."

"You got three weeks left. Try not to fug up any more than usual. Get out of here."

14

RIO RICHLIN—CAMP MARON, SMIDVILLE, GEORGIA, USA

"You shouldn't have too much trouble keeping track of the enemy today," Sergeant Mackie says. "The red team is actually black soldiers from across the river. Easy to differentiate. Like it will be if you're fighting Japs—easy to tell the good guys from the bad guys."

They are grouped into platoons and squads, combat formations different from the organization for other training. Rio knows most of the people in her squad, likes some of them, can't stand others, Luther Geer being prominent among that second group. Rio, Jenou, and an older woman named Arabella DeLarge are the only females in their squad. Cat Preeling is with a different group.

They carry full gear, including rifles loaded with blanks.

"They'll make noise, they just won't kill anyone," Mackie says laconically. "Only your own stupidity will get you killed. Try not to be stupid. The army would like you to get into the war before you get yourself killed."

They are deep in the trees and deeper still in the mosquitoes, which fly like dive bombers through the clouds of harmless but annoying gnats. The day is hot and, worse yet for girls from California, humid. Humidity at Camp Maron has been torture for Rio and Jenou.

Rio slaps a mosquito on her neck.

"Did you apply your mosquito repellant, Private Richlin?" Mackie demands.

"Yes, Sergeant," Rio says. "The mosquitoes don't want to be repelled."

"Richlin's just too sweet," Tilo says.

"Today's exercise is simple. The Red Team—"

"The coons," Luther interrupts.

"—will be coming from the east looking to take the only bridge over this stream. Then they will attempt to hold that bridge. You will beat them to that bridge and hold it."

"Hell yes, we will," Luther says loudly. He has left his contraband kitten back in its enclosure beneath the barracks.

"If we find this bridge," Kerwin mutters just loudly enough for Rio and a few others to hear.

"Your compass heading is north-northeast," Mackie says. "The objective is approximately four miles from here. We will begin . . ." She looks at her watch, waits, waits, waits. "Now!"

And no one moves.

"I take it from your cowlike immobility that you are waiting for me to show you the way," Mackie says. "I will not be showing you the way. The theoretical for this war game is that this platoon has lost its sergeants as well as its lieutenant, so, ladies and gentlemen, I will be back at my quarters filling out reports and drinking coffee while you are hiking through the woods. There will be proctors wearing yellow armbands. They will evaluate your performance and decide who's dead and wounded. And they will evacuate you when and if you break an ankle or are bitten by a snake."

Arabella DeLarge emits a small shriek at the mention of the word *snake*. So does one of the men. Sergeant Mackie grins, which is not a reassuring sight.

There are blank looks all around. The platoon consists of forty-eight men and women, and not one of them has any particular reason to think they're in charge. Finally someone actually pulls out a compass and says, "Northeast is that way," and makes a chopping motion.

Stick has just elected himself as guide. Some of the other men grumble and make a point of taking out their own compasses as if to double-check, but in the end the consensus is that they should all follow the young man with the widow's peak who spoke up first. They set off through the woods with all the discipline of a herd of sheep, and all the stealth of a brass band. They reach a proctor a few minutes after plunging into the woods. He nods as they pass.

Within minutes the complaining begins.

"If you soaked wool blankets in steaming hot water and then wrapped them around yourself, it would not feel as miserable as this," Rio says.

"Humidity," Jenou agrees darkly, catches her boot on one of the many aboveground roots, and trips.

"And snakes, don't forget snakes," Kerwin says, and snatches Jenou's pack, keeping her from hitting the ground face-first.

"Thanks, Cassel."

"Well, we're a team, right? I'm pretty sure I heard that somewhere."

Rio swats another mosquito. "I keep killing these mosquitoes, but they keep coming."

"So where are these Nigras?" Luther demands. "Let's find 'em, pretend-shoot 'em, and head back."

"Be careful they don't pretend-shoot you," Rio snaps. The contempt in Geer's voice sets her teeth on edge.

"No Nigra ever beat a white man," Luther says breezily. "Just like no woman ever beat a man."

Rio bites her lip, not wanting to waste energy on a

pointless argument. She does not like humidity, that's the main point; in fact, she hates humidity. It's grown steadily worse over the last few weeks, and she now thinks of the humidity and heat as personal insults. And she hates mosquitoes with an intensity of feeling she has never felt for anything before.

Rio comes out of her sour rumination on climate, and the insects that climate brings with it, in time to hear Geer say, ". . . we string 'em up."

"What?" Rio demands.

Luther grins and pantomimes a rope around the neck, yanked upward. He sticks his tongue out comically. "Nigra talks back, Nigra shows disrespect for a white woman, what else are you going to do? You get some boys, go around to their shack, frog-march them to the nearest tree, and watch 'em dance while you pass the bottle around."

"Shut up, Geer." This from Kerwin.

"Screw you, Cassel, I know where you come from, and it ain't any different there."

"Not every southern man is you, Geer," Kerwin says, and accelerates his pace to put distance between them.

"Tell you what," the unapologetic Luther continues, "it's a damn mistake giving Nigras uniforms and guns."

"There's one behind you! And he's got a gun!" Jenou yells.

Luther spins around, catches himself, and spots the grin on Jenou's face. "Yeah, screw you, Castain."

The mood has gone from sullen to resentful to downright angry as they march now through boot-sucking mud and swat at bugs and shy away from roots that look like snakes and just generally comport themselves like sullen kids on the worst field trip ever, which is not far from the truth.

"Oh, good: someplace to sit," Jenou says as they step into a triangular-shaped clearing. She pulls out her canteen and raises it to her lips. Three drops fall.

"I can spare a swig," Rio says, and hands her canteen to Jenou, not without some reluctance.

Stick surveys the trees around them, ignored by men and women who have flopped down onto the ground or are sneaking off to pee. Rio is one of the few interested when Stick says, "That's the direction. But we should send scouts out ahead."

"Yeah, you get right on that, GI Joe," someone says sardonically.

"I'll go," Kerwin says.

Rio can't pass up a chance to take a shot at Luther. "I'll go, as long as Geer doesn't."

She's not excited about walking ahead; she just wants to get away from the sound of people complaining. And, truth be told, she has carefully preserved her water and doesn't want to have to share what's left with Jenou. She loves Jenou, but Jenou needs to manage her own canteen; there are no soda machines out here.

She also half hopes and half fears that Jack will volunteer to join them. He's good company, she tells herself, and he carries his own weight and doesn't beg water off other people. Besides, she has had no second dream about him, but receiving a very affectionate letter from Strand has—she believes—put all thoughts of the Englishman out of her mind. She sees him now as nothing but a fellow soldier, more charming than most, less likely to smell— some of the men are not great fans of deodorant. Plus he tells amusing stories about England, about how they drive on the wrong side of the road, and how the king—who is definitely called George but may be either the fifth or the sixth, Rio can't be sure—came to be king only because his older brother ran off with an American floozy.

But as it happens Jack is in dire shape having split a bottle of moonshine with a corporal from supply the night before. He is lying flat on his back, helmet pulled over his eyes to shield them from the sun. From time to time he moans.

Rio and Kerwin agree with Stick that they'll start off ten minutes ahead and fire off a shot if they get into trouble, or come running back if they learn anything useful. Sticklin goes over the compass reading with them, and both Rio and Kerwin pull out their compasses and pretend to know what he's talking about.

Then they forge ahead, leaving the gaggle behind. The platoon soon disappears from sight and then sound.

"If you can get past the heat and the bugs, it's kind of pretty," Kerwin says, looking around.

Rio considers that. The trees are draped with Spanish moss, forming a great shroud that makes even young trees look ancient. A pure white bird with ungainly legs folded beneath it flies overhead, screeching a warning. Mushrooms the color of caramel erupt from decayed logs. The sky is a rich blue void framed by ornate patterns of branch and leaf. There are puffs of cloud but too little to offer any hope of relief from the sun.

"Uh-huh," Rio says, unconvinced.

"Freeze or I shoot."

The voice does not belong to Kerwin. It belongs to a young black man who rises from concealment behind a pillow of moss. He's holding a rifle leveled at them, and he is wearing a red armband.

Rio glances back, looking for a place to run, but two other black soldiers wait, each with rifle leveled.

"Well, I'll be damned," Kerwin says.

"Maybe, but first you'll be a prisoner." This from a small black woman soldier Rio has overlooked in her search for an escape route.

Rio and Kerwin exchange looks of consternation mixed with relief: now they don't have to keep marching through the damp forest.

"Put down your weapons," one of the male soldiers says. "You are officially prisoners of the Red Force."

Rio shrugs and slings her rifle, as does Kerwin.

"All right, Marr, you keep an eye on 'em till we can find a proctor."

The young woman shrugs. "There's a fairly dry log we can rest on over there."

On impulse Rio sticks out her hand. "Rio Richlin. This is Kerwin Cassel."

They shake briefly, and Rio glances at her palm.

"How you doing?" Kerwin says.

"Frangie Marr. And I'm doing fine now that I get to sit down." She sits on the log with Rio and Kerwin, who chooses to stretch out on his back, indifferent to the large beetle he nearly crushes.

"I don't suppose anyone's got a smoke," Kerwin says, looking up at the sky.

"Well, since you are my prisoner, I guess the humane thing . . ." Frangie Marr digs a slightly mashed cigarette out of her pocket and hands it to Kerwin, who lights it up.

"The humane thing would be a cool shower followed by a soft cot with an electric fan blowing," Kerwin says.

"But thanks for the smoke."

Rio notices Frangie looking at her and says, "What?"

"Nothing." Frangie shrugs. "It doesn't come off."

"What doesn't come off?"

"You looked at your hand after you shook mine. The black doesn't come off on you."

Rio feels a flush of embarrassment. "I wasn't . . . I was just . . ." And concludes with, "Sorry."

"I'm going to guess that you haven't met many colored folks."

"No," Rio admits. "I mean, I've seen colored people in movies."

"You like movies?"

"Sure I do. I go whenever I can afford it."

A silence follows and stretches until Frangie says, "Have you seen *Casablanca*?"

"No, I missed it! Last movie I saw was called *This Above All*. I saw it right before I enlisted. I saw it with . . . a friend."

"She means her boyfriend," Kerwin offers. "Haven't met him myself, but he's a Handsome Fly-Boy."

Rio rounds on Kerwin. "How do you know . . . Jenou. Of course." She curses Jenou under her breath.

"Yep, Private Jenou Castain. She's much more talkative than you, Richlin, plus I've seen you pull his photo out when you think no one's looking."

"He's not exactly a boyfriend," Rio grumbles. "He's just a friend. Who's a boy. A man."

"You kiss him?" Frangie asks.

"That's not exactly your business," Rio huffs.

Kerwin says, "I swear I would sell my mother to pirates in exchange for a cool shower."

Rio laughs, trying to lighten the mood after her sharp and defensive remark. "Pirates? A lot of pirates are there where you come from, Cassel?"

This leads into a general discussion of hometowns, home states, all the usual get-acquainted things. Cassel is from Teays, West Virginia, of course, coal country, as he has told Rio many times. That's about six hundred miles from their current location, a bit closer than Frangie's home. Rio has traveled the farthest to reach this misera-ble spot: twenty-five hundred miles.

"How you ever going to get home on leave?" Frangie asks.

"I'll walk if I have to," Rio says fervently.

"Maybe Handsome Fly-Boy will come fetch you in his airplane," Kerwin teases. "You got a man . . . um, Private Marr?"

"Nope. I got me two brothers and parents. And some-times some sick animals."

Mention of sick animals intrigues Rio. "What kind of animals? You have livestock?"

"Naw, Tulsa is a city, no one's got more than a chicken or two, but I tend to strays I find that are busted up."

"Like a vet?"

"More like a bad vet," Frangie says, and smiles at the memory. "But I do what I can with clean rags and iodine."

"Maybe you could put in for cavalry. They still got horses and mules and such," Kerwin says, and picks a praying mantis off his neck.

"There aren't any black cavalry, not anymore."

"Was there?"

"Back in olden times. Buffalo soldiers, that's what the Indians called them on account of their nappy hair making Indians think of buffaloes."

"Huh. My old granddad always says . . . ," Kerwin begins. Then he stops. "Anyone else hear that?"

"Probably a proctor coming to get us," Frangie says.

Kerwin sits up suddenly. "Uh-uh, city girl."

And with that there's a wild crashing sound of something bursting through vines and branches and—

"Run!"

The three of them launch from the log like someone's set off a hand grenade, leaving their rifles behind.

"What is it?" Rio yells.

"It's a tusker!" Kerwin yells back, leading the way toward a tree whose lower branches just might barely be within reach.

Rio shoots a look over her shoulder and sees something that looks like a small bear, but with a pig's snout, a rat's hair, and two curved tusks.

It's not huge, but it sure is angry.

Cassel leaps, grabs a branch with the dexterity of a monkey, and swings himself up. Rio is right behind him, blessing her push-up-strengthened shoulders as she scrambles and hauls, gasping for breath. Lying flat on the branch, feet and hands dangling, she sees that there is no way short of sprouting wings for the diminutive Frangie to make it.

Rio yells, "Grab my hand!"

Frangie grabs Rio's hand and Rio—with some help from Cassel—manages to pull Frangie up and out of range of the boar.

They are now six feet above the enraged pig. They gasp for breath, shaking, and then, suddenly, laughing.

Malevolent pig eyes stare up at them, and the pig circles, snorting and huffing, still furious at some imaginary insult. They edge closer to the trunk of the tree, finding more stable spots, not trusting the branch not to break.

"I shot one of his distant relations once," Kerwin says. "I reckon that's why he's so worked up."

"You're a hunter?" Rio asks.

"Where I live you are either a hunter or you don't see meat on your plate," Kerwin admits. "We live way back up in the hills. I say Teays Valley 'cause that's close as we get to a town, but I am pure hillbilly."

"What do your folks do up in the hills?"

"Well, my pap works the coal mine. Cooks a bit of mash on the side for spending money, but he generally drinks half of what he makes, and then gambles the rest." He softens his tone, fearing he's been too harsh. "He's a good man, my pap, never beats me more than a couple times a year, and he don't lay hands on my mom. But he does like a drink and a card game, that he does."

"I guess that's a hard life, coal mining." Frangie nods like she understands, though Rio is still digesting the fact that Kerwin finds it unusual that a man should not beat his wife.

"Yes, it is that," Kerwin says. "It'll be my life when this is all over." His tone is resigned. "Come home after ten hours spent a mile down, probably blacker than your own pap, Private Marr. That coal dust gets into your skin so after a while you can't wash it away, no matter how hard you scrub. By the time you're forty it's got you coughing up blood half the time. But it's a living, and there's plenty of folks ain't got that."

His tone of resignation irritates Rio, though she can't think why. Is it because he sounds like she feels? Like life is planned out in advance in ways that don't leave a lot of room for determining your own future?

"I'm going to try for college," Frangie says.

"A little Nigra girl like you?" Kerwin laughs. It's not a

mean laugh, more the sort of sound you make when you hear a child talking nonsense.

"It could happen." Frangie sounds defiant but not too sure of herself. "I have a cousin up in Chicago went to college. He's got a good job now."

"Well, that may be," Kerwin allows. "But most likely I end up in the mine and you end up taking in laundry and having a whole passel of little pickaninnies, and that's a fact. And Private Richlin, here, she's probably going to be an old-maid schoolteacher."

"Old maid, huh?" Rio recognizes his teasing tone for what it is, but she still doesn't like the image he's called to mind. "What makes you think I'll be an old maid?"

"Hell, Richlin, you're too ornery for any man to stay married to you."

It's the first time anyone has referred to Rio as ornery. Or any other synonym for ornery. It brings a reluctant smile to her lips.

Ornery.

"You want to hear a story, Private Marr?" Kerwin asks.

"I got time on my hands," Frangie says ruefully.

"See, there's this old boy doesn't like the ladies taking part in this here war, and he makes some rude suggestions to Private Richlin. Well—"

"Oh come on, Cassel, don't tell that story. I sound like some kind of crazy person."

"Well, now I have got to hear it," Frangie says.

For the next hour they swap stories, some funny, some not, and Rio's still grinning when the proctor finds them. He's a senior NCO armed with a clipboard and a pistol. He fires a round in the air, and the pig just stares at him. The NCO levels the pistol at the pig, which snorts derisively and finally trots off into the woods.

"What's going on here?" the proctor asks, drawling the words.

"These are my prisoners, Sergeant," Frangie answers.

Kerwin says, "Uh, Sergeant? I don't suppose you need to mention any details of this to anyone else, do you?"

"You mean you being caught by a tiny little Nigra girl and getting chased up a tree by a pig? My lips are sealed, Private."

Rio is prepared to believe this until later, when the badly beaten Blue Team is at chow and Jack slices into his ham steak, holds up a piece on the end of his fork, and says, "Richlin, I do hope this isn't a friend of yours."

Rio accepts the ribbing with good nature, just as the entire platoon has had to endure ridicule for losing the day's exercise to a colored platoon. She's still digesting the fact that she, little Rio Richlin from Gedwell Falls nowhere, is seen as ornery.

Well. Maybe I am.

15

FRANGIE MARR—CAMP SZEKELY, SMIDVILLE, GEORGIA, USA

"I got those Szekely blues, just as blue as I can be," Frangie sings to herself, freely adapting the W. C. Handy song "St. Louis Blues." "Oh, my sergeant's got a heart like a rock cast in the sea. Or else he wouldn't have been so mean to me."

She has not felt much like singing lately, but tomorrow is to be her first time off-post since coming to this steamy backwater, and she's walking toward the barracks, coming from the laundry with fresh uniforms and a spring in her step. Frangie's lucky that for her home is just a sixteen-hour bus and train ride away. For most of the soldiers at Camp Szekely, a three-day pass means staying with one of the black families in Smidville that will host lonesome soldiers for fifty cents a night.

Smidville isn't much of a town, and what there is of it is whites only. For black soldiers there's a juke joint out on the highway where for two dollars you can get pretty drunk and listen to some amateur musicians playing jazz or blues. But that's one thing for the men, a whole different matter for females: an unaccompanied woman at a juke joint is looking for trouble. Even an accompanied woman might not be so safe.

Most of the few women soldiers on the post live too far off to get home and back, so they stay in the barracks, even when they have a chance to get away, but Frangie has done her research and timed it all out, and there's a bus that will carry colored passengers in the last three rows to Atlanta, where she can catch a train to Tulsa. She's got leave coming; leave that, if everything works just right, will let her spend almost a day and a half with her family.

"If I feel tomorrow like I feel today, I'm gonna pack my trunk and make my getaway." Normally she sings in the church choir, the old standards like "Onward Christian Soldiers" and "Hard Trials" and "Go Down, Moses." Fond memories of warm nights practicing with the choir prompt her to begin a spontaneous rewrite of "My Way's Cloudy."

"Old Captain's mad, and I am glad, send them angels down! We're comin' on to '43, send them angels down. We're marchin' on to gay Paree, oh send them angels down!"

A day and a half without marching or KP or any of the other strains and indignities of military life sounds pretty good.

"Hey there, Private, that's a pretty voice you have. You want a ride back to barracks? Sweet thing like you shouldn't have to walk all that way carrying a box."

He's a white sergeant, driving an open jeep at walking speed, now keeping pace with her. A tingle of fear goes up her spine. His voice slurs from drink.

"No thanks, Sergeant. I don't mind the walk."

"Well, isn't that a hell of a thing. A white man offers you a ride and you turn him down?"

She glances at him. He's a tall man with a thin face and blue eyes that don't quite want to focus on a single point. "I don't want any trouble, Sergeant. I like to walk."

"Trouble? Who said anything about trouble?"

"It's not far." Maybe it wasn't far to walk, but now she is measuring the length of this dusty, deserted, hard-pack street with a whole different appreciation for distance. How far can she run before dropping her bundle? Can the jeep follow her across the parade ground if she gets off the road?

She accelerates her walking pace. He notices.

"You're not trying to get away from me now, are you?"

Fear is a hard knot in her stomach. The tension in her muscles crushes the cardboard box under her arm. There is no point in answering him; she's encountered his kind before, and he will not listen to reason.

"I'm thinking when a white sergeant offers a ride to

a Nigra private, she better just get her little black ass on board with the program."

"No, Sergeant," she says. Her teeth are chattering, and the distance to safety shrinks too slowly. If she runs what will he do? He might just laugh and call out names at her. Or he might race and catch up to her. He might even "accidentally" turn the car into her.

Best not to run until she has to. Best to just keep walking and pray God sends some help. She sees two black soldiers crossing the road, but they are three hundred yards off; anyway, what are they going to do?

Just keep walking.

The sergeant guns the car and yanks it right into her path. No question now that he's drunk; she can smell it wafting from him.

"You get your ass up here right now, Nigra, you and me are going for a little ride to somewhere private. Private, Private." He laughs. Then he switches to a friendlier tone. "Come on, honey, it won't be anything you haven't done before, it'll just be vanilla instead of chocolate."

She tries to pass behind the jeep. He grinds the gear into reverse and cuts her off. The fender strikes her thigh, a painful glancing blow, but she barely notices the pain.

"Sergeant, if you keep bothering me I'll take it to my captain."

He grins. "The word of a Nigra private against a white

216

noncom? How do you reckon that works out? Come on, little brown sugar, I'll make it quick, might be you'll even like it."

Two big deuce-and-a-half trucks come rolling by, and to Frangie's infinite relief, the soldiers in the back are black. They are not from her unit, but one of the NCOs sees what's what and raps on the hood of the trailing truck, bringing it to a shuddering, bouncing halt.

Ten black faces turn to watch, and none of those faces are amused.

"What's your name, Private?" the black sergeant calls down to her.

"Private Frangie Marr, Sergeant," she calls out in a trembling voice.

"Are you done giving directions to Sergeant Embleton?"

It takes her a few beats to realize what he's doing. She breathes a sigh of relief. "I believe so, Sergeant."

"Well then, you best climb up here and ride along with us."

Strong hands haul Frangie up over the tailgate, and she wedges in on the hard plank seat between a male and female GI. Her rescuer is only a few inches taller than she, but quite a bit wider, with bunched muscles straining his uniform. He has the stripes of a technical sergeant, three up-pointed chevrons, two arced ones beneath, which gives him rank over Embleton.

"Hey now, boy," Embleton yells, "that's my piece of tail there. You hand her right the hell back down."

Somewhat at odds with his hard face and body, Frangie's savior wears wire-rimmed glasses, and she watches, fascinated, as the eyes behind those spectacles shift from worried to angry.

"Goddammit, boy, you best hand her back down if you know what's good for you!"

The black sergeant is doing a slow boil, and she almost wants to tell him no, don't make trouble.

Almost.

What she says is, "Thanks, Sarge."

He ignores her and hops down from the truck, combat boots hard on the packed clay. He snaps fingers over his shoulder and is handed a rifle by one of his men.

"Sergeant Embleton, I believe you may be under the weather," he says. Embleton looks wary, glancing from the advancing man with a rifle to the truckload of black faces behind him.

"No harm meant, Green," Embleton says.

Green says, "Yes, I do believe you are drunk and driving a jeep, which could mean loss of rank, Embleton. Especially since you managed to bust out your headlight."

"I didn't bust out no—"

Crumpf!

Sergeant Green smashes the butt of the rifle into the

left headlight of the jeep.

Embleton watches, groans, and Frangie sees real fear on the white man's face. That simple reality amazes her. White men do not fear black men, not in her world.

"Now, I don't know what one-horse cracker town you come from, Embleton, but we aren't there. We're on an American army post. And I believe you have been warned about messing with female soldiers before."

"You don't talk to me like that, boy." Despite the drink, there is authority in that voice, a sense of right, a tone full of brutal history.

Sergeant Green stiff-arms the rifle back up to his corporal. He places his hands deliberately on the frame of the windshield and door of the jeep, looming over Embleton despite being the shorter man. "I find out you pulled anything like this again, and it won't be the headlight that gets a rifle butt. Do you understand me clearly? Now, you get this jeep back to the motor pool and hope they believe whatever bullshit story you come up with to explain the damage."

Hate, pure and undisguised, radiates from Embleton's face. But in the end, he drives away, wheels churning red dust.

Frangie closes her eyes and drinks in relief. She thanks Sergeant Green again.

"No idea what you're referring to, Private," Green

says after he's climbed back up in the truck. "Nothing happened here. Any of you fellows see anything happen here?"

There comes a false but cheerful chorus of "No, Sarge" from the truck's occupants, and even one smart-aleck who says, "I've lost my sight altogether, Sarge. Can I go back home now?"

The truck starts off again, and in a few minutes Frangie is safe and sound in her barracks. She sets her bundle down on her cot and goes to the latrine to vomit into the toilet bowl.

16

RIO RICHLIN—CAMP MARON, SMIDVILLE, GEORGIA, USA

"What is that filth on your belt buckle, Private Castain?"

It's inspection. It is the very last inspection they are to endure under Sergeant Mackie. The lieutenant has come to witness, as has the captain, two officers Rio has barely glimpsed during her weeks at Camp Maron.

Rio winces as Jenou makes the mistake of glancing down at her belt to see whether she can identify the "filth" in question. Jenou observes a single, greasy fingerprint and, in the process of observing this, realizes she has looked down while at attention—a sin, a crime, a travesty, an offense against all that is good and holy, quite possibly a form of treason, and the moral equivalent of offering to serve coffee and donuts to Mussolini, Tojo, and Hitler.

"Private Castain, after thirteen weeks I would have thought you understood what it means to be at attention! Obviously I have failed you, Private. I have failed you, I have failed the lieutenant, I have failed the captain, and

I have failed whatever sad unit ends up having you when you leave this place."

"Yes, Sergeant."

Neither the lieutenant nor the captain seems remotely upset, but the lieutenant makes a point of putting on his disappointed face, while the captain just looks as if he has an appointment elsewhere.

Once the inspection is complete and the officers—having done their duty—are gone, Mackie keeps them all lined up and at attention.

"In a few minutes you will be dismissed. At that time you will proceed to the bulletin board outside Company HQ to learn where you have been assigned." Sergeant Mackie's pacing has not grown less sinister, but Rio is used to it now.

"Some of you will man a typewriter. Some of you will drive a truck or a jeep. Some of you will go off to specialist training. A lot of you will draw safe and easy duty." Pace. Pace. A glance at this private or that, still judging, still searching for fault. "And some of you will be going to active frontline outfits. But wherever you are assigned, you will be soldiers in the army of the United States of America. You will be part of a history that stretches back two centuries. A proud tradition. The American army has never failed in its duty. You will not fail."

That last catches Rio by surprise. Suddenly she feels tears in her eyes.

Mackie stops in the center, arms clasped behind her back, a position that leaves her very close to Rio.

"Some of you may not make it back," Sergeant Mackie says. "But you will not fail me. You will not fail yourselves. And you will not fail our beloved army. You are far from being the best I have trained." She sighs. "But you're not the worst. Dismissed."

Rio turns away to hide the emotion that makes her feel silly and vulnerable. She glances over and sees Jenou rolling her eyes sarcastically. And beyond her, Stick, with a tear rolling down his cheek.

There should be a sense of elation. This is their last day of basic training, their next-to-last day at Camp Maron before heading home on a week's leave and then going on to their next assignment. But the few cheers and hoots die out quickly, and suddenly the rush to the HQ bulletin board is on.

"A nickel says it's a desk job," Jenou says. "And while I love your crazy dream of driving big trucks around between mortar shells, Rio, I think a nice office in which you and I are the only pretty girls surrounded by unattached officers would be just swell."

"Oh, come now, Jen. You know you'll miss all this."

There is a slight downhill slope to the one-story HQ building, and since so many have gone running on ahead, Rio and Jenou take their time, ambling along under puffy clouds with a blessed breeze pushing the humidity back into the forest.

"Have you heard from Strand?"

"He's going on leave at the same time we are. He'll be back in Gedwell Falls, so I imagine I'll see him."

"Oh, you imagine that, do you? Of course you'll see him."

"Most likely." Rio smiles to herself.

Jack and Kerwin come running up behind them, and Jack puts a hand on each of their shoulders, embracing them as if they were long-lost chums, despite having just parted minutes earlier.

"Are you as excited as I am? Or are you as anxious as I am?" Jack asks.

"We're giddy," Rio says dryly. "Can't you tell?"

"Think of it as a huge department store full of wonderful choices you might pick up and take home with you. There are motor pools on freezing arctic islands with walruses. There are dreary offices deep underground in London so you can keep typing right through the bombing. There's the unloading of ships, the handing out of gear, the care and feeding of outraged forest-dwelling pigs . . ."

"I knew that was coming," Kerwin says ruefully. "But you left out a few things. Like shooting and firing off howitzers. You know, all that stuff."

"Oh, that." Jack waves it off. "The army won't waste

four such intelligent and, may I say, pretty soldiers on anything so crude. I rather doubt we're going to the front lines."

"You think I'm pretty?" Kerwin asks with a grin that grows to consume most of his face.

"You were exactly the one I was thinking of," Jack says, and gives Kerwin a friendly punch in the arm.

Stick is twenty yards ahead.

"What about Stick?" Cassel asked.

"Not pretty."

"He'll most likely volunteer for some elite outfit. That young man intends to win the war all by himself."

"You don't?" Rio asks, still puzzling over whether "pretty" refers to Jenou or herself. Most likely Jenou. In fact, certainly Jenou. No one who sees the two of them together would pick Rio as the prettier one.

Well, maybe someone would. Not every man preferred voluptuous blondes to brunettes with impressive biceps.

It doesn't matter anyway: Rio is taken. She has a boyfriend. And while Jack is funny, charming, and not bad looking in a certain light, he is no Strand Braxton.

The bulletin boards are surrounded by a school of agitated piranhas anxiously shoving and pushing and exulting and bemoaning. Luther's overbearing voice demands, "What's a 745 designation mean? Why don't they speak plain English?"

"Hopefully 745 means permanent latrine duty," Rio mutters.

"Rifleman," Kerwin says. When he sees their surprised looks, he says, "Hey, I pay attention to the important stuff, just not the boring stuff. 745 is 'rifleman,' which is just the army's sweet way of saying, 'You're going to war, Private.'"

"Well, I pity the outfit that gets Geer," Jenou says.

They wait with growing impatience and nervousness as the crowd slowly thins out. Men and women cluster in little groups, discussing their assignments and what it might mean, and who else has the same. Words like *artillery*, *logistics*, *jump training*, and *motor pool* float by. There are numbers, meaningless but life-altering numbers, of classifications and also of units.

Finally Rio reaches the sheets stapled to the plywood board. She finds her name and puts her finger on it. Then follows the line to the right and sees her number.

No, she must have lost her place. She retraces. And then, just to be sure, she counts the lines and once again finds the number.

To her left Jenou emits a soft cry. A whimper. It's too vulnerable, that sound. Jenou is never vulnerable.

Rio cannot look away. She stares far too long at the number after her name. And beyond it the divisional number. The 119th Division. She stares at these two numbers until Jenou leans her head on her shoulder.

"Rifleman," Rio says dully. "It's that stupid Sharp-shooter badge."

"Maybe," Jenou says, "but that doesn't explain why I'm in the same boat."

Kerwin and Jack and a late-arriving Tilo are the same: riflemen. All assigned to the 119th. So are Cat and a girl named Jillion Magraff, who Rio has never warmed up to.

Stick joins them, looking worried, but not about himself. "I drew light machine gunner," he says, and nods as though it was not only inevitable, but correct. "Going to the one-one-nine. What did you guys get?"

Rio exhales a long, shaky sigh and says, "My parents are going to kill me."

She makes excuses for why she won't join the others at chow and heads alone back to the barracks. She finds it empty. Perfectly orderly of course, with blankets all tight and foot lockers all squared away, but empty. She goes to her bunk, conscious of the fact that tonight will be her last night here.

She sits down, careful not to pull the woolen blanket loose. Later, when she stands up to go, she will smooth it carefully and eliminate any slight crease. She spots a thread of lint, picks it off, and sticks it in her pocket for later disposal. Then she hears the steady tread of boots on tile and knows who owns those boots.

"What did you draw, Richlin?"

"Rifleman, Sarge," Rio answers. "The 119th."

Sergeant Mackie is quiet for a long time. Rio looks down at the floor, down at those perfectly spit-shined boots. She has the terrible feeling that she might cry, and she would rather Mackie not see that.

"What did you put in for?"

"Transport. I thought . . . Well, I've driven a truck before, back home, so I figured . . . I mean, a friend of mine, the air corps snatched him up because he'd flown a plane . . ."

Mackie says, "I guess the army needed riflemen more than drivers."

"I guess so."

"Are you scared, Private?"

"I'm scared of telling my folks. My sister . . . she was in the navy. Jap bombers . . ."

Rio waits, expecting the sergeant to tell her to knock it off, or else clean something or paint something. The old saw in the army goes, "If it moves, salute it; if it doesn't move, pick it up; if you can't pick it up, paint it." The mission of noncoms is to keep soldiers constantly busy, even if that means painting rocks, and Rio has done some rock painting during her weeks at Camp Maron.

"I knew you were from a gold-star family," Mackie says after a while. "It's in your file. But you know, the odds of getting hurt bad or killed are pretty low, even up on the line. Pretty good chance you won't even get a scratch."

"I'll tell my mother you said that."

"Well." For a pregnant moment it almost seems Sergeant Mackie might pat her on the shoulder, but no such touch occurs. "You have potential, Richlin. You're young—*too young*. But you never came running to me for help, and that tells me something. Keep your head down, your eyes open, listen to your sergeants—your squad sergeant, your platoon sergeant. They'll be trying to keep you alive."

Rio nods, unable to speak. *That tells me something*. It isn't the most effusive compliment, but it touches her.

She wants to thank Mackie, an urge she never expected to feel. Sergeant Mackie has never been abusive or harsh as some DIs were, but she has never shown Rio any favor either. She's pushed, tortured, and exhausted Rio the same as she has every other soldier, male or female.

The next words are out of Rio's mouth before she can stop and think. "I'm afraid I might be a coward."

Sergeant Mackie slows and stops. She turns and walks back, pace, pace, leather on polished tile.

"Private Richlin, every soldier is a coward some of the time." She sighs and for just a moment she isn't a sergeant, she's a woman, an adult woman, though probably no more than seven or eight years Rio's elder. For a moment she's just another human being. "I was at Bataan, Rich-lin."

Bataan, where American soldiers and marines were beaten by the Japanese. The captured soldiers were sent on a brutal death march that had become a notorious symbol of Japanese inhumanity.

"I was pulling desk duty when the Japs hit us, day after they hit Pearl. Bombing, strafing, naval shelling, and I hadn't even been issued a rifle. I found one. I took it off . . . off a fellow who didn't need it anymore."

She sits down on the edge of Jenou's cot, though even seated she looks spring-loaded, like she might leap up like a jack-in-the-box at the slightest provocation.

"They came ashore, and all of us were ordered to go and fight them. No plan. The officers were all dazed and confused. Training was . . . Well. Anyway. So, we fought them. And they beat us. Damned good fighters, the Japs. They beat us and they beat us, and we'd retreat, and they'd keep coming. They pushed us right across the island. Men dying everywhere. Heat. Malaria. We're telling ourselves help is coming, but deep down we know better. GIs start surrendering. Were they cowards? No, they were sick and hungry and exhausted."

"Did you surrender?"

"No." For a while she is silent, staring past and through Rio at memories. "No, I did not surrender, but it wasn't on account of me being braver than anyone else. Somehow I ended up close to General MacArthur, which was no picnic, but better than what was happening to the men taken prisoner. Then the president finally ordered Mac to abandon the Philippines. The general . . . well, I shouldn't say it, but he's a pompous ass and a showboat, but he's important to the war effort, so they ordered him to abandon the place and slip away on a PT boat at night. General took me along, part of his bodyguard supposedly." She makes a disparaging face.

"But you were ordered to leave, same as the general."

"Yep." Mackie slaps her hands down on her thighs as if signaling the end of the conversation. But then she goes on. "I'd have run if I could. I'd have surrendered if I could. Many good soldiers, brave men, strong men, after weeks of it, they were just done. Just done. And I was as done as any of them. If I'd had somewhere to run to, I expect I would have."

"I overheard Sergeant Etcher talking once. . . . He said he ran."

Sergeant Mackie makes a wry laugh. "Etch loves telling that story on himself, how he was a coward, broke and ran away. It's true, he did."

"Is he a coward?"

"Tell you what, Richlin." She does the knee slap thing again and this time stands up, as does Rio. "Tomorrow we have the ceremony where we send you off home and then off to the war. We'll all be in Class-As, fruit salad and all. So you find an excuse to get close enough to Sergeant Etcher and look at some of that fruit salad on his chest. You take a look at what's on his uniform and decide for yourself whether he's a coward."

Rio suddenly sticks out her hand.

Sergeant Mackie looks at the hand, obviously torn between disdain and acceptance. In the end she shakes Rio's hand.

"Thank you, for . . . I . . . You're . . ." And now the tears come, silent but unstoppable. Rio forces a small laugh. "I don't even know your first name."

"Sure you do, Richlin. It's Sergeant."

At that Sergeant Mackie walks away.

17

RAINY SCHULTERMAN—NEW YORK CITY, NEW YORK, USA

Rainy is pretty sure this will be her last opportunity for quite some time to enjoy New York. Her family lives on the Lower East Side, in a neighborhood that was once almost all Jewish but which has begun to change as many Jews have been driven by high prices to the refuge of Brooklyn across the river. Once almost all the store signs had been in Yiddish with smaller English subtitles, but now the Yiddish has grown steadily smaller and the English larger.

It is a neighborhood of four- and five-story brick buildings, narrow cross streets and broad avenues, cars parked haphazardly, wedged in between horse-drawn carts loaded with scrap to be taken away or barrels of ale to be brought in. Laundry lines are still slung across iron fire escapes, and rugs are still draped from open windows to air out, but this has come to seem low class and fewer pairs of underwear and nightgowns and baby diapers are on display.

It is a fine day, and people are out, taking what sun they can. A trio of shopgirls take their cigarette breaks on the sidewalk, sitting in rickety bentwood chairs, and pass a chipped pottery ashtray between them. Housewives in dowdy dresses and comfortable shoes haul string bags of canned goods and newspaper-wrapped fish. Wild young boys just released from school run and tease and shove, while their female counterparts, no older but far more mature, look on with disdain and trade secrets behind hands held over their mouths.

There are businessmen in suits and ties, ancient grandfathers with untrimmed gray beards, hurrying shopkeepers in stained aprons, teamsters flicking whips at their tired horses, taxicab drivers lounging and gossiping between fares. And the newest and most obvious addition to the life of the neighborhood: soldiers and sailors on leave, few entirely sober.

Rainy loves these streets. This is her home. But her affection does not diminish her restless desire to see very different places. She knows this place; she's spent much of her life running errands here: to the fishmonger, to the kosher grocery, to the sewing shop.

She knows it, she loves it, she's ready to see something new.

As she heads away from the Fulton Market, she sees three drunk sailors and one very sober young man. They are just inside an alley, and the situation looks a lot like a mugging.

Rainy stops. She scans around for police, but New York's Finest are not in view. One of the sailors pushes the civilian. He is putting up no resistance, but he is arguing loudly and without apparent fear.

"Hey, don't push. I just got this suit pressed."

"Don't push, huh?"

"Yes. You didn't hear me the first time?"

"Don't wise off to me, you dirty Jew."

"I apologize. I thought since you were pushing me, you would be the one to wise off to. Is there someone else I should be wising off to? How about you?" He addresses a second sailor. "Are you in charge here?"

Rainy sees what the young man is trying to do—he's trying to sow dissension among the three sailors. She doubts very much that it will work.

Sure enough, the second sailor punches the young man in the face. It's not a prizefighter blow, but neither is it gentle. Rainy hears the impact and sees the man's head snap back. Blood seeps from his lower lip.

Rainy looks again for cops, again sees none, but she does spot a trio of male GIs, two privates and a PFC. She sticks two fingers in her mouth and whistles sharply. "You three. Over here."

The three GIs are no less drunk than the three sailors,

but Rainy figures that's an advantage, as are the ser-geant's stripes on her shoulder. "Boys, there are some *sailors* down that alley who have been saying very bad things about the army. Talking about soldiers being lazy, good-for-nothing cowards. A friend of mine stuck up for the army, and now he's getting beat up."

The ensuing melee is satisfying to both the soldiers and the sailors, all of whom had just been looking for an excuse to get into a fight.

The beleaguered young man escapes with a cut lip. He nods appreciatively at Rainy.

"Thank you. I believe you may have saved me. My dig-nity is beyond salvation, but my body remains mostly intact."

Up close he's a good-looking fellow with thoughtful yet mischievous brown eyes, and he's younger than she'd initially thought.

"Think nothing of it."

"Um . . ."

"Yes?"

"I don't suppose you'd wish to repair with me to that diner and have a cup of coffee?"

Rainy is shocked and does nothing to hide it. "I don't even know your name."

"Halev. Halev Leventhal."

About half her instincts are telling her to say a polite

but firm good-bye. She listens to the other half. "You need some ice on that cut or it will swell up. They'll have ice at the diner."

The diner is like every other diner in the city—a narrow, greasy, noisy room with a grill down one side fronted by a counter with round stools, and a row of cramped tables along the other wall. It's mostly empty, it being too early for dinner and too late for lunch.

Rainy takes charge, ordering some ice and a towel and two cups of coffee. A kind waitress brings ice and a small bandage and clucks sympathetically for a while before being called away to another table.

"Hurt much?" Rainy asks Halev.

"It's mostly numb," Halev says, touching the wound experimentally, wincing, and replacing the ice bag. He twists in his stool to look Rainy up and down. "So, you're a soldier."

"Is it the uniform that gave it away?"

"Well, that and the steely-eyed determination. What's your name?"

"Rainy. Rainy Schulterman."

"Ah, so one of the tribe," he says. "A Jewish woman soldier."

"Is that disapproval I hear?"

"How could I possibly disapprove of you?" he says.

Rainy's not a fool; she knows a flirtatious remark when

237

she hears one, but she pointedly ignores it.

"That's a rhetorical question that avoids an answer," she says.

"Yes, but I think you're overlooking the obvious tone of admiration," he says.

He's enjoying sparring with her, and Rainy doesn't mind that at all. It's fun sparring with men who think they can make short work of her with leers and condescension.

"Misdirection doesn't work very well with me, I'm afraid. Neither does flirtation."

He leans toward her, cocking his head to one side, his eyes judgmental, amused, but not dismissive. "All right, you want a serious answer? My father would disapprove. My grandfather would disapprove. If you listen closely, you may hear the whirring sound of my great-grandfather spinning in his grave. But me?" The judgment and the sly mockery evaporate and a very different look now radiates from those really rather large and soulful eyes. "Me? I approve of anyone who means to rid the world of Adolf Hitler."

Suddenly they have a second thing in common, beyond sharing a religion and a background.

"I wasn't thinking of ridding the world of Hitler all by myself," Rainy says. "However, should the opportunity come my way . . ."

Halev's gaze is shrewd. "So that is it."

"Like I said: if I get that opportunity."

"You would take his life?"

"I would blow his brains out and dance a jig afterward," Rainy says. There is no doubt, no humor, no wise-guy attitude in her voice. She means it. She means it, and she wants to see the look on his face when he realizes she means it.

What she sees surprises her: raw envy, mixed with admiration. For a few minutes they sip their coffee and say nothing.

"I would join up if I could," Halev says at last, voice low. "Four-F. I broke my shoulder when I was seven, and it has never healed properly." He raises his left arm and winces when it approaches horizontal. And he says it again, the damning designation. "Four-F. Unfit for service."

"I'm sorry."

Halev drinks his coffee, eyes downcast, then says, "He means to kill every Jew on earth. He means to exterminate us. *Is* exterminating us."

"I don't think it's a good idea to exaggerate," Rainy says. "The truth is bad enough. Jews are being dispossessed, impoverished, dying on forced marches to concentration camps. That's enough."

"Rainy."

"What?"

"It's not an exaggeration."

There is a certainty in his tone. A sincerity and openness and pain in his eyes.

"You have proof?" she asks.

Halev shrugs. "Your family must know Jews in Germany and Poland. You must have family. Are you getting letters from those people?"

Rainy recalls the way her father pulled her aside to tell her that Cousin Esther has stopped writing. "I don't know." That is not an easy phrase for her to speak.

"No one is getting letters. Not in my circle, and we all have relatives. Relatives but no letters. Not from places the Germans have taken, anyway. A silence has descended on our people in Europe."

Rainy tells herself this is paranoia. She tells herself that the Germans have simply cut off all communication. But in light of her father's identical story, she is not so sure she's right.

Not at all sure.

"So what are we to do?" she asks.

Now he grins. "Two things. First, this." He taps two fingers on the stripes on her shoulder. "And also, you should come to a meeting."

"A meeting? I do hope you're not going to tell me you're a communist."

He laughs. "Nothing quite so conspiratorial. But I am a Zionist. In the end, we Jews must have a land of our own. You could come." Then, with a meaningful look, as if this is yet another flirt, "We are very progressive on women's rights."

Rainy is tempted but, after a moment's thought, shakes her head. "I can't attend meetings."

Halev waits, but she adds no explanation. He tilts his head to one side, looking at her now from an angle, as though this will reveal something new. "It is not that you don't care—you do."

"Of course."

"And it is not that you don't wish to know. No, I can see the curiosity in your eyes. It's as hard to miss as a bonfire on a dark plain."

"That was poetic." She's waiting now, watching him as intently as he is her. Just how smart is this young man?

Halev snaps his fingers. "You would have to report it."

Very smart indeed.

"It was a pleasure meeting you," Rainy says, and stands up.

She shakes his hand, but he does not release his grip. "You know the Garment District at all? Thirty-Seventh Street and Seventh Avenue. Zabno-America Button Company. I work for my uncle, in case you ever need someone to rescue. I'm sure I could arrange to get beaten up again."

"Zabno. I'll remember that," she says.

Halev laughs and releases her hand and looks at her shrewdly. "Oh, I have no doubt you will. You're a girl who remembers." He taps the side of his head.

Rainy walks away, sure she'll never see him again, and a little saddened by the realization. There is no time in her life for the male of the species, and definitely not for ardent young Zionists. No, the men in her life now will be wearing uniforms and carrying guns.

18

Rio sits at her usual place at the table. Her father is at the head, her mother to his right. Rio is across from her mother and down one place, leaving an empty seat for Rachel at her father's left hand.

She's been met with hugs and tears. The questions have been consciously put off till dinner, which consists of a small green salad from her mother's garden, milk from her mother's cows, a fat hen her father traded for with a farmer who was behind on his feed bill, mashed potatoes, boiled carrots, and a small but luscious cheesecake that was also courtesy of the cows.

Rio and her mother drink milk; her father drinks beer.

This place feels strange now.

"No steak, I'm afraid," her mother apologizes. "The only steak nowadays comes from Mr. Black."

"Mr. Black?" Rio asks.

"You know," her mother said with a knowing look that

borders on being comic. "The black market. That's where I go to get my stockings."

"Chiselers and thieves," her father says, politely wiping his mouth when a bit of lettuce escapes.

"Mother has fallen in with thieves?"

"Your mother has unexpected depths," Tam Richlin says, and winks.

"Are they feeding you at all?" her mother asks. "You look thin."

"Actually I've gained a few pounds."

"All of it muscle," her father observes disapprovingly. "You look . . ." He changes course upon receiving a warning eyebrow from his wife. "You look beautiful. Very healthy."

"And stylish too," Rio says dryly. She's in uniform, still proud of its shiny new adornment: the metal Sharpshooter badge.

Rio is happy to be distracted from the subject of food— the truth is, they had steak once a week at camp, pork chops or fried chicken most of the time. None of it had been well prepared or flavorful, and much of it was frightening to look at, but they did not go hungry. Rationing has been harder on civilians than on the soldiers.

She's tense, waiting for the inevitable question, and it isn't long in coming.

"So, you've made it through basic training.

Congratulations. Any word on what they'll have you doing?" her father asks, digging into his potatoes.

"I'm classified 745," Rio says, hoping that will end the discussion.

"Which is?"

She sets her drumstick down, mostly eaten. "Rifleman, Father."

Her father stares. Her mother says, "But what does that mean exactly?"

"It means that I will be carrying a rifle. Or maybe a carbine, it's lighter weight. But I'm a better shot with the rifle." She says that last part as if it's a throwaway line, like it doesn't matter, like her Sharpshooter badge is meaningless.

"But surely you won't be . . ."

"They're actually sending women into combat?" her father demands angrily. "Teenage girls? On the front lines?"

"Yes, Father."

A long silence follows her announcement. She can see that her father is suppressing a rising tide of anger that now is beginning to frighten her mother.

Suddenly her father slaps the table with the palm of his hand. Dishes jump and rattle. "It's a damned dirty rotten trick!"

"Dad, the war could be over before—"

"Don't feed me that line," he snarls. "It's too much like what your sister told me. 'It'll all be over soon,' she said. 'The Jap navy can't touch us,' she said. 'Stop worrying.' And now . . ." He looks at the empty place.

Rio's mother reaches to take his hand, but he shakes her off brusquely. "You don't know what you're getting into, young lady. Neither of you does. I do."

"Tam, there's no point in frightening Rio."

"The goddamned generals sit up there in their head-quarters, and you'll be nothing but a number to them. Some major will say, 'We anticipate only ten percent casualties,' and the general will say, 'Jolly good, we can manage that,' but the ten percent aren't names or faces to them, just numbers. And the generals are fools, most of them. They send young men to . . . to have their legs and arms and faces . . ."

He grits his teeth, angry at himself for losing control, angry at himself for showing emotion.

Rio sees the ruined face of the Stamp Man in her memory. She doesn't want to see it, has, in fact, pushed it to the far edges of her memory, but it is clear and vivid and real at this moment.

Rio wants to ask her father what it was like for him, his war. She wants to ask him whether he was brave—that question has begun to preoccupy her. And she wants to ask him what exactly happened with the Stamp Man on the terrible night of the fire. But she knows she mustn't—Tam Richlin's wartime experience is taboo in this house. It is not something the family is allowed to discuss, and a part of her doesn't really want to know, because his war was *his* war. For better or worse, this war is hers. It is *hers*.

Hers and Rachel's.

Hers and Jenou's.

And Kerwin's, and Jack's and Cat's and Stick's and Tilo's. It's even Luther's war. It does not belong to the men who fought that earlier war, that mockingly subtitled "war to end all wars." Their war, their fate, will not be hers. She will not live out her days sucking air through an absent cheek. Not her, not Jenou, not Strand.

"Mother, I like your chicken much better than the chow hall's chicken," Rio says gamely, moving the conversation to safer ground. Rio can see her father making an effort to be kind, to be patient, but the fear is very specific and very real to him. His fear frightens her because she cannot dismiss it.

Her mother's fear is no less real, but Millie Richlin's concerns are somewhat different.

"Just don't you forget all you learned in Sunday school," Millie says. "Just because you're in a uniform doesn't mean you're safe. It doesn't mean boys don't have certain urges. Secret urges."

Rio manages—just barely—to avoid grinning at the

notion of boys having secret urges. The males in her barracks have urges, all right, but they are definitely not secret. So do some of the females, including a certain Private Jenou Castain.

"Yes, Mother."

"One mistake can ruin your life. Don't forget: when this is over and you're home safe, you still have to find a good man, get married, and make a life together."

Mrs. Braxton. Mrs. Strand Braxton.

Mrs. Jack Stafford. Lady Stafford.

That's ridiculous, Jack is not a lord, and anyway, Strand! She'll be seeing him tomorrow.

"I worry about you."

"So do I," Rio mutters, before catching herself. "Don't worry, Mother, my own sergeant told me the odds of getting hurt are pretty low. Really. And Sergeant Mackie is not what you'd call a ray of sunshine."

"Is your sergeant going with you wherever you go?"

I wish she were.

"No, Mother, Sergeant Mackie already has another load of soft recruits to inflict pain on."

That truth causes Rio a pang of regret, a feeling almost like jealousy. Mackie with a whole new barracks full of gawky, awkward, ridiculous recruits, one of whom will be sleeping in Rio's bunk.

With the dishes done, Rio heads out to the porch. It is

unbelievable luxury to have time to slowly digest dinner without needing to study a manual or shine her boots or sew her uniform. At the same time, how strange not to have Cat tossing off some bit of poetry she's just made up, or Tilo doing his Frank Sinatra impression. Jenou is just across town, staying with her aunt, not her parents, for reasons Jenou has not explained. But the rest of the old crowd are spread here and there, slated to reunite in New York City.

New York City! The very thought is thrilling. New York City and then the slow boat to England. So long as a German U-boat doesn't spot their convoy.

Rio's father is on the porch, a cigarette in his mouth, gazing off toward the sun setting behind the church steeple. Rio noticed that he drank two beers with his dinner, not his usual one, and now he's holding a glass of brandy with the bottle near at hand but discreetly out of sight behind a potted plant.

She senses that he is nerving himself up for what he has to say. She feels him tense when she joins him. He seems at first to regret the brandy in his hand, but then takes a healthy swig. He sets the glass aside, pulls a pack of Luckies from his shirt pocket, and holds it toward her.

"Have you picked up the habit yet?"

"No thanks. Some of the guys have, but not me."

"Not yet," he says darkly. "Before you're done you'll be smoking and drinking too." He immediately shakes his head in regret. "Listen, I, uh . . ."

"Yes, Dad?"

He sighs, takes a drag off his cigarette, and exhales a cloud. "Listen, sweetheart. Don't be a hero."

Rio smiles. "I wasn't planning on it."

"No, listen to me." There is urgency in his tone. He insists she listen. He insists that what he knows she must know as well. "If they actually go through with this hare-brained notion and send you into the fighting, there will come a time when you'll have a choice between staying in your trench and crawling out of it to save a buddy. Or maybe you'll have had enough of getting shelled and decide you just have to run out there and shoot someone. That's what I mean. When that moment comes, you stay down. You keep your head down. You hug the ground."

She has the terrible feeling that his eyes might be filling with tears, but that's impossible, surely. She looks away.

He is seeing something in memory, playing it over again. He winces, swallows hard, and takes another puff and then a drink.

"Don't listen to your officers, listen to your noncoms. It's the sergeants that keep their men alive, the good ones, anyway. You find a sergeant you trust and stick to him like glue. An officer will throw your life away for nothing, but a good sergeant . . ."

"Yes, sir," she says, not even realizing that she's fallen into the military style of address, nor that she is standing at something like parade rest that is not quite attention, but not the casual stance of a teenage girl talking with her father either.

"I'm your father. That's your mother in there," he says, his voice gone rough. "We're your family. Whatever happens, we're your family. Whatever happens, this is your place, this house, this town."

He is seeing the Stamp Man too, she knows. And perhaps seeing much more.

"I know that, sir," she says.

"You'll need that." He nods to himself. "You'll need to know that. When you're scared. Or hurt. No matter what: we are your family."

Rio can't answer. This is as open as her father has ever been with her, the first time he has ever addressed her as an adult. This is him baring his soul within the limits his notions of masculinity allow. A tear rolls down her cheek, but she can't wipe at it without giving herself away.

"You'll need that," he says again, almost a whisper.

The doorbell rings at 0900 sharp.

"Strand!"

"It's too early, isn't it?" he asks.

He seems taller than she remembers, and his shoulders are definitely wider and stronger. But then, she supposes, she looks more muscular to him as well, and it makes her cringe a little.

"Not too early at all, Strand."

"I figured you woke up at, what, 0700?"

"Nonsense. I woke up at 0600—I'm real army, not air corps," she teases. "You know, in the real army we don't even have butlers to bring us our coffee in bed every morning."

"Oh, here we go," he says, playing along. "Now I have to listen to this from you. It's not true our butlers bring us coffee in bed. That is a dirty lie, a regular army falsehood. Our butlers lay the silver and the china out on a very nice table on the veranda, and *then* they bring us our coffee."

"It's awfully good to see you, Strand."

"You look swell," he says.

"So do you," she says. It takes her a moment to register that this is something she would never have said before. It's forward and blunt. She doesn't exactly regret it, but she does make a mental note to think about it later. "Speaking of coffee, will you come in and have a cup?"

"Oh, I don't want to use up your ration."

"Nonsense, we always have coffee for men in uniform," Rio's father says, coming down the stairs. He sticks a hand out, and Strand shakes it. "Am I to take it that you are here to court my daughter, young man?"

He pitches the tone perfectly between deadly serious and downright dangerous, so Strand swallows hard and shoots a panicky look at Rio.

"Father is having fun with you, Strand. Come in, come in."

"How's air corps life?" Tam asks Strand.

"It's fine, sir, aside from the matter of getting enough planes, which is FUBAR."

Rio, who has heard that term and knows what it means, sees horror in Strand's eyes and is torn between two wildly different emotions: fear of what may come next, and delighted amusement at the predicament Strand has just walked into.

Just let it go, Mother . . .

"What is FUBAR?" Millie asks.

Strand looks helplessly at Rio, who stares guiltily and paralyzed at her mother's innocent expression. It's her father who comes to the rescue.

"It stands for 'Fouled Up Beyond All Recognition,'" he says, casting a wry look at Strand, who rediscovers his ability to breathe. "It's a common soldier's term."

Yes, Rio thinks, though the *F* is usually taken to be a word that is a bit less appropriate for a mother's ears.

"I'm off to the store; I'm already late," Rio's father

says. "Oh, by the way, remind me that I need to clean my shotgun later. My twelve-gauge shotgun." He softens this with a manly hand on Strand's shoulder.

"Very funny, Father."

There. He seems like my dad again.

They take their coffee in the kitchen, seated around the comfortable old table where Rio's mother has laid out her dairy accounts and is industriously recording gallons of milk and dollars earned.

"I was wondering, well . . . ," Strand begins.

"Yes?"

"The thing is, my uncle's plane is being seized by the War Department. It's a tough break for him, although they're paying him more than the plane is worth. Anyway, he has it for another few days, and I thought, well . . ."

Sooner or later, Rio tells herself, she is going to have to get Strand to stop letting half his sentences trail off. "I'd love to."

But her mother isn't so sure. "Is it a two-seater?"

"Ma'am, the Jenny is designed with two completely separate cockpits. Also, ma'am, you'll be relieved to learn that it no longer has its machine guns from the last war."

"No crazy flying tricks or loop-de-loops!"

Strand makes the cross over his heart. "Cross my heart and hope to die," he vows. "It'll be more dangerous getting to the field than flying: we have to ride bikes. Those things are unstable."

Mrs. Richlin insists on making some sandwiches, as well as a tight-sealed Mason jar of lemonade, all packed into a small basket along with a checkered tablecloth to put down for a picnic.

"I don't have a blanket to spare," she says, looking a bit prune faced as she does so. "Careful if you lie on the grass, Rio—I'll have to get the grass stains out of your dress."

Rio carries the picnic lunch in her bike's basket; in Strand's basket is his prized camera. It's a four-mile ride from Gedwell Falls out into the countryside. The weather is that tenuous Northern California warm that turns chilly in the shadow of any passing cloud, and the hills are brilliant green from recent rain, though they will soon be the color of straw again. It's mostly an uphill ride on the way there, the sort of exercise that Rio might once have found tiring but now barely notices.

I could run this in full pack. Backward.

She's changed into a flannel skirt, white cotton blouse, and pink cardigan, and feels faintly ridiculous. She's used to her uniform trousers and the careless freedom they offer, but somehow she doubts that Strand wants to go riding or flying with a girl who looks like a soldier. Anyway, Jenou always says Rio's legs are her best feature; she might as well deploy them.

Deploy. Another word the army has insinuated into her brain.

"How are you liking being home?" Strand asks as they ride side by side. There has never been much traffic out this way.

"I feel strange, a little," Rio says. Her voice pitches high to reach him over the breeze and the sounds of sprockets and chains. "It's home, but it doesn't feel quite the same. I suppose it's me that's changed while home has stayed the same."

"Yes, the same for me. There they all were, my folks, and my old pals, and all the old places, and I would never say I miss barracks life, but the truth is, I have new pals now, and I'm even used to the chow."

"Have you started flight training?"

"No, that's up next. I mean, we've done some work on navigation and aeronautics."

"Aeronautics? That sounds very impressive."

"Yes. I just wish I understood what it is exactly."

Rio laughs. "I feel the same about small unit tactics."

"Talk about impressive sounding!"

"We're meant to care a great deal about enfilade and defilade."

"Which are . . . ?"

"Well, of course, being air corps you wouldn't be expected to understand such things," she teases. "Enfilade is where you don't wish to be. It means the bad guys can shoot at you along your longest axis. If you're lined up like the upright of a letter *T*, see, you don't want Japs or Krauts to be the cross of the *T*."

"I should think not."

"And defilade is when you've gotten yourself behind some cover and can shoot at the bad guys."

"So as to not be in enfilade," Strand said. "I think I've got it."

"Yes, well, it's a very different matter when you're in the woods and all tangled up in blackberry thorns and some sergeant is shouting at you."

We're so easy together.

"Sergeants shouting?" Strand jokes. "Why, I never. In the air corps the noncoms are all very polite and helpful, offering to iron our uniforms and such."

"Is that before or after the butler brings you coffee?"

"I hate to say it, though, but some of them are all right."

"Some are," Rio admits.

They have the identical tone when discussing sergeants: rueful, reluctantly admiring, perversely proud of their toughness.

A truck comes rattling by loaded with empty barrels.

The driver stares at them, unsmiling, not approving of them at all, so naturally they both grin and wave enthusiastically.

"So what is aeronautics?"

"I'm not quite sure, but the essence of it appears to be that you should not crash the army's airplanes, or the army will be very cross with you."

"I've heard it's months of training, so maybe the war will be over before you can be deployed."

"Yeah, well, predictions of quick and easy wars have a history of being wrong, Rio."

"It's almost as if it's a fairy tale meant to encourage us to sign up," Rio says dryly.

"You're becoming cynical."

"Or realistic."

A perverse part of her wants to tell Strand about seeing the Stamp Man, but that would just make him worry, and what's the point in that? Besides, this is supposed to be fun.

They reach the airfield, which is nothing but three battered old biplanes parked on a dusty field. There's a cylindrical fuel tank standing aboveground on a rusted iron platform, surrounded by brand-new barbed wire. And there is a large tin shed that is the field's closest approximation of a hangar. A triangular flag on a pole rustles fitfully, suggesting the breeze is out of the west.

Strand points to a plane painted yellow. Written in uneven script along the fuselage is *Braxton Air Service*.

"That's ours, and that is the whole of Braxton Air Service. But my uncle has ambitions, you know, or had, anyway. He's a bit at loose ends now."

They park the bikes on a grassy spot with bare cover provided by two tall palm trees. Each time the breeze blows the palm trees sway, causing them to be alternately in cool shade and brilliant sun. They spread the table-cloth and set down the picnic basket. But Rio is more fascinated by the plane than she is hungry and, after a few minutes' rest, heads toward it, confident that Strand will follow.

"I'm afraid I may have misled your mother," Strand says, wincing. "I didn't lie, I was careful not to, when she asked about the cockpit. The Jennies do have two cock-pits; however, my uncle has adapted the passenger cockpit to carry the insecticide tank for spraying. So I'm afraid there's just the one cockpit, and we'll have to squeeze in together."

"Oh, indeed?" Rio says archly.

"Unless you'd rather not."

There is no safe and proper way to answer that directly. The fact is that so much physical contact would be just the sort of thing to give Millie Richlin fits.

Up close the Jenny is a fragile-looking thing with the

upper wing longer than the lower, a wooden frame with fabric stretched and lacquered to form the surfaces. The propeller is polished wood, and the top of the engine and its muffler stick rudely out of the cowling.

"It's not exactly a P-38," Strand admits. "But there's the advantage that I actually know how to fly this one."

"How is it different?"

"Well, for one thing, this engine here will be lucky to hit one hundred and twelve horsepower, while the P-38 has two engines with thirty-two hundred horsepower total and a ceiling of almost forty-five thousand feet, whereas this old girl will be struggling at half a mile."

"Forty-five thousand feet! That's eight miles up. Why do you want to be eight miles up?"

"Because that's where the German bombers fly. Of course they're much lower when they drop bombs—you can't hit anything from eight miles up. The idea is to ride that P-38 up there and wait until you see a nice fat Heinkel or Junker poking along a mile below you as it comes in for a bomb run. Then you come swooping down, guns blazing."

There are of course accompanying hand gestures. And even a sound effect: *taka-taka-taka-taka!*

"Is that what you'll be doing?"

He shrugs. "I'd like to fly a fighter, the P-38, or the P-40, if I have the stuff for it. Otherwise, I guess if I don't wash out altogether, I'll be driving a bus: a B-24 or B-17. Bombers."

He indicates the hard spots where it is safe to place her feet. Rio climbs cautiously and slides into the snug, wood-ringed space with its handful of gauges and knobs.

Strand leans over her and shows her the throttle and choke. "We'll just set these . . . All right, that should do it. I'm going to go start her up. All you have to do is push this in about halfway once I give you the sign. Oh, and don't fly it away."

Rio raises her hands. "I won't touch a thing except . . . whatever that is."

Strand walks around the wings to the propeller. He turns it slowly by hand a couple of times, pumping fuel to the cylinders. Then he swings the propeller hard.

The engine sputters and sputters some more, then catches and chugs along, sounding very much like any average car with a bad muffler. The propeller spins until it is just a faint blur and Rio feels the wind of it on her face.

Strand climbs up and awkwardly wedges himself behind her. Her back is against his chest, and her bottom is pressed back against something she doesn't want to think about at the moment, though thanks to her famous latrine raid she has a far-too-clear picture in her mind. Strand's arms reach around her and his long legs twine through hers to reach the pedals. His camera is on her lap, and all in all there is scarcely room to take a deep breath.

She pulls on the goggles he gives her, and they are off, bouncing across the grass, picking up speed. Ten miles an hour. Twenty. Thirty.

The engine roars to a higher pitch, though it still seems pitifully unlikely to enable actual flight, and yet suddenly the bouncing is gone, the wheels spin in air, and they are aloft.

Rio looks over the side, wind whipping her hair and making her cheeks vibrate. The ground falls away, trees shrink to become bushes, a tractor looks like a toy, cows are reduced to black-and-white mice.

"I'm flying!" Rio exults.

"Is this your first time up?" Strand says. His mouth is quite near her ear, and she can hear him clearly. She can also feel the rise and fall of his every breath, and even, when she focuses her attention, the beat of his heart.

"My very first!" she shouts into the wind.

"You're taking it well," he says. "Some girls might be nervous."

"I'm not some girls."

"Sorry? Couldn't hear you."

"I said, I'm not some girls!"

She feels rather than hears his laugh.

They fly over hills and over lakes. They fly over farms

and orderly vineyards and then turn toward Gedwell Falls.

"Take the stick."

"No!"

"Just hold it steady, I'm going to take some pictures." He takes her hands in his and places them on the long, upright wooden baton. She instantly feels the life of the plane in her hands and with it the urge to move the stick, to make the plane obey her, which she sensibly resists.

Strand twists to one side, holding the camera with his left and straining to get his right arm around her to reach the shutter. He has to reach beneath her arm, pressing his strong bicep against her breast.

She wonders if he can feel her heart accelerate. She wonders if he notices that she is no longer breathing. Certainly he cannot see the blush that spreads up her neck to her cheeks, but he is certainly noticing something, because there are subtle changes in his breathing as well, and he squirms a little to lessen contact that she might find . . . improper.

She is in the air. She is in the arms of a boy, no, a man. Something dark and insistent is awake in her, a feeling like pressure, a feeling like hunger. She has never been this physically close to a man, never felt *this*, never known she would or could feel this. And she would never have believed how much she does not want it to end.

"Shall we make a strafing run on your house, then do

some loops over town square?" Strand asks.

"Not unless you want my mother to have a heart attack!"

"God forbid!"

They fly for an hour, all the aviation fuel they can afford, and finally land back in the field.

Once on the ground, Strand begs her to stand beside the plane. "I want a picture."

"Of me or the plane?"

He takes several shots: Rio with her hand resting on a strut, Rio back up in the cockpit, and quite by accident Rio slipping so she ends up sitting with legs splayed out on the ground beneath the plane.

So much for avoiding telltale grass stains.

"That last one was pretty good, but would you mind tripping again? I'd like to—"

She gives him a playful shove. He takes her hand and, in a single deft motion, draws her to her feet and into his arms.

And kisses her.

It doesn't last long, that kiss. But when it is done she senses that a profound change has occurred in her world. She has imagined being kissed, but she has never before craved it. Now she wants very badly to kiss him back, to put her arm around his neck and pull him down to her, and for the kiss to go on longer, much longer.

But Rio Richlin is a good girl; she is not Jenou, though

she bitterly regrets that fact at the moment. Instead she laughs with forced gaiety to conceal a needier emotion and dances away.

She manages to take a decent picture of him, which she is sure will be much better than the high school yearbook picture she's been carrying. It becomes the photo she will hold close to her breast: happy, grinning rakishly, leaning against the Jenny.

He does not look at all like a younger, happier version of the Stamp Man.

No, not at all.

19

There is a thick book and a less thick book. The thick book is titled *The Medical Field Manual—Medical Service of Field Units*.

The army, Frangie notes upon receiving this book, is not good at catchy titles.

The manual is printed on cheap paper and is 294 pages long. Where one might normally find the copyright page, there is instead a statement that the manual has been prepared on orders of the army chief of staff, a creature so far above Private Frangie Marr that he might as well be the fourth member of the Trinity.

The contents page shows such enticing entries as "Medical Service in Camp and Bivouac," "Medical Service on Marches," and "Individual Equipment of Medical Department Officers and Enlisted Men."

The moment when she is issued this book feels almost holy to Frangie. This will be her sacred text. This will teach her to save lives. And, with a lot of luck and even more hard work, it may pave the way, someday, to Dr. Marr.

"Yes," Frangie whispers, "the doctor will see you now."

GENERAL DOCTRINES—a. Commanders at all echelons are responsible for—

Frangie is not clear on exactly what an *echelon* is. But she makes a note to find out.

—the provision of adequate and proper medical care for all noneffectives of their command.

Okay. Sure. Whatever that means. She scans down the page.

e. Casualties in the combat zone are collected at medical installations along the general axis of advance of the units to which they pertain.

Frangie sits at an outdoor table, a sort of wooden picnic table, at Fort Huachuca, in the emptiest part of the empty state of Arizona. For hundreds of miles in every direction there is sand, and there are rocks, and there are desolate hills, and there are multiple types of cactus: the cactus that looks like a bunch of sword blades pointing out in every direction, the cactus that looks like a totem pole, the cactus that looks like a cluster of teddy bear ears with spikes.

And there is sun. No more Georgia humidity for Frangie; it's nothing but dry, hot, blazing sun.

Inevitably Fort Huachuca becomes *Fort Whatcha Got?* to the black soldiers stationed there. There is no town nearby, just a few Indians who suffer like the blacks from the contempt of the white soldiers. No one is happy to find themselves at this post in the middle of nowhere, but despite the isolation and the boredom, Frangie finds herself relaxing a bit.

She is here to learn medicine.

And, it seems, Sergeant Green is here now as well. She spotted him in line for chow, and saw him again later, running alongside a platoon and calling out cadence.

"My honey heard me comin' on my left, right, on left.
I saw Jody runnin' on his left, right, on left.
I chased after Jody and I ran him down,
Poor ol' boy doesn't feel good now."

"MPs came a runnin' on their left, right, on left.
The medics came a runnin' on their left, right, on left.

He felt a little better with a few IVs.
Son, I told you not to mess with the infantry."

He had given her a tight nod of recognition as he passed, and that had pleased her. And she had felt a particular pride watching soldiers who looked like her go passing by, so fit and disciplined. This fort had once housed the buffalo soldiers who had fought the Indians in the surrounding nothingness. What her big brother, Harder, used to sneeringly describe as "black men killing red men for white men."

Now she glances up from the manual to look around at the sun-blasted landscape, at the barracks nearby—one of which is reserved for the tiny number of black medical trainees and the few black doctors and nurses who do their training—and at the row of jeeps and civilian cars over by the HQ building, and then up at the sinister, tumbleweed-covered hills that seem to wedge the fort in.

Not that she is looking for Sergeant Green. She would have nothing to say to him unless it was to repeat her thanks, and Green rather intimidates Frangie, so she knows idle chatter is not a good idea.

Still . . .

She returns her attention to the manual. Unfortunately *The Medical Field Manual* does not contain any information pertaining to actual medicine. That is to be found in the somewhat smaller (seventy-eight pages) manual with the title *Bandaging and Splinting*.

Bandaging and Splinting is a real page-turner, heavily illustrated with drawings of everything from the *"cravat bandage of eye"* to *"triangle of foot bandage"* to the rather pretty *"roller bandage"* to the *"basic arm splint."*

This is, without the slightest doubt, the most interesting book Frangie has ever read. As she reads and looks closely at the diagrams, she plays out the moves, winding and tying around imaginary arms, legs, necks, and heads.

Bandages should be applied evenly, firmly, and not too tightly. Excessive pressure may cause interference with the circulation and may lead to disastrous consequences.

This makes her laugh, though she's not sure why.

"You find it entertaining, Private?"

Frangie looks up, shielding her eyes against the sun, spots captain's bars on a shoulder, jumps to her feet—not easily done at a picnic table—and snaps a salute.

"Sir?"

He's a black man, an actual black officer, stocky, not very tall, probably in his forties, almost totally bald with just a fringe of hair that looks like it's doomed to continue retreating.

"I asked if you found it amusing."

"No, sir. I mean, I guess I did, sir."

He reaches past her, flips though a few pages in the book, nods. "This is good information. I assume you're hoping to be a nurse."

"No, sir. I'm hoping to be a doctor. But first a medic. I want to be a medic."

"Do you?" he asks skeptically. "Has anyone told you what the job entails?"

"Entails, sir?"

He belatedly returns her salute, allowing her to put her hand down.

"You know, medics end up in bad places, Private. They end up in very bad places."

Frangie shrugs with one shoulder—the other shoulder remembered that you do not shrug at superior officers. "I didn't figure many colored outfits would be allowed to fight."

That causes him to tilt his head and look at her appraisingly. "Well, that may be. Then again, it may not. I'm not sure the brass will always be able to keep colored units back like they did in the last war. But I can't help but notice some up-to-date cannon and such appearing, and I doubt that's just for show. Might be you'll end up at the sharp end."

"Yes, sir." You rarely went wrong saying "Yes, sir."

"You think you could handle that? Trying to keep a

wounded man alive while you're getting shot at?"

She starts an automatic "yes, sir" but stops herself. Something about this captain does not strike her as that sort of officer, the kind looking to be saluted and "yes, sir'ed" regardless of circumstances.

She takes a chance. "Are you a doctor, Captain?"

"Now what makes you think that?"

"I . . . I don't know, sir."

"Is it the somewhat unmilitary look of my uniform?"

Now that she thinks of it, his uniform isn't exactly a model of perfection. There's a small soup stain on his olive drab tie, his shirttail is trying hard to escape his waistband, and his boots are not boots. In fact, they're carpet slippers.

The captain is wearing slippers out of doors, while in uniform. No, that is not quite military. But the shoulder patch of the caduceus—two snakes twined about a pole beneath a dove's wings—definitely indicates that he's in the medical service in some capacity.

He winks, understanding that she cannot say anything critical, being just a private. "I am a doctor, as it happens. I'm a thoracic surgeon by trade, and an army captain by virtue of my local draft board."

"Yes, sir."

"You haven't answered my question. Do you think you can kneel beside a man whose intestines are lying on the ground and tell that man he's going to be all right, and sew him up quick and slap on a bandage and get him to an aid station while German artillery is dropping all around you?"

"I don't know, sir."

There's a sad twinkle in his eye. "Good answer. I don't know either, I have not been asked to do that. What I do know is that as a medic you won't be carrying a gun, you won't get to shoot back, and you'll have a nice big red-and-white cross on your helmet that lets everyone know you're a medic. If you think the enemy won't take aim at that cross, you're mistaken."

She squares her shoulders, feeling pushed by the doctor, feeling challenged. "I don't know, sir, but I don't think I'm a coward."

"Hmm," he says thoughtfully. He pulls a thankfully clean handkerchief from his pocket and hands it to her. Then he sits down beside her and lays his arm on the table. "Bullet wound. Lots of blood. What do you do first?"

For just a second she freezes. What is this? She hasn't even taken a single class yet, she barely knows where her cot is, and she wouldn't recognize her new sergeant if he walked up and said howdy.

"First thing, see if it's an artery or something smaller."

"And?"

She presses the ball of her palm down on his arm. "It's

an artery. It's pulsing. I press down to slow the blood."

"It hurts. Give me morphine."

"Not yet, sir." Then, unsure of her snap answer, she says, "Right?"

"Morphine might put me into shock," he says. "Priorities. First priority, don't let me bleed to death while you're shooting me up with morphine."

"Yes, sir." And now, strange as it seems, she's enjoying this. "Pressure to slow the bleeding. Sulfa powder." She mimes tearing open a package with her teeth and sprinkling powder on the wound. Then, with her one free hand she folds his handkerchief just like the illustration she saw earlier and wraps this around his arm.

She mimes something else, and he interrupts to say, "What are you doing?"

"Sir, I'm making a thick square of gauze to place under the bandage to help keep the pressure on." She wraps the actual handkerchief over the imaginary gauze and ties it off.

The doctor inspects her work. "Well, I'll bleed to death most likely."

Frangie is crestfallen.

"You didn't check the other side of my arm, Private. Bullets go in, but they often come out, too, and when they come out they make a much bigger mess than when they go in."

"Yes, sir."

He stands up. "I'm Dr., er, Captain Washington. And I'm going to guess that you have applied bandages before."

"Just on animals, sir."

"Ah. Tender heart, eh?"

"Sir, I . . ."

"A tender heart is not a bad thing in a medic, or a doctor."

"Yes, sir."

"Well, you study hard, Private . . ."

"Marr, sir. Private Frangie Marr."

"Okay, Marr. You study hard. You study so you know it all, not just in your head but in your fingers. That's where the real memory is. In your fingers, in your hands. When you're getting shot at your brain may forget and only your hands remember."

"Yes, sir."

"All right." He blows air out, making a fluttery sound with his lips. "The instructors are mostly hard-asses and they will be all over you, you understand, you being a female. Most of them don't much like the notion of a young woman out in the action."

"But not you, sir?"

"Well, Private, I don't like the idea of judging people by superficial criteria. I'll judge you the same way I judge every other candidate who comes through here."

Only then does it dawn on Frangie that this doctor, this captain, is in charge.

"I'll judge you by your work, and on whether I think you can send boys home alive who by rights should be dead. If you screw up, if you don't memorize those manuals, and more besides, I'll wash you out. That may sound harsh—"

"No, sir."

"No?"

"Either I'm good enough or I'm not, sir."

He nods and smiles. "Good talking to you, Private."

They salute, and Frangie sits back down, shaking. Then she notices the handkerchief.

"Sir!" she holds it up.

"Keep it. Practice with it. That was a sloppy cravat. Sergeant Peel will scalp you if you show her that kind of work."

She says "yes, sir" again and opens her manual. And once she's sure the captain is out of earshot, she grins hugely and says, "This is going to be fun."

20

"Okay, deck six, forward eight, row B, bunk number seventeen," Rio reads off the paper in her hand. She carries sixty pounds' worth of gear, has just waited three hours to begin boarding, and then spent two hours just shuffling along in rows of packed bodies to find her spot.

"So this is luxury travel," Jenou says.

"Biggest, fastest, fanciest ship afloat," Cat says.

"It is magnificent," Rio agrees. "I especially like the way they've managed to stack the bunks four high."

The *Queen Mary*'s once-lovely cabins and staterooms have been largely stripped out, bulkheads knocked down to transform the lower decks into vast steel boxes stuffed to an almost comical degree with bunks. The bunks are four high and touch end to end, so a person could crawl the entire length of the hold without ever touching the deck. Not that anyone would want to. The aisle between two rows of bunks was just two feet wide, which barely allowed the heavily laden GIs to move to their assigned locations.

"I'm on the top level," Rio says glumly. "So a nice, close-up view of that pipe up there."

"I'm right below you," Jenou says with matching glumness.

"It'll be just like sleepover camp, kids," Rio says with mock cheer. "We can light a campfire and roast marshmallows."

"You've never gone to sleepover camp."

"No," Rio admits. "But the other comparison I could make is to sardines in a can."

"She's fast, that's all that matters," Cat offers.

"You in a hurry, Cat?" Jenou asks.

"She's faster than Kraut subs," Cat says. "That's the point."

This is a sobering thought. Reassuring, but also sobering.

The hold is already hot when they come aboard. It grows hotter over the next few days. The hold already smells of paint, varnish, and ancient body odor at the outset, but those are good times fondly remembered a few days later when the hold reeks of vomit, overflowing toilets, sweat, farts, cigarette smoke, and more vomit, as well as the paint and varnish. At times Rio is convinced the air in the hold is no more than 10 percent actual, breathable air.

This particular section is occupied solely by women, but the open-air decks are available to all, with the result that masses of frustrated, nervous, bored, and seasick GIs regularly pack the upper decks from rail to rail.

Under a chilly sun Rio and Jenou take the air, straining every nerve to ignore the incessant catcalls and lewd entreaties of male soldiers.

"Hey, girls, my bunk's pretty crowded, but I can make room for both of you."

"Come here, honey, there's something I want to show you."

"Oh yeah, Daddy likes what *she's* got."

"Hey, Joe, that private has titties."

"Come on, honey, just a little kiss."

Some of the men from Rio's company try vainly to stop the harassment, but this has led to several fistfights. The ship's captain has several times made announcements over the public address system, but GIs ignore sailors, even captains. So if Rio intends to breathe actual oxygen she has no choice but to endure a stream of abuse so constant it becomes background noise, like the thrum of the engines or the howl of the wind in the wires.

"Ladies, I've got something for you. It's right here in my pants."

"Come on now, sweet things, what are you doing, holding out for an officer?"

"Officers got tiny dicks; you want a real man."

"Holding out till the Germans get her, then we'll see how long she can hold on to her chastity."

All of this is accompanied by hoots, whistles, gestures, and, on occasion, dropped trousers. Rio is used to a certain amount of this, but being trapped in close quarters with thousands of keyed-up men who do not know her has made it all much, much worse.

They are three days out before Rio hears a familiar male voice.

"Rio? Is that you?"

She turns warily to see Strand Braxton.

"Strand!"

"How long have you been . . . Well, I guess it's obvious, isn't it, that you've been aboard the whole time. I never saw you!"

He is as tall as ever, as good-looking as ever, his smile as dazzling as ever. He moves as if to take her in his arms but she glances meaningfully over his shoulder to the stacked rows of avidly observant men on the deck and on the stairs and the officers watching just as avidly but with more decorum from the upper decks.

Strand quickly grasps the point and extends a hand, which she gratefully takes and holds longer than necessary.

"You look swell," she says.

"So do you. I can't believe you're here. I wish—" He stops when he realizes there's a soldier literally at his knees, gazing up at the two of them. "Come on," he says. Then, "You too, Jenou."

But Jenou knows better. "No, I think I'll just stay here and breathe the fresh air and fresher comments."

"You can take the brunette," someone shouts, "but leave us the blonde."

Jenou rolls her eyes. "My public demands I stay. You two go catch up. Hey, wait!"

Strand and Rio turn back to see Jenou snapping a salute.

"Oh, Lord, I—" Rio says, blushing, and then salutes Strand, who now wears lieutenant's bars.

"Yeah, that's enough of that," Strand says, returning the salutes. He taps his insignia of rank. "All this means is I've got a high school diploma. We have enlisted pilots, but they're stuck flying transport, and well . . . the pay's better."

Strand guides Rio through the mass of men, up a set of steel steps and another to the lifeboat deck. Here the big lifeboats—enough for less than half the men aboard—hang on davits. The boats are covered with canvas tarps drawn tight with ropes passed through brass grommets. But the boat farthest aft has had its canvas covering loosened.

Strand shows her how to climb up and into the boat. Inside, four men, all flyers like Strand, lounge in the shade playing a desultory game of cards. There are cans of beer and a half-empty bottle of whiskey and makeshift ashtrays piled to overflowing with cigarette butts.

"Hey, guys, meet my girl. Rio, these are some of the boys. Lefty, Choke, Bandito. Not their real names, of course. We use nicknames so when we're talking on radio we don't confuse ourselves; we've already got two Smiths."

"Hello," Rio says uneasily. They're all officers, but she's pretty sure an officer lying shirtless with a bottle of beer in one hand and cards in the other does not require or want a salute.

"How come you get a girl and all I've got is a bottle?" Lefty demands.

"That's not true," the one named Bandito says. "You got your hand."

"Hey, hey, come on," Strand says sharply. "There's a lady present."

"Looks like a GI," Bandito says, but adds, "Sorry, miss."

"Bunch of savages," Strand says, disapproving but not angry. He leads Rio to a plank seat as far from the game as they can get. It's not privacy, but it's the closest thing available on the ship.

"I was just going to write you tonight," Rio says.

"How have you been?"

"About as well as can be expected," Rio says, but then flashes a smile. "We were supposed to ship out weeks ago. The usual hurry up and wait. But I'm a whole lot better now."

He reaches for her hand, and she takes his.

"Isn't that cute?" Lefty says.

"Shut up, you apes. This is my girl. From back home. We grew up together."

Bandito is on the verge of letting go with a crude line but thinks better of it and contents himself with looking at the gambling stakes, saying, "Okay, who hasn't anted up?"

There's "a girl," and then there's "a girl from back home," a much more revered status.

Bandito says, "So is it true that Fish is captain of the football team, homecoming king, and all-around hero back in, where is it, Fish? Getwell Flails?"

"Gedwell Falls, smart-ass," Strand says tolerantly. "Fish. That's my call sign."

When Rio looks baffled, Choke, the oldest of the men at twenty-six, says, "He dived into the river to . . . um . . . Anyway, we call him Fish. Miss."

Rio is pretty sure there's an off-color story behind the dive into a river.

"I fold. Come on, guys, let's take a walk," Lefty says. "Give Fish some privacy." In a few seconds they are alone in a lifeboat beneath a canvas tarp, sitting on hard wooden planks.

"So. How's air corps life, Lieutenant?" Rio asks.

"It's fine," he says. "How's army life, Private?"

"Cramped and smelly," Rio says.

"Couple more days until we get to England. Then we'll have room."

"Do you know where you'll be stationed?"

He shakes his head. "Just somewhere in England. Then it's more training while we wait for our planes to catch up. Then I suppose we'll be escorting bombers over Hitlerville. You?"

She shrugs. "They don't tell us much. But more training in England, for certain. Then who knows? I guess we're not going to liberate France right away. Some people say we'll head to Italy, others say no, we're going to North Africa. Some think it's all a clever ruse and we're really going straight on around the bottom of Africa to kill Japs."

He looks troubled. "So you're going through with this?"

"Going through with what?"

"With playing soldier."

Rio is struck dumb for a long minute. "I . . . I don't

think I'm playing, Strand."

He leans toward her and now gathers both her hands in his. "Of course you're not, you know what I mean. Come on, you must have noticed by now that this is not a game for girls."

Her hands are limp and unresponsive in his. "Well, actually, I haven't noticed that, no. At basic we had a lot of girls wash out as physically unfit, but I didn't wash out and neither did Jenou or Cat."

Strand releases his grip only to wave off her reply. "Rio, is this really what you want? I heard those GIs up there talking to you and Jenou."

"Is that what they were doing? Talking?"

"Well, what do you expect? You're a beautiful girl on a ship full of . . . of . . . rambunctious"—he sighs in relief at having found a safe word—"men and barely men."

Rio does not overlook the use of the word *beautiful*. She files it away for later enjoyment.

"Strand, even if I wanted out, that's not the way it works." She waves her hands down her front to indicate her uniform. "I'm in the army. I would go to prison if I tried to leave. You must know that."

He starts to argue, realizes she's right, and settles for a lame, "I just don't want you to be hurt."

"I don't want you to be hurt either."

He shakes his head ruefully. "This stupid war. FUBAR."

On that they agree. Rio moves the conversation to safer topics, but as they talk of home and mutual acquaintances they are moving, by incremental shifts of weight, ever closer. Neither acknowledges it when their knees come to touch, but they chat on, though with voices newly weighed down by feelings that rise from within. Surprising feelings, to Rio, unsettling feelings. She wants to touch his face. She wants to push her fingers through his hair and . . .

It's the suddenness of desire that unnerves her. She's thought about him often during the long weeks of training. Being around loud, unruly men has not soured her on men, at least not on this one. But every part of her relationship with Strand has been like this: sudden. And now she wants him to stop talking and saying stupid things and kiss her.

She wants him to kiss her, and now as he goes on and on, she's thinking more and more about just doing it herself. She could, couldn't she? No. No, no, that isn't done. Girls do not make the first move.

But why? Surely he wants to kiss her and is just being a gentleman. Surely he'll enjoy it. After all, he must be . . . rambunctious . . . too.

Her fingers twitch, her hands move, but she stops herself. He'll be shocked. He'll think all this army stuff has changed her.

Maybe it has.

"Do you think your friends will be back soon?" she asks, interrupting him in midsentence.

"What? Oh, um . . . I suppose so."

"Mmm. It's nice having a little privacy, even if it won't last long." This is not subtle. It takes him a while to figure it out, and when he does she sees that slight shock, that slight note of disapproval on his face. But she doesn't care.

"Are you . . . Do you . . . ?" Strand asks.

At that she loses patience, leans into him, tilts her head, and leaves him with no practical choice but to kiss her. She doesn't make the first contact, so she has deniability; she hasn't quite become a hussy, but she has at last made her desires clear.

It is a very nice kiss. It lasts several seconds, and then Strand pulls back. But Rio is not done. She does not pull away. She remains so close that he cannot possibly mistake her intentions. This time when their lips meet it is with open mouths, and her hand does push through his hair. He knocks the service cap from her head and she puts her other hand behind his neck and he covers her cheek with his hand. He slides over to sit beside her, never breaking contact, eyes closed. His tongue is in her mouth and a sound like an animal growl somehow comes from her, a sound she has never even imagined making before, and an answering sound in a deeper register comes from him, and now hands are going to places only Rio has ever touched and—

"Knock, knock." It's Lefty's voice. To drive home the point he raps his knuckles on the side of the boat. "Permission to come aboard."

"Oh sure, of course, um—" Strand says.

"Yes, we aren't . . . yes," Rio manages.

Lefty's face appears above the gunwale. "I see you're discussing war strategy," he says flatly.

"I have to . . . um, better get to chow," Rio says, unconsciously pushing her hair back in place and fumbling around for her cap. "They, you know . . . check on us."

"Ri-i-ight," Lefty says.

"Okay, so. It was good catching up, Strand."

"Yes, it was," he says stiffly.

They shake hands, a move so patently false that Lefty guffaws loudly.

Rio climbs out, helped down by Strand's two other friends, armed now with a small canned ham they must have "liberated" from the mess kitchen.

Rio heads toward her berth, ignoring the usual male catcalls, ignoring even the outstretched hands, the kissy-faces, and all the rest. She finds Jenou in her bunk.

Jenou takes one look at her and says, "You've got a little slobber on your cheek."

Rio climbs up and slides into Jenou's bunk beside her. There's very little room as they lie on their sides, face to face, like the old days.

"We kissed," Rio confides.

"No kidding."

"I've never done it that way before."

This brightens Jenou's eyes. She's like a hungry cat being presented with a dish of milk. "You mean . . . tongue?"

"Eww! Do you have to be so disgusting?" Then, in a whisper, "Yes!"

"Did you like it?"

Rio hesitates. She's not uncertain as to whether she liked it; she's searching for the right way to put it. "Better than ice cream."

"Better than—"

"Better than chocolate."

"Wow."

"You know how you told me that girls can have those feelings too?"

"Those feelings?" Jenou repeats, being deliberately obtuse to provoke her friend. "Which feelings are you talking about exactly?"

Rio swallows. She bites her lips. Then, "I wanted him to kiss me. In fact, I think I almost forced him to. Poor Strand."

"Yes," Jenou drawls with heavy sarcasm. "Poor Strand."

"I've just never . . . and it was all of a sudden. It was like, well, there he was, and he was right there."

"Uh-huh."

"And he just kept talking. And I wanted to say 'Shut up and kiss me.'"

"My little Rio," Jenou says proudly. "You're growing up."

"And now . . ."

"And now you're tingling all over."

Rio nods vigorously and rolls onto her back, leaving Jenou even less room and pressing her against the steel bulkhead.

"I think I'm rambunctious," Rio says.

"Did he try to . . . you know."

"No! Of course not. He's a gentleman. He would never."

"Never? I hope that's not true. I'm still hoping to be Auntie Jenou to your children."

"You'll have children of your own; you won't need to be Auntie Jenou to mine. Ours."

"Oh my goodness, whatever happened to my favorite naive farm girl? You just talked about sex without blushing."

"No I did not!" Rio said hotly. "Take that back!"

"Sweetie, when you start daydreaming about children,

you're daydreaming about 's-e-x.' You do know the two things are connected, right?"

"I may be naive, but I know how a cow and a bull come to have calves."

For some reason this causes Jenou to sputter in amazement and then start to giggle. Soon Rio is giggling as well.

Cat pokes her head up. There's a strange look when she sees the two of them lying side by side. She seems almost jealous, or maybe just left out, but she quickly conceals it with a request to borrow some boot polish.

The PA crackles to life, announcing chow time for their company, and there is no dawdling when meals are announced—the navy serves good chow, and eating is about the only thing that punctuates the long days of doing nothing.

They file out to stand in a long, slow line for dinner, where Rio eats her fried chicken and mashed potatoes with unusual energy and enjoyment. And that night she lies in the dark after lights-out, staring up at the steel pipe over her head, and recalls every detail, every single detail, savoring, wondering, replaying.

But she replays, too, Strand's insinuation that she is merely playing soldier. She'll have to have a talk with him about that someday.

First another kiss, then a conversation, because

somewhere along the line, Rio has ceased to see this as any sort of game. She never wanted to really go to war, but now it seems she is, and a part of her, a small but growing part of her, is almost looking forward to it.

PART II

WAR

THE OPENING DAYS OF 1943

The Nazis and their collaborators control all of Europe except for a handful of neutral countries. Italy's buffoonish dictator, Benito Mussolini, has suffered one humiliation after another, and now the remains of his army in North Africa are increasingly dependent on the Germans. The French Vichy regime, Nazi collaborators allowed to control the southern parts of France and French overseas colonies, have begun shipping French Jews to the extermination camps. The German army, the Wehrmacht, has been stopped by the Soviets at Stalingrad, with staggering casualties on both sides.

A direct attack on Germany is not yet possible, but the Americans are anxious to strike a blow. The target is the Mediterranean, where the tiny British-held island of Malta has held out against impossible odds, keeping Allied air power alive. The Royal Navy, strengthened by the output of American factories, now dominates the western Mediterranean. The British fortress of Gibraltar, the gateway to the Mediterranean, remains firmly in Allied hands.

In Egypt the great British general Bernard Law Montgomery, known as Monty, has turned the tide against the equally skilled German general Erwin Rommel. Monty drives the Afrika Korps and what's left of the Italian army from the east across Libya. The Americans have arrived in Morocco and Algeria and lie in wait. The trap is set.

The Allies are sure that the Germans, Italians, and a handful of remaining Vichy will have no choice but to surrender or be wiped out.

The Germans have a different view.

In her first entry for 1943, Anne Frank writes, "All we can do is wait, as calmly as possible, for it to end. Jews and Christians alike are waiting, the whole world is waiting, and many are waiting for death."

But the US Army is not waiting. It goes looking for death and finds it at a place called Kasserine, Tunisia.

"*I want to impose on everyone that the bad times are over, they are finished! Our mandate from the Prime Minister is to destroy the Axis forces in North Africa. . . . It can be done, and it will be done!*"
—*General Bernard Law Montgomery, British Eighth Army*

"*We have come into North Africa shoulder to shoulder with our American friends and allies for one purpose and one purpose only. Namely, to gain a vantage ground from which to open a new front against Hitler and Hitlerism, to cleanse the shores of Africa from the stain of Nazi and Fascist tyranny, to open the Mediterranean to Allied sea power and air power, and thus effect the liberation of the peoples of Europe from the pit of misery into which they have been passed by their own improvidence and by the brutal violence of the enemy.*"
—*British Prime Minister Winston Churchill*

Interstitial
107TH EVAC HOSPITAL, WÜRZBURG, GERMANY—APRIL 1945

Thus do our young heroines train and prepare and ship off for war, Gentle Reader. Enfilade, defilade, bandaging, and spy craft, but the war is not yet real to them. It is out there, waiting for them, but they have no sense of what it is, really. It is vague. Indistinct. It's something concealed from view by fog so thick that even the sound of cannon would still easily be mistaken for thunder.

What do you think of my soldier girls, Gentle Reader? Aimless, naive Rio and sexy Jenou; smart, determined Rainy; and gentle, conflicted Frangie.

Could you see yourself sitting down to tea with these girls? Will it surprise you to learn that one of them went on to gun down three unarmed German prisoners? Will it shock you to learn that one lit her cigarette from the flames of a burning German SS officer?

We understood nothing, you see. We thought we were soldiers, but we were still civilians dressed in khaki and

OD. None of us had yet felt the fear so overpowering that you shake all the way down to your bones and your bladder empties into your pants and you can't speak for the chattering of your teeth. None of us had yet seen the red pulsating insides of another human being. We had not yet killed, and that, Gentle Reader, that is what we had been trained to do.

We had made friends among our fellow soldiers, male and female, but we as yet had no idea what those men and women could do, for we had as yet no idea what would be required of us.

It seems impossible to me now as I sit here deciding whether to bully an orderly into bringing me coffee, scratching the itch beneath my bandage, typing away in this dark and gloomy place and . . . dammit, the screaming again, someone trapped in a nightmare or in some more present physical agony.

I was attempting eloquence, Gentle Reader, and was interrupted by the raw urgency of another woman's pain. It serves me right, I suppose.

My own leg hurts, my breast hurts, but I'm not that poor woman screaming in the night, am I? Will you understand if I tell you that there are times when it is better to feel the pain yourself than to see it and hear it in another?

Helplessness is a big part of war, helplessness and

confusion and boredom, too, so that at times you tell the woman or man beside you that you'd rather be getting shot at. But that's always a lie, something you say to . . .

I'm getting ahead of myself. I am not here to ruminate and philosophize, or to attempt eloquence, I am here to tell the story, our story. Much of the time my fingers fairly dance over the keys and the sheets of paper go flying in and out. But right now as I write this, each letter is a struggle. For now our story leaves behind the sweet before and enters the darker after.

Where is this war, you wonder? Enough of the familiar; show me the blood and guts. When do we get to the killing and the dying?

Well, it is very near now, Gentle Reader, for we are going to North Africa, to the deserts where the Brits have the famed German Afrika Korps on the run after many battles. The Americans have landed against some resistance from the Vichy French, most of which crumbled soon enough.

It was supposed to be a pincer movement; Brits to the east in Egypt and Libya, Americans to the west in Morocco and Algeria, with the Germans, a few Italians, and a sprinkling of unrepentant French collaborators— running out of fuel, tanks, and ammo—trapped helplessly between the two.

We had yet to learn war, and we had yet to learn that

the Kraut was never helpless.

One more boat ride and we will arrive at the front lines in Tunisia. And there, Gentle Reader, you'll get your blood and guts.

Dear Pastor M'Dale,

I hope you won't mind me writing to you. I am writing to my parents and brothers as well, but I can't worry them. I suppose I shouldn't be worrying you either, but I need to do this, I need to write to someone. I talk to the other folks in my unit, but none of them has become really close. The men don't talk to us women, and the women mostly want to talk about what dress they'll get for the big victory party we all keep saying we'll throw someday. Or else they talk about boys, and that's not on the top of my mind. I guess you'll be relieved to hear that.

After an uneventful sea voyage, I'm in ███████. I think I can say that without getting censored. They put me on a ward for badly injured English soldiers as practical training. The Tommies aren't as concerned about black folk tending their white wounded since a lot of their nurses are already from colonies where folks are mostly brown or black. It's not like the white boys treat us as equals, but they seem happy to have any soft hand regardless of color to apply a salve or inject morphine.

I saw some bad things, sir. I don't really know how to explain without making you see what I don't suppose you want to see. But I think if I don't tell someone I'll crack up.

There was this one white boy. I can't tell you his name so I'll make one up: Errol. I've always liked that name.

Anyway, Errol had got hit by a passing 88 shell. It didn't explode because it was fused for armor not flesh, but it took off a chunk of his face, including his nose and part of a cheek. His buddies had found the missing flesh and bandaged it back on and sent him off to their field hospital and they had tried to sew it back on. And when he got evacuated here to ▮▮▮▮▮▮ the doctors thought maybe . . . But it didn't take, so the sewed-on part grew septic and morbid.

Pastor, they had to cut that boy's face back off. They were trying to keep the infection from spreading, but now it's all down his neck and his hair is falling out and when I saw him again he was raving. The infection was in his brain. He kept screaming and trying to tear the bandage off. Finally he died. Maybe it was one of the doctors deliberately ████████████████████████████, and maybe that's wrong according to the Bible, but now Errol can be in heaven where he will not have to scream.

I know you said helping keep these soldiers alive means they can go back to killing, but lots of these boys will be lucky to have any kind of life, let alone go back to war.

I guess I wanted to tell you that. And I wanted to ask you how God lets this happen. I was angry with God over that. I blasphemed. I repented as best I could, but in my heart I'm still angry.

I can't tell my folks that or they'll worry, so I'm telling you.

Keep praying for me, Pastor. Don't forget me.

Frangie

Dear Father,

I am well, though somewhat damp and oppressed by gray weather in a place I shall not name but which you may reasonably deduce. You'd think given my name I'd be better at enduring rain. I don't believe we shall be here for long, though I have no idea where the army may send me next.

I have to tell you some things that may disturb

you. Let me start by saying I know about the numbers running—they found out during an investigation of my background. I was surprised and disappointed, I guess, but I'm not upset now. You've always been a good father, and you did what you had to do to keep us all fed and together during the Depression and since then too. The commandments say we should honor our parents, and I do honor you, and I don't think I have anything to forgive.

But I'm going to tell you something now that you need to know in case something happens to Aryeh. You have a grandchild on the way. (No, not mine!) Aryeh fell in love and one thing led to another.

And, Father, the girl, his wife, is not a Jew. Her name is Jane Meehan. I've arranged to give her some of my pay and so has Aryeh, of course, but who knows what may happen in a war.

Next letter I promise will have fewer surprises.

Love,

Rainy

Dear Strand,

It was wonderful being able to spend some time with you on the ███████. I so wish it had been more. I suppose there are good things about a fast ship, but the time did fly by.

We spent ▮▮▮▮▮ in ▮▮▮▮▮ doing more tedious training, and I had hoped to see you there and be able to spend time with you in ▮▮▮▮▮▮▮. But I'm afraid I'm off yet again to parts unknown and the rumor is that ▮▮▮▮▮▮▮▮▮▮▮▮▮ ▮▮▮▮▮▮▮▮▮▮▮. So this may be ▮▮▮▮▮▮▮.

I don't mean to seem contrary or argumentative, but I suppose it got under my skin a little when you said I was "playing" soldier. Maybe I was a little, in the beginning, but I think now it won't be any kind of play. I'm not sure I'm ready for what lies ahead, but I mean to do my best. I want you to understand that, and I hope you'll be proud of me. Even when I'm a grizzled old veteran. Funny, huh?

I keep your picture with me and look at it often. I will think of you up there in the sky, somewhere, being very brave and dashing. I will think of you every day.

Maybe this is silly and too sentimental, but I hope the day will come when we can find ourselves back at the Jubilee, sharing popcorn and watching a movie. Would you like that? I would.

Please take care of yourself, Strand. Please.

Your girl,

Rio

21

"Jesus save us!" Kerwin cries, perhaps being funny, but perhaps scared as hell too.

The *Tiburon*—a much, much smaller ship than the *Queen Mary*, and much, much more likely to be tossed around like a cork—reaches the top of a wave and then shoots down the far side like a boulder rolling down the side of a mountain. For a few seconds Rio feels as if gravity has been canceled. But gravity comes right back with a vengeance as the ship bottoms out, nearly collapsing Rio's knees.

"I never knew being in the army meant so much time on boats," Jenou says. "And if we have to be on boats, why can't it be the *Queen* instead of this old tub? I liked the *Queen*."

"Yes," Rio says wryly, "you had a very good time on the *Queen*."

"Oh, I wouldn't call one young ensign a very good time. More like a . . . diversion," Jenou says, and attempts to toss her hair coyly, an effect ruined by the fact that her hair—and the rest of her as well—is quite wet.

Rio, Jenou, Cat, Kerwin, Luther, Tilo, Stick, and Jack have been formed into a squad with the sullen and unfriendly Jillion Magraff, a gloomy corporal named Hark Millican, a very Japanese-looking and instantly distrusted Hansu Pang, and Buck Sergeant Cole, who is to be their squad leader.

Most of the squad is in bunks trying desperately not to vomit. But Rio, Jenou, Cat, Stick, Tilo, Kerwin, and Jack are either immune to seasickness or else have already emptied every possible fluid from their bodies. The seven of them have found a tiny, cramped space beneath an overhanging gangway on the port side. They are shielded from the direct blasts of the weather and catch only spray rather than the massive, deck-clearing gray-green waves that roll over the bow and the starboard side.

"This is bad," Rio shouts above the wind. "Not as bad as down below."

"At least there's some oxygen up here," Cat agrees. "Somewhat damp, though."

Their outer layers are soaked despite the ponchos they wear. Tilo has for once abandoned vanity to tie a red plaid scarf—a gift from an aunt—around his head. The scarf is soaked, and Rio can see each breath he takes as it draws wet wool into his mouth.

"You know your problem," Jack says, shouting to be heard over another moan from Cassel. "You're not a seafaring folk, you Yanks. You don't know how to cope with these mildly blustery conditions."

Stick, normally the most stoic of the group, says, "I don't want to punch you in the nose, Stafford, but I will."

"Ah, but being of proper English seafaring stock, I have managed to obtain a cure for all our ills," Jack says, and with that draws a bottle of whiskey from beneath his poncho.

Rio has sipped the occasional beer at home in Gedwell Falls, has drunk entire beers during the bleak, wet, dull two weeks of training in England, but has never before tasted whiskey. Jack hands the bottle to her first, and though she has her doubts, she doesn't want to be a stick-in-the-mud.

So she tilts the bottle back and takes a deep swig of what feels like liquid fire.

"Good, eh?" Jack asks.

To which Rio replies, "Cchh . . . Ah . . . Mmpf . . ." and gasps out several painful breaths.

Jack grins happily, sticks his fists on his hips, widens his stance, and begins to sing at the top of his voice.

"When Britain f-i-i-irst, at heaven's command,
Arose from out the a-a-a-azure main,
Arose, arose from out the azure main;
This was the charter, the charter of the Land
And Guardian A-a-a-angels sang this strain . . ."

Tilo says something that sounds like an exasperated threat, but it isn't intelligible through his scarf. Rio, however, is charmed to discover that Jack has quite a good singing voice.

"Rule Britannia, Britannia rule the waves!
Britons never, never, never shall be slaves.
Rule Britannia, Britannia rule the waves!
Britons never, never, never shall be slaves!"

"I'm going to kill him, just as soon as we finish his bottle," Kerwin says, taking a drink.

In short order they are seven quite drunk soldiers, stumbling helplessly into one another with each big swell. And now they are an impromptu chorus belting out the chorus, "Rule, Britannia, Britannia rule the waves," despite some querulous looks from passing sailors who, being Americans, are not pleased to be celebrating the Royal Navy.

Yes, Rio thinks, Jack has a very nice singing voice. And

she likes his accent too.

Rio has no experience of being drunk. Jenou is a bit more knowledgeable and is amused by the sight of her friend growing more garrulous and more friendly. And less steady on her feet.

And Jenou is also more observant when it comes to men. She has noticed several lingering looks from a seriously inebriated Jack—looks aimed not at Jenou but at Rio.

Well, Jenou thinks, *there's no accounting for taste.* She tilts her head and gives Tilo a speculative glance, but Tilo has just collapsed in a heap, completely unconscious. Stick hauls him away by the only means he can manage on the pitching deck: he's got one of Tilo's ankles in each of his hands and is dragging him as if he's pulling a wagon.

Jenou says, "Maybe we better get below too," and takes Rio by the arm.

Rio laughs as if that's a joke and peers around owlishly, surprised to discover that her little group has already attrited, reduced now to just herself, Jack, Jenou, and Kerwin.

"Come on," Rio says, "party's just getting started!"

Jenou rolls her eyes, torn between a never-very-strong sense of responsibility and amusement. Then the matter is settled when Kerwin seems to freeze solid in midsentence, eyes fixed, jaw slack.

"Wha's Cassel starin' at?" Rio asks.

"Absolutely nothing," Jenou says. She sighs. "The care and feeding of drunks. All this way to deal with drunks. I could have stayed home and helped pour my father into his bed. Come on, Cassel, let's get you to where you won't wash over the side."

Rio watches them stagger away and is overwhelmed by a wave of sadness for Jenou. Both Jenou's parents are heavy drinkers. Rio's known that since she was eight and witnessed the two of them throwing dinner plates across the dining room. It's a burden for Jenou.

Jenou leans close to Rio, puts her mouth right up close to her ear, and says, "You're drunk, honey. Don't do anything you shouldn't do."

"Wha' should I . . . should not, shouldn't I do?"

"Okay, I'm coming right back for you," Jenou says, pointing a warning finger at Rio. "Don't get washed overboard before I get back."

"M'be righ' there," Rio calls after her friend.

"Uh-huh," Jenou says, and guides the comatose Kerwin away like she's leading a blind man.

"Where are they . . . huh . . . ," Jack says, and sways into Rio, causing her to giggle, which causes him to giggle, and the two of them roar with laughter when a wave sneaks up the port side to slap at them and barely misses.

"Almost got us," Rio says.

"Nazi wave. Thass wha' that was," Jack says.

"I thought Britannia ruled them. The waves."

"Not tha' one. Tha' was a bloody treasonous wave."

It is the last assault of a sea that is calming by degrees. Rio and Jack lean back against the steel bulkhead and stare blearily out at the convoy around them. A Royal Navy destroyer is a mile off, eternally patrolling for submarines. A second troopship is nearer, in line just astern. The sky is ragged, scudding clouds below a silvery moon, sky and moon both untroubled by the storm below.

"I've got . . ." Jack holds the bottle up to see that it has less than an inch of auburn liquid left in it. "That much lef."

"No more," Rio says.

Jack upends the bottle, swallows all that remains, and then belatedly says, "Sure you don't want some?"

He is suddenly standing very close to Rio, or perhaps she's standing very close to him, close enough that they no longer need to shout.

"You sing . . . good," Rio says.

"You shoot good," Jack says. "You shoot, I'll sing."

At which point he launches into a largely incomprehensible version of a song Rio has never heard.

"Come, come, come and make eyes at me, down at the old Bull and Bush, la-la-la."

"Make eyes," Rio says, and follows it with a snorting laugh. "I don't even know wha' tha' means. Make eyes."

"Hah!"

"Jenou, she . . . I don't . . ." Something has gone wrong with her brain and her body, the sober voice buried deep inside her inebriated brain notices with alarm. Her body is way too cold and wet to feel this warm.

Jack turns to her and looks directly into her eyes.

"What. Are. You. Doing? Jack Stafford?" Rio enunciates as carefully as she can.

"Making eyes at you," Jack says.

Rio is going to laugh but doesn't. She's about to give him a playful shove but doesn't do that either. Instead she feels herself falling toward him, as if some kind of gravity wave is beaming from his suddenly serious eyes.

"I can do that," Rio says. She steadies her head, which has a tendency to want to loll back and forth with each movement of the ship. And she looks into his eyes.

"Wow," Rio says.

"Mmm?"

"It's like . . ."

"Like?"

"Um . . ."

She closes her eyes when he kisses her.

The first kiss is tentative and a bit sloppy. Jack pulls away. He seems to be trying to focus his eyes, then gives up and in the end closes them, and moves forward blindly for a second kiss.

It would be easy for Rio to push him away. But she doesn't. Nor does she close her eyes this time, but watches him, watches him with minute attention, and when it begins to look very much as if he will miss his target, she takes his face with her two cold hands and holds him still. Holds him still, and he opens his eyes, heavy lidded, somehow innocent and lustful at once, and for what feels like a very long time the two of them just look, inches separating them.

The distance between them lessens, and Rio feels the warmth of his breath on her nose and cheeks. His lips are parted, waiting, and she draws him closer, fraction of an inch by fraction of an inch. She tilts his head to the right, and her own to the left, because that is the opposite of how Strand kissed her, and she is aware of that memory, and aware that what she is doing is very wrong, but this is not a moment for fine moral considerations. Of far greater importance right now is the feeling in the pit of her stomach, and the trembling of her hands on his face, and the realization that they have both stopped breathing.

He does not kiss her, she kisses him, lips parted so she can taste him.

Which is when Jenou reappears to say, "Uh-oh."

*   *   *

Your father got a job!

Frangie clenches her teeth as her bunk passes through all the angles between 45 and 135 degrees. On the downswing she extends her feet to stop sliding in that direction, and on the upswing she sticks a hand over her head to brace against sliding in that direction.

In her free hand she holds the letter she's already read through several times. Obal has taken over his buddy's paper route, Pastor M'Dale has won an award from the NAACP, and the labor shortage as men and women flood into defense plants has created an unexpected opportunity for her father.

Her father is dispatching taxis, a job he can do from a chair. He is earning a living. The family finances are saved. They aren't well-to-do, certainly, but neither will they lose their home or go hungry.

You can come home now, baby.

That line is as sickening as the effects of the waves. Frangie enlisted to save the family. So she could contribute her allotment. It is the sole reason she signed up, the sole reason she is here on her way to North Africa in this follow-up to the successful American landings at Algiers and Oran.

She wants to ball the letter up and throw it away. Or burn it. Or rip it into tiny pieces and scatter them overboard.

Camp Szekely, Fort Huachuca, that hellish hospital ward near Manchester, two reeking, miserable ships, all to save a family that no longer needs saving. And her mother writes as if this will be happy news.

You can come home now? Frangie pulls the rolled-up coat she uses as a pillow from beneath her head, wads it up over her mouth, and screams into the rough wool.

The letter reached her in England as she was being herded along with thousands of others from ship to truck to train to truck to ship. Mail call, normally the happiest of times, had turned very dark very quickly.

As she's screaming a hand roughly shakes her shoulder. She pulls off the "pillow" and stares at an amused white sailor.

"What?" she snaps.

"Your lieutenant volunteered you. Sick bay is ass-deep in bruises and broken bones, dumb-ass coons not knowing you keep a hand for yourself and a hand for the ship, falling down hatches and—"

"What?"

"They need a Nigra medic to help with some of the coloreds. Tag: you're it."

She follows the sailor down labyrinthine corridors whose walls and floors will not stand still, up stairs that almost seem to change direction as the floor falls away, across just enough open deck to leave her drenched, and finally arrives at the sick bay.

Sick bay is roomy by contrast with her berth, but still no bigger than a pair of parlors. One room is distinctly for whites, the other definitely for colored. There's a white doctor muttering to orderlies as he moves between the white beds, pointing at fractures, prodding at bruises, and ignoring anything said to him.

The injured black soldiers are receiving even less care, with one sour-faced white orderly and two black privates who are clearly at a loss. Frangie spots a familiar face. Sergeant Green has just heaved a loudly complaining soldier off his shoulders and onto a gurney that is already occupied.

It's the wounded man who, despite having what looks like a sprained ankle, recognizes Frangie.

"Hey, it's the little soldier girl."

Sergeant Green looks, sees Frangie, and greets her with an annoyed, "Help me with this fool."

Frangie helps to prop the wounded man in place beside the other man on the gurney and, seeking no further conversation with the obviously seething Sergeant Green, gets to work with gauze and tape and splints. She works for two hours without letup, caring for perhaps fifteen injuries, and by then the sea has gentled and Sergeant Green surprises her with a cup of hot coffee.

"Here."

She does not drink coffee. Until now. She takes the cup.

"Thanks for helping out," Sergeant Green says. Then, checking to make sure that he is not being overheard, he says, "I didn't mean to snarl at you."

"It's fine, Sergeant," Frangie says, taking a sip. He has added sugar to it, and some milk, and it tastes delicious.

"I'm going to get some air and have a smoke. You?"

She doesn't smoke, but she would like some fresh air, so she follows Sergeant Green out onto the deck to get a cold, wet, salty slap in the face that makes her laugh.

"Where you from, Private Marr?"

"Greenwood." And when he shows no recognition, adds, "Tulsa, Oklahoma. Also, most people call me Frangie."

She winces, embarrassed by her name. It's a little girl's name, really, and she wishes she'd said Francine.

He extends a hand and says, "Walter," earning a giggle from Frangie that she instantly regrets and tries to take back by covering her mouth.

"It's all right," he says tolerantly. "I guess I don't look like a Walter. Everyone gets a laugh at that." Then, staring at her sideways, he adds, "One laugh. Just one."

"And you're from . . ."

"Iowa."

"You're joking. Walter from Iowa? I didn't know there were any colored folks in Iowa."

"Well," Walter says laconically, "now that I'm here I guess we're down to about three left in the state: my mom and my two little sisters."

"Do you mind if I ask what you do in real life?"

He shakes his head slowly, as if he can't quite believe what he's about to say. "During the week I design trailers. You know, what we call mobile homes. I'm an engineer."

Frangie nods. That at least fits, somehow.

"On weekends I play a little bass."

"In a jazz band?"

"Well, I don't know I'd call us a band. More like four fellows who like to get together of a Saturday night. Play some Dixieland for the white folk, and maybe some blues for the college kids."

Frangie looks more closely at him. He's removed the glasses and stuck them in his pocket—they'd steamed up—and without them she sees the laugh lines they'd concealed. He doesn't look so old now, probably no more than twenty-one, maybe a year in either direction. She notices as well the tiny veins of gold within the deep brown of his irises, and then quickly looks away, feeling very confused.

Apparently Walter Green feels equally confused, because he flicks an only-half-smoked cigarette into the wind and says, "Well, I better get back to it. Good evening, Private."

"Good evening, Sergeant."

And just like that they are sergeant and private again, not Walter and Frangie.

Back at her bunk, Frangie draws the offending letter out again. She is still angry about it and wants to revel anew in that anger. But instead she whispers, "Walter?" And then, "Iowa?"

Rainy Schulterman is in her own bunk, one just slightly less fetid as befits her rank. She is reading an Italian-to-English dictionary and whispering her attempts at pronunciation.

"*Birichino . . . biscia . . . bloccare . . .*"

A sailor passes by carrying a length of thick hose. He stops, walks backward, puts on a big, toothy grin, and rests his free hand on the side of her bunk.

"Well, hello there, pretty girl," he says. "Are you trying to learn Italian? The language of love? Because I could help with that. My folks were right out of Pontassieve. *Capisci?*"

Rainy stares at him and says nothing, which unsettles the sailor a bit.

"So," he says. "What's your name, babe?"

"Mussolini," she says.

"Ah, you've got a sense of humor. I like a girl with a sense of humor, likes a laugh. Where you headed?"

Rainy points toward the front of the ship. "South," she says.

Which is when the sailor realizes he's getting nowhere, and walks on.

Several hours later, deep in the night, Rio wakes suddenly.

"Oh my God, did I . . . ?"

From the bunk below comes Jenou's voice. "You did. But hopefully he's too drunk to remember."

22

RIO RICHLIN—OUTSIDE TUNIS, TUNISIA, NORTH AFRICA

"All right, Second Squad, gear up." Sergeant Cole speaks around the cold cigar in the corner of his mouth. He's broad rather than tall, with a potato of a nose, a wide mouth with gapped teeth more or less always clenching a cigar, which is seldom lit. He'll be bald at an early age; his dishwater-colored hair is already beginning the retreat. He is not loud or overbearing as some sergeants are, but he has the gift of authority, despite the fact that he is quick to break out a grin. Where Sergeant Mackie was stern with a tight-wrapped and seldom-glimpsed sense of humor, Sergeant Cole is a man who is prepared to be amused by life.

GIs being GIs, Cole's announcement is met with the usual grumbling and the busting of chops.

"Aw, man. Haven't even had any hot chow."

"More hurry up and wait, probably."

"What happened to mail call? That's what I want to

know. I was supposed to get some cookies from my aunt," says Jenou.

"Anyone got a spare bootlace? I've already knotted this thing twice."

"Sarge," Cat says, "Private Castain can't fight without cookies."

"My boots still ain't dried out," Kerwin complains. "Be a hell of a thing fighting in wet boots in a damn desert."

"I'd sell my soul for a cup of hot coffee and real milk in it."

"You ain't got a soul, none of us do. The army wanted you to have a soul, they'd of issued one."

Rio digs the butt of her rifle into the mud, wraps her hands around the barrel, and heaves herself up off the relatively dry rock she's sitting on. Then she kicks the thick mud from her boots and shakes the mud from the butt of her weapon.

Shouldn't really be mud, should there, she thinks, *this being a desert?* Humid Georgia to a steamy *Queen Mary* to waterlogged England to the storms of the trip south, by rights shouldn't she have come at last to a dry place?

She swings her pack up off the ground, shoulders into it, and shifts around until it feels as right as it is going to get. The weight of it bites, and she has to lean forward a little to stay upright.

They do not form neat lines as they march; in fact, it's not what the drill instructors back at Camp Maron would even call marching, it's more of an amble, a stroll. They are soldiers in theory, but in reality they are still just civilians wearing uniforms.

Rio stays close to Jenou, who is on about her usual whine: "What happened to females being given typewriters and rich, handsome lieutenants, that's what I want to know."

"Yes, well I requested something in the technical field, something of great significance but with only the bare minimum of danger," Jack says in his poshest English accent. "Imagine my surprise when the army failed to fulfill my every wish."

He says this to Rio. Everyone hears, of course, but he says it to her, especially the last part. *My every wish.*

"No one gets everything they want," Rio says, keeping her voice bland, implying nothing—at least nothing that anyone else will understand. Except Jenou, of course, because Jenou was there when *the incident* occurred, a week ago.

"So true," Jack says ruefully, smiling his simultaneously cheeky and abashed smile. "But it never hurts to dream big."

It was his smile that first got to Rio, all the way back at Camp Maron. The accent hadn't hurt either. But this is not the time and not the place. Memories of a drunken moment—a shameful moment, really, given the place Strand Braxton holds in her heart—are out of place here and now.

The transport never happened. There was no kiss.

And anyway, I was drunk, so it doesn't count.

But Rio grins anyway. It's good to have an excuse to smile, no matter how much effort it takes when your insides are churning and your imagination is painting lurid pictures of amputations and cries of pain. The grin freezes in place. She's clenching her jaw, and now consciously unclenches it.

Imagination is not your friend in war, Rio knows. It's too easy to imagine yourself dead: shot or torn to shreds by bomb shrapnel. Or mauled but left alive to suffer another thirty years of misery, like the Stamp Man.

And why is she here? Why exactly is she here on this desert-front beach in a country she's barely heard of? It is decidedly not for the purpose of flirting with Jack Stafford, especially when Strand's picture is in her inner pocket, wrapped in waterproof oilcloth alongside the picture of her parents and her sister.

Strand is there, close to her heart.

Jack is there, close.

"Well, when I think about it, the army did fulfill my every wish," Rio says, trying gamely not to sink into a funk. "But that's because I wished to be cold and confused and surrounded by smelly, unwashed apes."

People laugh. That's good. Laughter fights worry.

"See, Private Richlin here has it figured out," Stick says. Stick is still the closest thing to a real soldier in the squad, aside from the sergeant. "You just have to wish for something lousy and the army is sure to arrange it." He shifts his big, heavy BAR from one sore shoulder to a slightly less sore shoulder.

The sky is losing the last of its gloomy, gray glow as night turns silver to slate. The desert around them begins to lose its form and color as shadow swallows it up. Ochre becomes gray, muted reds become gray, the world shifts from color to grayscale, a prelude to blackness.

"That's a cheerful thought," Rio mutters under her breath.

Rio carries a pack and gear that weighs thirty-five pounds all told, one-third her own weight. The pack contains one spare khaki uniform, four pairs of khaki socks, one khaki bra—not the sort of thing one finds in the average department store—one clean khaki undershirt and one that smells like an animal has crawled into it and died. There is a personal care kit, which is basically a comb, a few hairpins, a toothbrush and dental powder, lice-killer, a thinning bar of soap she'd had no chance to use recently, and a bottle of fingernail polish that she now regrets.

The heaviest thing in Private Richlin's pack is three days' worth of combat rations consisting of canned beef stew, canned corned beef hash, canned pork and beans, and canned cheese. The cans are olive drab, the food is not. The food is a sort of mealy tan hue unless it's the cheese, and then it is bright yellow.

Other food items consist of dehydrated lemonade, dehydrated coffee, and dehydrated cocoa. There is also something called a D-ration bar, which is alleged to be related to chocolate and has a tendency to break teeth and give soldiers the runs. GIs claim the D-bar is the enemy's secret weapon.

Tied to the back of Rio's pack is an entrenching tool, which a civilian might call a shovel. Rio's experience of the war so far—at Camp Maron, at two separate training bases in Britain, and thus far in Tunisia—has involved extensive use of the entrenching tool and no use at all of her weapon outside of the firing range.

It is all, all of it, khaki or light-olive drab. Khaki and OD alike are liberally decorated with mud splatters from passing deuce-and-a-half trucks.

Her fingernails—what is left of them—are pink. She's been unable to find fingernail polish remover, so the pink she applied seven days ago on the transport coming down from England is just slowly chipping away, another few flakes every time she digs a hole or cleans her rifle or unscrews the top of her tin canteen to take a swallow of brackish water.

The fingernail polish was a stupid decision. Rio was talked into it by Cat. *Amazing what boredom will drive you to,* Rio thinks.

Sergeant Cole, upon first seeing the nail polish just after they'd landed in Oran, stared at Rio with a look that reduced her height from five eight to just eight. He spoke not a word, just stared at her in disbelief and head-shaking disappointment.

The only reason Rio did not immediately toss the bottle of polish away is that she is saving it for a special occasion—like the end of this war, maybe. This will most likely be within a few months, because now that the Americans are in this fight, the Germans and Italians will give up pretty quick.

At least that's the consensus among the eight men and four women of Second Squad, Fifth Platoon, Company A, 119th Division based on precisely zero actual combat experience.

Their British allies, with two years of hard experience of the war, do not share this high opinion of the Americans, a fact that has been conveyed at times forcefully, even obscenely, from passing British forces.

Yet Second Squad, Fifth Platoon has remained cocky. Wet, cold, dirty, sore, hungry, tired, and endlessly disgruntled, but cocky.

Except now they are marching away from their temporary camp into the African night, the full desert night under a dangerously clear sky still dominated by the German Luftwaffe.

I could die tonight.

Second Squad and the rest of Fifth Platoon march, grumbling all the while, through slow-to-dry mud to an assembly area where Third Platoon is already standing around looking scruffy and unhappy. There's some sort of ongoing beef between Fifth and Third Platoons, dating back to the *Tiburon*. Rio doesn't know what it is, nor does anyone else (though it may involve a missing case of fruit cocktail), but it is for certain that Fifth Platoon is in the right. All forty-five soldiers in Fifth Platoon, including the twelve in Second Squad, are pretty sure of that.

The assembly area is a field once sparsely covered with desiccated grass, now trampled into the mud with such thoroughness that it almost seems like deliberate vandalism. They are within sight of the beach, an endless and barely visible stretch of sand that would no doubt be a playground in better times.

Sunshine and lovely warmth is what they all expected when they were told they'd be fighting in North Africa. Wasn't Africa all lions and elephants and jungles and sunshine? It seems not. This part of the continent is sand and rock and gloomy stone hills and squat, desperately poor villages that survive on date palms and an olive tree or two, with a fair number of mules and the occasional camel, but nary an elephant let alone a lion.

"Maybe there'll be lions wherever we're heading," Jack says, knowing better, but too nervous and too bored to stay silent.

"Lions got too much sense to get theirselves into a war," Kerwin says, to which Cat says, "*Themselves*, you dumb hick," to which Jenou says, "If you two start in again, I will shoot both of you," to which Tilo says, "Well, you're both safe. Castain couldn't hit a barn with a brick at two paces."

And so it goes, an endless round-robin of complaints, jokes, grudges, and absurdities, all punctuated with rude bodily noises, sudden laughs, snatches of song, and curses. The sound of soldiers standing around waiting for orders.

Cat recites some poetry she's come up with.

> *"They march us here*
> *They march us there,*
> *Where we going?*
> *No Damn Where."*

Cat's bit of doggerel may be correct and they may well be heading to "no damn where," but it doesn't feel that way, no, it sure doesn't, not to Rio. There is an edginess to the NCOs, even Cole. The sergeants have all been to a briefing earlier in the day and came back with long faces and extra ammunition.

The squad is either oblivious to this darkening mood or perhaps simply refusing to yield to it. The horseplay, the whining, the ridiculous rumors all go on, but to Rio's ears it's all in a lower register, a shadowed tone. Rio looks from her squad's sergeant, Cole, to Platoon Sergeant Garaman to Lieutenant Liefer—representing as they do the chain of command for Fifth Platoon, and thus Rio's leaders, mentors, and tormentors in varying degrees—and sees the signs of nerves. Cole relights his cigar. Garaman is chain-smoking some awful-smelling smokes he bought off an urchin in Algiers. Neither looks happy. Their counterparts from Third Platoon don't look any more cheerful.

Down on the beach two dozen boxy landing craft cough and sputter as they come ashore, appearing as darker shapes against a faintly luminescent sea. And coming down the beach toward those landing craft is a troop—about sixty men—in the khaki shorts and knee socks of the British army. The Tommies march in their usual, swaggering swing-step, and cast dismissive, pitying glances at the green Americans.

Lieutenant Eelie Liefer, Fifth Platoon's commander, is joined by the lieutenant from Third Platoon and the various NCOs are now yelling to everyone to listen up, listen up, you mugs. Notably they do not call for anyone to come to attention since somehow all of that spit-and-polish stuff seems to have been abandoned once they reached the actual war.

Lieutenant Liefer is a sight. She is the living, breathing poster girl for recruitment of female soldiers. She stands straight as a flagpole, her blond hair cut almost man-short, her blue eyes piercing, her skin glowing and perfect. Her uniform is improbably clean and still shows evidence of having been ironed at least once. There is something about Lieutenant Liefer that makes one think of girls who organize the homecoming dance, serve in student government, and are chosen as homecoming queen. She is a blonder, posher Sergeant Mackie with a lot less quiet assurance and a lot more shrill insistence.

"Okay, GIs, here's the scoop," Liefer announces in her penetrating alto voice. "Third and Fifth Platoons have been detailed to accompany a troop of commandos on a mission."

"Commandos?" Jenou whispers.

"That ain't good," Corporal Hark Millican mutters under his breath. "No, that ain't good at all. Them fellows get shot at." He sighs. Hark Millican is a gloomy, hangdog man who possesses an entire vocabulary of sighs.

Sergeant Cole aims a silencing look at Millican.

Liefer goes on. "We will embark on the landing craft you see there, move approximately a hundred and fifty miles down the coast under cover of darkness, go ashore, and advance inland to take out a German communications station. The trip will run approximately eighteen hours. Then we will return to the boats and be back here within seventy-two hours."

"Eighteen more hours in boats," Jenou mutters, just loudly enough for Rio to hear.

"Thirty-six if we make the round-trip. I wonder if the navy gets to stay on dry land?" Rio says.

"SNAFU," comes the inevitable summation from Suarez.

Situation Normal: All Fugged Up.

Liefer seems to think all this sounds just swell, although the Third Platoon's lieutenant, a beanpole of a twenty-nine-year-old named Helder, is looking a bit green around the gills. In real life he's an advertising man, another civilian playing at soldier, like most of both platoons.

"You've been issued extra ammo and three days' rations. Now, this is a joint operation with our allies, and the British captain will be in overall command. Needless to say, the eyes of the brass are on us, so let's not screw this up. Do you wish to add anything, Lieutenant Helder?"

No, Lieutenant Helder does not. Lieutenant Helder

looks like he just wants to find a warm bunk and crawl into it, a sentiment shared by 99 percent of both platoons, probably even by Stick.

The ramps of the landing craft drop to allow the GIs to board, which they do with the usual pelting disorder until the navy coxswain starts to bawl everyone out for tramping mud aboard.

"Goddammit, you fugging GIs think I'm going to swab all that mud out? Kick your fugging boots before you climb aboard my fugging boat! And if you're smoking, toss them over the rail, I ain't policing up your butts, neither!"

"Friendly, these navy boys," Jack says.

Now Second Squad hunkers down in the boat, which is nothing but an open gray-painted plywood box just big enough to fit two dozen soldiers or, in this case, a twelve-person rifle squad, a jeep, and a strapped-down pile of jerry cans full of gasoline.

Lieutenant Liefer and Platoon Sergeant Garaman sit in the open jeep. Buck Sergeant Cole is offered a nice dry seat as well but opts to stay with his people. Second Squad sit on their packs, pull their ponchos over themselves, and settle in for a long, long damp ride accompanied by seasickness and the usual vomiting. There is not a man or woman in the platoon who has not puked more in the last six weeks than they have in the rest of their lives put together. They're getting used to it.

The diesel engine roars, the water churns, and with a scraping sound the boat reverses and pulls itself off the beach. Once afloat the boat turns sharply to head southeastward, away from the faint, shrouded glow of the setting sun and toward onrushing darkness.

Rio Richlin wipes salt spray from her face. Her jaw clenches. Her fingers are cold and sore from gripping her rifle too tightly. And she wonders whether, once they reach the landing beach, she will be able to force herself to get off the boat. Already the sick dread is spreading through her like a poison. She has felt this before, but she was a child then. Since then she has aged. Matured. She has been trained. She has learned to . . .

She has *not* learned not to be afraid.

Her face is wet but her mouth is dry. Her heart is beating heavy and slow. Her breaths are shallow. She observes all these signs. She knows what they mean. She remembers the fear.

Am I a coward?

"Well, I guess I'll find out," Rio Richlin whispers.

23

Am I a coward?

Soon now. Soon they will be there, wherever there is. It is a mission, it is a commando raid. It will almost certainly be combat.

It all leads to this.

"I do not like the water at night," Jenou says.

"You figure it's wetter at night?" Tilo asks, just to start an argument and have something to do.

"No, Suarez, I figure if it's light maybe I can at least see which direction to swim in," Jenou says, perfectly willing to spend half the night arguing nonsense with Suarez.

"If you go into the drink sharks will get you, Castain," Tilo says.

"Nah, not Castain," Cat says, butting in. "She wouldn't taste good."

"At least if they ate me they'd get a full meal," Jenou

says. "You, Preeling? You're all bones. Just a big old shark belly full of big old bones."

"Sharks'll eat garbage, I've seen them do it," Kerwin offers, not meaning to compare Jenou to garbage, just talking to keep his teeth from chattering. "Back on the transport, cooks' mates would toss the garbage off the rail and in would come the sharks." He makes some accompanying hand gestures meant to be swarming, diving sharks, but mostly lost for being largely invisible in the dark.

An hour passes, during which the relative tastiness of various members of the squad is fully examined as related to sharks, and then, just for good measure, lions. Because, dammit, they are not giving up on lions, not just yet.

Then, in water that calms a little as they turn to move with the current, the smokes come out, and a deck of cards that can barely be seen. The players hold their glowing cigarettes close to read the cards, which makes for a very slow poker game, but what's the hurry? The glow also briefly illuminates their faces, mostly young, some old, all nervous. Sergeant Garaman bestirs himself from the jeep and joins in. Garaman wants to win back some of the smokes he lost in a previous game. That plus Garaman has never seen a card game he could pass up.

Rio does not take part in the banter, the card game, or the smoking. Her stomach is touchy from bouncing along at nine knots in a craft that reeks of oil and unbathed bodies. And she cannot turn off her imagination; she cannot stop thinking of pain and death. She cannot dismiss the lurid memory of the Stamp Man. And worst of all, fear itself, just like old FDR said. "The only thing we have to fear is fear itself." Well, maybe not the only thing.

Rio can imagine herself panicking. She can imagine refusing to get off the boat, having Jenou coax her, having Sergeant Cole pry her fingers loose, she can imagine it all in terrible detail, down to how cold her fingers will be as she cries and pleads and holds on for dear life.

But boredom begins to wear down her fear. Hours go by. The night wears on, and she falls asleep wedged between her pack and the side of the boat, waking whenever a gallon or six of cold water comes sloshing over the side, which is too often. She wakes as well when someone steps on her, and as she prepares an irritated response she sees that the sun has come up.

Rising to her feet she is greeted by the sight of the little flotilla spread raggedly across a couple miles of green sea. The land must be off to their right somewhere, and she sees what may be a line of brown—or may not be.

The squad is frowsy, soaked, and in a foul mood. Hark Millican has given up keeping his glasses dry, and now, spectacles tucked away, he looks like an owl, blinking and squinting. Cole has a nice spot for himself, legs stretched out, leaning against the front bumper of the jeep on deck. The lieutenant is up with the boat's crew, scanning the horizon with binoculars.

Luther lost his original kitten to the English countryside. He managed to not only replace her with a nearly identical calico but to smuggle her all the way here. The kitten, who Luther has named Miss Pat for reasons he has never volunteered, seems quite at home in his jacket pocket or occasionally stuffed down under his shirt. He takes her out now and feeds her tiny bites of C-ration cheese. Rio notices Liefer apparently just now becoming aware of the cat and watches the conflict play out on her smoothly sculpted face: make an issue of it? Or pretend not to notice?

There being no practical way to dispose of Miss Pat, the lieutenant opts to look away.

"See any submarines out there?" Jenou asks as she climbs stiffly to her feet and leans on the gunwale beside Rio.

"Don't sweat subs," Stick says. "These boats don't draw enough water. A torpedo would pass right under us. But you might want to glance up at the sky every now and again."

"Planes? Out here?"

"Well, hopefully the Luftwaffe is busy elsewhere, but sure, sure there could be planes."

"What do we do if one comes at us?" Jenou asks, head swiveling to scan the sky.

"We get our asses shot up," Luther says. "Hope that doesn't disturb you ladies."

More card games. More smoking. More grumbling. Cold food and suddenly there's a shout from the coxswain. The engine throttles down, and the boat slows.

"What the hell?" Hansu Pang yells, breaking his habit of complete silence.

The boat turns sharply, and they all soon see what the hell. One of the boats has been swamped by the agitated sea. The LCM is stopped, way too low in the water, with British commandos climbing out to hang over the side and inflating their Mae West life jackets while the other boats veer in like bees heading back to the hive.

The swamped LCM is more heavily loaded than the others as it carried one of two half-tracks, meant to give the commandos some speed on land as well as the use of its heavy machine guns.

"It's going!" Jillion Magraff yells. Private Jillion Magraff is blond, medium-height, and has the sullen eyes and outthrust chin of a young woman with a chip on her shoulder. Rio took an immediate dislike to her. But Magraff is right, and the boat, which had never enjoyed more than nine or ten inches of freeboard, is swamped. Only its stunted bridge and the upper half of the half-track are still visible. The sounds of lusty British cursing carry across the water as the commandos release their grips on the sinking boat and are picked up by other boats.

The entire operation eats up more than an hour. To make matters worse, the accident plus the freshening seas force the navy to slow their speed from a healthy, but not exactly rip-roaring, nine knots to just six. Now they are poking along at slightly better than rowing speed, a gaggle of boats as exposed and helpless as slugs on a sidewalk.

Lieutenant Helder's boat sidles up alongside Rio's. Helder shouts over to Liefer, "This is FUBAR, Liefer. We'll be landing in the dark!"

All conversation from the squad falls silent as they savor this opportunity to eavesdrop.

"Can't turn back," Liefer shouts, taking a face full of spray.

"That boat had most of the mortars, a bunch of the ammo too."

"I'm not in command of this mission; talk to the captain."

"I intend to," Helder yells back. "I wanted to have a united front."

Lieutenant Liefer shakes her head vehemently. "I'm not turning tail so the goddamned Limeys can call us chickenshit!"

"We have no business being on this mission in the first

place! This is a commando raid. We are infantry, and green."

Liefer shakes her head no. And after a hard look and a worried shake of his head, Lieutenant Helder and the boat he's on veer away.

"Well, that was encouraging," Jack says.

A second boat is swamped that afternoon, this time one of the American boats. Two soldiers from Third Platoon drown. Only one of the bodies is recovered.

Rio's worries, blunted earlier by boredom, come back full force now. She checks her Mae West, and plans mentally for what gear she can ditch to avoid drowning if her boat founders.

And then . . .

"Plane!"

Rio spins, tries to see who is yelling, tries to spot the plane, head swiveling, Jenou now doing the same. The coxswain hits a klaxon, which echoes across the water and then points in big choppy arm motions toward a sort of black X outlined against a falling afternoon sun.

"Is it coming or going?" Jillion Magraff cries.

"Can't tell."

"I think it's going . . . wait," Jenou says.

"Shit! It's coming! It's coming!" Kerwin yells.

One of the sailors hops onto the machine gun mounted beside the conn, tears off the protective canvas cover, and racks in a belt of ammo.

Cole says, "Everyone down, stay down!"

Rio can hear it now, a high-pitched insect whine.

"Could be one of ours," she says.

"Could be," Cole says, "but don't count on it. Get down. Take cover."

The plane roars overhead, and there, plain as day, are the black crosses of the Luftwaffe. As it zooms past every machine gun opens up, crisscrossing its wake, missing to the left, missing to the right.

Taka-taka-taka-taka-taka!

Everyone is on their feet now, eyes straining, tentative, praying, shouting impotent threats, shaking irrelevant fists.

The plane is in view for several long minutes, but it does not return. Instead it arcs away to the east again, toward Sicily.

Sergeant Garaman is beside Cole, both men keeping their eyes on the retreating plane.

"Well, they've spotted us."

"That they have."

"Loot's not turning back, I don't suppose," Cole said.

"I reckon not," Garaman says. "Not and be called out as a weak sister."

Rio scans until she spots the British captain's boat. There is no sign it is turning from its course.

"One hell of a secret mission we got here," Garaman says. "That Nazi bastard either sends a fighter back after us or radios ahead to the beach."

"I'll take a fight on the beach over getting sunk and shot up in the water," Cole says sourly.

"Six of one."

The British captain's boat surges to the front of the pack, and with hand gestures he indicates that everyone is to follow him. He changes course, then gathers speed, back up to the craft's maximum of nine knots, but not toward home, rather heading northwest toward a peninsula.

"What in hell is he about?" Kerwin wonders aloud.

Sergeant Cole answers. "He figures the Krauts have our course. Figures Jerry pilot radios back to Sicily, they get a plane up in the air in ten minutes, takes that plane maybe half an hour, forty-five minutes to get airborne and cover the hundred and fifty or so miles to where he can intercept our course. So we got half an hour, maybe a bit more, to see if we can't throw him off the scent."

"The sun goes down in ninety minutes, after that we'll be hard to see. So . . ." Garaman shrugs. "He's got at best thirty minutes on target to find us again."

As it happens, if a second plane has been launched to locate and destroy them, they never see it. Eyes strain to catch any sight of a plane, and it is a very hard hour, an hour of nervous chatter and whispered prayers, but when darkness falls, the boats turn back south, moving again at safer speed, but now hours behind schedule.

"They'll be waiting for us when we land," Tilo says nervously.

"Could be," Cole says, nodding in a sort of sideways, back-and-forth way that signals skepticism. "But there's a lot of coastline. Lot of beach. They won't know exactly."

Rio looks around at her companions, her squad. Reliable Stick; obnoxious Luther; the funny and pugnacious Cat; big, friendly Kerwin; Tilo, looking startlingly young despite his tough city-boy airs; sullen, standoffish, and barely known Jillion Magraff; jaunty Jack. Hark Millican, looking sick and sad, as if he's already been shot and he's just waiting for someone to tell him to die; and the most recent addition, the presumed Japanese American Hansu Pang.

Jenou catches Rio's eye and winks.

Jack catches her eye and just holds her gaze, sharing some emotion that neither of them can hope to name.

Rio breaks eye contact to look at Sergeant Cole. He's showing nothing. He does his three-stage move where he shifts his cold cigar from side to middle to the other side of his mouth. It reminds Rio of a horse chewing on its bit.

Rio wants to hide behind Cole. She wants to grab

Jenou and say, "This is all a stupid mistake; we have to go home now."

She wants to be with Stafford.

No, far better, she wants to be with Strand, because he's not here in this boat. She never should have spent time with Stafford.

Jack. His name is Jack, and you know it.

Those emotions—shameful, lustful, conflicted, unfaithful emotions—just add to the weight that bears down on her soul. She feels it that way, as a weight. A heaviness that crushes her heart and extends, leaden, to her limbs.

The flotilla has turned toward a shore invisible in the darkness. No one has to tell them they're going in, they can all feel it in the air. The heaviness in Rio's soul grows more oppressive. She closes her eyes and prays.

The prospect of imminent combat should erase all other concerns, it should leave Rio free of all doubts, all second-guessing, but of course it doesn't. She will carry all of it with her. The picture of Strand in her pocket, the image of Jack belting out "*Rule, Britannia*," the imagined images of Rachel, her lungs filling with salt water. The Stamp Man.

The sea grows more agitated; short, steep waves that slap loudly at the sides and fire fountains of spray into the air. The boat rolls, side to side, triggering a new wave of nausea. The latest card game folds up, and now, as they near the target, the coxswain calls for all cigarettes to be put out.

"Fugging German gunners see that light, and we all get blowed to hell."

Rio has been cold, miserable, sick, and scared for twenty-four hours now, and is in no way prepared to fight. She hasn't even started, and she's already exhausted. She has an overpowering desire to check her rifle to make sure, doubly sure, triply sure, that it works, and she repeatedly touches the pockets of her ammo belt, reassuring herself that she has a full load. Despite the wet everywhere else, her mouth is dry.

She does a deep-knee bend then stands up, shakes out her hands, stamps her feet to get some feeling back in her numb toes. The other boats are strung out ahead and behind, all running along in almost total darkness now under a sky playing peek-a-boo with patches of cloud beneath a jeweler's display case of diamonds. There is a single bunkered light on the stern of the lead boat with all the others following it.

The sea itself is almost as bright as the sky, with phosphorescence sparkling green from the wave tops, but these hints of color only make the underlying sea seem blacker.

The Mediterranean Sea, cradle of human civilization. All the ancient empires have fought their wars here; Rio's heard Stick talking about it.

"The bottom of the Mediterranean is piled deep with bones and weapons and lost gold from long-ago wars between countries and empires that no longer exist," Stick once told Rio. Rio hoped then, and hopes even more fervently now, that her bones will not be joining that vast collection.

The lead boat turns sharply to the right—starboard, as the navy boys say—toward the still-invisible shore. This brings the wind and spray around to almost directly in Rio's face, so she shivers and drops back down behind cover. The boat is heaving and bucking, hitting wave tops and falling into troughs.

Sergeant Cole, speaking calmly, without inflection, and as usual somewhat muffled by his unlit cigar, says, "Okay, ladies and gentlemen, we are heading in. Anyone wants to throw up one last time, get it over with."

Kerwin does exactly that, leaping to his feet in a vain attempt to project his vomit away from the boat. The wind blows it right back in his face, but the spray soon washes it away.

"No one smokes, no one talks, and sure as hell no one shoots unless I say so. You all got me?"

Cole's probably done this before.

"Yes, Sergeant," came the rattling-teeth responses.

Rio licks her lips, tasting salt water.

"Let's go over the call sign. The challenge is *mustard*. And the response is *ketchup*. Do it with me."

"Mustard."

"Ketchup."

"Mustard."

"Ketchup."

"You see or hear something that looks like a person, you call out *mustard*. If that person does not give back *ketchup*, you shoot him. But let me repeat: we are not looking for a fight. We have an objective."

Cole always pronounces it "OB-jective," which usually makes Rio smile, but not now, this is not a time for smiles, this is a time for clenched fists and gritted teeth.

"We want to get to the objective without the enemy spotting us. So quiet it is. Like a mouse sneaking past a cat, right?"

"Right, Sarge."

Cole then looks around at his squad, eyes just faint glitters in the dark as he tries to assess each of his charges. "If you all remember your training and don't lose your heads, you'll likely be okay."

Likely. How likely?

A navy crewman comes forward, walking with an ease the land-loving GIs could never master aboard a wet, rolling matchbox. He says, "All right, five minutes to the beach. God be with you, Army."

"Thanks for the ride, Sailor," Cole says.

"Next time I want a first-class berth," Rio says through a tight-clenched jaw, just to show she's not afraid, not so afraid she can't speak, anyway. The words chatter and break up a bit on the way out of her mouth, and the laughter that follows is strained and nervous, but laughter just the same.

Don't screw up, Rio, that's all.

Sergeant Garaman fires up the jeep's engine, making everyone jump.

"Load your weapons. Safeties on!" Cole says. "Let's not shoot ourselves getting off the boat."

Rio draws a clip from her belt. Her fingers are numb with cold, and she almost drops it. Jenou does drop hers, but no one is in the mood just now to tease her about it.

Rio racks back the slide and thumbs in the clip, pushes it all the way down and yanks her hand back quick. She extends her index finger, touches the safety, assuring herself that it's on.

"Hey, Richlin," Kerwin says. "You think there'll be any angry pigs on that beach?"

"As long as there's a tree for us to climb, it'll be okay," Rio says.

"Okay, Second Squad, brace!"

They brace, hands grabbing anything solid, knees tense, heads low, insides quivering.

"Soon as the ramp drops, go. Stay low, stay quiet. Run fifty yards up, split left and right, keeping the egress clear for the jeep. Then drop and wait."

Just don't screw up, Rio, just don't screw up.

Now she sees a snaking line of phosphorescence marking the crashing surf, shockingly near. The engine changes tone and the vibration increases as the coxswain slows for impact.

Rio has to pee badly.

Her breath comes short and fast. Her chest pounds out a panicky, irregular drumbeat. Her hands clutch her rifle, left hand gripping the forward stock, right hand wrapped around the neck, index finger lying on the safety, just like she's been taught.

Lord, make me brave.

And then she glances at Jack, not wanting that thought to enter her head right now, not right now, because right now she's about to hit the beach and she wants moral clarity, she wants to be the good girl who will deserve the protection of an approving God.

"I guess it'll all be nothing," Jenou says.

"Right."

Rio feels Jenou's hand fumbling for hers. She releases her trigger finger and takes her friend's cold fingers. They squeeze hard, reminding each other that they were still here, together, alive.

The surf seizes the small boat and hurls it forward. The bottom of the boat scrapes suddenly, and immediately the ramp rattles down.

"Go, go, go!" Cole says in an urgent whisper.

The first row leaps forward, Corporal Millican taking the lead, with Tilo and Jillion flanking him. Rio is in the second row with Jenou and Stick, and the three of them surge behind the leaders.

There comes a shout from the darkness ahead, barely audible above the vehement throat-clearing sound of the engines and the shushing of the waves. A distinctly non-American shout.

Rio lands waist deep in a retreating wave. The water is like molasses, grabbing at her uniform, tugging her back toward the sea with disturbing force. It nearly unbalances her, and if she falls she'll drown because the weight of the pack and the weight of the ammo have suddenly been doubled by the water. But Cole's hand shoves her upright and she slogs forward, forward and up an incline, and now the water pushes with her as the wave rolls in, lets her move, lets her run up onto sand, rifle at the ready.

A noise like a very big zipper being yanked down hard and streams of tracer fire arc from the darkness, a bright line of death.

"Down! Down!" Cole yells.

"Clear the egress!" Liefer is yelling in her shrill alto,

because they have to get the jeep off the boat and she doesn't want to drive over her own soldiers.

"Go, go, go!"

"Look out!"

"Get the fug—"

"They're shooting!"

Rio lurches to her right, three steps, four, five, ten, fifteen, counting them off, drops to her knees, plants the butt of her rifle, and lies facedown on her belly with her weapon pointing toward where she thinks the machine gunner might be.

Fifteen hundred rounds per minute. The standard German machine gun fires fifteen hundred rounds per minute.

The machine gun opens up again, loud but distant, followed by softer but way-too-near *Pfft! Pfft!* sounds as the bullets hit sand. Soft whimpering noises are coming from her throat, unlike any sound she's ever made before.

A split second slower than Rio to hit the ground, Kerwin cries out. He says, "Oh!"

Just that. Oh.

Rio sees him fall backward. His head lands in the edge of the retreating foam, legs folded beneath him.

"Cassel! You hit?"

No answer.

God no, God no, God no.

The jeep roars and splashes out of the landing craft

and instantly draws the fire of the enemy machine gun.

"Are you hit? Cassel! Are you hit?"

"Doc! Doc!" someone yells.

The jeep swerves left and goes nose-down in a hole, rear wheels spinning and throwing up a plume of sand.

"Richlin! Give Doc a hand with Cassel!" Cole yells. "Stick, get that BAR onto that dune there and put some fire on that machine gun, take Geer with you. Castain, Pang, Suarez, stay low and follow me!"

Rio crawls toward her stricken comrade, elbows digging, knees pushing, heart gone mad. The doc, who came ashore with Fourth Squad, is hunched over Cassel. He grabs at something in his medical kit, and now Rio sees that Cassel is flailing spasmodically, arms and legs jerking, torso heaving. An advancing wave covers his face in foam.

"Pull him back, pull him back, goddammit, he'll drown!" the medic shouts.

Rio grabs Cassel's legs and has to rise to her own knees in order to get leverage. She is acutely aware of her exposed back but hauls him out of the surf.

"Hold him down," the medic says through gritted teeth as he tears open a bandage. "Gotta stop the bleeding. His neck."

"Take it easy, Cassel, take it easy," Rio says.

Blood pulses from Cassel's throat, like a garden hose

that someone is kinking and releasing, kinking and releasing. The blood looks like chocolate syrup in the darkness.

Kerwin is making guttural sounds, words full of urgency with no vowels.

Rio rises again, just high enough to place her hands on Kerwin's chest and hold him down, but as she does this she feels slippery warmth and realizes that large quantities of blood are gushing from his upper chest. He's been hit twice, not once.

"Gotta take it easy, Cassel, let Doc work."

Would sound better if my teeth weren't chattering.

But Kerwin isn't hearing her. He jerks wildly, tries to say something that comes out as a plaintive grunt, then lays back down, quieting. Doc slaps a pressure bandage on, but the artery in Cassel's neck is barely slowed.

Like trying to block a fire hydrant with your fingers.

Doc rips Cassel's uniform shirt open and there's the second hole near, far too near, to his heart.

The medic curses and then covers for that by telling Cassel, "It's okay, it's okay, soldier, you'll be okay, going home is all, going home." It's a lie, but Kerwin never hears it anyway.

Rio feels his heart stop. One second there's a wild beating thing in his chest and then nothing.

Kerwin's last breath is a slow wet wheeze of exhalation, as if he's sinking back into an easy chair after a long day.

The machine gun chatters and digs divots *Pfft! Pfft! Pfft!* in the sand near Rio, so she has to roll away, clutching her rifle to her chest with blood-slicked hands.

Kerwin is dead without even getting a chance to speak. His final intelligible word just that single syllable, "Oh."

24

FRANGIE MARR—TUNISIAN DESERT, NORTH AFRICA

The same northern African night that envelops Second Squad on its beach covers Frangie Marr and the colored 403rd Artillery Battalion. They are not on a beach but in the shadow of a stark, bare hill with just a number for a name.

Frangie hears the sounds and sees the flash of artillery fire in the distance. That would be a white battalion sending 105 and 155 shells toward the Germans, who Frangie has neither seen nor heard. Something is up, she can feel it. The pace of firing—at night, no less—is too great for it to be a minor fire mission.

Doon Acey—Buck Sergeant Acey now—is already busy about the sights of his 105, carefully wiping the glass in the eyepiece, checking the set screws with a flashlight, fussing like a backyard mechanic working on a jalopy.

Rough wooden boxes of shells are eagerly manhandled down from the trucks, which go roaring off the instant they are empty, spraying mud from their fat, heavily treaded tires. More trucks come carrying more ammo, water, tents, chow, all the paraphernalia of an army as the 403rd races to get set up.

There are six guns in this battery, four batteries in the battalion, twenty-four tubes in all, served by a total of just under five hundred men, of which ten are white officers and the rest black privates and NCOs.

There should be at least a half-dozen medics throughout the battalion, but there are just three—trained medics are in short supply, especially black ones.

Frangie mentally goes over the contents of her medical bag. Plenty of bandages and tape. Enough sulfa powder, hopefully. Sutures? Probably, and if not she has a sewing kit her mother insisted on sending with her. Morphine? Someone has stolen some of her stock, but there is enough, most likely. She sees the water truck with its oval seven-hundred-fifty-gallon tank. Water is as important as any medicine; she's been taught that, and here in the desert with nary a brook or stream, she feels it.

An instructor, an old sergeant from the last war, had told the medics-in-training, "When they're injured they'll ask for water. When it's bad they'll pray to Jesus. When it's over they'll ask for their mother."

Medicine she has. Water she has. She can do nothing about anyone's mother.

Everyone says the artillery doesn't get shot at. Much. So maybe she won't need anything. But she does the mental checklist anyway, a result of training plus a desire to not screw up. To be ready. Always ready. Because this is it. This is the war.

Already tired but keyed up by the atmosphere of controlled panic, Frangie watches the jiggly dance of flashlights as the crews set up the firing stakes and square the 105s and 155s, digging in the split trails that will absorb some of the shock of firing. Men and some women stack shells, dig foxholes, rig shaggy fishnet camouflage, position defensive machine guns, and set up a small command post.

They are in hill country, desert hill country, with hills that are little more than bare rock and low, scruffy bushes. The air smells of dust, diesel fuel, bug spray, and Cosmoline, the thick petroleum jelly used to keep metal gun parts away from salt spray and other corrosive things. The wind is cold, the particularly cutting cold of the desert at night. Frangie has located her little aid station near the narrow, paved road behind them, and in just the last hour American soldiers have appeared on that road, walking toward the rear. Some are bandaged. Some of the wounded are on stretchers atop jeeps that honk their horns carelessly to clear a path.

But most of the soldiers who pass by are not wounded.

Some have lost or thrown away their weapons. Many look abashed or even frankly scared—it is not hard to guess that something out there in the desert went poorly.

A dusty, dirty-looking buck sergeant comes toward Frangie's station calling out, "You boys got any water you can spare?"

"You can have a swig off my canteen, Sergeant," Frangie says, "and there's a tanker truck just over behind the command tent."

Only when he's a few feet away does the sergeant focus and notice that Frangie is black and female.

"I ain't drinking water out of no coon's canteen," he says, and rejoins the jittery, mournful parade. He's not alone in his hostility. Some of the passing soldiers take the time to stare at the all-black artillery and some take the time to marvel loudly at, "All them Nigras with big old guns."

"No wonder we couldn't get no arty support, it's nothing but jigs and jugs," a phrase Frangie hears for the first but not the last time.

"Doc! Doc Marr!"

Frangie searches in the dark for the source of the shout, trying to place it. It's from Doon's gun, nearby. She grabs her bag and runs the fifty yards to the emplacement. One of the gunners has crushed a couple of fingers in the breech.

"I'll put on a splint. But you won't have much use of that hand for a while, Private."

"That's your jerking-off hand too," another private says, laughing. Then he realizes what he's said in front of a woman and hastily retreats. "I meant, um . . . Well . . ."

Doon comes around, gives the splint a critical eye, winks at Frangie, and says, "Likely to get noisy around here pretty soon, Frangie."

"Any word on what's happening?" she asks, tying off the gauze and ripping it with her teeth. She jerks her head toward the passing white soldiers and says, "That doesn't look good."

"Looks like getting our butts kicked is what's happening," Doon says. He seems cheerful despite that gloomy assessment. "But I guess we'll see how much the Germans enjoy the mail we're going to send them."

One of the very few advantages to segregation is that despite being only recently attached to this unit, Frangie has already run into two people she knows: Doon Acey and Sergeant Green. Sergeant Walter Green of Iowa. Finding Doon with the big guns is not a surprise, but Green is infantry. She and Green managed only a brief surprised nod of recognition before Green's platoon was dispatched up the looming hill to keep a lookout and presumably defend the vulnerable but valuable big guns.

Lieutenant Penche, an impossibly young-looking white

boy with a very deep-woods accent, comes running, a grin spoiling his attempt to look mature and officerly.

"Men, we have a live-fire mission!" he announces.

He's written the coordinates in a small, spiral-bound notebook. Doon's gun crew and the other five in the battery, having only just gotten into position, begin the backbreaking work of digging the tails back up, hefting them, and walking them to the right, bringing the cannon tube to the left. This is the crude aiming—the exacting work is setting elevation and traversing the gun with a hand crank and a wheel. As a soldier spins the wheel, Doon calls out, "Yeah . . . Yeah . . . Almost. Hold it. Yeah. Now give me another two mils elevation."

"Back up, Doc," someone says to Frangie, "this girl kicks."

Frangie backs away ten yards but wants to see the gun in action, up close. Best to get used to the noise now—she has not yet been exposed to close-up cannon fire. This changes with a shout of, "Ready," followed by the high-pitched voice of the lieutenant yelling, "Fire one round."

The explosion causes the entire howitzer to jump. It digs the tails into the gravel and bounces the cannon and its undercarriage on the two big tires. A jet of red flame shoots from the muzzle, lighting the crew like a lightning flash. Smoke billows from the muzzle, and already the crew has popped out the spent casing, hot and smoking.

It rolls toward Frangie.

A runner comes from the command post, which has heard from the forward position by radio. "Two hundred short!"

A second round is fired, and after a few minutes comes word that it's a hundred yards long. Frantic adjustments left and right, then from each of the six guns in the battery comes a shout of "Ready!"

"Fire for effect!" the young lieutenant yells, and the whole world becomes one big explosion as all six howitzers fire within a split second of each other.

Out slides the hot brass, in goes a new shell, and *ka-boom!* It makes the ground beneath Frangie's feet bounce, and out slides a smoking shell and in goes its replacement, and another *ka-boom!*

The other batteries, spread in an arc across a quarter of a mile, watch with envy.

The battery fires off six rounds per gun, then stops. But within seconds a second battery opens up, its guns elevated higher. Again a total of eighteen rounds are fired. Red lightning, like camera bulbs from hell, a strobe of light now, up and down the line. The lingering smoke seems almost to hold on to that red light for a while.

Then, another target and a battery down the line opens up, getting their chance to rain death on the unseen Germans. The more distant batteries are loud, but Doon's, right here, right on top of Frangie, is shattering as the battery fires again, and this time it runs on longer, and at such a rapid clip that it's like some massive drum beating out a frantic rhythm.

Frangie is called to treat a burn, and then the shattered kneecap of an unwary soldier who stood too close as his gun fired. It means evacuating the soldier—Frangie is not a surgeon—but he'll keep the leg and may even get sent home.

She's feeling pretty good, really; nothing has occurred yet that is beyond the scope of her training. The noise is stunning, and she soon discovers that neither she nor the soldiers can really hear much, certainly not normal conversation, and the flashes shrink her pupils until the darkness between explosions is impenetrable. She's treating men who can only point and wince, but it's nothing terrible or overwhelming, and she breathes a tentative sigh of relief.

There's a lull of a few minutes in Doon's battery. He turns and shoots a grin at Frangie.

Then Frangie hears something she doesn't understand. She yells, "What's that?" But the high-pitched whine she hears is not audible to men who've been standing right up close to the firing guns, nor for that matter is her worried cry, so no one else hears the scream of incoming shells until they land.

The explosion of a German 88 that lands just a hundred fifty yards to their right between Bravo battery and Charlie battery. A fountain of dirt erupts into the air.

As the dust settles, men and women scramble, running and diving into the nearest foxhole, because if there's one thing artillery men know, it's that a ranging shot will be followed by total devastation.

It's not long in coming.

Frangie has already located the nearest hole and dives into it just seconds before Doon Acey.

"See," Doon says. "I told you the army was fun."

"You said no such thing," Frangie manages to say before the whole world explodes. The impacts are so powerful that the ground around them, the dirt and rock walls of their foxhole, punishes them, hammering their feet, their arms, their behinds when they fall to the bottom of the hole.

The noise is catastrophic. Frangie's ears scream in pain from the noise but more from the sucking away and rushing in of air following each explosion. Her mind is scattered, unable to form a thought. Just a series of flashes, segments of thought. Scared. Tears. Terror. Like some mythical thunder god is beating the earth with a hammer the size of a house, hammering on her, her personally. A flash of flying dirt. Flash of foxhole collapsing. An incongruous image of her room back home. A flash of

Doon's terrified face, looking almost green.

She and Doon hold each other like frightened children in a thunderstorm, but this thunderstorm is unlike anything they've ever experienced. This thunderstorm has malice behind it. This thunder and lightning are bent on murder.

Spent shrapnel rains down into the foxhole, burning hot, singeing clothing and exposed flesh. Frangie screams now, screams unheard, "Stop it! Stop it! Stop it!"

There's an enormous metallic *clang* that's almost musical and the twisted, smoking barrel of a howitzer lands across the top of the foxhole, cutting off any escape, hissing hot.

A burning smell flows down into the foxhole, a toxic, chemical smell. Frangie is suddenly afraid that she's on fire, slaps at her uniform, checking, *Where's that smell coming from, am I burning?*

It's never going to stop.

Round after round. It's never going to stop until she's dead. She's going to die. Right now she's going to die.

And then, slowly, she realizes it *has* stopped. It's stopped. Silence. She can't hear anything but a loud ringing sound that's no sound at all. She feels her own heart but surely no heart can beat that fast and go on beating?

Her body trembles. Every cell of every muscle shakes, shakes like she's freezing, like she's going to die, *Oh, Jesus, take me, take me to heaven.*

"Are you hurt?" She can't hear Doon, just see his mouth moving, a sort of unreal hole just inches from her face. He leans in, brings his head into contact with hers, and now she can hear through the skull, through the bones of their bodies. "Are you hurt?"

Hurt? She's destroyed. But she shakes her head no.

The side of the foxhole has collapsed in one quadrant, opening up a space through which they might just crawl past the barrel of the destroyed artillery piece. Doon loses all self-control now and begins clawing at the dirt, tearing his fingernails as he yells, "Hey! Hey! We're down here!"

Frangie joins him, shouldering in beside him, tearing at clods of loose dirt that fall and cover their boots. Doon decides enough is enough and pushes his way up, kicking at the dirt, frantic, reaching up to grab the red-hot metal of the barrel, yelling soundlessly in pain, to be replaced by Frangie, who digs and scrambles, and panic feeds panic now, fear swallows fear and grows more desperate.

All at once Frangie's head is up and out in the air, the blessed air, the air filled with fire-lit nightmare images of twisted cannon and running soldiers and smoke. She crawls up the rest of the way and lies for a while, flat on her belly in the dirt. Then she turns and offers a hand to Doon, who takes it weakly.

She pulls, and he loses his grip.

She grabs his wrist with both her hands and pulls, but

there's something wrong. He can't hold on. He's crying now, she can see the tears, and she can feel the weakness in his grip. Sobbing, big wracking sobs.

"Help me, someone! Help!"

But no one can hear; it's a landscape with no sound but the droning tone in her ears.

She releases her grip on Doon and stands up, amazed she still can. It's wreckage and destruction everywhere. Trucks and cannon lie like some failed attempt at sculpture, twisted, blown into pieces, jagged edged, smoking. The water truck drips the last of its water. Men and women wander lost and confused, looking for nothing, looking for something, around in circles. The young lieutenant stares down at a twisted hunk of steel and cries.

"I'll get help," Frangie tells Doon. She grabs the lieutenant and jerks her head toward the foxhole. "Help me."

The lieutenant doesn't understand, but he's willing to be led. Together the two of them kneel by Doon's foxhole. They reach down, each taking an arm, and pull Doon up.

His intestines remain behind.

He sits on the edge of the hole looking at the horrifying mess that slips down his lap. With limp hands he tries to reel his intestines back up, but they're slippery and he's crying, tears rolling down his cheeks. Frangie tries to help, tries to pull the pulsating wormlike tube up, but she's crying and making sounds that are not words.

Doon looks at her. He says something, words she can't hear. Then he dies.

Someone is shaking Frangie's shoulder roughly, yelling at her, a sound she cannot parse, cannot understand. But the face looking at her is anguished. She nods.

She leaves Doon and the weeping lieutenant behind and in a trance follows the soldier who guides her by the hand to a second soldier. He's lying against an unharmed howitzer. His foot is gone.

"Traumatic amputation." That's the term for it. Something has been blown off. Something is missing.

His ankle is a mess of red worms, arteries and veins and shreds of meat and a circle of white bone oozing marrow, but half of it has been cauterized, seared shut by the heat of the shrapnel. It saved him a lot of blood, that's a good thing. She tightens a tourniquet around the stump. Instinct. Training.

Humanity.

She slaps a bandage on, inadequate, laughable if laughter is ever possible again. She stabs a morphine syrette into his thigh.

There's more. A dead woman. Frangie cannot raise the dead, not this PFC, and not Doon Acey.

A man with shrapnel in his chest and belly roars in pain, the first real sound she's heard since the bombardment. More morphine. The man has to go to the field aid station; there's nothing she can do with a belly wound. She sends him off on a cloud of morphine.

There's a broken arm, a scalp laceration, a few small burns. And there's a body without its head. The head is never found. A male soldier with a superficial wound—hot shrapnel grazing a thigh—demands to be sent home.

"Can't do it," Frangie says as she sprinkles sulfa powder on the wound. "That doesn't even rate stitches."

"I coulda been killed."

"And if you had been, you'd be going home." She's pleased with the steadiness of her voice, she likes the toughness of it. And she's coping, that's the important thing, she's coping.

Despite the hammering they've taken there's only three deaths: the PFC, the headless man, and Doon Acey. He was the only one she knew in the outfit, the only one she could talk to.

If I were a real doctor, maybe . . .

After doing all she can for the urgent cases she sets up an examination office of sorts, an upturned ammo crate for a chair, another one for her patients. Three men and one woman line up, all with minor injuries.

Frangie is in charge. She's the doc, at least for this part of the battalion.

All around her there is frantic activity as soldiers run a length of chain to a surviving truck and haul an overturned howitzer upright. The battery must be moved if they are to avoid another barrage.

"Sergeant Acey." It's the young lieutenant. His pale skin is covered with dust, so even in firelight he looks more gray than white. "There was nothing you could do for him?"

She is busy picking at a stubborn roll of medical tape. "No, sir. It was . . . Um." She grabs the tape end and pulls. "It was . . . It was bad."

"He was a good soldier." The dust on Lieutenant Penche's face reveals the track of a tear. He is shaken up.

He's not much older than I am.

"Yes, sir," she says. "I knew him. I know his folks. I can write them."

He shakes his head. "No, I'll write them. And the others. I mean, of course you can, but I must. It's my duty."

"That's the captain's job, isn't it, sir?"

"The captain . . . Well, he's not . . . I mean, with colored troops and how . . ." Lieutenant Penche realizes he's said too much and finishes lamely by saying, "Let's both write to his folks, you and me, Doc."

"Yes, sir."

"Is there anything you need here?" He doesn't seem to want to leave.

"Water, sir, if there is any."

He's relieved to be given something to do. "I'll do what I can."

She watches him walk away. He looks lost, somehow. He's swallowed up in the rush of soldiers and vehicles, and Frangie figures that's it, he's done what he thought he had to do and having discharged his duty she'll hear no more from him. But within ten minutes a five-gallon can of awful-tasting but satisfyingly wet water is delivered.

It takes the battalion an hour and a half before they can relocate and begin the job of doing unto others what's been done to them, and by then half a dozen soldiers have disappeared, melting into shadows and heading toward the rear.

Frangie has seen the insides of her hometown friend. When she writes his parents, she will not mention that. And she will try to forget it.

Then, as if she is receiving a vision, a glimpse ahead in time, like a newsreel of her future, Frangie knows that blood and bone, spasms and shrieks, terrible, terrible things will be her future so long as she is in this war.

She looks longingly back down the road, back toward safety, and thinks, *Let them court-martial me. Let them lock me up and call me a coward. I don't care. I can't do this.*

I can't.

Dear God in heaven, you know I can't.

25

RIO RICHLIN—A BEACH NEAR SOUSSE, TUNISIA, NORTH AFRICA

"Off the beach, off the beach! Come on!"

The person yelling sounds authoritative, and Rio responds, moves, moves, anything to get away from the scene of Kerwin Cassel's death, from the salty smell of his blood, from the memory of a beating heart come to full rest.

It's a panic reaction, a visceral need to get away, to put distance between herself and death, and it almost gets her killed. She stands up and instantly earns a shout of, "Stay low, you stupid bugger!" in a British accent. It's Jack. "Sorry, Rio, didn't mean—" His unnecessary apology stops abruptly when they hear shouts and gunfire and then . . .

Crump!

Crump!

Two grenades go off in rapid succession, and the

machine gun falls silent. Shots. Slow, aimed, deliberate. Someone is finishing off whoever the grenades didn't kill. Shooting bullets into human beings.

Liefer yells something about getting the wounded onto the boats, but most of the boats are gone already, racing away to safety in deeper water.

What will they do with Cassel? He has to go home. He has to go home.

A coal miner and his haggard wife, that's what Rio pictures. Pictures them getting the telegram all the way up in the steep, green hills of West Virginia.

"Second Squad, over here!" Sergeant Cole, somewhere in the darkness ahead, for once not mumbling.

Rio can't see where "over here" is, but she runs toward the sound of his voice, runs hunched over until she plows into a seated soldier and hits the sand face-first.

"What the hell?" Cat's voice.

"Sorry, Preeling."

"Jeez, Richlin, you kneed me in the neck."

"I said sorry."

Rio spits sand and struggles into a kneeling position. After a moment it occurs to her that she should probably level her rifle. She adopts the textbook kneeling firing position, with one shin flat on the ground, the other vertical with her knee up, elbow on knee, rifle leveled. At Cole.

"Excellent position, Richlin," he says, looming up out of the dark. "But if you shoot me, I will be irritated at you."

"Sarge got the machine gun!" Suarez says, running up and kicking sand as he does. He's excited. Giddy. "You should have seen him, it was—"

"Knock it off," Cole snaps. "The Tommies say we're on the wrong beach."

"What?" half a dozen voices chorus. Followed by variations on, "Lousy navy," and "It figures," and assorted curses and nervous witticisms.

"We want to be that way." Cole points with a chopping motion. "About two miles."

"Two miles? We're off by two bloody miles?" Jack demands. "Well, that's a bit much, what?"

Jack is playing up his posh-sounding British accent for laughs.

"Don't you know this is Uncle Adolf's's private beach here," Cat says. "No GIs allowed."

"Where's Cassel?" Jenou asks, looking around at the dark faces.

Rio has the answer and it's on the tip of her tongue, but when it comes down to it, she can't say the words. She does not want to say that he is dead. She isn't ready to believe it herself. Kerwin dead? No, that's nuts. But there's a mix of sand and blood grit between her fingers.

"Cassel's not coming." She doesn't mean to sound terse but she's feeling sick, and one more word and she might be sick. Jack makes eye contact, moves slightly as if he would comfort Rio but thinks better of it and instead pulls off his helmet to push his unruly red hair back.

The jittery smartass talk dies out then for a while. They straighten their gear, take long pulls from their canteens, cast worried looks around, and follow Cole as he feels his way forward, leaving the beach.

"Topping this dune, keep low. Don't give them a silhouette."

They keep low.

Cassel. Dead.

Beyond the dune there's a dip, a sort of natural ditch partly choked with straw-like beach grass. The depression runs parallel to the beach and they follow this, relieved to be able to stand up. A low, reassuring conversation starts up again.

"Sarge blew the hell out of that machine gun."

"Is Cassel hurt?"

"Are they evacuating him?"

"Who was shooting, was that a German?"

"Cassel bought it."

"Bought what?"

"Just some fugging Italian, I heard, not Krauts. But Sarge got them with grenades, boom, boom."

"Keep quiet," Sergeant Cole says, and there's a raggedness to his voice. "Shut up and whoever's got their canteen banging, tighten it down. Keep your interval."

Keeping an interval is easier said than done moving through pitch darkness where the person in front of you disappears within twenty yards.

Rio follows Jenou and, as far as she can tell, is followed in turn by Sticklin.

I'm lost. We're all lost. Cassel most of all.

A runner from Lieutenant Liefer comes huffing and puffing up behind them and only barely avoids being shot by yelling, "Mustard, mustard!"

Jenou says, "Ketchup!" She's the only one to remember the call sign.

Rio bends down and wipes the blood off her hands onto a sparse tuft of sere grass. But it's on her rifle as well. So she tries to wipe that with the tail of her shirt, which is soaked with salt water and coated with wet sand. Not good for the mechanism of her rifle, but necessary. She feels wrong, feels like she's destroying evidence of Kerwin's life, like she's trying to forget him, insulting his memory by needing to get his blood off her.

Luther Geer, his voice quieter than usual, asks, "Is Cassel dead?"

Rio's stomach heaves, and she vomits off to the side. Trying to be discreet. Trying not to look weak. Like a girl.

"Let it go, Geer," Stick says quietly.

The runner is with Cole, and in defiance of orders the squad gathers around to eavesdrop.

"Loot says this is the wrong way," the runner announces nervously, anticipating a hostile reaction. "Go inland. She says there's a road."

"I'm in a nice sheltered gully here," Cole answers. "I've got cover. She wants us on an open road instead?"

"Orders from the limey captain. Plus they can't drive the jeep down this gully."

"The half-track can do it."

"Bit of a SNAFU there, Sarge: our only remaining half-track took a round right through the engine block. We got a jeep. One jeep."

"Uh-huh," Cole says, and spits. "And what squad is taking point on this little stroll down a wide-open road where we don't know where we are?"

"You're farthest south," the runner says, and shrugs to show that it's not his decision, he's just the messenger.

"Swell," Cole mutters. He grabs Rio's sleeve and pulls her aside. "You all right?"

"Yeah, just like delayed seasickness or something."

"You can't dwell on it, Richlin." The way he says it makes it clear he knows this is not about seasickness. "You put it aside. You put it all in a box, and you don't open that box until after."

"Right, Sarge. I'm fine."

"Yeah, we're all just great," Cole says. "Okay, Geer? You take point. Richlin, you have his back. Castain and Pang take the rear. The other squads will be on our six, so Castain and Pang, do not shoot them. They will be irritated with us if we shoot them."

"Right, Sarge."

Rio has a moment to wonder which is worse: being in the front, or bringing up the rear. Then again, if you happen to be a German gunner you might aim for the middle of the column, so . . .

"Don't watch Geer," Stick mutters so only Rio can hear. "Look past him. Right? And use your ears too."

"Yeah, Stick," Rio says, hoping she sounds tough and confident, but secretly glad of any advice. Private Geer (and his kitten) is on point, but she neither likes nor trusts the big redhead.

Stick, on the other hand, pays close attention and takes soldiering seriously, but he's humping the BAR so he can't be walking point.

He hasn't talked much about it, but once in a tipsy pub conversation back in Britain during extended training, Stick let slip to Rio that he came from money. With his connections and smarts, Stick could easily have arranged a soft job far, far from the front lines. He could have had an officer's commission without too much effort, and could have found a place on some general's staff where he would sleep in a feather bed every night. He has chosen instead to serve as a private and to request the infantry.

No one *requests* the infantry. Rio sure as hell didn't.

Luther seems to think he's being singled out for his skills, and he puffs out his chest as he swaggers out in front, his face too bright against black night. Rio hears the soft rattle of something in his pack, the crunch of his boots, the sloshing of water in his canteen. She even hears when he farts. But she can see him only as an indistinct gray shape.

Rio is next in line. Behind her Tilo, then Stick, then Sergeant Cole, who will make a habit of never being far from point, but never so far up front that he's the first guy shot.

Absolutely no one but no one wants Cole shot. As far as Rio can tell, Sergeant Cole is the only one who knows what's going on, or at least can pretend to. Corporal Millican has a little rank, but Rio worries about him, and the truth is, Millican worries even more about himself. Corporal's stripes do not a leader make.

They stumble around in the sand until they find the road, and, while it might be more exposed, it's a whole lot easier to walk along mostly dry, hard-packed dirt interrupted in low spots by shallow patches of slick mud.

Rio peers deep into the darkness on either side of the

road, head swiveling, just like she's been taught. Is that a German helmet or a rock? Is that a bush or a man squatting behind a machine gun? Are there eyes out there in the night seeking just as eagerly for her?

Geer walks with his weapon resting in the crook of his left elbow, right arm looped through the strap. Rio does the same, though she occasionally blows into her hands or sticks her fingers under her arm to ward off the chill. It is cold, cold in the desert night, which they all agree is a travesty, a violation of the laws of the universe, and a damned dirty trick for the god of weather to play on them.

At first they move slowly, cautiously, then word comes forward to pick up the pace, they don't have all night, so Geer takes longer strides and the rest follow.

"How'd he go?" Tilo stage-whispers. "Richlin. How'd he go?"

Rio considers pretending not to understand, but she understands fine, and Tilo and the others have a right to know. Kerwin had been everyone's friend. Well, mostly. Luther never liked him much, and not being at all good-looking, he'd been all but ignored by Jenou.

"Two bullets, chest and neck," Rio says at last. The callous tone of her voice surprises her. She doesn't feel callous. She feels like her soul has been sandpapered raw.

She listens to her news being whispered back down the

line. She waits for Cole to put an end to it, but he remains silent, knowing they need to digest this new reality.

"Was it . . . ?" Suarez doesn't know quite how to finish that sentence.

"It didn't take long," Rio says. "Doc did his best, but the whole thing, maybe two minutes." A very long two minutes. Two minutes that will resonate, that will spread into all the minutes to follow.

There is no follow-up question. The remaining eleven members of the squad ruminate on the fact that a man can be alive and talking and normal, and a second later be bleeding on the sand, and dead within two minutes.

Two minutes.

A long time for a dying man to think about the things he'll never experience.

There are photos in Rio's inner pocket, wrapped in oil-cloth to keep the wet at bay. She wants to look at these pictures. She wants to remember those memories. She wants to push the other thing, this new and terrible thing, down below those gentler memories, dismiss it, put it in a box, like Sarge said.

In some way she cannot explain, Kerwin's death makes Rachel's death more real. Until now death has been an idea, a thing she could examine from a safe distance. It has touched her, but only through loss, not physically, not graphically, not with blood on her hands. One day Rachel was alive in Rio's mind, the next she was gone, and Rio misses her, but Rachel's death happened far away. Rio has had to imagine Rachel's death. Cassel's death requires no imagination.

"Probably didn't hit the dirt fast enough." A barely audible whisper from Jenou, bunching up like she shouldn't. Instinctively moving closer to Rio.

"He never was quick," someone else offers. "Still . . ."

"Yeah . . ."

"Okay, knock it off," Cole says, finally shutting the whispers down now that everyone had at least been told the basics. "Back in line, Castain, and keep your goddamn intervals."

What else should I tell them? The way his last breath made a sound like a straw at the bottom of a milk shake? The way he emptied his bowels so that he stank? The slickness of his blood? The way it looked like chocolate syrup in the dark?

They march on, miles passing beneath sore feet. Now the sky is clearing as thick, low cloud gives way to the higher, thinner stuff. The moon has set, but the stars are able to peek through in patches, so now Rio can actually see where she's going and even see a bit beyond Luther.

Heel, toe. Heel, toe. She hears the cadence call in her head. *Your left, your left, your left, right, left.* The soft crunch of boots on hard dirt. The squishy sound when they hit mud. The many sounds of straps chafing, and uniform pants rubbing, and packs straining, and her helmet riding on the tops of Rio's ears, which means she needs to adjust her helmet liner, though not just now. Definitely not taking her helmet off just now.

They were taught in basic that a helmet is not there to stop bullets. It is just there to stop ejected rifle brass and falling shrapnel from hitting your head. A bullet? A German rifle bullet will pass right through the steel helmet like a hot knife through butter.

Rio isn't taking her helmet off to adjust it, no, not just yet; she'll take what armor she can get. She's seen now what bullets do. But after a while Rio's mind travels away. It goes to that far-off movie theater. It goes to the last letter from Strand, the one where he sounded just the slightest bit distant, as though maybe he had not really been in the mood to write to her.

From there it goes to questions of whether she was a fool thinking that one real date, a few stolen kisses on the *Queen Mary*, and a couple of letters mean they have a real relationship. What are they, even? Boyfriend and girlfriend? Absurd. Going steady? Those are school notions. Those terms are from another life.

And from there her memory inevitably wanders to the *Tiburon* and Jack. She glances back at him but sees nothing but his helmet over Sticklin's shoulder.

It was nothing, really. Nothing. *Really.* Even Jenou said it was nothing. Forget it. Rio is Strand's girl. But that definite statement leads her imagination to questions about women in the air corps. They are almost certainly pretty. Why wouldn't they be? Of course they are: a smart, good-looking young woman would naturally choose air corps over army, if she could, and if she had a lick of sense.

In my own defense, I just wanted to drive a truck.

Strand is probably already bored with the idea of her, of little Rio from Nowhere, America. Yes, he is from that same nowhere, but that will just make some bold floozy from the big city all the more enticing to him.

She chews on that for a few miles and then begins to think about life after the war. What would that be? First, she will finish school, of course. Then . . . Well, what then? College? She would be only the second person in her family to ever finish high school, and if she went to college, the first Richlin ever to do so.

Or she could forget schooling, get married, and have children. And cook. And clean house. Help the children with their homework. Say things like, "Just wait till your father gets home."

Not yet. First this. First war.

Gradually, as the long, slow miles pass, Rio stops thinking about anything really, and just walks. She's had practice at that. Walking doesn't take much thought after the first few miles.

The sun turns the horizon pink, then golden, the light picking out random objects—a single big boulder sitting all by itself, a stump, a misshapen tree, the peaks of the mountains in the distance off to the right. A random beam of sunlight peeking just for a moment through the clouds brightens half of Jenou's face but leaves her eyes in the shadow of her helmet. But the dawn has not penetrated the space directly ahead of the column; they march still toward darkness.

Somewhere out there artillery is blasting away, a sound like far-off thunder. Someone was catching hell, and she hopes it's them, the enemy.

Kill them all, artillery, kill them all before they can kill me.

"Geer, fall back. Richlin, take point," Cole says.

"But, Sarge, I'm—" Geer starts to complain.

"Private Geer, when I tell you to fall back, fall back." No yelling, no threat, just that calm authority Cole always seems to convey.

And suddenly Rio is walking point.

Behind her stretch two American platoons and one British platoon. Ahead of her, presumably the enemy. Or maybe just more desert.

Possibly lions.

We're out front because we're expendable, she realizes. It's the British commandos who matter; they're the experienced soldiers and thus more valuable.

The platoon's been briefed on the basics of the mission: a crossroads, then a detachment of *Nachrichtentruppe,* the communications arm of the German army. They were believed not to be defended and were expected to be easy prey.

"Shoot 'em up, blow up their radios, and run like hell," that was the short version of the mission.

Run like hell back to boats that may or may not be there.

She freezes. Something ahead. On the road.

It takes several frazzled seconds, several tentative steps, before she recalls the hand signal for "freeze." She cocks her left elbow, raises her left hand, and makes a fist. Nevertheless Tilo Suarez, who has been sleep-marching, plows into her.

"Hey," he protests.

"Shut up, Suarez! Sarge!" This in urgent whispers.

Sergeant Cole holds his palm out to the soldiers behind him, then motions for them to drop and take cover. The squad, and then the rest of the platoon, takes a knee and waits. Sticklin trots off the road, drops, and readies his BAR.

"What do you see, Richlin?" Cole is at her side, hunched low.

It's still just early morning. The hope of a colorful sunrise fades, and now the light is the gray of raw oysters as cloud covers the horizon.

Rio peers down the road through the gloom, squints, and lowers her head slightly, trying for a different perspective.

"I think it's a man, Sarge. I think he's got a light."

Cole draws a deep breath. "I think you may be right. I make it a man and some kind of lantern. You've got good eyes, Richlin. Okay. Advance slowly."

Advance?

"Sarge?"

"Go on, Richlin. Keep your eyes open, issue the challenge, anything happens hit the deck and we'll open up. Stick? Heads up with that BAR."

The man—if that's indeed what it is—stands about two hundred yards up the road. There is a hut off to the man's right, a low adobe structure no bigger than a garden toolshed. But there could easily be a couple of German infantrymen in there. There could be a machine gun.

It can happen so fast. Instantly. Without warning. Like it had to Kerwin.

To him. But not to me.

"Mustard!" Rio yells, louder and shakier than she intends.

No answer. She raises her rifle to her shoulder. She

sights on the figure. She flicks off the safety.

Elevation? Windage?

"Mustard! Answer or I shoot!"

"Is it shallots? Do not shoot, I beg you!"

The words are heavily accented. German accent? Or Italian?

"Why shouldn't I shoot?"

"Because I am not your enemy."

"Put your hands up in the air!"

The lantern, if that's what it is, rises from below waist height to above head height. This has the effect of spilling yellow light down on the head of an old man dressed in an aged uniform that he has not been able to button all the way.

"I'm moving up, Sarge." Rio's mouth tastes of bile. Her heart pounds, but instinct reassures her: it's just one old man. But then again, there is the hut, a closed door, a window dark in shadow.

"Stick!" Rio yells.

"Yeah!"

"Watch that doorway." Then, to the man with the accent, "I'm coming forward. Anyone comes out of that building, we open up."

"You have nothing to fear, *mon ami*."

I have plenty to fear.

Keeping her rifle sighted she walks steadily forward.

"It's just a man," Rio yells back to Cole. "One guy. He's not armed."

Cole barks orders for Magraff, Suarez, and Pang to rush the building. "Look out for booby traps." Then he trots up to Rio. Together they look the man in the road over.

He is perhaps fifty-five or sixty-five years old, with weary, heavily bagged but humorous eyes, and a magnificent handlebar mustache that's eaten the lower half of his face. He's holding a lantern and having some difficulty keeping it up in the air. There is no weapon visible, and the uniform, while aged, carries a patch with the flag of France. The old flag, the one before the occupation. There are medals on his chest.

In the middle of the road he has placed a stone, smaller than Rio's helmet. Leaned against this stone is a small child's slate chalkboard with the word *Barricade* written on two lines. *Barri* and *Cade*.

"Okay, bud, what's your story?" Cole asks.

"May I lower the lantern? My strength is not what it once was . . ."

"Fine. Now who the hell are you?"

"I am Sergeant Maxim LeFevre, of the army of France."

"Okay, Sergeant Le . . . whatever," Sergeant Cole says. "Why are you standing here in the middle of the goddamn road?" Cole still has his tommy gun trained on the man.

"I have been returned to active duty through no desire of my own, I assure you. And I have been tasked to set up a barricade to slow the advance of any American troops on the roads."

For a full thirty seconds neither Rio nor Cole can think of anything to say to that.

Jillion Magraff calls out, "Building's clear, Sarge."

Rio and Sergeant Cole lower their weapons.

"You're here to slow our advance?"

The Frenchman shrugs, and with the fine nuance of his people manages with that shrug to convey helplessness, cynicism, and amusement. "I must follow orders, yes? So I have set up a barricade. *Une barricade symbolique.* A symbolic barricade."

"A symbolic barricade?"

The man indicated the rock and the sign. "*Comme vous voyez.* As you see."

"And you lit a lamp so . . ."

"So my American friends should see the barricade and not stub their toes en route to killing the *Boche.*"

Rio notices Cole peering closely at what GIs called fruit salad: the medals that adorn the man's chest. Rio is on the point of laughing in a mixture of relief and condescension, but Cole straightens up and extends a hand, which the old man shakes firmly, decorously.

"Sergeant LeFevre, I am Sergeant Cole, this is Private

Richlin. I'm sorry to say so, but I'm afraid I gotta take you prisoner. Don't you know all the Vichy people have come over to our side?"

"Of course, Sergeant, that is understood. But my commander, regrettably, has not. I regret to say that he is a true *collaborateur*, and in time, I hope to see him hanging by the neck." The old Frenchman indicates the building. "Will you and the lovely Private Richlin do me the honor of sharing a glass of brandy with me?"

"It's early for a drink."

"It is war, Sergeant, how can it be too early?"

"Point taken. The honor would be mine," Cole says. "Millican! Take point, keep 'em moving, we'll catch up. Preeling? Double-time back to the lieutenant, tell her we have an honored prisoner."

Rio follows the two into the building, shrugging at Jenou's unspoken question as they pass.

Inside is a bare room with the unmistakable feel of a place that has not been inhabited in some time. There is a rickety wood table with one leg missing, propped against a wall. On the table, a wedge of cheese, a heel of crusty French bread, and a bottle. The ceiling is so low that Sergeant Cole's helmet scrapes a crossbeam and he removes it and sticks it under his arm.

Cole breaks out his canteen cup, and Rio follows suit. The Frenchman pours Cole a healthy shot, and, after a disapproving glance that takes in Rio's age, he pours her a bare mouthful.

"To Free France and the American army," LeFevre says, raising his own glass.

"Free France," Cole agrees. At the moment he is not entirely pleased with the American army.

Rio is extremely leery of alcohol, clearly recalling the results of her first episode of drunkenness. But it would be impolite to refuse.

The burn in her throat leaves her wheezing embarrassingly. It's worse than whatever it was Jack gave her.

"We had some trouble coming ashore," Cole says.

"Indeed?"

"We lost a man. And we killed the gunner and two others with him. It looked like an isolated outpost, though word will be out and the Krauts will be on our tails before long."

"I am grieved by your loss," LeFevre says. "We are still somewhat divided, as you have seen. The generals in Algiers have joined the Free French, but not all are ready to abandon Vichy. Many fear what the Germans will do in Occupied France should we aid the Americans here in the colonies."

"SNAFU," Cole says, and when the Frenchman looks uncertain, explains, "Situation Normal: All Fugged Up."

LeFevre breaks into a big grin that pushes his mustache

up around his nose. "SNAFU. Hah! Delightful."

Liefer and Garaman arrive. The lieutenant looks around suspiciously. Garaman's experienced eye goes straight to the bottle.

"Better tie this man up and march him back to the beach," Liefer says.

"Lieutenant, a moment?" Cole asks. He draws her aside for a whispered five-minute conversation, during which the Frenchman smiles at Rio and says, "So it is true, that even the young women of America fight in this war? I do not approve. War is no place for a young woman."

"No place for anyone, far as I can tell," Rio says. She glances unconsciously at her hand. Chipped fingernail polish and, in the creases of her palm, blood.

Liefer, looking annoyed, comes over and says, "My sergeant here says you'll give us your parole. You won't fight or inform your superiors of our coming this way."

LeFevre's smile is not warm; the lieutenant lacks charm. "My orders were merely to erect a barricade. They neglected to order me to bring sufficient men as there were none available, and I have no orders to report back. My superior"—and at that he spits onto the floor—"is far from Algiers and still obeys his German masters like a faithful dog."

The lieutenant accepts that, though without grace and with a hard look at Sergeant Cole. "On your head, Cole," she says, and leaves.

Cole sticks out his hand again for the Frenchman, and they shake solemnly. He nods at the medals on the older man's chest. "I had two uncles in that war, sir. One came home. I intend to visit the other's grave should we make it to France."

"That was a very bad war," LeFevre says, too much feeling packed into such a short sentence.

"So I've heard."

"When you get to France, take care of your men—and women—Sergeant. Leave no more dead Americans in French graveyards."

Cole holds out his canteen cup. "I'll drink to that."

The two soldiers share a last drink of brandy and a silence that leaves Rio feeling very much like an outsider.

Then, Jenou's voice from outside. "Sarge! Tanks!"

26

RIO RICHLIN—A BEACH NEAR SOUSSE, TUNISIA, NORTH AFRICA

There are many words that an infantry soldier does not want to hear: *patrol*, *dig*, *march*, *volunteer*, *air raid*, *incoming*.

And *tank*.

Rio runs from the old French soldier's hut followed by Cole. Liefer is standing up in the jeep scanning the road ahead as a hazy dawn picks out details of the surrounding countryside.

No tank is in sight, but there's a sound, a sound Rio has heard before but only from friendly tanks during training. It's the sound of a barely muffled engine, punctuated by occasional backfires, the grinding of gears, and an unmistakable rapid metallic *clank-clank-clank-clank-clank* of treads.

"What's that sound like to you?" Liefer snaps at Cole and Garaman.

"Sounds like tanks, Lieutenant," Garaman says, shooting a meaningful look at Cole. "And not far off." They are the professionals, the sergeants; they share something that does not include Lieutenant Liefer, still less Private Rio Richlin.

"Okay," the lieutenant says. "I'm scouting forward, see what I can see. Cole, deploy your squad. Garaman, send a runner back to the captain and Lieutenant Helder. And get the rest of Fifth Platoon into defensive position."

She drops herself smartly into the passenger seat of the jeep, which her corporal driver guns, slamming her back.

Garaman spits tobacco juice and says, "I imagine the Tommies will form up back down the road. So, Cole, I figure your people fire a couple of rounds to keep the Krauts' heads down, then fall back, hope to draw them in. Is that how you see it?"

"Yep," Sergeant Cole says.

"And make sure your people don't shoot the Loot when she comes hightailing it back."

"Sure about that?" Cole says dryly. He snaps out orders. "Second Squad, right-hand side of the road. There's not much cover, so dig while you can. Millican, get the bazooka set up on that little hump there where you can cover the road. Pang, you load; Magraff, watch their backs. Stick, farther off by that, whatever the hell that is, that stumpy tree. Dig in, don't fire until you have targets, and let Corporal Millican get off the first shot with the bazooka. Preeling with Stick. Castain, you're running ammo. Get a box of thirty-caliber up here and another pouch of bazooka rockets if you can handle it. Richlin, Suarez, you're with me."

For a moment no one moves. Then, in a perfectly calm, even pedantic voice, Cole says, "Not next week, now."

The bazooka team runs for the very slight elevation, while Sticklin and Cat race, heads low, for the tree that is a whole lot more like a bush once they look at it.

"All right, Richlin and Suarez, we're taking the left side of the road."

The three of them run forward, boots loud on pebbly soil, Cole in the lead, a scared and excited Rio in his wake, Suarez bringing up the rear.

Rio sees Jenou and the others across the road, on their knees, wielding their entrenching tools with unusual vigor, scraping away enough crusty sand and rock to provide at least some sort of cover. They have a slight bit of elevation, not a hill or even a rise, but the road slopes downward and curves away behind a second rise, so while it is slightly lower than the platoon, it is mostly out of sight until the last half mile. The tanks will have to emerge from the shadow of that rise to follow the road past Rio's position. This should give Millican a clear shot with the bazooka.

"Down," Cole says, pointing at the ground. "Make

sure not to shoot toward our people, they will be irritated if you do."

"I'm shooting?" It comes out as a squeak.

"That's why the army invited you two to this little war. Aside from Stick, you two are the best shots in the squad."

"Swell," Suarez mutters under his breath.

Rio sees the squads of Fifth Platoon digging in a couple hundred yards behind them, and presumably Third Platoon is behind them. They only have a little more cover than Rio, but they're farther from that relentless *clank-clank-clank* and the hollow growl of the tank engines, and she thinks she'd rather be back there. Or back anywhere.

Won't be a paper target this time.

Suddenly the jeep barrels back down the road going flat-out and kicking up a plume of dust.

The jeep brakes in a shower of dust and gravel, and Liefer yells, "Two German tanks and a whole goddamn company of Italian infantry!" before tearing away again toward the rear.

She has given no orders. She has shouted a warning and disappeared. Rio sees a dark look in Cole's eyes. Suarez looks nervous, but Rio is pretty sure he'll do what he needs to do. Tilo Suarez might be a pain in the butt sometimes with his tiresome Lothario act, but he'll do what he has to do.

Will I?

The sound of tank treads grows louder and louder, nearer and nearer, like the slow approach of a movie villain. Rio manages to push about ten inches of dirt and rock in front of herself and lies down in the laughably shallow depression. She rests her left hand on the dirt and points her rifle. Suarez has followed suit. He's twenty feet to her right.

"Set sights for two hundred yards," Cole says.

Rio hasn't even thought of adjusting her sights. It shames her being reminded, and she quickly clicks the elevation wheel. There is no breeze to speak of, no need to adjust for windage.

And suddenly there they are.

They seem almost to rise out of the desert, two tan steel monsters come to destroy, Panzer IIIs, two-inch main gun, two machine guns. The barrel of the lead tank's gun is pointed directly at Rio.

It sees me!

The absurdity of facing a tank with just a rifle comes home full force. The tank doesn't care about her pitiful rifle, or the human being holding it. The tank doesn't care about anything made of flesh and blood.

The Italian soldiers are a ramshackle mob walking in front of the tanks with more on the flanks. If the column on the left side just keeps walking the way they are they'll walk directly into Rio, Suarez, and Sergeant Cole.

Five hundred yards, a quarter mile. The enemy infantry are sketched figures, two legs, two arms, a circle of head, just sticks, no face, no expression, no individuality. Yet there's an air of weariness about them, a sense of exhaustion.

"At least they didn't spot the jeep," Cole mutters.

"How do you know . . . ?" Rio starts to ask, but then decides she probably isn't supposed to be asking questions at a time like this.

Cole answers anyway. "From the way they walk. They haven't sent out flankers, their heads are down, rifles slung."

Now that she looks more carefully, Rio sees the same thing: the Italians are not expecting to be fired upon, or perhaps they are and have just given up caring. And yet, they are coming on, and they are bringing tanks with them.

"Maybe they'll stop," Tilo says, which makes no sense to Rio. Of course they'll keep coming, they'll keep coming at the same leisurely pace until someone fires on them.

They'll be surprised, the Italians, as well as the German tankers. But surprise wasn't going to gain the Americans much, not with just two platoons of green troops. The enemy column stretches as far as she can see, a full company of men, easily two hundred or so. Twelve hundred Italians might be manageable by themselves, but they aren't by themselves. They are very definitely not by themselves.

Clank-clank-clank-clank-clank.

Four hundred yards.

Rio swallows dust. Her hands sweat on the stock of her rifle. Cole is on his knees like a prairie dog, watching the enemy, glancing toward his men, glancing back at the rest of the force. The British commandos are way back, out of sight. The Americans are as dug in as they're going to get in bare rock, sand, and pebbles.

"We'll bang on 'em, then fall back," Cole says.

"Right."

"No time for a decent ambush. But make your shots count. Discourages the others if you shoot a few."

"Uh." That short grunt is all the speech Rio can manage. Suarez is silent.

Three hundred yards. Millican and Pang are the bazooka team, and they are roughly fifty yards closer to the enemy. Millican will fire at two hundred yards. Bazookas are pretty accurate at one hundred to two hundred yards, not much use beyond that unless you get lucky.

Watch your breathing. Slow it down. In, out, slow.

"Okay, Millican, get ready," Sergeant Cole mutters, as if willing his corporal to strike at the right moment. "Wait till you've got 'em . . ."

"Unh?" Rio grunts, thinking he's talking to her.

She remembers firing the bazooka a few times back at Camp Maron. They are surprisingly simple weapons, a 54-inch section of pipe just 2.36 inches in diameter, with a chunky wooden trapezium stock and a stubby grip for each hand. Two batteries hide inside that primitive wooden stock—a tiny bulb will light up if you pull the trigger when the launcher is empty. The light on means you have enough juice to fire the round.

Pang carries two bazooka pouches, each containing three cylinders that hold the 3.5-pound rockets. He's already pushed one in the back of the tube and pulled the safety clip clear.

Suddenly there's a hollow bang, like someone striking an empty steel barrel with a hammer, and a puff of smoke.

The rocket flies right over the top of the lead tank.

"Damn it!"

The bazooka round has knocked the casualness right out of the enemy. Rio sees them diving off to the sides of the road. They may be tired, but they run and jump with impressive speed.

Good. Just stay down.

But they don't stay down, because now a German staff car, an open, gray-painted saloon, comes tearing up the side of the road, bouncing madly, and nearly driving right over cowering Italians, who have to roll from cover to avoid being hit.

A somewhat portly German officer in the backseat of the staff car yells a blue streak at the Italians, a shrill and tinny sound at this distance. He gesticulates furiously, gestures that very clearly mean, "Get up there in front of the tanks!"

Some of the Italians heed his demands, and some do not but instead stay flat on the ground, very much like Rio and Tilo.

A second round flies from Hark Millican's bazooka. And this time it hits the side of the leading tank's turret . . . and glances off. It explodes harmlessly two hundred yards off in the dirt. But it seems to have grazed or perhaps just frightened the lead tank commander who'd been heads-up in the hatch, because he drops out of sight, as does his counterpart in the second tank, both as fast as whack-a-moles. Now slowly, slowly but inexorably, the tank's big gun comes swinging toward the bare bit of elevation where Millican, Pang, and Magraff squat. Magraff backs away fast, trips and falls, jumps up and runs.

"Millican! Get out of there! Move!" Cole yells. Millican jumps up, drops the bazooka, and hightails it after Magraff, but Pang snatches up the bazooka and run-hobbles away, trying to balance the long tube on one shoulder while pressing down on the ammo pouch to keep it from banging against his hip.

BANG! The tank fires. That flat, metallic sound is followed instantly by a larger explosion as the shell blows apart the ground where Millican was just seconds before. Dust hides Hansu Pang from view.

Is Pang hit?

"Fall back!" Cole roars through cupped hands, but falling rock and dirt from the explosion and the shouts of the Italian infantry drown him out. "Put some fire on them!"

It takes Rio several seconds to realize what he means. That he means that *she* should shoot. The sergeant is armed with a tommy gun, useless at this range: this is rifle work. This is M1 Garand work.

Across the road the cloud of dust from the tank round blocks Sticklin's view, which means there are only two rifles in a position to be fired. One is in Rio's sweaty hands, the stock pressed to her cheek.

She takes aim. They've taught her never to fire without picking a target. One individual target.

One man.

That one? The one to the left?

Her finger is on the trigger. The safety is off. The rifle has a two-stage trigger. Pull first to take up slack. Then just the barest movement to fire. Five pounds of pressure on stage one. The same but a shorter pull for the actual firing.

Her heart seems both too slow and too fast, like a car being run through the gears regardless of the engine.

The first pull.

Pull the trigger again and—

"Shoot!" Sergeant Cole yells.

Convulsively Rio pulls the trigger.

The recoil punches her shoulder, but she's used to that. She does not see where her shot goes—no way to be sure since she has not really aimed. Not really. Not like she did when she earned her Sharpshooter badge.

Cole yells again. "Second Squad, fall back! Fall back!" and in a quieter tone, "Not you two."

The tanks are moving again, *clank-clank*ing down the road, shifting through the gears. They'll be here in thirty seconds. Their shells will arrive sooner.

"Richlin! Suarez! Lay down some fugging fire," Sergeant Cole yells.

Now he's firing his tommy gun, .45 caliber slugs in short bursts, a *chug-a-chug-a-chug* sound, but it's nothing but a noisemaker at this distance.

Shoot, Rio. Shoot.

She aims. A man in a yellow-tan uniform. Two hundred yards away.

He's perfectly centered between the two curved uprights

of the front sight, chest resting on the stubby center post, all contained within the circle of the rear sight.

She draws a breath and lets it out as slowly as her racing metabolism will allow and—

BAM!

The familiar kick to her shoulder. The familiar cordite smell. The metallic *clang* as the spent brass spins through the air before dropping to the ground.

The Italian soldier trips. He falls to one knee.

He tripped. That's all.

The Italian drops his rifle. He clutches his thigh.

My God, I hit him!

"Keep it up, pour it on!"

Chug-a-chug-a-chug-chug-a-chug-a-chug!

Take aim.

Choices. Three or four men in view. Which?

You. The one with the mustache.

Breathe in, out sloooow . . .

BAM!

A miss. She breathes a sigh of relief, only no, no, now the Italian is falling. Straight back. Like he's falling in slow motion, an optical illusion that makes it seem that he's shrinking not falling, until suddenly his knees buckle and his entire body crumples.

A sob escapes her. She looks desperately to her right. Suarez is a ghost, pale, staring down the barrel of his rifle. Has he fired?

Beyond him she sees the rest of Second Squad falling back, Hansu Pang alive still and hauling the bazooka, all of them are running low, holding their helmets with one hand, Millican alive too, Jenou with steel ammo boxes in each hand, struggling to run. The lead tank turns slightly and—

BOOM!

This round sails harmlessly over the squad's heads to explode beyond them.

"Keep it coming, Richlin!"

Another target. Find the man. Find the one man who is going to die.

No, I don't want to, no, I don't want to.

Her body is a single tensed muscle, she's hard as a board, her teeth will break if she clenches any harder.

Tougher now. They're running.

The Italians know now they're being fired on, they know they're exposed and no matter what the Kraut officer yelled, they are ducking, running, cowering behind the tank, some preparing to return fire, most just trying to make themselves as small as possible.

You.

BAM!

"Aaaahh!" Rio cries, and the sound is something animalistic, some terrible blend of terror and triumph.

"Okay, Richlin, let's go!" Cole grabs her shoulder, and she is aware in a distant, disconnected way that he's had to repeat it a couple of times, so she rolls over, gets awkwardly to her knees, then jumps up to run with bullets whizzing by overhead.

They run, the three of them, and ahead now she sees the rest of the squad. Jenou, still okay it seems, still hauling ammo though she's lost her helmet and her short-cut blond hair is like a bird in panicked flight. The rear tank sends another round after them, blowing another hole in the desert, and lends speed to Rio's legs.

It is flat-out, undignified running, track and field, kicking divots in the dirt.

Italian soldiers see them fleeing and now aim, aim at her, willing their bullets to find her, to blow a hole in her, to see her fall, to see her die. They're shouting in their foreign tongue, angry, scared shouts, firing fast, bullets everywhere.

Rio runs, Cole just behind her, Suarez ahead, runs and up ahead some rocks and the other squad is up in there, squinting from beneath their helmets, aiming their rifles but not shooting yet, not wanting to hit Second Squad.

Rio pants and sweats though it is still cold, even with the sun coming up now in a clearing sky. She runs to catch up to her own long shadow.

Suddenly the rest of the platoon opens up, blazes away at the advancing Italians as Rio, Suarez, and the sergeant rush past them, but already Rio sees some breaking, pelting away from the advancing Panzers.

Rio falls into a bare scraped depression in the ground, each frantic breath painful in her raw throat. Her heart pounds like it will physically break her breastbone. Tilo Suarez drops beside her.

"Fugging tanks!" he yells.

"Unh," she grunts in response.

"Never even got a chance to get off a shot," he says, like he's making an excuse, like he's defending himself.

I shot at them.

Tilo says, "On us too fast. We're going to have to pull back. Tanks." He sounds panicked.

The Italians hang back a little now as the rest of both platoons fire into them. They hold back, letting the tanks run on ahead, but now there's the German officer again in the staff car, yelling, berating them in harsh, German-accented Italian, clearly audible despite the cacophony of rifle fire. He waves a baton of some sort, a riding crop, waves it furiously, demanding the infantry advance.

But the Italians, the distant descendants of the greatest empire the world has ever known, do not seem in a hurry to get shot at in this particular place at this particular time.

Yet there's no stopping the tanks. Someone from another squad fires a hasty bazooka round that does explode this time, but with all the apparent destructive effect of a cream puff thrown against a brick wall.

The tank fires back, and as the explosion fades Rio hears screams. She starts firing, somewhat wildly, not targeting, not picking out individual targets now, just shooting off the remaining rounds in her clip, which pops out with a musical *clang*. She cannot at that particular moment, cannot, just cannot coldly locate and target an enemy. She can manage to fire, she can make noise with her rifle, but she cannot right then take careful deadly aim and end another life.

She fumbles a clip from her belt and first tries to shove it in backward before turning it around and, with numb fingers, inserting it as she had done long ago in training, long ago, weeks ago, in the world of paper targets.

BANG! and *ka-boom!* A tank fires and punches a round into the dirt just thirty feet from Rio, pelting her with debris that rattles on her helmet and dusts her shoulders and clogs the air.

Cole yells, "Where's the Loot? Where's Liefer?"

If the lieutenant is around, no one knows where she is. But Platoon Sergeant Garaman comes running up just then and says, "Come on, Cole, we're falling back."

"Yeah," Cole says, because there isn't much else to say. It's GIs versus tanks, and the bazookas aren't doing a damned thing, so it's fall back or die. "Fall back to where?"

Garaman shakes his head. "I'll be damned if I know, Jedron."

It is the first time Rio has ever heard anyone call Sergeant Cole by his first name. It's a bad omen.

"Well, I guess we aren't knocking out any goddamn Kraut radio," Cole mutters as Garaman stumbles away, looking for the lieutenant.

All of Fifth Platoon is falling back. Running away. And seeing their backs, the emboldened Italians are hot on their heels and the tanks *clank-clank-clank* behind, the sound of doom.

Rio runs with Sergeant Cole, who, like a magnet passing through metal filings, draws the rest of Second Squad behind him. Panic threatens to take over, Rio can feel it, can feel the razor edge of her own panic. Her combat boots seem unnaturally loud scrambling across loose rock and sand, sometimes silent as she leaps small depressions, panting, panting, gasping for breath in a burning throat.

Ahead she sees a gun of some sort, like a howitzer but smaller. It has a vertical rectangle of steel plate pierced by about four feet of barrel. British commandos man it, four of them, judging by the shallow soup-bowl helmets crouching behind the gun. One of the commandos is improbably smoking a pipe.

"Get past that two-pounder, join up with the Tommies," Cole yells.

Rio goes tearing past the two-pounder, runs on another twenty feet and sees that the commandos have dug in, and drops herself into a foxhole no more than eighteen inches deep and just wide enough for her to cower in.

But the commando sergeant in the hole isn't having it. "You can bugger off, mate." Then he looks at her and does a double take. "Sorry, miss. But you still aren't taking my hole. Keep running, we'll take care of Jerry."

Rio hesitates, searches for Cole, and sees him in heated argument with the British captain, who keeps hacking at the air in a way that makes it clear he'd like the Americans to just keep on running.

Cole has no choice and yells for Fifth Platoon to fall back. He's not the platoon sergeant, still less the lieutenant, but he's there and seems to have some idea what he's doing, so both American platoons gladly accept his order and now all of them, all the Americans, run away. Run down the road. One soldier throws away his rifle the better to run.

It is a rout. It is panic, outright panic now.

It is about to get worse.

27

RAINY SCHULTERMAN—MAKTAR, TUNISIA, NORTH AFRICA

"Do they no longer teach spelling in school?" Sergeant Rainy Schulterman waves a paper in the air. "*There, their, they're.* Three different words! They are not interchangeable."

Steam comes from her mouth as she speaks. It is cold. She has been typing with fingerless gloves on, and, in addition to two T-shirts, two pairs of socks, her regular uniform, and a field jacket, she wears a sweater knitted by her aunt Zaz. Aunt Zaz (short for Zlota) is an indifferent craftsman, but she has had the great good sense to knit the sweater using olive drab yarn, so it does not scream civilian even though the crew neck peeks out from beneath Rainy's jacket.

She is assigned to a small, forward detachment of General Lloyd Fredendall's headquarters, largely, she believes, because she can type sixty words a minute with few errors, and she speaks fluent German. All too often for Rainy's taste this ends up meaning that she's just a glorified secretary.

In fact, she's noticing that the secretarial duties keep growing, while work related to her training and skills is handled by male soldiers.

The Detachment has an official numeric designation as part of II Corps, but is never called anything but "the Detachment" or occasionally, Maktar—the nearest Arab town—familiarly rendered as "Mucked Up."

General Fredendall has not endeared himself to his soldiers with his decision to keep his own headquarters very far to the rear, where he is rumored to be expending prodigious engineering energies and resources in building tunnels in mountains to safeguard himself from air raids that never come.

There is one good thing from Rainy's perspective. The general's distance has led to the establishment of various outposts—like cavalry forts in the Old West—around Algeria and Tunisia in a system that makes it still harder for the general to track or respond to events in the area of his command, which is essentially all of North Africa this side of Casablanca.

Having formed a harsh opinion of the general, Rainy is relieved not to be in the general's new cave.

On a couple of occasions Rainy has ventured into Maktar itself to see the magnificent Roman ruins dating back to Trajan. And from some of the windows in the Detachment's walled compound, Rainy can gaze out on a still-more-ancient Roman aqueduct. The area is neck-deep in history and unfortunately completely lacking in heat.

"What is it now, Schulterman?" Staff Sergeant Pooley, seated at the desk across from Rainy's, asks wearily.

"A report that says, '*They're—t-h-e-y apostrophe r-e*—tanks are coming through the gap,' is not the same as a report that says, '*Their—t-h-e-i-r*—tanks are coming through the gap.'"

The staff sergeant nods. He is twenty years older than Rainy and forms the calm counterpoint to her passion. He doesn't seem to dislike her, but neither does he see much use for her. He is old army, and absolutely no one old army favors women soldiers. Neither do 90 percent of new army officers and noncoms, but among the old guard it is unanimous. Nevertheless, Sergeant Pooley has never been unpleasant about it.

"Your language skills are commendable, Schulterman. Therefore consider yourself commended."

Rainy aims her big eyes at him and considers a smart-ass retort. But she likes Pooley. He has tolerated her, and she is aware that she's a person who requires tolerance, and not just because of her gender. The phrase "does not suffer fools gladly" very definitely applies to Rainy. She makes a note to herself to attempt greater tolerance for fools in the future.

Pooley's phone rings. He listens, says, "Yes, sir," and hangs up. "You're up, Schulterman. Staff meeting. They need someone to take notes."

Rainy jumps up, arranges her uniform, tries to squeeze the bulk out of her sweater, checks her hair, grabs her notebook and three sharpened pencils, and is on her way in fifteen seconds. Buck sergeants do not keep colonels waiting.

She slips unobtrusively into the conference room where Colonel George Jasper and his staff are gazing thoughtfully at a map spread out across a long, rectangular table.

The colonel is not an impressive figure. He is nearly as small as Rainy herself, is often indifferently turned out, has a lugubrious hound dog face, and despite being third-generation military and a professional soldier who graduated in the respectable middle of his West Point class, seems to have no gift for commanding respect. His staff officers range from incompetent to excellent, but the colonel, much like the general, his boss, has no great talent for differentiating the two.

They are discussing intelligence reports that the Germans are either launching or about to launch a full-scale attack. Rainy faithfully writes down the essentials of the conversation, using her own version of shorthand. "C" is the colonel. "S2" is his intelligence chief, Lieutenant Colonel Courter Clay, a sour-faced, brush-mustached, cold fish of a man with wide-set eyes that stare challengingly out from beneath impressive iron-filing eyebrows. He has the look of an unpleasant private school headmaster.

The other major participants in the conference are: 1) a British major named Wiltshire (W), who is supposed to be the liaison with the Britain forces but spends most of his time frowning at documents he doesn't read; 2) another lieutenant colonel, Kanly Coffee (KC), whose main duty appears to be acting as General Fredendall's spy; and 3) a major from the air corps named Bencell, abbreviated not as B but as (A) for air.

C—Likely just probe.

S2—Don't believe so. Three forward units report contact w/ German or mixed Germ-Ital units.

C—Reports like this before. What sense wd it make? Germans between us & Monty's whole army. No sense.

KC—If we panic at every report . . .

C—Maybe if we had air recon.

A—No planes to spare for recon.

C—Wiltshire?

W—Nothing. Monty does not see evidence of attack.

Rainy at this point could very well stop taking notes—she doesn't—because she's been around long enough to recognize the sounds of paralysis. The only officer she really trusts is the one she likes least: the S2, Colonel Clay.

Lieutenant Colonel Clay is, as Sergeant Pooley has observed, "a humorless prick," but he has energy and determination, which set him apart from the lethargy at this outpost, and indeed the lethargy throughout II Corps.

Eventually the colonel will decide to do nothing other than forward a memo to the general, who will also decide to do nothing. It takes Colonel Jasper another half hour to reach that point, but the conclusion Rainy writes down is not a surprise. Nor is it a surprise when the colonel moves on to a much more passionate discussion involving kerosene heaters.

Is it treason to suspect that the men commanding II Corps are incompetent? Surely the powers-that-be in Washington would not send incompetents to oversee America's first real contact with the German foe.

Rainy tells herself that, but she fails to convince.

When she returns to her desk to type up her notes, Pooley looks up questioningly and gets a terse "They're going to wait and see" from Rainy.

She types up her notes and puts them in the "out" basket on her desk. They will be collected by the corporal, who will take them to the staff sergeant—Pooley—seated just five feet away—who will take them to the colonel's aide, who will, as far as Rainy can tell, file them away, never to be seen again.

At times she envies the frontline troops. At least they know what they are doing.

"Where's the goddamned interpreter?" This is from Colonel Clay, the S2, who now looks around the stuffy office with an irritated gaze. He is referring to Lieutenant Belfurd who, Rainy knows, is in town visiting a prostitute.

"Colonel, the lieutenant's out of the HQ," she says discreetly.

"I'll just bet he is."

"Colonel, I speak and read German."

Colonel Clay stares at her as if she is a dog who has suddenly announced a talent for plate spinning. His two bushy gray eyebrows become one.

Pooley speaks up, saying, "Colonel, she is fluent. She sometimes helps out Belfurd . . . Lieutenant Belfurd, I mean."

"What is your clearance? Your security clearance, miss."

It is not protocol to address her as miss. It is protocol to address her as sergeant. Or by her last name, Schulterman. But Rainy does not have quite the cheek to reprove a lieutenant colonel. Not right away.

She reassures Colonel Clay that she is cleared for sensitive documents. He sniffs, sighs, and finally crooks a finger at her.

Rainy leaps from her chair and follows him out of the room. They go to Colonel Clay's office. The walls there are festooned with the usual maps, but interspersed in unused spaces are drawings of fish, done in oil crayon. Quite good pictures, Rainy thinks. Some are only partly finished.

"Steelhead," Rainy mutters, not thinking.

"Did you say steelhead, miss?"

"Sorry. Yes, sir. I didn't mean . . . it's just . . ." and she waves vaguely at one of the fish. "That's a steelhead trout. Rainbow trout, some call them."

The colonel stares sideways at her and lights a cigarette without offering one to her. "And what would you say that was?" He points to a second drawing.

"I'm not completely sure, Colonel. Some type of salmon, but I'm not as up as I should be on salmon species."

"It's a Coho salmon. I caught him in Scotland. Twenty-nine inches. No record, but a fine fish that cooked up very nicely over a campfire."

For a moment he seems lost in memory. Rainy is fascinated at the possibility that an actual smile might appear beneath the unfortunate mustache, but no. He is content to smoke and contemplate his various fishes. "You must be a country girl."

"No, Colonel, I'm from New York City. But every summer we had Jewish camp up in the mountains. We fished a bit, and I got so I liked it."

Almost as if his primacy has been challenged, Colonel Clay says, "I tie my own lures."

"It's a skill I wish I had, sir."

He still looks sourly at her, but she senses that she has passed some kind of test and been found to be of at least marginal intelligence and wit. He waves her over to his desk. "These are transcriptions of a dozen unguarded German radio intercepts. They've been written down phonetically since we are short of German speakers. Can you make any sense of them?"

She gathers up the flimsy sheets and, without being asked or given permission, sits down in the colonel's chair and frowns in concentration.

For five full minutes she ignores the colonel as he stands, impatient and annoyed by the effrontery of a mere three-striper, a female at that, sitting there like a schoolgirl working out her homework.

"This one is a Kraut lieutenant asking about some crates of brandy. He says he is short of brandy, and if he is to move as ordered he will need more."

"And what would you make of that?"

"There's another one here from a tanker also talking about brandy, so I think unless the Wehrmacht is composed of drunks, they are not talking about brandy. Either ammo or fuel, most likely fuel."

Colonel Clay's eyes narrow. "Cigarette?"

She takes one but sticks it behind her ear to trade later. "The others are more obvious, I think. This one is a fellow asking about an injured soldier. This one asks whether there has been any mail." She hesitates. "No, wait, there are two asking about mail. . . . It's hard to be sure since these are just phonetic but yes, I think they are both asking about mail. *Post*. Is *post* available."

"Artillery support," Colonel Clay says. "A sort of crude code, barely disguised. They lack landlines, but they haven't got the latest code, I suppose. Dismissed."

She nearly misses that last word, but after a moment's hesitation, jumps up, snaps a salute, and walks away, deflated.

Later that day she learns that she has been reassigned to Colonel Clay's staff.

It is a step down in the sense that she'll be working for a lieutenant colonel of intelligence rather than a full bird colonel in charge of the detachment, but she allows herself a satisfied grin. She has a feeling Colonel Clay might put her to better use.

And there is the added advantage of not working for a complete fool.

Clearly some sort of major German attack is coming. It may already have started, and General Fredendall is in "Speedy Valley" obsessing over his new headquarters construction, and Colonel Jasper is not inclined to make waves. Only Colonel Clay seems to have a clear notion of what he's doing.

Somewhere out there in the vast reaches of the trackless Sahara, someone is very likely catching hell and perhaps about to catch a great deal more of it. Now at least Rainy Schulterman may be able to help them.

28

They run.

Rio and the rest of Fifth Platoon run from the gunfire and the intermittent *BOOM* of the tanks' cannon and the relentless *clank-clank-clank* of the tracks.

They run past Third Platoon, which promptly bails out of its shallow holes and starts running too.

They are a mob, feeding on their own fear, tensing against the bullets that can at any moment pass through their defenseless bodies, tensing against the shrapnel and flying rock that can rip and batter them to death in an instant.

Months of training and preparation, months of bragging that they are tough, that they can take it. *Hey, the Krauts better look out now that the Yanks are here.*

It takes two German tanks and two hundred indifferent Italian infantry to send them all fleeing for their lives.

Behind them they hear the metallic crack of the British

antitank gun firing, joined by the hollow *ka-tooo!* of mortars firing, followed after a pregnant pause by the flat *crump!* of the shells landing amid the Italians.

But Second Squad, Fifth Platoon, as well as the other squads, and Third Platoon, all the Americans in this particular section of the Tunisian desert, all run until they run into Lieutenant Eelie Liefer in her jeep. Her driver looks scared. The lieutenant looks no better.

"Sergeant Cole!" the lieutenant yells. "What's going on?"

"We hit 'em, they hit back, and now we're running," Sergeant Cole says, disgusted.

"Where's Garaman?"

"I thought he was with you, ma'am. We need to form up."

The GIs have mostly paused to see what light the officer can shed on the situation, particularly whether she has any better idea than just running away. They mill around the jeep, worried glances cast back toward the shooting, now just out of sight but very definitely audible.

"There's no defensible ground here," Liefer pronounces.

"Ma'am," Cole says, "there's those rocks over there, we can set up firing positions, defilade the road, backstop the Tommies. And try for some air support or naval gunfire. Artillery. Something."

Lieutenant Liefer stares at him as if he's lost his mind. "Hide in the rocks? From tanks?"

Rio can see exasperation on her sergeant's face. "Lieutenant, let's at least radio in, see if we can get some arty."

"None of our artillery is in range, and there's no air cover," she says, sounding as though she knows what she's talking about. "We have no choice but to pull back."

"Ma'am, we'll be leaving the Tommies hanging."

"They're commandos, experienced troops. They're not our concern. Our concern is the safety of our own men."

Cole's mouth hangs open for several seconds in pure disbelief. He makes one more try. "We can carry out a fighting withdrawal, we can set up in those rocks and—"

"Sergeant Cole, I'm well aware that you used to have five stripes on your sleeve, but now you have three, thanks to your habit of insubordination. Unless you want to be minus another stripe, you will follow my orders."

Half the GIs who've gathered around take this as a signal to keep moving. They don't run, they're tired, but they walk plenty fast, away from the sounds of a battle that has grown louder and more desperate. The British antitank gun is no longer firing, just the tanks and the mortars and rifles, lots of rifles. A terrible scream rises high in the air and is cut off in midnote. A pillar of dust rises from the direction of the fight.

"Yes, ma'am," Cole snaps. "Where would you like us to stop running?"

"I'll have your stripes if I hear one more goddamned word from you!" Liefer yells, and points down the road, back in the direction they came from, back to the rear. Her driver guns the engine, spins into a dusty turn, and roars away, showing them all the line of retreat.

"I guess that's the other reason officers need jeeps," Luther says. "Female officers, at least."

Cole snaps, "Private Richlin has one confirmed kill, Geer, and another probable. What do you have?"

One confirmed kill. One probable.

Geer stares daggers at Richlin, and Suarez occupies himself lighting a smoke. Jack is there as well, and he frowns at Rio as if just noticing something about her face that troubles him.

They run and they walk and they run some more, putting all their PT to a use none of them expected. Finally, after hours, they manage to outrun the sounds of the fight. Or else the fight is lost and the Tommies are wiped out. Rio doesn't know which.

She walks fast; Jenou at her side now, a strange echo of times walking together around the square in Gedwell Falls, or halfheartedly running the track at school. Rio and Jenou, two high school girls out for a stroll, but with slung rifles and pounds of ammo and gear, and mortal dread in their hearts.

"I never wanted to be in the fighting," Jenou says, her teeth chattering either from cold or fear. "I lost my helmet. I'm supposed to be at a desk. Now we're going to have to surrender and spend the rest of the war in a POW camp."

"Surrender?" Rio tries the word out and doesn't like it at all, but maybe Jenou is right. They're licked, aren't they? They've been sent packing. Where are the American lines, even? None of them really knows where they themselves are right now, aside from it being a miserable place in a country they'd never even heard of before arriving here.

They keep moving, moving, always away from the German tanks, which they can no longer hear, fleeing an enemy that is farther and farther behind them. Fleeing to . . . where? Where is safety?

"We just have to get back to our lines," Rio says.

"We have to get back to Gedwell Falls," Jenou says savagely.

"You shot one of them?" Tilo Suarez asked Rio.

She shrugs.

"She killed one for sure," Hark Millican says. "I saw him drop. Sarge saw it too. Mighta been two. Maybe."

"Probably just tripped," Rio says through gritted teeth.

"Like hell," Millican says. "You shot him. You shot him good."

Confirmed kill.

Rio accelerates her pace, wanting to get away from him. She feels panicky, more panicky than when she was running away from actual enemy fire.

"I probably got me one or two," Luther says. He's angry as well as scared. Scared of the Germans, angry that Rio has a confirmed kill and he does not. "Maybe more, I mean, I was shooting like crazy, but the smoke and all . . ."

Something is buzzing. Jillion Magraff and Cole yell at the same time. "Plane!"

And there it is, a plane, coming in low. Hopefully it will make short work of the tanks and save the Tommies, who sure weren't going to be saved by Fifth Platoon.

"Scatter!" Cole yells.

A few seconds pass before it dawns on Rio that no, this is not Strand Braxton flying out of the clouds to rescue her, nor any friendly pilot.

She glances left, right, no holes, no shelter. She starts to run, sees that Jenou is frozen, runs back to grab her friend's shoulder, a handful of uniform, pulls her along, and the two of them plunge off the road, run a few steps, and hit the dirt.

The Stuka—unmistakable once it is close enough—fires

its twin wing-mounted machine guns and rips up a quarter of a mile of dirt road like some devil-possessed backhoe, and the plane roars by overhead, the black-and-white crosses and the swastika on the tail all too visible.

The Stuka flies on, and Rio sees two bombs detach from the undercarriage.

Out of sight, but in the area where they last saw the commandos, the bombs explode, a single massive earth-shaking detonation.

"Move out!" Cole yells. "He may come back around!"

But the German plane has lost interest in them and now circles to rain more machine gun fire on the commandos. The Americans leap up out of the dirt and start walking fast again, glancing over their shoulders every few steps to see if the plane is coming back.

But it isn't the Stuka chasing them now, it's the tanks, that terrible *clank-clank-clank* distant but audible. The tanks were slowed by the determined resistance of the British commandos, but the bombs have taken care of that.

They run and when exhausted slow to a walk and then, hearing the distant *clank-clank-clank*, start moving again. Some packs are shed by the road, abandoned to buy more speed. Ammo is dropped, even rifles.

They run and walk for five miles, and there at last is Liefer and her jeep again, and beyond her three dusty trucks. The Americans pile gratefully into the trucks and join what will turn out to be a much larger rout.

The Germans had been squeezed between Field Marshal Montgomery's fabled Eighth Army and the cocky-but-green American forces to the west and, by all logic, should have either given up or run for the nearest beach to seek a desperate escape. Instead, they have attacked, pushing west against the Americans and north toward Tunis.

They're tougher than we are.

29

RAINY SCHULTERMAN—MAKTAR, TUNISIA, NORTH AFRICA

"Colonel Clay wants you, PDQ." The news is delivered to Rainy by a lieutenant who is the spitting image of her brother, Aryeh, just with less muscle.

"Yes, sir." PDQ—pretty damned quick—means now, so Rainy jumps up, grabs her notation pad, and fast-walks down a busy hallway past women at typewriters and men shuffling papers; past tea being brewed by the dark-skinned batman of the British liaison officer; and past two majors laughing loudly and smoking like chimneys.

In addition to Colonel Clay there are two men Rainy recognizes but has never met in his office, and one who openly grins at her.

She manages to avoid letting her mouth hang open and salutes properly.

"Sergeant Schulterman," Captain Herkemeier says.

"Captain, it's good to see you. I didn't know you were in theater."

"Just a week behind you, Sergeant."

They shake hands while Colonel Clay looks on in disdain. He says, "I understand I have Captain Herkemeier to thank for your services here," he says.

"Yes, sir," Rainy says. Thus far she assumes this is just some sort of awkward reunion, though Colonel Clay would be the very last person she'd suspect of arranging any sort of social event.

"He speaks highly of you," Clay allows, studying papers in his hands. "Says you come from criminal stock."

"Sir, I—"

"Which I consider to be a plus," the colonel goes on. "There are far too many well-bred gentlemen in military intelligence and not nearly enough aggressive Jewesses with a potential for criminality."

The first part of that was a shot at the other two officers, both of whom Rainy knew to be from upper-crust families and schools. The second part is by all rights offensive and derogatory, but Rainy is sure it wasn't intended that way, and also indifferent, because it sounds like the prelude to something worthwhile.

Still, she's a bit at a loss for how to respond so she falls back on the always reliable, "Yes, sir."

"Captain, proceed."

Captain Herkemeier has a map, which he unfolds and spreads across the colonel's desk. All five of them form a circle, heads down, eyes searching.

"My division is in full retreat, getting hit hard, hoping to dig in and make a stand here." The captain taps the map and they all nod. "But we picked up some radio chatter from the enemy; we didn't have any German speakers on the radio, but I speak some Italian."

Rainy blinks, and Herkemeier notices. "Yes, Sergeant, Herkemeier is a German name, but my father never spoke it, while my mother is an Italian immigrant."

"Yes, yes," the colonel interjects impatiently.

"The short of it is that I sent what we had to HQ, where I understand Sergeant Schulterman was able to make some sense of it. We got some triangulation on the signal, not very good, unreliable frankly, but nevertheless, we have a working theory."

"A supply column," Rainy said. "Probably crossing open desert. A rendezvous with some element of the German armored thrust."

The colonel's eyebrows shake hands with each other again at that, and the other men equally stare in open disbelief, all but Herkemeier, who winks at Rainy.

"Where would you guess that rendezvous would take place, Sergeant?"

It's a challenge, a sign of his confidence in her. He is showing off his star pupil.

Rainy takes several minutes to study the map,

muttering to herself as if no one else is in the room. "He'll send his flanking force right across open desert, this wadi here. German supply depot . . . this road . . . say they make thirty miles an hour . . ." She taps the map. "The two roads intersect here . . . crossroads . . . middle of nowhere . . ." Rainy shrugs and steps back, suddenly self-conscious.

Captain Herkemeier is keeping a straight face, and anyway it's Colonel Clay's reaction that matters.

The major clears his throat and gets a nod. "Sir, we have nothing to put up against that armored column. If we had air cover we might be able to intercept the supply column, and that would likely stop 'em dead in their tracks. But we have nothing in the area but a few scattered elements."

Now it is the lieutenant's turn to clear his throat—very polite, very upper-crust, Rainy thinks, very much not the aggressive Jewess with criminal tendencies. "Sir, there's a small force. Two platoons that were sent in to buttress a British commando mission. The commandos have been beaten up pretty badly, and what's left of them are heading out cross-country to try to circle back to the beach, but they last saw our two platoons on this road, heading back toward Sidi Bouzid, which means they'll most likely run right into the Kraut main force." He shakes his head doubtfully. "They aren't much, but if the Brits are right, they're within ten miles, give or take."

"Who's in command?" Colonel Clay asks.

"A Lieutenant Liefer and a Lieutenant Helder. I believe Liefer is senior, so with the Tommies out of the picture, she'd be in command. But, Colonel, we have no radio contact. Their set must have been knocked out."

"We could send someone," the major says, stroking his chin thoughtfully. "A German speaker with a radio might just make it; he could stay in touch and monitor any continuing chatter."

"See who we have," Colonel Clay says.

"Sir," Rainy interrupts.

She's forgotten now that the officers are speaking. Sergeants in the company of senior officers are like children: best seen and not heard. But something about having been labeled an aggressive Jewess . . .

"Sir," she repeats when the conversation continues uninterrupted.

"Yes, Sergeant, what is it?" the colonel snaps.

"Sir, we have someone who can get there with a radio and who speaks German."

Out of the corner of her eye she sees Captain Herkemeier, concerned, shaking his head slightly and mouthing the word *no*.

"Me, sir," Rainy says. "Get me a jeep and a driver, I'll carry the orders."

"Very commendable," Colonel Clay snaps dismissively. "But this isn't a drive in the country. In fact, it won't be a drive at all. It would mean jumping."

"Jumping, sir?"

"Out of an airplane," Colonel Clay says.

And before Rainy Schulterman can think through the implications of what she is saying, out come the words "I can do that."

30

FRANGIE MARR—TUNISIAN DESERT, NORTH AFRICA

For the better part of a day, retreating American troops and some scattered units of Brits stream past Frangie and the shattered but still-functioning remains of her unit. Trucks, jeeps, battle-scarred Sherman tanks, one with its turret blown clean off, come rattling by, steel beasts pushing past scared and beaten men and equally scared and beaten women. The GIs come as slumping groups that look like they've never seen a parade ground, or as individuals with heads down, and occasionally as more or less ordered squads and platoons.

Some in that passing show are wounded, and there is no surplus of medics, so some, a few, have spotted the cross on Frangie's helmet and come in search of help.

About half turn back once they see the color of her face. But she's still not short of patients to treat—bullet holes and shrapnel, broken bones and burns, but also diarrhea from bad water, and fevers from infections.

There are some who just can't go on but reach her tent and fall down, fall straight down like felled trees, their last reserves of energy utterly drained.

Frangie is using forceps to dig painfully into the meat above the collarbone of a wounded soldier, looking for the lead. It must have been a nearly spent bullet since it went in and did not come out the other side. For the most part the bullet wounds she's seen are like this, suffered at a distance, not close up. And many, like this wound, are in the back or the back of legs, arms, or buttocks—the wounds of those fleeing, not advancing.

"Gotta sit still, Corporal, and Private? Keep that light still."

The sun is up, but inside the tent it's all soft-green shadows and canvas-filtered glare. The private holding the flashlight—Frangie knows him only as Ren—is tired, everyone is tired, but she can't hope to see what she's doing unless he holds the light still.

"It hurts, goddammit," the injured corporal says angrily, twitching again. Tears stream down his face, but they're not tears of pain or sadness, they're tears of helpless rage.

"Listen to me, Corporal, this ain't going to kill you unless you jump around and make me nick an artery, so sit still."

"That's what I get," he says bitterly. "Nigra skirt trying to kill me."

It's not the first time Frangie has heard some variation on that theme. The worst refuse to accept any help. Others like this angry corporal will take the help but curse her while she's delivering it. Others, though, are just grateful for anyone of any color who will ease their fear and pain.

"Give me some damn morphine!"

"We're short of morphine; we keep it for those that need it worst." She shouldn't be wasting breath. The wound is bleeding freely, and she can't swab fast enough to get a look inside the hole. She's feeling for the bullet, gently moving her probe from side to side, hoping to feel a click. She feels a click but it's bone, and the corporal howls.

"Saving it for your Nigras, more like!"

"Shut the fug up, Brattle, I'm tired of hearing it." This from a white male sergeant who's escorting the wounded man.

"This Nigra's going to finish what the damned Krauts started!"

It's been like this hour after hour. Frangie has no time to wash her hands between patients, no water to be spared for washing even if she had time. She's got first draw on water supplies, but it doesn't matter much because there isn't any more than a few mouthfuls for anyone.

In the back of her mind she keeps a running inventory. So many pressure bandages, so much tape, so many splints, so much gauze, so many ampules of morphine. She's begun "charging" for her services, requiring patients to give up most of the contents of their emergency medical kits. But it's not enough, and she's already put out the word that she needs T-shirts. Her orderly, Ren—in reality just a passing white private whose nerves collapsed under the strain of combat—cuts them into strips when she doesn't have him holding the flashlight.

Her patient, Brattle, says something that's obliterated by the shattering noise of the remaining guns opening up again after a brief interlude.

Frangie doesn't know anything about artillery, but she knows the pace of outgoing shells has slowed. Some of the cannon have barrels melted and twisted, others are jammed, many were lost to the German 88s, but mostly it's the fact that they are running out of ammunition. "Ordnance," as the artillerymen call it.

BOOM!

Everyone knows the battalion is going to have to withdraw, soon as they get orders. They are way too far forward for an artillery unit. The barrels of the big guns are trained ever higher, creating steeper but shorter arcs for the shells, a sure sign that the enemy is close, way too close.

Frangie's probe clicks, a dull feel more than a sound. Ever so carefully she widens the tips and slides them around the slug. She grips it tightly, wipes sweat from her forehead with her free hand, and begins to tease the bullet out.

BOOM! BOOM!

The earth shudders from each outgoing package. She pulls the bullet free, drops it in the dirt, sprinkles on a precious few grains of sulfa powder, far too little but all she can spare, and wraps the arm in white gauze and a black man's T-shirt.

"Thanks, Doc," the sergeant says between eruptions. "Brattle, let's go."

There's a rush of feet outside, and Frangie sighs, knowing that it presages yet another casualty.

Four dirty soldiers, two men and two women, come rushing in, carrying a fifth man on a makeshift stretcher of tied-together field jackets.

The white man on the stretcher is wearing captain's bars. Blood saturates his crotch and spreads down his legs.

"What the hell? It's a Nigra!" one of the stretcher bearers yells.

"Put him on the table," Frangie snaps.

The table is a makeshift affair of empty ammo crates topped by a jagged but almost flat piece of a blown-up water tank.

"Get him undressed," she orders.

"What the hell?"

"You have knives, don't you? Cut his clothes off, and be careful not to cut him."

One of them turns away to retch. A chunk of the captain's thigh is gone, as if a shark had bitten it off, just a gaping nothing where muscle should be. A curious flap of skin is peeled off the front of his hip and now drapes over his privates. Blood is everywhere, not pumping, not spurting, but seeping from too many places at once. Frangie looks at his face. He's not just white, his brown eyebrows look like caterpillars crossing a sheet of paper. His eyes are wandering, seemingly sightless.

The wound is far too grave for her skills, far too grave for anyone's skills, and she knows she should follow the laws of triage. There are three categories: those who will likely live without treatment, those who may be saved by treatment, and those who have no chance of survival.

Hurt, hurt bad, and goners, in the shorthand version.

"What's his name?"

"Captain Schrenk," a soldier answers.

"He got a first name?"

"Sol, I think. Some Jew name like that. But he's a good officer."

"Good captain," another confirms.

"Ren, get me sulfa, scrap sponges, and water," Frangie says.

"You know what you're doing, Nig . . . Doc?"

"No, I do not," Frangie says. "You want to take over?"

That's the end of the second-guessing.

"Two of you stay in case I need to hold him down," Frangie says. "The other two, take off, it's tight in here."

The matter is decided with looks between the four soldiers. One woman and one man stay behind. Frangie guesses they're the two with the strongest stomachs. At least she hopes so.

There's an artery, a big, fat glistening artery that ought to be pumping but is merely draining. There's very little blood left in the captain. Frangie pulls out his dog tags.

"AB Negative? Jesus, I don't have any AB anything. Ren, hang some plasma."

It turns out the woman soldier has type AB negative, a rare bit of good luck. "At least it'll be white blood," she mutters.

"Pretty sure it'll be red," Frangie says, now feeling her way with bare fingers around the chewed meat that is the captain's thigh.

Suddenly the captain shouts; at least he intends to shout, he's too weak to make much noise.

"Morphine?" Ren asks.

"No, weak as he is it'd kill him for sure."

"You, AB: pull that chair over here, sit down as close as you can get. Ren?"

Ren has learned enough in the last twelve hours to

know where the needles and tubes are. He uncoils a plastic tube and fits a used hollow needle to one end.

"You, pressure right here," Frangie orders the male soldier, only now noticing that he's a senior NCO, and that he, too, is bleeding from the side of his face, bleeding but walking wounded, likely to survive on his own. "Your thumb. Right there." He looks a little sickly, so Frangie adds, "If you need to throw up, don't do it on my patient."

She manages to find an artery on the female soldier, but the captain's system is collapsing and she wastes precious seconds finding a vein. Finally red liquid surges through the piping. She stops it with a clamp. First she needs to sew up the hole in the femoral artery—no point pumping blood in only to have it drain out.

"You tell me if you get light-headed," Frangie instructs the donor as she pushes the NCO's thumb aside, clamps the artery, and places three quick sutures. They won't stop all the bleeding, but they'll slow it down.

She unclamps the transfusion and blood flows from the woman to the captain.

"Now, to—"

The tent flap flies open. It's Sergeant Green. "Doc, orders: we're bugging out."

"Can't," Frangie says.

"Orders," he says, insisting on the word. "They're going to blow the tubes."

"What?"

"We're tossing grenades down the last few artillery tubes and skedaddling."

This obviously gets the full attention of the man and woman who came in with Captain Schrenk, but they stay, though their body language telegraphs a desire to go.

Frangie hadn't even noticed that the artillery was no longer firing. The only explosions she's heard in the last sixty seconds have been muffled bangs—grenades.

"I have a patient," Frangie says, now tracking smaller bleeders.

"Doc . . . Private Marr . . . that man isn't even one of ours."

"Well, he's one of my patients, Sarge. Go, go, take care of yourself, I'll catch up soon as I have this man stable."

Sergeant Green looks torn. He takes off his wire-framed glasses to wipe them off with his shirttail, obviously considering his path. "Look, I would . . . But it's no good, I have to stay with my men."

"That's your duty, Sergeant Green, this is mine."

"God keep you safe, sister."

"You too, Sarge. Wait, give me your medical kit."

He does, nods, and is gone.

From outside she hears more muffled bangs, running feet, a jeep engine, shouts, and urgent orders.

The reality of it hits her. She will be alone here with the captain, alone waiting for the enemy. Everyone who can leave has left. "Ren, you take off too. You done good, now get the hell out of here."

The raw, exposed flesh under the captain's torn skin oozes with some thick, green-brown liquid, black in the minimal light. Bile, maybe, or the contents of his lower intestines. The wound is deeper than she can see, there is almost certainly shrapnel up inside his belly, and it is septic—she can smell the intestinal contents. There's no way the captain survives, not even at a field hospital, most likely. But Frangie does not believe for a moment that she can leave him. Medics do not only care for the wounded, they comfort the dying.

Outside, the last jeep takes a load on its engine and begins to draw away. There's a shockingly loud explosion and a flash of light that turns every seam and gap in the tent bright yellow for a second. They've set off the last of their ammunition, keeping it from the enemy.

Frangie ties off as many bleeders as she can. Is that a hint of color returning to the captain's face? Must be, because he sits bolt upright, stares in horror and confusion at the mess of his crotch, and cries, "They shot my dick off!"

"It's still there—"

"Kill me now, kill me now, kill me now!"

"Like hell I will," Frangie snarls.

"Sergeant! Sergeant! I order you to shoot me!"

"Captain, you're okay, you're okay, take a look!"

Frangie draws the skin flap back, exposing the captain's genitals.

"It's all there, Cap, it's all good," the white sergeant says.

But of course it's not all good. Frangie has not the faintest clue what to do about what may be a perforated intestine or gallbladder. She is not a surgeon, not a doctor, not even close.

A silence descends. Outside, the feet no longer rush. There are no more small explosions. The only things Frangie hears are the captain's labored breathing, almost a sob, and the sound of blood dripping onto dirt floor.

Then, in the distance, engines.

31

"You're a girl."

"No, sir, I'm a sergeant. I'm a sergeant carrying orders from Colonel Clay." Rainy tugs the single sheet of paper from her pocket and opens it for the skeptical sergeant.

"You some kind of paratrooper?" He doesn't seem mean as much as amused.

"I am no kind of paratrooper," she says. "This will be a first for me."

"Well, I have to tell you, Sergeant Schulterman, this here is what we call FUBAR." But he extends a hand, shakes hers, and says, "But I'll fly you. Call me Skip."

"Skip?"

"Warrant Officer Elihu J. Ostrowski if you prefer, but Skip rolls off the tongue a bit easier."

Rainy manages a grin, a shaky, tenuous grin, and says, "I'm Rainy. And I know it's FUBAR, Skip, and I'm sorry to drag you into it."

451

He's an older man in his early thirties, with a face creased by a lifetime in the sun. He doesn't seem happy about flying a young woman barely more than half his age, but he's not hostile, and Rainy has learned to welcome anything short of open contempt. And after all, she's dragging him into a bad situation, so he'd be justified in a little resentment. She reminds herself not to mention that this whole mission is largely her idea.

They stand before an Army L-4, basically just a Piper Cub. It has a single engine and a single overhead wing, without weapons, armor, or speed to protect it. It has two seats, one behind the other, and only one cramped door that requires Rainy—newly bulked up with not one but two parachutes—to squeeze in with great difficulty.

Though she's not a big person, Rainy is squashed in a sandwich between her own seat back, her main chute, her belly chute, and the pilot's seat back. This does nothing to calm her, but, she reminds herself, she'll have lots of fresh air as she plummets toward the ground.

Skip revs the engine, which is not a reassuring sound, and the tiny plane goes bouncing down the dirt field, swerving to avoid a mud puddle and then lifting off in a sort of crablike, half-sideways fashion.

The cockpit is tiny and freezing but at least there are ample windows, and with the wing above them the view of the ground is good. They fly over the town of Maktar, on overcultivated fields now fallow as they head into winter. It's interesting enough for a while—Rainy has not only had no experience with parachutes, this is her first time up in a plane—but it soon becomes monotonous as signs of human habitation disappear and the ground below becomes one long stretch of sand and rock.

She passes the time replaying her hasty instruction in the use of the parachute. Climb up into the doorway, legs dangling out. Push hard away from the plane and for God's sake don't pull the rip cord too soon. Or too late. Or forget to pull it at all.

And if the main chute should fail to deploy, she should calmly and without panic go to her emergency chute. Calmly. While falling like a rock.

They run into some turbulence, and the little plane starts to rise and fall just like a boat on the waves, elevator up, and a playground slide down. Up . . . down. Up . . . and the combination of the movement and the fear, the growing fear of jumping, turns her stomach acid. She needs to pee. She needs to vomit. She needs to not be here, not be in a tiny plane on her way to the middle of nowhere, and not be contemplating a parachute jump with zero experience.

Skip yells something back to her that she cannot hear, so he makes a chopping motion off to their right, and when Rainy looks she sees vehicles on a road, heading north. They're nothing but tan rectangles, but she's had enough training in reading recon photos to recognize German tanks and trucks. They're leading a long plume of dust.

Those are the Germans she'd have run into had she tried to reach her destination by jeep. Unfortunately this means she will almost certainly be cut off once she drops, retreat barred by the enemy.

Skip holds the stick with his knees and jots notes into a notebook, tapping his compass to check their bearing and unfolding a map to compare what he's seeing and what the map wants him to be seeing.

Skip reaches back to tap her leg and get her attention. Then he holds up one hand, fingers splayed.

Five. Five minutes.

This is a terrible idea.

This is crazy.

This is suicidal.

She feels like something large is stuck in her throat, like she tried to swallow a hamburger in one bite and now can't get it down. Her heart is pounding in her chest.

Skip motions again, and now he unlatches the door, which will be hard to push open against the wind. Harder still is climbing up there. Left leg forward, squeezing, sucking in her breath while all the while she feels she can't breathe, leaning into Skip, her weight on his left shoulder, her face practically pushed into his bald spot. He's scrunching over as far as he can get while still keeping a hand on the stick, and then she slips. Her hand reaches instinctively for anything solid—the stick—and the plane plunges right and down. Something much bigger and much, much faster goes blazing by.

Backwash buffets the plane, it's rattling, the engine is coughing, the door is unhitched, and in the wild careening Rainy sees the flat-nosed Focke-Wulf 190 banking into a tight turn to come back at them.

"Now or never!" Skip yells.

She's got her back to the door, hunched over like a cooked shrimp.

"Are we there?"

Skip strong-arms her, pushing hard on her chest. Her hands tear loose from their hold, the door bangs on her thigh, air pressure like a hurricane hits her full force, and she's falling, tumbling, head over heels, head over heels, like an acrobat.

She does not scream but wants to, her mind a blur, her body in a state of rigid panic. But a part of her brain, some cold, calm, reasoning fragment, says, *Pull the rip cord, you* meshuggeneh *fool!*

She pulls the cord. Nothing happens. She's stopped

breathing. The desert is whirling around, blue sky, beige dirt, blue sky, and then there is a sharp, almost brutal jerk that digs straps into her crotch and gives her whiplash as the chute brings her upright, feet dangling.

But she's still falling, falling to her death . . . No. No, she can see the white-silk canopy above her, so she's done it, she's done it, she's parachuted.

You still have to land!

A quarter mile above her and away to the south, the spotter plane comes apart, pieces flying as the Focke-Wulf pours machine gun fire into it. She watches but does not see Skip getting out, does not see a second chute blossoming, just the plane falling nose-down in wild loops. Part of the wing comes off, and the loops become a disorganized tumble.

She looks away as the plane hits the ground, a puff of dust, soundless.

And the ground is rushing up at her, and she forgets everything she was told about landing, no bracing, no bent knees, no rolling to spread the impact, she hits hard, bone-jarringly hard, and falls over. The chute, still full, drags her on her back for a few feet before she can roll over, get first to her knees and then to her feet, and the chute collapses.

She works her way free of the parachute harness. Rainy Schulterman has just parachuted behind enemy lines.

And gotten a man named Skip killed.

Featureless desert sand in every direction. She lies on her back, panting, willing her heart to slow down enough to actually pump blood rather than just hammer at her rib cage.

"Get up," Rainy orders herself. "Move!"

Direction is easy enough: she can see the sun. And she remembers seeing a road on her way down. East. That's right, east. She walks a few steps, collapses to her knees, pushes herself back up, and heads on again.

The unit she's looking for is out there somewhere, a somewhere that looks a whole lot larger from ground level than it did on a map.

She has survived the jump, she reminds herself, and that was the hard part, surely. How hard can it be to find fifty or so soldiers in a million miles of trackless emptiness?

It takes a half an hour just to find the road. She flops beside it, nervous and scared as hell, but alive. If only she knew . . . anything, really, about the survival skills a soldier should have. If only . . . The plan had been to spot the platoon, fly low, give them a wing wag to get their attention, then jump.

That did not happen. But the fortunes of war that had turned against her and dropped her here, lost and abandoned, now capriciously come to her rescue.

There is a jeep coming down the road, hell-for-leather, a single soldier at the wheel.

Rainy climbs heavily to her feet and then, composing her face into a calm and, she hopes, authoritative expression, steps out into the middle of the road.

32

Two fears vie for the upper hand in Frangie's mind. First, that she might do something stupid and kill the wounded captain. He's almost certainly dying anyway, but the Hippocratic oath is pretty clear: first, do no harm. She has done what she can; now she can only offer comfort and morphine.

The second fear is simply of the sounds of trucks and men approaching.

She does not want to serve out the rest of the war in a prisoner of war camp. It is inconceivable that the racist Germans would be any better than the racist Americans in their treatment of blacks.

She wants to flee. There would be no shame in it, not really; the captain is doomed. The sergeant who stayed to help finally leaves with a terse, "Thanks for taking care of my captain."

Ren remains behind still.

"Ren, get the fug out. Seriously, go. Go! I'm ordering you, go!" It is the first time Frangie has ever cursed, and she marks it in an abstract sort of way as something she will later pray over.

The bottle of plasma hangs from a lanyard dropped from a seam in the tent. It joins the transfused whole blood and flows now into the captain's arm, slightly more going in than comes out, though soon enough the plasma will be empty and there's no more whole blood to be had.

"Am I dying?" the captain asks in a shaky but rational voice.

Frangie wants to tell the truth, maybe then he'll order her to leave, to escape. But that isn't how it's done. A medic does not tell a soldier he is dying.

"You'll be fine, Captain. Just sewing you up is all. Sew you up, bandage you up . . ."

"Okay, listen . . . I'm going, Doc," Ren says, looking tortured but relieved.

"God keep you, Ren."

"You, too, Doc. I'll say a prayer for you."

"I'll need it."

He grabs a canteen and runs for it. Frangie listens for the sound of gunfire and blessedly hears none. But the sound of truck engines and tank treads and the rattle of soldiers' gear fill her hearing and her imagination.

Her hands are steady as she sutures, but tears flow and

she is having difficulty swallowing. Maybe the Germans will see that she is a medic with a patient and do the decent thing and leave her to it. After all, they can't really all be the monsters the propaganda makes them out to be. Surely there is something to the notion of soldiers' honor, surely—

The tent flap flies open, and three German soldiers rush in yelling incomprehensibly, leveling their submachine guns. They look tired and dirty but keyed up, blue eyes searching every corner of the tent.

"*Schwarze!*" one says, his look contemptuous. He shoves the barrel of his machine pistol into her stomach, hard enough to double her over. The suture slips from her hand, she struggles to get it back, and the stock of the gun smashes against her forehead.

The whole world spins. Her knees collapse and she falls to the dirt, landing on her side, still struggling but unable to focus, unable to see anything but swirling, doubled reality. A blow to her kidneys, a kick, has the paradoxical effect of clearing her mind so she can focus on the agony that radiates up and down her spine. She lies on her side, panting, seeing in the dirt before her the bloody, twisted lead slug she took from the earlier patient. Bloody rags are all around. Some sort of rat is carrying one off.

Frangie does not yet expect to die, but she expects to be hurt, she expects a second boot and it is not long in coming, this time smashing her tailbone. The electric agony she'd felt before is worse now. Her stomach heaves, but it is empty. She gasps and inhales dirt, which starts a coughing fit. She pushes at the ground, trying to rise, knowing it will just set her up for another blow.

But the next blow does not come, and she manages to get to her knees, head hanging down, lungs burning for oxygen, nerve pain zapping through her, tingling her hands and feet.

Someone new is in the tent, and his presence has calmed the excitable soldiers. Frangie twists her head and sees an expensive-looking pair of leather boots. They are caked with mud and adorned with spurs—she's only ever seen spurs in cowboy movies and their presence here seems like a hallucination.

Powerful hands grab her shoulders and haul her to her feet. Blood sheets down over her eyes, and she wipes it away with her arm. She cannot stand fully erect, not yet, leaving her to look and feel even smaller than usual.

She tries to look at the man in the boots but her eyes will not focus and all she can make out is that there are three soldiers in butternut-colored uniforms, and the spurred man wearing dusty black.

The man in black speaks. Is it German? No, the words are accented but familiar. English, but pronounced like a war movie villain. She struggles to make sense of it, to get her brain to work properly, to understand—

A hard slap across the face knocks her against the table. She is almost facedown in the captain's ruined belly.

"Where have they gone?" the spurred man demands.

"Gone?" she mumbled, uncomprehending.

"Your unit. Your men. Where have they gone? Where is their rendezvous?"

She blinks and wipes away more blood and turns with slow, arthritic dignity to face her interrogator. Her vision focuses on silver collar patches, each marked by the SS lightning bolts.

She does not then recognize the significance of those emblems, nor can she decipher the insignia of rank on his uniform, but she knows him to be an officer by the stiffness in the poses of the soldiers.

"I will strike you again, if—"

"They ran off," she says.

"Where are they going? What is their destination? Are they joining another unit?"

She shakes her head and cries out sharply at the pain that swarms her. "I'm just a medic. Just trying to sew this man up."

"You stayed behind to care for him?"

"Leave her alone, she's just a Nigra," the captain says from the table.

The German officer jerks his head, and before Frangie can protest, one of the soldiers steps close, presses the barrel of his rifle against the captain's head, and fires once.

Bone and brain explode from the opposite side of the captain's head. A piece of skull shatters the hanging bottle of plasma.

"Damn it!" Frangie cries. "You didn't have to do that! You didn't have to do that, he was dead anyway!"

"Then no harm has been done," the officer says, and grins, revealing uneven but bright-white teeth.

He snaps orders to the soldiers, who immediately begin to gather up what medical supplies remain.

His next order will be to shoot Frangie, unless rape is on the menu first, and from the look in at least one of the German soldiers' eyes, it is. He is anxious, she can see it, anxious lest the officer order that she be killed before he can have his fun.

The officer says two things, neither decipherable, but it makes the soldier with the hungry eyes grin. The officer laughs indulgently, as though he's jolly Saint Nick handing out presents, then he turns and leaves.

Before he has cleared the tent flaps, Hungry Eyes' belt is unhitched and the other two are crowding in close.

"No, don't," Frangie says, knowing it won't help, knowing in her heart that the officer has told the men to have their fun and be quick about it, and then shoot her.

The tent flap opens again, a second officer, this one in

gray. His uniform is stained with blood as well as mud. He speaks in German, as harsh as the first officer, but with more irritation in his tone, more like a stern schoolteacher addressing stupid pupils.

The soldier with his pants down around his ankles remonstrates, but this just sets off a torrent of derisive abuse. Reluctantly and angrily he pulls his pants back up, creating mirth among his fellows, who follow him as he rages out of the tent.

"I am Oberstarzt Hefflewezen. Doctor-Major to you," He leans over the dead captain. "These are your sutures?"

Frangie grunts a yes.

"The wound is septic, he would not have lived."

"I know that."

He sighs, not a sympathetic sound, an annoyed one. "Your officers are fools leaving a medic behind. They will come to regret it."

I already regret it, she thinks bitterly, though despite everything she does not quite believe it.

"You are my prisoner." There is subtle weight on that word *my*. "My company has several cases of typhus. I have no time for routine bandaging and suturing."

Lest Frangie believe she has fallen in with a sympathetic medical professional, the doctor grabs her by the back of the neck, squeezing painfully hard, and shoves her toward the tent flap.

She is startled to see that the gray light of morning is in

the eastern sky. German soldiers pick over the remains of the abandoned camp, looking carefully for booby traps, scrounging for food and water, hoping for alcohol.

The German unit is a long column of trucks, most of them tankers carrying either water or fuel. There are two half-tracks—lightly armored vehicles with tank tracks at the rear, conventional tires up front, an open bed that carries nine or ten German soldiers, and a machine gun mounted over the low, sloped roof of the driver's compartment.

The column is starting to move again, engines roaring, gears grinding. Frangie sees the SS officer in an open staff car, drinking something from a thermos bottle.

Doon Acey's body lies still unburied, laid out on the ground beside the road with three other American dead, awaiting graves registration units. A bored-looking German soldier methodically shoots each corpse in the chest and head. *Bang, bang. Bang, bang. Bang, bang. Bang, bang.* Making sure the dead Americans stay dead.

The column jounces and sputters past, truck after truck, until a green-painted ambulance adorned with a red cross very similar to the one on Frangie's helmet appears. Behind it, just ahead of the final half-track, an open, slat-sided truck full to overflowing with wounded Germans.

"You," the Doctor-Major orders, and shoves Frangie

toward the truck. She catches the tailgate and climbs aboard on shaky legs to be met with hostile stares from men with every variety of battlefield injury. One man winks at her and grabs his crotch suggestively. Another spits in her general direction, though with insufficient force, so it lands on the helmet of a man who is either unconscious or dead.

Frangie sits as far back as she can from the more threatening enemy soldiers. A private running from the ambulance tosses her a small box marked with the red cross. It contains bandages, tape, scissors, and sulfa powder. There's a smaller box that should contain morphine, but it's been emptied, presumably to keep her from killing one of the Germans or herself.

That last thought lingers in her mind. She is a prisoner. She is a woman. And with sick dread she knows what to expect.

But for now there's a man with a bandage the color of old meat. She will change that bandage and worry about the rest later.

33

"Nothing we could do up against tanks, right?" Tilo says.

"Fugging bazooka bounced off," Corporal Hark Millican says, not for the first or last time. "How we supposed to stop tanks with that? Like throwing a fugging water balloon." He has previously compared the bazooka shell to a baseball, a rock, and a watermelon.

"What do you expect?" Luther snaps. "We're fighting with girls against men. I always said this was doomed. I always said that."

Stick says, "As far as I can tell, the only one who inflicted any casualties on them was a girl."

"Because the men are too busy looking out for the women, that's what," Geer insists furiously. "Girls and a goddamned Jap. We're cursed."

Hansu Pang cannot help but hear this. He clamps his jaw tight but says nothing and no one comes to his defense. The fact that Pang did exactly what he was ordered to do and performed as well as anyone means nothing; he has the face and the hair and, above all, the eyes of a Jap. And scared, beaten men need an excuse. Blame the women, blame the Jap, blame the officers all the way up the chain of command, blame anyone but themselves.

They've lost Cassel. They've lost their medic. And, to make matters worse, everyone has earlier overheard the furious British captain reaming out Lieutenants Liefer and Helder, before leading his men off.

"You ran, you silly bastards," he raged. "We could have managed a fighting withdrawal, but you broke and ran."

To which Liefer had responded by making things worse. "I can only be as good as my people. These are green troops."

"Young lady, it's a bloody poor officer that blames her men," the captain shot back savagely. "I've got five of my boys dead and one so shot up he won't be long joining them. And you were well in the rear, Lieutenant. That fact will be in my report, you may count on it."

And with that the British commandos double-timed past them, not without harsh words from some of the Tommies.

"Soft Yank bastards."

"Americans, my arse."

"You fight like women. Oh, too right: you *are* women."

Rio does her best to ignore the taunts. She ignores, too,

the unsettling mix of respect and resentment that comes from being the only one in the squad to provably hit an enemy soldier.

She watches it in her memory. She sees the Italian through her sights. She feels the pressure of her finger on the trigger. He trips. He falls. Just a stumble.

No, he's hit. He's fallen. He's bleeding into the sand. Just like Cassel.

She wants to walk with Sergeant Cole, but she resists. It would be like clinging to her parents, and she's past that, she's not a little girl needing her father. She's a soldier, right? A soldier.

Instead she walks with Jenou, good old Jenou who can always perk her up with chatter about boys and girls and clothing and hairstyles and . . .

"What was it like?" Jenou asks her.

There's no doubt in Rio's mind what her friend means. "It's my job, right? I just did my job."

Jenou lets a few paces pass. "You were pretty cool under pressure."

"No different than anyone else," Rio says, trying to shut her friend down. She's feeling, feeling way too much now that the fight is past. She's like a steam boiler, pressure building up inside, a churning feeling. She wants to scream.

Everyone just shut up.

"Bet there's lions out here, up in those rocks. Mountain lions." Cat walking just a few steps behind.

Again with the lions. Give it a rest, Preeling, shut up, just shut up and let us march.

"Probably eating the guts out of that Italian you shot," Cat says.

Rio spins to face her. Rio is vibrating, all of her body straining to contain the pressure. She wants to snarl at Preeling, but can't find the words. Her clenched and cocked fist hovers, trembling, before dropping to her side.

Rio grits her teeth and starts walking again. Jenou has at last realized her friend is upset. "Don't pay any attention, Rio. Let it go."

Rio pulls out her canteen. Why are her hands trembling now when they were so steady before? She can feel the lightness of the canteen. There's no more than two inches of water in it. *Save it, don't drink until you can't stand it.*

But she drinks, just a mouthful, just enough to wash some of the grit from her teeth.

"Sarge," Sticklin calls out. "Off to the left at eight o'clock."

Cole halts, and the squad bunches up behind him. He's like a mother duck with newborn ducklings; they follow him, go where he goes, stop when he stops.

They all turn to look.

"It's a car," Jillion Magraff says. "Probably coming to get us to surrender."

"It's not German, it's a jeep," Hansu Pang says quietly.

Geer unlimbers his rifle. "If the Jap says it's a jeep, it's for sure a German."

Sticklin levels the BAR at the approaching dust plume.

"Hold your fire," Cole says. "It's a jeep."

Rio sees two people in the vehicle, a man and a woman. She looks ahead up this endless dirt road to nowhere. The Tommies are no longer in sight. Lieutenant Liefer has stopped. She's shading her eyes, staring at the approaching vehicle. Behind them in the direction they've come from, Helder and Third Platoon. They, too, are watching the jeep, which pulls up in a skid.

A female buck sergeant jumps out. "Are you from the 119th?"

Lieutenant Liefer glares at her. "Have you forgotten how to salute an officer, Sergeant?"

The sergeant does a double take, sighs, and snaps an entirely correct salute that Liefer takes her time returning. "This is Fifth Platoon, Charlie Company, 119th Infantry. You're looking for us?"

That last is said with an incredulous tone.

"Excellent, our relief is here," Jack says. Jack remained silent during the taunting by his fellow countrymen—this has earned him respect from the squad. He could have said he was English, he could have distanced himself from the disaster around him, but instead he remained loyal to his outfit.

"Sergeant Schulterman, ma'am, and this is Corporal Seavee. May I ask if you are in command here, ma'am?"

Liefer does not like her tone. The sergeant is not so disrespectful that she can make an issue of it, but it's clear that Rainy Schulterman is not impressed. The lieutenant holds out her hand. "If you have orders for me, let's have them."

Two folded sheets are drawn from within the sergeant's shirt. She hands them to the lieutenant. Helder comes trotting up, and the two officers, as well as Garaman, peruse the two paragraphs and peer closely at the signature.

Lieutenant Helder says, "Are you out of your fugging mind, Sergeant? We're to turn north? Across that?" He waves at the desert and the looming hills. "And attack a German supply column? We've got two platoons, no armor, no artillery or air support."

"Sir, those are the orders," Rainy says simply. Then adds, "The colonel's orders," and points at the signature.

Rio notices the way Liefer's face turns rigid as it dawns on her that the orders are for real and that failure to obey will mean the end of her career. If she still has one.

"Then Colonel Clay has lost his fugging mind," Helder

473

snaps. "My men are not going to march across nine, ten miles of wasteland to get killed."

But Liefer has reached a different conclusion. "I'm in command here."

"You're a second lieutenant, same as me," Helder says.

"What's the date of your commission?"

They compare commission dates, the day on which they were promoted to lieutenant, and Liefer has seventeen days' seniority. Lieutenant Helder curses, but he's powerless unless he wants to disobey clear, written orders.

Garbled repetitions of everything being said filter back through the GIs, who grumble, and more than grumble, about the stupidity of charging off into the desert with practically no water and damn little ammo. At least here on the road they may be taken prisoner by the Germans, who, by all accounts, treat prisoners humanely and according to the rules of war. But out in the deep desert, who knows?

"I'm already almost dry," Jillion Magraff says.

"Almost? Hell, I've been out of water for a couple hours, at least," Suarez says. He rattles his canteen to make the point.

As the lieutenants and NCOs discuss their fate, Second Squad sits or sprawls or lies down beside the road.

Rio closes her eyes. Closes them and sits there slumped over, her butt cold on the ground, swaying back and forth with exhaustion. It's hit her all at once. No sleep last night, no sleep today, and it's noon. Sleep, food, a hot shower, in that order, that's what she wants. Top it with mail from home, and it would be a foot soldier's paradise.

The next thing she hears is Cole sounding bitterly unhappy. "All right, Second Squad, gear up."

"Are you kidding me?" Jenou groans.

"I knew it," Hark Millican says, his eternal gloominess validated.

Jenou is standing; she offers Rio her hand and pulls her friend up.

"Bloody march in the bloody desert." Jack Stafford's usual good humor has deserted him.

An argument has broken out between the two lieutenants and Corporal Seavee. The officers are requisitioning his jeep.

"I'm only here because she"—the newly arrived sergeant—"popped up and shoved those orders in my face, but I got other orders, orders to get this jeep back to my captain," Seavee says, standing with arms crossed.

"Do you have written orders to that effect?"

Seavee shakes his head, amused in a bad way, pissed off but defeated by the relentless logic of officers. "Goddammit. Goddammit. We don't know what the hell's out there, Lieutenant, all due respect."

"Welcome to the war," Liefer snaps, and seems quite

pleased with that terse response.

Sergeant Cole and his counterparts from the other squads do a water and ammo count. It quickly becomes clear that there's nowhere near enough water, and half a dozen soldiers out of maybe sixty, seventy men and women left in the two platoons have lost or thrown away their rifles, though in Second Squad only Jillion Magraff has done so. Food is short as well. The jeep brought some cans of water, but barely enough to take the edge off.

"Okay, ladies and gentlemen, we are on short rations," Cole says. "We've got a good nine, ten miles at least, assuming there's a pass through those hills over there."

"Are they sending us some supplies?" Stick asks.

"Hell, Stick, we've got a military disaster going on here, the whole front is being rolled up. We are no one's top priority. If we find this column, maybe we can drink their water." It's a peevish joke, and no one laughs.

"What's this column we're supposed to find?" Luther demands, angry because he has a blister from poorly worn-in boots, and because his kitten is kneading his chest with her sharp little claws.

"Supposed to be ammo trucks and fuel tankers rendez-vousing with a German armored column."

"A what? An armored column? Tanks?"

"If we get there fast enough, maybe we get the trucks and skedaddle before the tanks show up."

"If we don't, we're fugging dead," Jack says. "Infantry against tanks? In open desert? That's mad!"

Cole does not argue with him. Stafford's summation and the sergeant's silence begin to sink in. The two green platoons are going off on a suicide mission with no help coming. There's mutiny in many eyes, but the problem is that there's nowhere to run. They are separated from any other force, and in the middle of a major German attack.

"I'd sure like to know who the hell dreamed up this hair-brained scheme," Geer demands belligerently.

"I did." It's the female sergeant who brought the orders from headquarters.

Her announcement earns her looks ranging from skepticism to resentment to outright hate.

"Great, another woman soldier," Luther sneers. "Thanks. Fugging excellent."

The complaints continue, but in the end they carry as much weight as a soldier's complaints generally do: none.

Sergeant Schulterman has been kicked out of the jeep so Liefer can take her place, with a PFC from Third Platoon perched on the back to employ the .50 caliber machine gun.

The jeep takes off at a walking pace with Second Squad behind it eating the dust it kicks up, and the rest of the two platoons behind them eating still more dust. This does not improve anyone's mood. But gradually Cole stretches the distance between the squad and the jeep. It's not quite enough to save them from a fine coating of dust that gets into their clothing and noses and eyes and mouths.

"Maybe we should get off to one side, Sarge," Jillion Magraff suggests.

"No, I think we best follow the jeep's tracks," Cole says.

"But the dust is—"

"You can get used to the dust," he says. "Can't get used to land mines."

The entire squad misses several steps. It would be funny if they weren't talking about mines.

"See, the good thing is, if there are mines they're most likely antitank not antipersonnel. So it'd take something heavier than a man to set one of those off." Cole reluctantly spits out the butt of his cigar, now no more than half an inch long. He pulls a replacement from his breast pocket and looks at it regretfully. He draws his knife and cuts the end off, then lights it with a Zippo. "But maybe there's antipersonnel mines, in which case something heavy will set them off too. Either way . . ."

Stick is the first one to grin, and it spreads throughout the squad as more GIs realize that they are basically letting Lieutenant Liefer ride in comfort . . . and check for mines. It's the sort of thought that brings a bit of joy to a foot soldier.

Rainy Schulterman walks beside Rio and Jenou, drawn by gender not rank.

"Has it been rough?" Rainy asks.

"It's been cold," Jenou allows.

"Too cold for mosquitoes. That's good, anyway." Tilo is giving the woman the once-over. Rio almost has to admire his single-mindedness, but she doubts the sergeant is Suarez's style. She's small, dark haired, olive complected, with what is probably a nice figure beneath a crisp but oversized uniform. *She looks clever,* Rio thinks, *smart.* Rainy has very alert eyes and seems interested in the people around her. Somehow that doesn't seem like Tilo's style.

And credit where it's due, Rio thinks, *she can't have been expecting to get dragged along on this mission. She's an office worker, probably some kind of clerk or something, who's been sent off to deliver orders.*

But no, hadn't Schulterman said this whole thing was her idea?

"What do they have you doing?" Rio asks.

"I work in intelligence," Rainy says.

"Office work? Headquarters work?" Jenou asks. "That's what I wanted. A desk, a telephone I could answer in a kind of sexy, breathy voice, hot showers, and hotter young officers."

Rio sees Rainy's nascent laugh before it comes and

says, "No, she's entirely serious."

"I am," Jenou confirms. "I did not volunteer for the infantry."

"No one volunteers for the infantry," Tilo says. "Except Stick. Stick, you always wanted this, right?"

"Maybe not exactly this," Stick says gloomily. "I was thinking we'd be going forward, not backward."

"It caught everyone by surprise," Rainy says. "The attack, I mean. Besides, you're no longer retreating, you're counterattacking."

"Counterattacking when everyone else is retreating sounds just a bit loony," Jack says.

The day is running out, and soon they'll be marching in darkness. The officers are anxious to reach the pass before night falls, so the jeep accelerates just a little, pushing the pace. They're climbing up a long slope now and the grumbling has turned specific: when are they going to get a break? When are they going to get a chance to eat? Even walking off to one side to take a bathroom break is impossible because at this pace they won't catch up without running and no one wants to run.

The sergeant from headquarters—now, in fact, nicknamed Headquarters—is having a particularly rough time of it because she's not in the shape the infantry men and women are.

"Where are you from?" Rainy asks.

Rio makes a gesture indicating herself and Jenou. "We're from a little town in Northern California that you've never heard of."

"Have you seen a lot of action?"

Rio shrugs. "Well, we took on a couple of tanks. I guess you can see how well that turned out."

"It's not just your outfit," Rainy says. "The whole front is collapsing. FUBAR."

It dawns on those within hearing that they have here that rarest of creatures: someone who actually has some notion of the big picture. Rio, Jenou, Tilo, and Jack move closer.

"Tell us," Tilo says.

Rio says, "See, we don't exactly know why we're here or what's going on."

"No, I guess you wouldn't," Rainy says with just a trace of condescension. "What's happening is that the Germans did what they were not supposed to do. They were supposed to realize that with the American army in front of them and the British army behind them, they were surrounded and cut off, and would be best off just surrendering. Instead, they attacked."

"Yeah, we noticed that much," Tilo says.

"If we don't stop them, they could push us all the way out of Tunisia, all the way back to Oran, or even clear out of North Africa, though that's unlikely. We have the edge in numbers and supply. Their big weakness is fuel for those tanks," Rainy goes on. "They're desperate. This fuel column is absolutely vital to them. They lose that fuel, this part of their thrust will peter out."

"Why us?" Jenou asks.

"You were in the right place."

"Wrong place, more like it," Tilo says.

Far up ahead the jeep has reached the pass.

It blows up.

34

RIO RICHLIN—TUNISIAN DESERT, NORTH AFRICA

The ground beneath the jeep just explodes upward, sending the jeep cartwheeling. It turns in midair. Rio sees bodies thrown like dolls.

"Hit the dirt!" Cole yells.

The jeep slams down and explodes again. This time it slams into the wall of the canyon. A body, Rio can't tell whose, flies free and smashes against the canyon wall. It slides down like some figure in a cartoon. Like it's adhesive.

"Minefield!" Cole shouts. "Everybody freeze. Nobody moves."

GIs strain to see if anyone is moving up ahead. The pass is in shadow but the jeep burns now, burns and casts an eerie orange light that does not show movement other than the drift of disturbed sand and a small, indistinguishable desert creature that sensibly scuttles away.

Lieutenant Helder from Third Platoon along with the

various sergeants huddle up, once they're sure this isn't artillery or an air raid. The general consensus is that they have to send someone forward to check for survivors, but once that's done they should abandon this stupid mission, get back to the road, and find their way to the main body of the army, wherever the hell that may be.

Rainy disagrees. "The orders I'm carrying come from Colonel Clay, with the full authority of General Fredendall." This is a bit of an exaggeration, but only a bit. "Those orders say we go find this supply column. And it's through that pass."

"You want to stroll through that pass, Headquarters?" Sergeant Garaman demands. "That's a minefield. Now, maybe it's just antitank mines, but maybe it's antipersonnel mines, too, and I don't see any engineers here."

"Don't go through the pass? Then climb the hills on either side."

"In the dark? Shadows are already long, and night comes on fast out here, this time of year. We'll lose half a dozen men just from broken bones."

"The orders are clear," Rainy shoots back.

"Well, your colonel isn't the one who has to find a way through, now is he? He ain't here, he's in the rear with some A-rab whore pulling his pud."

Garaman and Schulterman continue to argue, and Helder continues to show every sign of being a man overwhelmed, while Cole borrows a pair of binoculars and scans the two sides of the pass.

"Anyone here ever done any mountain climbing?" Cole asks, interrupting the increasingly heated flow of invective.

Rio has not, but Hansu Pang raises his hand. So does a corporal from another squad.

"What are you thinking, Jedron?" Garaman asks, relieved to have an excuse to end the absurd shouting match with a woman half his size.

"I'm thinking that cliff right there isn't but thirty, forty feet high," Sergeant Cole says. "A man could carry a rope up there."

The NCOs pass the binoculars back and forth, pausing to cast suspicious glances at Private Pang.

"We're supposed to trust a fugging Jap?" someone asks, making the suspicions explicit.

"He's an American," Cole says, casting his own suspicious look at Pang, who stands stock-still, jaw clenched.

"I'm actually—" Hansu begins, but is cut off.

"He could get to the top and signal anyone on the other side," Garaman says. "He could bring them down on us."

Silence stretches as everyone considers the situation. Finally Helder sighs and says, "I don't like it. But if we don't try it, this headquarters girl, sorry, Sergeant Schulterman, here, is going to have us up on charges."

"That's right," Rainy says, playing her part.

"Yeah, that's about what I thought." Sergeant Garaman is disgusted. It's a feeling shared by everyone, including a visibly angry Hansu Pang. "Someone's got to climb with the Jap. And if there's any funny business . . ."

The implication is unspoken but clear: if Pang looks cross-eyed, someone has to be there to shoot him.

"I'll go with Pang," Cole says at last. "See if we can't find a way forward that isn't through that pass. Maybe at least get a picture of what's on the other side. Could be more mines, could be a battalion of Waffen SS waiting for us."

"Okay. And we need a detail to check on the jeep, see if anyone's alive. Salvage any water or ammo. Any volunteers?"

"I'll go." Dain Sticklin, of course.

"Pick two people from your squad to go with you," Sergeant Garaman says.

Sticklin's eyes widen in shock. "I'm not a noncom, I'm—"

"I don't really give a goddamn," Garaman snaps, his patience worn out. "It's a three-man job. And, Cole, before you give me any crap about your squad doing the hard part, your man volunteered. I want him to have people he knows. Pick your team, Stick. Pang, get a fugging rope."

"Sorry," Stick says to Rio.

Rio is flattered, but she's more tired. She groans. So does Jack when he intercepts Sticklin's abashed look.

"Oh, lovely," Jack says. "Just bloody lovely."

The idea is simple enough: stay strictly within the jeep's tire tracks. But those tracks are only about eight inches wide and the distance to be covered is a quarter mile.

Sticklin takes point. He's handed off his BAR to Geer, both because it's an ungainly weight to carry when trying to walk a perfectly straight line, and because they can't risk a useful weapon.

Jack is next in line, with Rio behind him. They keep a hundred-foot interval. If Sticklin hits a mine it will only kill him and not the two behind him.

Heel, toe, heel, toe. Rio wobbles. Rights herself. Heel, toe. Like walking a balance beam. Like a tired, thirsty, exhausted gymnast walking a balance beam.

And with each step they are closer to a devastation that Rio does not want to see. She never liked Liefer, but she never wanted her blown up.

Sticklin stops.

Rio freezes. Advances slowly, cautiously.

Something on the sand. Just to the right. Just ten feet beyond the safe zone. A charred object, black, tattered.

An arm.

A human arm. It can't be anything else given the length, given the way it bends in the middle. Given the way it ends in what looks like a bird's claw more than a hand but must nevertheless be a hand, a human hand.

"Who is it?" Jack asks. His voice is hushed. It's a church voice.

Sticklin shakes his head slightly.

They move on, no longer keeping an interval because they need each other's presence for what lies ahead. The terra-cotta-colored walls of the canyon are close around them now, the ground steep and the walls steeper. The passage is narrow at this point, no more than thirty, forty feet from wall to wall. The jeep lies upended, engine down, wheels in the air. It's bent, as though it were one of those die-cast metal toys, and twisted in the middle.

It's burning, but not all of it, mostly just the rear wheels, sending up a column of black smoke, filling the air with the stink of burning rubber. Burning rubber and a smell that's just a little like bacon.

Corporal Seavee is still in his seat. It seems impossible, but he slumps there, bent over the twisted frame of the windshield. His arms hang down like he's pointing at the ground. His back is burning.

It takes Rio a few seconds to realize that his head is gone and when she does realize she cries out, a sound of fear and horror. She looks around wildly trying to find it, like that would help, like she might be able to reattach it.

Stafford retches. Rio wishes she could, but her stomach is empty and anyway a numbness has come over her. A distance. She's not there, not really. She's nowhere, in fact, a disembodied ghost of herself floating beside the appalled white-faced girl in a uniform.

I'm so young.

"Anyone see the Loot?" Sticklin asks after a minute. His voice is far away, but spirit Rio sees that the young girl is looking dutifully, scanning left and right.

"Is that . . . ?" Stafford says.

Twenty yards away there's a lump of something black. It's smoking like a recently extinguished campfire. There is nothing recognizably human about it, but it cannot be metal, it's too soft in the edges.

Rio can't look any longer. She looks up and sees two vultures circling high overhead.

How do they get here so fast? Who tells the vultures?

"I say that's Lieutenant Liefer," Jack says. He wipes his mouth but misses some of the vomit. He unlimbers his canteen, and Rio sees his hands shake.

"Where's the guy from Third Platoon?"

"I think that arm . . . ," Jack offers.

"Yeah," Stick says. "No way we can get anyone's dog tags."

"No," Rio agrees.

"So, we all agree that we identified all three bodies, right?" Stick asks. His voice is ragged, insistent.

Rio and Stafford make eye contact. Both nod.

"We can't even . . ." Stick licks his lips and looks a little desperate. "We'll send the info to graves registration. We'll give them the location. They'll come in with an engineer unit, clear the mines, retrieve the bodies."

"I never liked her much," Jack says of Liefer.

Rio shakes her head. "No."

"Feels bad though."

"Yeah."

"Anyone see anything salvageable?" The jerry cans of fuel are burning. The ammo must have been blown clear, a good thing since otherwise it would cook off, maybe kill one of them.

Rio is back in her body, seeing the world through her own eyes. She shoots a look at the two understrength platoons. Just short of a hundred guys, well, less than that counting those who got separated during the initial rush to escape the tanks. Seventy guys? Maybe. They're a pitiful-looking bunch. They look small in the open desert, small and scared, armed with rifles that look like toys from this distance. Like children playing war and armed with sticks. Like they'll all just yell, "Bang! Bang!"

They're smoking and opening cans of rations. Many are stretched out on the ground, grabbing rest while they can.

"It was quick," Rio says. "They didn't feel anything."

Jack nods. "Never even knew."

The cooking-meat smell is sickening—and all the more sickening because it starts Rio's mouth watering.

"That could be a water can," Jack says, pointing to something half-buried in the dirt off the track.

It could be sitting right next to a mine.

"I don't see anything," Stick says pointedly.

"No," Jack says. "No, you're quite right. Nothing."

Without further discussion, they turn and start the long walk back out of the pass.

As they emerge, Rio sees Pang climbing with impressive confidence up a rock face, a rope tied around his waist. Cole and a private from the other platoon are ten feet below him, moving more slowly.

Rio, Stafford, and Sticklin reach the relative security of the group. Sticklin gives Helder their report.

"Three dead bodies. Nothing salvageable."

Hansu Pang and Cole have topped the cliff. Additional ropes are being sent up, so in half an hour, as darkness falls, there are three ropes hanging down and the GIs begin to climb.

Rio and Jenou are among the last to go up. Big knots have been tied in the ropes, making the ascent easier, but still by the time she reaches the top Rio has chipped the last flakes of pink from her nails and her knees and knuckles are scraped raw.

No one has fallen. Everyone is safe atop the height. They march slowly, two men out front with bunkered flashlights trying to see any ravines, but everyone is stumbling and cursing, all making too much noise. If there are Germans on the other side of this hill, they won't have any difficulty guessing that Americans are coming.

But after an hour of twisting ankles and curses they reach the far side and there's nothing to be seen there, just darkness. They advance slowly down a mercifully gentle slope.

Then someone calls out, "I see lights!"

Everyone squats down, and the GIs on point switch off their flashlights. Yes, there are definitely lights, slitted headlights that cast pale pools on what must be a road.

"Could just be locals."

"No. It's trucks," Garaman says.

Distance is almost impossible to gauge; the desert is just a dry ocean with few landmarks or reference points. It could be five miles, it could be twenty. The noncoms huddle with Rainy Schulterman and unfold a map, which they read in the light of a flashlight shining red through fingers.

"Could be we're in the right place," Garaman says. "Sheer dumb luck."

"Could be another minefield between us and them

too," Hark Millican says with one of his more worried sighs. "Could be antipersonnel this time."

"We either do it or don't," Cole says, looking to Helder, who says, "Goddammit," several times.

No one doubts the answer. They've come too far. They're late getting here, but the way back isn't much better than the way forward at this point. Everyone is thirsty, seeing the presumed German trucks as a possible source of water. Or death.

"If it was tanks we'd hear them," Cole says, reassuring his squad.

Rio is not reassured. She hadn't even thought of tanks. They were looking for trucks, the tanks weren't supposed to be there ahead of the fuel. But now it's all she can think of. She's had all the tanks she ever wants to see.

Garaman says, "How do you see this, Jedron?"

Cole considers. "If there are mines we're better off sticking to single file until we get close. Keep intervals. No light. When we're within a hundred yards or so of the road we spread right and left. They get into the crosshairs, we fire off some flares. We light them up and open up."

Sergeant Garaman nods. "Yeah." Then he turns to the lieutenant.

The lieutenant sighs. "Not much else we can do, is there? Can't even see if there's any cover."

"Wish we had a couple more mortars and a few fifties," another NCO says.

"Wish we had a couple of fugging tanks and some planes overhead," Garaman says, and there's low, anxious laughter.

"Light 'em up, blow 'em up, be ready to run like scared rabbits."

"Hero time," Sergeant Cole says dryly.

Rainy Schulterman says, "It's awfully dark." There's fear in her voice.

Yeah, it is, Headquarters. It sure is.

35

RIO RICHLIN—TUNISIAN DESERT, NORTH AFRICA

Lights crawl toward her across the black and featureless desert, out of the southeast, heading north. Both platoons are dug in facing east.

Lieutenant Helder is in command, but he's self-aware enough to know that this is not a job for a ninety-day wonder with no combat experience, so in effect, Sergeant Garaman is in command, with his counterpart, Sergeant Coffey from Third Platoon, as his second. Between the two platoons there are eight NCOs, not counting the female sergeant from headquarters. "Headquarters" is instructed to dig a hole well back and stay down.

Rio has had time to dig a decent hole, not deep enough to stand in, but she can squat on her knees. A hundred feet to her right, Jenou has her own foxhole. A hundred feet to her left and taking advantage of a few feet of elevation, Stick has the BAR ready.

Millican and Pang are a hundred yards out front,

practically on top of the presumed line of travel for the convoy. But even in the dark Rio can see that the convoy is not staying in line but spreading out across the desert.

"That's good and bad," Cole opines. "Means they don't think they have mines here."

"What's the bad part, Sarge?" Jenou asks.

Cole is walking the line, making sure everyone in the squad is tucked in, talking calmly, doing his best to project a confidence Rio knows he doesn't feel.

"The bad part is the bazooka teams could end up having bad guys behind them as well as in front."

"Will they be okay?" Rio asks.

"Sure, Richlin," Cole says, a little sarcastic and a lot worried. "Day at the beach. The other bad news is worse: our right is hanging in the air. Third Platoon's on the left, and that's a bit better because at least they've got some dry gullies on their left. Our right flank is you people, Castain, Richlin, Stick, and that's open ground."

Day at the beach is an unfortunate turn of phrase: Rio's most recent day at the beach ended with Kerwin's blood in the sand. She wipes unconsciously at the blood that has long since sweated off her hand.

"Sun will be up soon, in a couple hours," Stick says.

"Not before they get here," Sergeant Cole says. "We'll light 'em up with the flares. Then the bazookas and the mortar." He squats beside Rio. "Richlin, their

496

commanding officer is either going to be in a half-track or a staff car. He's your target. If you can pick him out, you keep fire on him."

Why me?

"Yes, sir," Rio says.

Cole snorts a laugh, as he was supposed to. "How many times I have to tell you? I am not a sir. I work for a living."

Rio, like every other soldier in the platoon, is secretly glad that Liefer is not here to direct this battle. Not that she wanted Liefer dead, not even a little, but in a desperate firefight she feels safer with cranky old Garaman and steady Cole, and Helder who's got enough sense to let them handle things.

The thought takes her back to that evening with her father on the porch. *It's the sergeants that keep their men alive, the good ones, anyway. You find a sergeant you trust and stick to him like glue.*

There's a feeling of doom over her. A feeling that what is to come will be very bad, that this is a suicide mission, one for which they are wholly inadequate. She recalls her father's warning that generals sitting far from the battlefield will spend her life for nothing. Isn't that just what's happening here?

Headquarters' fault, the pushy little sergeant. No one asked her to drive out here and get them into this.

Cole has walked on, and now Jenou, in a stage whisper, says, "Rio? If I don't make it . . ."

"Shut up, you're going to make it," Rio snaps.

Look for the officer. Keep fire on him.

Kill him.

"Yeah, well, if I don't, promise you'll marry Strand. And if you have a girl, name her after me. Jenou. It can be her middle name, that's okay."

"If I have a girl I'm going to name her Jenou, all right, but I'll make her pronounce it with a hard *j*."

There's no laugh in response, instead a long silence in which they can begin to hear the clank of half-track treads, not as insistently frightening as a tank, but not nothing either, and the grinding of truck gears.

"I'm scared," Jenou says in the voice of a much younger self.

"We're all scared."

"Yeah, but I'm too cute to die," Jenou says. "And, uh, I'm sorry I got us into this. It's just . . ." She shakes her head. "My home isn't like yours, honey. I needed to get away."

Rio has long sensed something dark about Jenou's family, but though they have talked of many things, shared many things, Jenou has seldom spoken about her parents other than to dismiss them as a pair of drunks. Jenou has built a wall around whatever her secret is.

Someday I'll get her to tell me, Rio thinks. *If there's a someday.*

"You didn't twist my arm, Jen."

"Goddammit, Rio. This was not what I had in mind."

"FUBAR," Rio says.

Jenou manages a short laugh. "How did we ever get by without that word in civilian life?"

"Folks weren't shooting at us."

"You're my best friend, Rio. I would not have made it without you. Not back home, not in basic."

Rio feels emotion rising in her. There's a lump in her throat. But this is not the time. This is not the time for emotion.

"You'd have been fine," Rio says curtly. She wants now to focus on the job ahead. On enfilade and defilade. On windage and elevation. Not feelings, not even friendship.

Waiting in her hole in the Tunisian desert, with German trucks and half-tracks, Kraut soldiers and their machine guns that fired fifteen hundred rounds per minute, twenty-five lead slugs every second, each one traveling at 2,461 feet per second, Rio does not want to remember home. She is here.

Here.

"I don't want you to die, Rio. You're all I've got," Jenou says.

"Everyone's scared," Rio snaps. Then, desperate to

ease the tension, she adds, "Everyone except Stick."

Stick, in his hole to their left, says, "Well, I haven't pissed myself yet, but the day is young."

The lights crawl. The sound of engines grows. The head of the column is even with them now, somewhere between a hundred feet and a mile off, distances still impossible to judge well in the inky black.

Blow up the supply column, and run like hell before the tanks get here for the rendezvous.

Stars are visible now, as scattered high cumulus clear just enough to let starlight edge the clouds in silver. If only the moon had not set. Rio suddenly craves the reassurance of the moon.

She prays for survival, for courage. For a drink of water in a mouth as dry as the sand.

A shout!

Flares shoot up into the sky, long, red, smoky trails that zig and zag as they climb.

And . . . burst!

Eerie red light reveals a half-track, a line of trucks—six, eight—a staff car, another half-track, and lagging a little behind, still almost invisible in darkness, an ambulance.

Hark Millican's bazooka fires. *Fwooosh!*

It hits the lead half-track dead center. The explosion ejects German soldiers like popcorn.

Find the officer!

If their commander was in the lead half-track, he's either dead or definitely distracted, because fire is raging up through the vehicle. And now Stick opens up and there's fire all down the line, M1s and carbines and BARs.

"Two fifty yards!" Sergeant Cole shouts above the sudden eruption of shattering noise.

With trembling fingers Rio clicks the wheel on her rifle. No wind.

The staff car. She sees it, sees three indistinct shapes, sees that the driver has gunned the engine. She sees the light of the flares is dying, more are launched, and already the Germans are shooting back, aiming blind, but firing at where they guess the flares came from. Soon they'll sight on the sources of tracer fire, but the Germans are in the open and the Americans are in holes.

A second bazooka round from the other platoon and the hollow sound of the sole mortar and Rio lines her sights up on the staff car.

Bang!

No way to tell if she missed or where the bullet fell.

Bang! Bang! Bang! Bang!

Jenou is blasting away now on Rio's right, Sticklin's BAR rattles out a stream of bullets, red tracers rising across the sand as he finds his range and pours lead into one of the tanker trucks.

We light them up and open up, Cole said earlier.

Rio has lost sight of the staff car. She pushes her helmet back to get a better view, rises in her hole; where the hell is it?

There! Racing to get out in front of the burning half-track.

Rio fires after it. It's a tracer round, and she can see it hit but can't tell whether it hit steel or flesh.

Bang! Bang! Bang! Clang!

Empty clip. She pulls another from her belt and slams it home. *Bang! Bang!*

The staff car is still moving, but it tips into a ditch or depression and rolls partway onto its side.

Ba-woosh!

A tanker truck explodes, spraying flaming fuel. It looks like a deadly flower blooming at accelerated speed. Rio hears screams. A man is on fire, running, a torch in the dark. The burning gasoline outlines the staff car. She sees a helmet.

Bang! Bang!

A mortar round stops a second tanker. It does not explode, but it's not moving either, and out of the corner of her eye Rio sees the driver leaping from the truck.

Everywhere are shouts and cries, both sides yelling versions of *kill them* and *help me* and cursing, but they are small sounds in contrast with the steady staccato of rifle fire and the intermittent roar of the BAR.

The second half-track is making a move toward the front. It goes around to the east side of the column, visible now only in the gaps between trucks.

"I got movement here!" It's Jenou, the dangling end of their too-short line.

Suddenly, seemingly out of nowhere, rifle and machine pistol fire erupts, fast but disciplined fire, veteran troops for whom this is not their first ambush. They are trying to flank the line, crossing the T that will let them roll up the line, foxhole by foxhole, while the Americans can't shoot for fear of killing their own people.

A scream. More fire.

"Suarez, Preeling, Stafford!" Sergeant Cole shouts. "On our right, on our right! Castain, Richlin, drop back behind Stick. Stick, you open up soon as they're clear!"

Jenou pops up out of her foxhole and runs past. She's forgotten her rifle.

Rio has been ordered back, but she knows she's not in Stick's line of fire, and she thinks she sees a head that is adorned not by a helmet but by a peaked cap. She aims.

The BAR, Suarez, Preeling, and Jack open up on the advancing Germans, but the fire coming back the other way is just as intense.

Rio cannot look at that, cannot waste the time to look

at the Germans now just a hundred yards away, she has a target.

Bang! Bang! Two shots, the first one carefully aimed, the second sloppier, but a peaked cap flies off the distant head.

Now, Rio twists to face the advancing Germans. There must be twenty of them, twenty against five while the remainder of the squad continue to fire on the column.

Rio aims, fires, aims, fires. Germans fall but they keep coming, heads low, firing from the hip, running straight into the BAR and rifle fire, and Rio thinks, *They're better than we are. My God, look at them!*

Another clip gone and the reload jams. She feels frantically, pushing, pulling, banging with the heel of her hand until the clip slides free. She reloads carefully this time, carefully, but the butternut uniforms are right there, right there. *Bang! Bang! Bang!*

Something fast dings her helmet. Something else plucks at her collar.

She keeps firing, firing, and reloading, and now the Germans are hesitating, two drop into Jenou's abandoned foxhole, but the German fire still comes fast and accurate, and there's nothing to be done now but to keep shooting back.

The battlefield is silent.

The sound of her own heart.

The sound of her breath.

The silent impact of the rifle butt on her shoulder as she fires round after round, reloads, fires.

Off to her left another tanker truck explodes.

Have we done enough? Can we run away now?

Suddenly Rio is shaking, her entire body, every muscle so weak she can't stay up, she slumps into her hole, drawing her helmet down out of the line of fire as the BAR's tracers arc overhead to seemingly bounce back as German bullets.

Rio is praying aloud now, praying gibberish interspersed with the kind of curses that once would have made her blush, stars in the sky above, God up there somewhere, three clips left, three clips, twenty-four bullets.

And three grenades.

There's a tunnel in space, a warping of the fabric of reality between Rio and the Germans. She sees nothing but the end of that tunnel, nothing else exists. Just that space directly before her, just the enemy.

The location of Jenou's foxhole is clear in her mind. She unhooks a grenade and crooks her finger through the pin.

She pulls the pin. Her hand, tight now, strong in a kind of spasm, holding down the lever.

Release it. Release it and throw. Release it and throw, Rio, do it.

Rio releases the lever, which cartwheels away as the fuse pops and now just four seconds. She does not throw. One. Two. And . . . she stands up, head just inches below the BAR fire, and throws.

36

FRANGIE MARR—TUNISIAN DESERT, NORTH AFRICA

Frangie changes every bandage. She sews up a split finger, irrigates an eye crusted shut with blood, and manages to do it despite rude thrusting fingers and groping hands.

The column is driving on relentlessly, no longer on anything resembling a road but pushing out into open desert. The overcast skies keep Allied air power from spotting them, but there are many nervous glances skyward from wounded and healthy soldiers alike.

Eventually she is given a can of tinned meat and crackers. It's what the German soldiers are eating, and grumbling as they do so. The grumbling is not comprehensible, but is nevertheless familiar to Frangie. Soldiers complain; German, American, every kind of soldier.

An open staff car carries the black-uniformed officer who ordered her patient shot and a second officer in the more familiar butternut khaki. There is clearly no love lost between these two as she learns from their body language, each on his own side of the car, each avoiding looking at the other.

A young German who is missing his right foot rides along in the truck and offers her a half cigarette. Frangie doesn't smoke, and in any case fears if she takes it she'll be accepting some unspoken bargain. She shakes her head no.

The soldier shrugs, says something to his companion, gets a laugh in return.

The ambulance is just behind them and off to one side to avoid the vast clouds of choking dust the truck tires throw up. The ambulance driver leans out of his window and yells something that Frangie does not understand but contains one word she has learned: *schwarze*.

Black.

The cigarette soldier gives her a light shove and waves her toward the ambulance, but they're moving at a steady twenty miles an hour. Maybe she can jump off the truck, but she can't climb onto the ambulance.

Another shout, an impatient wave, and Hungry Eyes, the lowering brute who seems more or less in charge of the wounded, says something that causes cigarette soldier to shove her again, harder.

She stands up, bracing against the lurching, spine-jarring assault of the truck's suspension, climbs as far down as she can, down onto the bumper, takes a deep breath, and jumps the last two feet. Unsurprisingly she stumbles, falls on her back, and rolls onto her side to stand up.

The ambulance comes to a halt beside her. The back door now flies open and the Doctor-Major yells, "Get in here, American."

The inside of the ambulance reeks of sweat, vomit, human waste, and fear. The sides are lined with stretchers hinged to the walls, three on each side, but there are two men in each cot, lying head to foot, and three more sitting hunched over against the front of the rectangular space.

Frangie frantically runs through what she knows about typhus, but that turns out to be almost nothing.

The Doctor-Major says, "Lice," as if answering her query. "We raided a village, not knowing . . . Some of the men passed their time with the women, many of whom turned out to be louse-ridden with *rickettsia typhi–*bearing lice. It's a nasty little disease that displays as a very severe headache, fever, cough, muscle pain . . . death in usually twenty percent or so of healthy men, but these are not healthy men, these are exhausted men who have gone too often without food or water or sanitation."

The men are either stripped down to their underwear or buried in blankets, depending on the state of their fevers. Frangie sees rashes from the illness, but also protruding ribs and injuries in various stages of healing . . . or not healing.

"I have had no sleep in three days," the Doctor-Major says. "I must sleep."

His eyes are glassy, his whiskered face sallow.

"Have you taken your own temperature, Doctor-Major?"

He hesitates, bites his lip. "One hundred point five. And yes, my head aches and my muscles as well. I pray it is not typhus or who will care for these men? It is only me."

He pulls a blanket from a man who, Frangie now sees, is dead. He spreads the blanket out on the filthy floor, lies down, mutters something about rationing the water, they always want water, and falls asleep.

Wasser. That was the German word for *water.* There is a tin ten-gallon tank bolted to the wall behind one of the seated men. A tin cup hangs from a chain and rattles softly.

Schwarze, *give me water . . .*

I want morphine, kaffer, *this pain . . .*

I am so cold . . .

They are the enemy, and they have come down with this disease as a consequence of attacking a village and raping the women. They are abusive, despite being sick, arrogant though prone. These are not fresh recruits, that is clear from their disease-yellowed tans, the ancient scars, and the tattoos that proudly advertise the names of battles they fought against the British and the French before them.

First: love. That was what my faith has taught me.

Love even those that hate you.

Well, Frangie Marr is nowhere near summoning love for these men, but she can dole out water and hold the bucket for men who vomited, and she can spoon-feed potted meat and rehydrated cabbage to the men who can eat. She can do that.

Hour after hour the column lurches on. An especially sharp jolt wakes the Doctor-Major, who rises groggily to check on his patients. A new one arrives to be manhandled into the back of the ambulance, and is laid on the blanket the Doctor-Major had vacated, both Frangie and the German doctor straining weary muscles.

Frangie leaves the door swinging open, squeaking and banging as the ambulance hits ruts and gullies and climbs soft hillocks of sand with grinding gears. The fresh air is worth the noise. Night has long since come and is now threatened by just a hint of gray in the east. A half-track is behind them and to one side, headlights slitted, machine limned by silver starlight.

"How much longer?" Frangie asks.

The Doctor-Major has slept seven hours and awakened at last to find his charges all well cared for. And the mood has changed. Frangie is no longer *Schwarze*, at least for some of the men, she has become *Schwester*: sister.

Nurse.

The Doctor-Major shakes his head. "I don't know. We are to rendezvous with a tank unit. But that is only the next step, America, it never ends, you know. It never ends, this war. You'll see."

But two hours later, as Frangie sits scrunched in a corner catching a catnap, it does end, at least for most of the men around her.

The first explosion wakes her.

The rattle of gunfire propels her to her feet.

"What's happening?"

"War," the Doctor-Major says sourly.

The rear door is still open. Frangie shoots a terrified glance at the Doctor-Major and at the door, now an eerie red rectangle in the light of the flares.

"No," the Doctor-Major snaps, grabbing her by the back of the neck. "There will be more wounded, and I cannot—"

A noise, several rapid sounds like a knife being stabbed into a tin can, and red holes appear in the side of the ambulance and spray blood across Frangie's chest and arm.

It is a sheer panic reflex that sends her stumbling out through the open door to land hard on the sand.

In a shocked instant she takes it all in: a burning vehicle up ahead, shouts, a storm of rifle and machine gun fire coming from the left, the zing of bullets flying in search of soft targets.

She begins to stand up but thinks better of it and lies flat, her belly in the dirt. Tracer rounds pierce the ambulance again and again, like flaming arrows. The men on the stretchers twitch and jerk, try to stand and fall, collapse, roll out of the back of the ambulance to crawl or lie still on the cold ground.

She sees the Doctor-Major twist, slap at a hole in his buttock made by a .30 caliber round, then drop to his knees as more rounds pierce him again and again.

Frangie rolls away, rolls and rolls like some game she would have played in the park with Obal, frantically aware of the half-track rushing toward her with a roar and a grinding of gears, a bear maddened by bee stings, desperate to escape the deadly fire that pursues it.

It careens past, the tracks missing her by inches.

She comes to rest, hugging the sand as the battle rages on ahead of her, drawing slowly away as the column continues to try and escape. She remains flat as a platoon of German soldiers race past, rushing to flank the attackers.

The ambulance rolls on for a bit, slower, slower, and finally comes to rest. A tire is burning, billowing toxic black smoke that rises to obscure the stars.

In the east the faint gray dawn is a signal of more terrible sights to come.

37

The grenade lands at the lip of what had been Jenou's foxhole. It lies there looking like a small steel pineapple, two seconds gone, two more, *tick-tock*.

The nearest German sees it, reaches for it, picks it up, starts to throw it back. The explosion amputates his arm at the elbow and shreds his helmet and face.

The German stands there, already dead but not yet fallen, frozen in the flare light, looking as if some gigantic tiger with claws of steel has ripped the side of his face.

Rio stands, staring. Her rifle leans against the inside of her foxhole, forgotten. She is looking at a monster. There is a terrible curiosity, a can't-look-away horror blended with denial because such things simply did not exist, her mind will not accept it, and a second German soldier farther back roars hatred and raises his machine pistol toward her, the deadly barrel spitting bullets.

And . . . empty.

She hears the metal-on-metal click of an empty chamber and the soldier throws his machine pistol aside in rage, draws a dagger from a sheath strapped to his leg, and runs at her.

He is a big man, brown eyed. She notices that because so many of the Germans have blue eyes, but no, these are brown. He is missing two teeth, which makes his snarl seem almost comical. His uniform is filthy, streaked with mud and coated with a thick layer of dust. His hands are big, thick fingers gripping the hilt, big boots slamming the sand, propelling him forward, roaring, always roaring, like a beast.

"Richlin! Down!"

The voice is far away and means nothing.

In three steps she will—

Down, down, down!

Where has that voice come from? Is it a voice at all? For a fleeting split second she thinks it's her father, and then, a sudden, urgent spasm, like a lightning strike, and she drops to her knees as Jack fires. She feels the breeze of his bullets.

The big German staggers forward, carried by momentum. He swings the knife and Rio feels something like a punch in the arm, and then is buried beneath the German's body.

She is on her back, squashed down into her shallow

foxhole, crushed by two hundred pounds of dead man exhaling his final breath into her ear.

Something snaps. Rio hears it as a snap, feels it as a twig breaking, and all at once she is pushing and punching and screaming foul curses and blasphemies, while all around her the guns blaze on. A second grenade goes off, and at last she breaks free and pushes herself up, drags her rifle from beneath the dead man, and starts firing again, screaming all the while, screaming, "Die, you fugging bastards!"

She fires until her clip pops.

Then . . . silence.

"Hold your fire, hold your fire!" Cole's voice.

A single shot followed by a louder Cole, yelling, "Goddammit, I said hold your fugging fire!"

Morning has come.

A white flag has appeared.

Rio stands with her rifle in her hand, legs still pinned by the dead man at her feet.

The man with the face ripped apart by Rio's grenade slides slowly down into Jenou's foxhole.

"Are you okay?"

Rio's hearing is half gone, her comprehension gone further still. The world around her seems to vibrate. The light is unreal.

A hand touches her arm and she flinches; the hand

does not pull away but tightens its grip. "Honey, are you okay?"

Rio stares at Jenou, blinks at her as if there is something about this person she should recognize, but she can't quite place the face.

"Who shot him?" Rio asked.

"What?"

"Who shot him? This one." She looks down and carefully begins disentangling her feet.

"I think it was Stafford."

A sharp sob. Rio takes several deep breaths, but the trembling is upon her again, the same as her first shots, her first kill. Tears come fast and hot, streams of mud down her cheeks. She dashes them away and shakes her head and throws off Jenou's comforting hand.

"I'm okay," Rio says.

"Yeah, well, I'm not," Jenou admits softly. "I can't do this, honey. I'm not made for this like you are."

It's not meant as an insult, it is admiring and a little awestruck, but Rio flares and says, "Don't say that, Jen. Don't say that, we are . . . we're . . . I'm okay. I'm okay. You'll be okay."

For that moment Rio has convinced herself that she is done, that she has performed her duty. She has done all that can be asked of her. She closes her eyes and she is home. She is home, she is in the barn with her mother, and they are laughing while the cows moo in outrage, demanding to be milked.

Her father is there, too, but not laughing. *We're your family. Whatever happens, we're your family. Whatever happens, this is your place, this house, this town.*

You'll need that.

Sergeant Cole yells to Luther and Pang to check the German bodies. "The dead ones, make sure they're dead, then strip them of their water and food. Any that are alive take their weapons, use their bootlaces to tie them up."

"Aw, why can't Richlin do it?" Luther complains.

"She's the one who made them dead, most of 'em," Cole says. "You just make sure they stay that way."

38

RAINY SCHULTERMAN—TUNISIAN DESERT, NORTH AFRICA

Three German vehicles are burning, more are disabled, and the dramatic pink light of morning highlights a white flag flying from the antenna of one of the surviving tanker trucks.

"Well, I will be well and truly damned," Sergeant Garaman says to Cole, shaking his head in disbelief at the carnage there at the end of their line. "You got some people who can fight, Jedron."

"That I do."

Rainy, no longer able to tolerate hugging the sand at a safe distance, has crawled forward. She sees helmets barely poking above foxholes. She sees Garaman standing, shielding his eyes, peering intently. Then she sees the bodies, maybe a dozen in German uniform, lying in the weird and horribly comic poses of violent death.

"I need ammo!" Sticklin shouts.

"Magraff, distribute ammo!" Cole shouts. "Pang, give her a hand."

Geer, his voice choked, says, "My kitten! Miss Pat!"

Rainy risks standing herself and realizes the toll fear has taken on her: her muscles scream from tension and rigidity.

"What now, Sergeant?" Rainy asks Garaman. "Where's Lieutenant Helder?"

"Deader than hell, Headquarters."

"Shit," Cole says. "He was okay. I guess you're it, Garaman."

"I fugging know it," Garaman says bitterly. "Okay, I'll tell you what's next, Headquarters, we blow the hell out of the remaining trucks, scrounge what we can, and get the fug out of here before that tank column shows up."

Off to the southeast a sandstorm whips up intermittent tornadoes, a brownish smear across the horizon, dirtying the sunrise, but it's a mile off and not heading this direction.

Rainy says, "Sarge, I'm with S2 and I want to look for papers, maybe interrogate some prisoners."

Cole snorts and shakes his head. "Well, I sure wouldn't want to harm the war effort by denying you the opportunity, Sergeant . . . what was your name?"

"Schulterman."

"We're just going to make sure this isn't a trick and . . ." He falls silent because three German soldiers are carrying the white flag forward. One appears to be a senior officer.

Weapons are trained on the advancing enemy but

520

no one fires, and a sort of collective sigh of relief rolls down the line. Rainy hears relieved laughter, nervous and uncertain.

Cole lights his stubby cigar with his Zippo and to Garaman says, "All right then, boss, what is the protocol for accepting the surrender of an enemy officer?"

Garaman lights one of his foul cigarettes. "See, that's why we need officers, to handle this kind of—"

"Sarge," a man from Third Platoon says, high-strung and upset. "We got wounded. Six men, two of which is a woman. I mean, two are women, plus four men."

"Well, we ain't got a doc, so you're going to have to do what you can. You got any medical skills, Headquarters?"

"No," she says. Rainy is not about to let herself be turned into a nurse. That is a German colonel advancing under the flag of truce, and she is determined to do her job as a military intelligence sergeant.

Said German colonel stops fifty feet away. He speaks no English, so Rainy avoids nursing duty by stepping in as translator.

"He says he's Colonel Von Holtzer and he wants to see our commanding officer," she says.

"Tell him we ain't got a commanding officer, just us lowly noncoms."

This news is not well received. There's a desperate look in Colonel Von Holtzer's eyes, a kind of panic that is quickly papered over by practiced arrogance. Through Rainy, he says, "I cannot surrender to common soldiers."

"I see," Garaman said, cracking a rare grin.

Cole said, "Tell the colonel we are going to blow up his fugging trucks and he can either disarm his fugging men and send them down the road and no one gets hurt, or we can resume fire."

After a brief back and forth, Rainy says, "He'll do it, but only if you don't insist on formal surrender."

Garaman said, "You tell the colonel—"

"Sarge," Rainy interrupts, "I need to be able to question any officers."

Sergeants Garaman and Cole blow different fragrances of smoke toward her and favor her with nearly identical looks of irritation. But then Garaman shrugs.

"Tell the colonel we reserve the right to question any officers. But aside from that we have no interest in taking prisoners. We'll leave him with what food and water we can spare, and nothing else."

The colonel is clearly worried and unconsciously glances back toward his burning vehicles and men.

Rainy says, "I'm not sure this guy's in charge. He seems awfully nervous. I would suggest we take his offer, but keep our eyes open—there may be another colonel—even a general—hiding among the men."

It is a shrewd guess, and Rainy is flattered by the

surprised appreciation in Garaman's eyes. Cole nods agreement.

"All right, Headquarters. We'll secure the column; you take a couple of Cole's people and check it out. Tell the colonel here to order all his men to drop arms and move north away from the vehicles. If there's any trouble—I mean if we see so much as a souvenir dueling pistol—we will open up on them and kill every last one of the bastards."

Which is how Rainy ends up trudging across the desert toward the Germans with Rio Richlin and Jack Stafford, once Cole has waved an all-clear.

They have covered half the distance when a single person appears, walking out of the sunrise.

Stafford trains his rifle. Rio levels hers from the hip.

Rainy calls out something in German, but almost immediately realizes that this is definitely not a German.

"She's a Negro," Rio says.

"Yes, I just noticed that," Rainy says. "And a woman."

"The Germans are not fond of blacks, or women," Stafford points out.

Rio calls out, "If you've got any weapons, drop them right now."

"Private Frangie Marr. I was being held prisoner."

"Put your hands down, Private," Rainy says. She looks closely at the small young black woman. "You look like you've been through it."

"Hey," Rio says. "Don't I know you?"

Frangie tilts her head and looks at her quizzically, then her face brightens. "Seen any wild pigs out here?"

"I have not," Rio says, breaking into a grin.

"Where's that big old hillbilly who was with you?"

That kills the smile on Rio's face. "Kerwin Cassel. He, uh . . ." She shrugs.

Frangie understands immediately. "I am sorry to hear that. He seemed like a good guy."

"Yeah. Yeah, he was. He was a good guy."

The four of them stand awkwardly until Jack says, "I'm not sure I'm enjoying this war."

That coaxes a rueful nod from Rio and Frangie. Rainy fidgets impatiently, but she says nothing, acutely aware suddenly of a yawning gap between herself and these soldiers who have seen real combat, who have fired guns in anger.

Rainy looks thoughtfully at Frangie. "You were a prisoner? You see that colonel standing over there? Is he the commanding officer?"

Frangie closes her eyes, an aid to memory, and a response to exhaustion, exhaustion somehow made more profound by the relief she feels at being back with American troops. "Him and another guy in a different uniform. Black uniform."

Rainy feels predatory excitement. "An officer in a black uniform?" She points at her collar. "SS?"

"Yep," Frangie confirms. "He's the one that shot my patient, lying on a table, his stomach all messed up. Ordered one of the soldiers to shoot him in the head."

"Waffen SS. They're a whole separate army. Fanatics. The worst of the worst." To Frangie she says, "I imagine you'd like to grab some chow and take a nice long nap, but can you walk with us through those Krauts?"

So they are four when they enter the mass of angry, resentful, worn-out Germans. The Germans are under the guns of a dozen Americans armed with rifles and sub-machine guns. Other soldiers are gleefully looting trucks, digging out anything that can be eaten, drunk, or considered a souvenir.

Rainy speaks German as she walks through the sullen mob. "You men have nothing to fear, we don't shoot prisoners. As long as you cause no trouble, we're going to let you walk away. I just want the officers."

She watches eyes flick involuntarily, but not toward the two lieutenants and the major standing together and trying to look dignified in the face of defeat. Nor do they glance toward Colonel Von Holtzer, who stands aloof, face mirroring the self-justifying internal dialogue he's assembling for his superiors.

No, the eyes dart toward a corporal in blood-stained

khaki who sits on the sand surrounded by other men, all stiffly ill at ease.

Rainy walks directly to this man, who refuses to look up.

"That him?" Rainy asks Frangie.

"I can't see his face."

Stafford steps forward and uses the barrel of his rifle to push the man's head back.

"That's him, and he speaks English," Frangie confirms. "What happened to the fancy boots, Colonel?"

"Go on, shoot me," he said, rising to his feet, defiant. "Kill me and be done with it."

"Doc, they've got chow and wounded back there," Rainy says to Frangie, who gratefully takes the hint.

"I wasn't planning on killing you, Colonel . . ." Rainy lets the question hang.

"SS Colonel Von Kleeberg," he says. "Where are your officers? I demand to see them."

"Nah, you don't want to see them," Jack says.

"So I am to be questioned by a . . . a . . . female sergeant?"

Rainy does not see the smile on her own face, but Rio and Stafford do, and their opinions of the sergeant from headquarters change dramatically. Headquarters does not like SS officers, no she does not.

"Not just a female, Colonel. A Jew. Sergeant Rainy Schulterman. Hebrew."

The colonel's hauteur slips and there is a mix of hatred and dread in his eyes that Rainy enjoys immensely.

That's right, asshole, one of those people.

The colonel spits at her. It hits Rainy on the cheek and slides down her face, cleaning a path through the dust as it does.

"Happy to shoot him for you, Headquarters," Jack says cheerfully.

"No, that's what he wants. Then his little blond children and his wife and his mistress can all tell themselves he died a warrior's death." Rainy does not bother to wipe off the spit; she leaves it there, evidence of her indifference.

She considers for a moment, then says, "I won't kill you, Colonel, you're a potentially valuable asset. You weren't here for the supplies, you were joining the tank column. Replacement commander, right? You're coming with us. But first you're taking off those boots and the pants too."

"I don't take orders from filthy Jews."

Rainy gives no order and is frankly shocked when Private Rio Richlin swings the butt of her rifle into the side of the colonel's face. It's not enough to kill or even render him unconscious, but it staggers him and blood seeps from his ear.

Rainy gives a slight nod to the fierce young woman and notices a troubled frown on Stafford's face.

In the end they march a bootless, pantless SS colonel back to the platoon and present him to Sergeants Garaman and Cole.

"This piece of shit is an SS colonel who had an unarmed, wounded American captain shot through the head. We're taking him with us," Rainy says, defiant, expecting them to argue.

The two sergeants nod contentedly as they peer at the swelling bruise on the side of his head, then at his state of undress, and finally, as though they have synchronized their movements through long practice, turn to look at Rainy Schulterman.

"One other thing, gentlemen," Rainy says. "Some of those trucks are still working. If you squeezed your people in tight . . ."

"We could ride on out of here," Sergeant Cole says. "Yeah, we already thought of that."

"Might not be room for the prisoner, though," Rainy says.

"Might not be."

"Might be you could tie him to the bumper. He looks healthy enough to run."

"Now I know why they never let women fight wars," Sergeant Garaman says. "Too mean."

39

RIO RICHLIN, FRANGIE MARR, RAINY SCHULTERMAN— TUNISIAN DESERT, NORTH AFRICA

Luther's kitten, the inexplicably named Miss Pat, took a piece of shrapnel in her paw.

"Well, she won't be able to count to ten on her paws, but she'll do fine," Frangie says after bandaging the wound.

Luther Geer takes the kitten back from her and after some grimacing manages to say a civil, "Thanks." And then, after some kind of internal struggle, amends it by saying, "Thanks, uh, Doc."

The German prisoners are set to digging graves for the American and German dead. But they are not given any precious water or food because the sandstorm has cleared, revealing a line of two dozen German tanks that Cole estimates in the light of day to be five miles away.

"Time to skedaddle on outta here," Cole says. "Move, people! If we don't get the hell away before those Panzers get within range, I will be irritated."

The two platoons are down to a total of just fifty-one men and women and no officers. The gravely wounded, those who will never survive being moved, are left behind in the hope that the Germans will do the decent thing. The walking wounded are laid out on the beds of the trucks while the healthier folks, including Rio and Jenou, Frangie and Rainy, Cat and Jillion, Jack and Stick and Suarez, Pang and Geer, all end up standing on seats, their feet between the heads and shoulders and legs of the injured. It's not a comfortable way of traveling, and the GIs keep up the usual steady stream of complaints, liberally salted with the inevitable obscenities and blasphemies, but no one is anxious to climb down and try to walk away from the approaching German tanks.

Those tanks fire one shot after them that explodes harmlessly, but perhaps because they've noticed an SS colonel (forcibly uniformed in the tell-tale black) being dragged along on a rope at a desperate trot, or more likely because they don't have orders to go wasting fuel, the tanks give up the chase.

The fortunes of war had their fun getting the platoon involved in an ill-conceived commando mission and then sending them into battle unprepared. The fortunes now relent and give them safe passage to reach and join the flight of the Americans through the mountain passes and eventually back to safety.

Safety, hot chow, and plenty of water.

Rio stands in line for that hot chow, a stew of some sort containing God only knows what species of meat. She is exhausted, too exhausted even to make small talk with Jenou or Jack or Stick, each of whom has now become something more to her than they were before. They are welded together in a way that each of them feels and none of them could explain. And some of that rubs off on the outsiders who shared the terror and thrill of combat with them, Frangie and Rainy.

Rio is weary to the point where a choice between eating and just throwing herself on the ground and sleeping is a tough one to make. In a dull and distant sort of way she is aware that something profound has changed within her. She both fears and welcomes this change.

A white PFC with a clean uniform, clean, shaved face, and bright eyes objects to Frangie being in the chow line ahead of him. Rio turns hollow eyes and a blood-spattered face to him and says, "Fug off."

And when the PFC says, "Figures a woman wouldn't know any better than to eat with a Nigra," it's Luther who growls, "You know what's good for you, boy, you'll do like she said and fug off."

There is a weight that comes from surviving combat, an authority that soldiers serving honorably in the rear may resent but cannot ignore.

They sit hunched over their tin mess kits, shoveling food mechanically, saying nothing, staring at nothing, and one by one fall back onto the dirt and sleep.

When they are roused by insistent shoves and kicks by Sergeant Cole, it is to board still more trucks and head farther to the rear to rest, rearm, reorganize, and prepare for whatever the brass has in mind for them next.

Cole pulls Rio aside before they board. "When we get our new lieutenant, I'm putting you in for a medal, Rich-lin."

"Oh, Jesus, Sarge, don't do that. I didn't do anything everyone else wasn't doing."

Cole smacks the side of her helmet. "Hey. Medals aren't just for you. They're for other men—and women—to see and to want to be more like you."

Rio laughs and yawns simultaneously, not an attractive look or sound. "Forget it."

"You got something, Richlin. I'm going to tell you what it is, and you're probably not going to like it."

This gets Rio's attention. She sighs, but she listens.

"A lot of guys go to war. A small percentage of them end up in the shit. A small percentage of those end up being good soldiers. And a smaller percentage still become what you're on your way to being, Richlin."

"Tired?"

"Killers. I don't mean crazy glory-hounds or heroes. I mean efficient, professional killers."

"That's not . . . ," Rio says, trying to work up a dismissive laugh. She shakes her head no, not liking that at all, not liking it one bit. That's not her. That's not Rio Richlin, confused and aimless teenager from Gedwell Falls. She's going to be a wife, marry Strand, have kids.

"When the war's over, you put all that in a box," Sergeant Cole says. "You go on with whatever else you want to do in life. Get married and have lots of babies. But right now, Richlin, you're a killer, and killers are what I need. So I'm putting you in and that's it."

Rio says nothing, just turns away and walks back to her squad, who are busy packing up, smoking, cursing, and annoying one another for no good reason. A fist fight breaks out between Tilo and Luther, and everyone watches for a while until it becomes clear that both men are just blowing off steam. The fight ends when Jillion Magraff arrives with a purloined bottle of German schnapps, and the squad quickly adjusts its priorities.

Jenou intercepts the bottle on its way to Rio. "Oh, no you don't. I saw what happened last time you started drinking."

Rio holds her hands up and lets the bottle pass by.

"At some point you're going to have to spill," Jenou says.

"What? Spill what? The bottle?"

"The straight dope. The inside scoop. You have now had . . . interludes . . . with two different males. It's time for detailed comparisons, Rio."

Rio glances guiltily toward Jack, who is dusting Suarez off and getting Geer's helmet, which Suarez had knocked off.

"Let's just pretend it was only one . . . interlude," Rio says. "Strand is the one. Jack is . . . He's a fellow soldier."

"Right. You think I'm going to let you get away with that? There are a lot of boats and trucks and long walks ahead of us, Rio. You will tell all. Oh yes, you will tell all."

Rio has a sudden, overpowering desire to hug Jenou, so she contents herself with patting Jenou's back. "You and me, right?"

Jenou turns and notices tears in her friend's eyes. "Of course you and me, honey. All the way through."

After a while Rio says, "You know what I wish I had right now?"

Without a moment's hesitation, Jenou answers, "Sure. Same thing I want. A big basket of fries and a milk shake."

Rio gasps and then shakes her head ruefully. "I was going to say a big *plate* of fries and a Coke. But close enough. You know me too well, Jen. I don't even need to tell you anything."

Jenou gives Rio a playful shove and says, "Nice try. But you will tell all. I will absolutely resort to torture." Then Jenou's focus shifts to someone beyond Rio. "Well, hello, who is that?"

Rio glances over her shoulder and sees a young lieutenant in a torn and dirty uniform carrying an M-1 like an enlisted man. He could use a shave, but he's not bad looking despite that. He's trading salutes with Sergeant Garaman.

"Law of averages says it's someone with orders for us to go off and do something stupid," Rio speculates.

"That's a coincidence, because I just happen to have something stupid in mind," Jenou says.

Rainy Schulterman is brought to the nearest thing this dusty, chaotic assembly area has for an S2. Captain Jon Joad demands to know what the hell she thinks she's doing out here, separated from her unit.

Rainy shows him her orders.

The captain sneers. "Yeah, and how did that go for you, little lady?"

"Pretty well, sir."

"Well?" He throws the orders at her; she fumbles the catch and has to pick the page up out of the dirt.

"Yes, sir, quite well."

"The hell are you talking about, lady?"

"Sir, we were able to intercept a supply column and

destroy it just before a German tank column rendez-voused. That's why there are those German trucks parked out there. And, sir, I have a request."

"A request?"

"Yes, sir, I have a prisoner I need to get back to Maktar. I need a jeep and a driver, and an MP to keep an eye on the prisoner, if you have any MPs, otherwise any soldier you can spare."

"What, some beat-up sergeant surrender to you?"

"Sir, I have a Waffen SS colonel as my prisoner, and I request—pursuant to the orders I've just shown you—to have appropriate means made available for transport so he can be interrogated ASAP by Colonel Clay."

She is given a jeep, a driver, and a corporal to ride shot-gun.

The corporal is the gloomy Hark Millican, volunteered by Sergeant Cole, who taps Stick to step up into that role.

Rainy is tempted to stop by Fifth Platoon and thank them. But it was her bright idea that got their lieutenant killed, and others besides, and on reflection she decides that would not be wise. She was the bringer of ill tidings, and soldiers are not above blaming the messenger.

She and her battered, exhausted, sore, and dirty pris-oner drive away.

Frangie no longer has a unit to return to. Whatever was left of her battalion is far from here, and no one seems clear on where it might have gone. She seeks out Sergeant Garaman.

"Sarge, I'm kind of up in the air right now. I don't suppose I could tag along with your platoon until I figure out where I'm supposed to be."

Garaman shrugs and flicks away the butt of his cigarette. "Well, we need a doc, that's a fact." He sighs, anticipating some world of trouble he's buying for himself by an impromptu integration of his platoon. Then says, "Go hook up with Sergeant Cole. His squad's all broads, Limeys, Japs, and misfits anyway, might as well add a Nigra."

So Frangie gathers her small stash of medical supplies, sneaks by the hospital tent where additional supplies happen—purely by accident—to fall into her pockets, and finds Second Squad climbing on a truck.

There's another squad with them, and naturally one of those soldiers makes an angry remark about her race.

"She's not a Nigra," Luther says. "She's Doc."

"How's Miss Pat doing, Geer?"

Luther pulls the kitten from his shirt, holds her up, and says, "Not Miss Pat anymore, she's a veteran, she gets a better name. Calling her Miss Lion from now on."

Rio looks at Jack, guessing what's coming next. Jack winks at her and says, "See? I told you there were lions around here."

Interstitial
107TH EVAC HOSPITAL, WÜRZBURG, GERMANY—APRIL 1945

Well, Gentle Reader, I had a bit of joy today. Sergeant Richlin—Rio—came by to check on me, see how I was doing. I think she scared some of the nurses; she has that effect on people now. She's hard and she's foul-mouthed and she's got that thousand-yard stare that I suppose I do as well. Or maybe it's just the fact that she came in straight from the front line, grenades hanging off her like ornaments on a Christmas tree, tommy gun on her shoulder, her prized souvenir, a German Luger, stuck in her webbing belt, and that big knife of hers strapped to her leg.

But if you looked hard, Gentle Reader, you'd still see something of that freckle-faced tomboy who grew up milking cows and thought "golly" was a curse word. Some part of the sweetness of her is still alive underneath it all, or at least I think so, hope so. Same as I hope there's still some part of a different me hidden away under the hard shell of cynicism.

I wonder how I look to her. I know I'm damaged in more than body. The fever that pushes me to write this is not the symptom of a mind at peace. Can she see the invisible damage inside me, as I see it in her?

Won't be long now, I think. The Russians are in Berlin, going street by street. The Krauts will have to fold up shop, though not until Hitler's dead, I guess. They are still in thrall to that mad bastard, even now with their cities burned down around their ears, what a goddamn waste. A lot of German units have surrendered, and what's left is mostly old men and kids. Kids. Like we were not long ago.

It's coming to an end, this war, but I still have a lot of story to tell. There's Sicily and Italy and France yet to write about. A whole lot of war there.

North Africa was where we were bloodied, where we became real soldiers, but in the grand scheme of the war it was small beer. The Krauts taught us a lesson we needed to learn, though; they knocked the cockiness right out of us, that they did, and we were better soldiers for it. One hell of a lot of Krauts died in the stony hills of Sicily and Italy because we had begun to learn our profession.

The battle of Kasserine Pass will not go down in history as the finest moment in the history of the US Army. Although what's funny is that when we were in it we didn't know that's what that debacle would be called.

We just knew it was FUBAR. It shook me, that's for sure, shook me all the way down to my bones. There's nothing like the feeling of running away to feed the beast of fear inside you. That took its toll. Still does.

But that's all down the road. We'll get there, Gentle Reader, we will.

If you're wondering what happened with Rio and Strand and Jack, or wondering whether Rainy ever met up with that nice Jewish boy again, or whether Jenou ever met her longed-for handsome officer, or whether Frangie and Sergeant Walter Green . . . Well, not now, that's all for later. Right now I have to go and cause a ruckus because they're talking about shipping me stateside. I won't have it. I'll go AWOL before I let that happen. I got this far with our little band, and I'll be damned if I miss the final act. I don't expect we'll celebrate, celebration doesn't feel right, but I would sure love to sit down and have a quiet beer with my pals.

Besides, like I said, there's a lot more for me to write.

THE BATTLE OF KASSERINE PASS

"The weaknesses the Americans showed were those usually demonstrated by inexperienced troops committed to battle for the first time. Beforehand, they were overconfident . . . once committed, they were jittery . . . They lacked proficiency in newly developed weapons such as bazookas. They had difficulty identifying enemy weapons and equipment . . . They were handicapped by certain poor commanders . . . reactions were slow, cautious, and characteristic of World War I operations. Units were dispersed and employed in small parcels instead of being concentrated. Air-ground cooperation was defective. Replacement troops were often deficient in physical fitness and training. Some weapons were below par. . . . Higher commanders shirked the responsibility or lacked the knowledge to coordinate units in battle . . ."

—US Army Center for Military History

"In Tunisia the Americans had to pay a stiff price for their experience, but it brought rich dividends."
—*German Field Marshal Erwin Rommel*

I write fiction. In writing this piece of fiction I have attempted to accurately capture the flavor and the feel and as much of the detail of actual historical events as is practical, but any conflicts between my version of events and the work of historians should unquestionably be resolved in favor of those worthy academics. In writing this book I have relied on dozens of histories, memoirs, newsreels, museum exhibits, and photographic archives, but all errors or deviations from fact are mine alone.

Operation Torch and the battle of Kasserine Pass? Real. Tulsa? Real. New York City? I'm pretty sure that exists. Gedwell Falls is my own invention, though I suspect it's located quite near Healdsburg, California. Similarly, Camps Maron and Szekely, while suspiciously close to Fort Benning, Georgia, are made up. Other things, things you might not expect, actually happened. A lot of American troops really did go to war on the luxury liner *Queen*

Mary. And the bit about a French soldier who erected a *barricade symbolique?* That scene is actually based on a true story. Nothing is more unexpected than reality.

In the course of portraying the attitudes and notions of social justice prevalent in the United States in those days, I have used language and portrayed attitudes that all good people now find abhorrent. But it was another time, and I can't whitewash history. In those days, racism and sexism and anti-Semitism were all right out there in the open. Some people had begun to see beyond those destructively irrational notions, but it was very much a work in progress. The generation that won World War II saved the world—no, really, *saved the world*—but they were not saints.

There's a bunch more to be found on our website, www.frontlinesbook.com, and our Facebook page, Facebook.com/frontlinesbook, including videos, photos, maps, music, additional stories, and more.

I'm to be found on Twitter @MichaelGrantBks.

Questions of legal rights and permissions should be directed to Steve Sheppard at Cowan, DeBaets, Abrahams and Sheppard, but please don't send him fan mail—he's a lawyer, and he'll charge me to read it.

Thanks. Please consider checking for digital shorts wherever you buy ebooks and stay tuned for book two of Front Lines.

—Michael Grant

BIBLIOGRAPHY

This is very much a *partial* bibliography.

A lot of my sources were online. I have only to wonder, "How do you fire a bazooka?" and ten seconds later I'll be watching the official World War II–era army training film. How great is that?

A quick shout-out to some wonderful museums: the Imperial War Museums in London, the National World War II Museum in New Orleans, and the Smithsonian Institution in Washington, DC. You can understand intellectually how intimidating a tank is, but standing in front of the real thing, running your hands over the armor, that certainly drives the point home.

Pride of place goes to the series that inspired me to write this trilogy: the Liberation Trilogy by Rick Atkinson. It was reading that trilogy that first caused me to think I'd like to write about World War II.

I also want to mention *Code Name Verity* by Elizabeth Wein. I'd already started writing *Front Lines* when I read

Verity, but it certainly caused me to want to work harder to come up to that very high standard.

Okay, on to at least some of the books:

Berubé, Allan. *Coming Out Under Fire*. Washington, DC: The Free Press, 1990.

Blumenson, Martin. *Kasserine Pass—Rommel's Bloody, Climactic Battle for Tunisia*. New York: Cooper Square Press, 2000.

Calhoun, Mark T. *Defeat at Kasserine—American Armor Doctrine, Training and Battle Command in Northwest Africa, World War II*. Pickle Partners Publishing, 2014.

Cowdrey, Albert E. *Fighting for Life—American Military Medicine in World War II*. Washington, DC: The Free Press, 1994.

Franklin, Robert "Doc Joe." *Medic—How I Fought World War II with Morphine, Sulfa, and Iodine Swabs*. Lincoln, NE: Bison Books, 2006.

Hartstern, Carl J. *World War II: Memoirs of a Dogface Soldier*. Xlibris, 2011.

Hirsch, James S. *Riot and Remembrance: The Tulsa Race War and Its Legacy*. Boston, MA: Houghton Mifflin, 2002.

Johnson, Hannibal B. *Tulsa's Historic Greenwood District*. Mount Pleasant, SC: Arcadia Publishing, 2014.

Kelly, Orr. *Meeting the Fox*. New York: John Wiley and Sons, 2002.

Kerner, MD, John A. *Combat Medic: World War II*. Donald S. Ellis, 2002.

Kershaw, Alex. *The Liberator*. New York: Broadway Books, 2012.

Mauldin, Bill. *Up Front*. New York: W.W. Norton, 1945.

Muth, Jörg. *Command Culture*. Denton, TX: University of North Texas Press, 2011.

Pyle, Ernie. *Brave Men*. Scripps Howard Newspaper Alliance, 1943.

———. *Here Is Your War: Story of GI Joe*. New York: Henry Holt, 1943.

Reitan, Earl A. *Riflemen—On the Cutting Edge of World War II*. Bennington, VT: Merriam Press, 2014.

Robinson, Sergeant Don. *News of the 45th*. Norman, OK: University of Oklahoma Press, 1944.

Rottman, Gordon L. *SNAFU—Situation Normal All F***ed Up*. New York: Osprey Publishing, 2013.

Smith, Daniel D., and Frank T. Barber. *Memoirs of World War II in Europe*. CreateSpace Independent Publishing Platform, 2013.

Tobin, James. *Ernie Pyle's War—America's Eyewitness to World War II*. Washington, DC: The Free Press, 1997.

Urban, Mark. *The Tank War*. New York: Abacus, 2013.

Watson, Edward. *A Rifleman in World War II*. Digital Unlimited, 2015.

Zaloga, Steven. *Kasserine Pass 1943—Rommel's Last Victory*. New York: Osprey Publishing, 2005.

1943

Three great Axis powers: Germany, Italy, and Japan. Italy's Benito Mussolini began as Hitler's mentor, but after failure upon failure it has become clear that Mussolini's Italy lacks the resources and the will to fight effectively. The war in Europe will be fought between the Allies and Germany, with Mussolini more a hindrance than a help.

For too long Britain stood alone while the Soviet Union's paranoid dictator, Stalin, purged his own army and worked backroom deals with the Nazis to seize Finland and divide Poland. But in one of the great mistakes of history, Hitler attacked Stalin. The Soviet Union's vast size, terrible winter, and the astonishing courage and

1

endurance of its people have proven too much, even for the Wehrmacht.

And now, thanks to the Japanese bombing of Pearl Harbor, the United States of America is in the fight, bringing staggering industrial might and a military that will, in just a few short years, go from being a negligible force of 334,000 to a 12 million strong juggernaut.

In the Pacific, the US Marines have survived a protracted living nightmare on Guadalcanal. Japanese expansion is halted. Australia and New Zealand are safe, but China, the Philippines, and Southeast Asia still bleed under brutal Japanese occupation.

In Europe, the Soviet Red Army has fought the German Wehrmacht to a halt at Stalingrad. Hitler's mad order allowing no retreat will lead to the death of a third of a million Germans and the surrender of 91,000 more. The greatest tank battle in history will be fought at a place called Kursk, and by dint of sheer numbers and steely determination, the Soviet T-34 tanks will beat the German panzers back.

London is still struggling to recover from the Blitz, and now German cities cringe beneath falling bombs. In Poland, the Jews who had been herded into the ghetto to be starved to death rise up against their Nazi oppressors and, despite great heroism, are exterminated.

The Americans, British, British Commonwealth, and

Free French forces have pushed the Nazis out of North Africa. Benito Mussolini is weakened and discredited but not yet destroyed.

No one is certain about the next objective, including Allied leadership.

The Germans have been bloodied, but Nazi Germany is very far from beaten. And in places called Dachau, Bergen-Belsen, Buchenwald, and Auschwitz, the killing gas still flows and the ovens still burn hot.

107TH EVAC HOSPITAL, WÜRZBURG, GERMANY—APRIL 1945

Welcome back, Gentle Reader, welcome back to the war.

I've got quite a pile of typed pages now, quite a pile, and I'm not even a third of the way through. But I've already got some readers, some of the people here in this hospital with me, and, well, they've stopped complaining about me being up typing at all hours. So I guess I'll keep at it.

I'm still not quite ready to tell you who I am. I'm not being coy or cute, I just find it easier to write about all of it, even my own part, as if it happened to someone else. And if I put myself forward you might start thinking of me as the hero of the story. I can't allow that because I know better. I know who the heroes are, and who the heroes were, and I am neither. I'm just a shot-up GI sitting here typing and trying not to itch the wound on my chest which, dammit, feels like I've got a whole colony of ants in there. I suppose this means I'll never be able to wear a bathing suit or a plunging neckline. That will bother me someday, but right now, looking around this ward at my fellow soldier girls, and at the soldier boys across the hall, I'm not feeling the urge to complain.

I hear civilians saying we're all heroes, heard someone . . . was it Arthur Godfrey on Armed Forces Radio? I can't recall, but it's nonsense anyway. If everyone is a hero, then no one is. Others say everyone below ground is a hero, but a lot of those were just green kids who spent an hour or a day on the battlefield before standing up when they shouldn't have, or stepping where they shouldn't have stepped. If there's something heroic about standing up to scratch your ass and having some Kraut sniper ventilate your head, I guess I don't see it.

If by "hero," you mean one of those soldiers who will follow an order to rush a Kraut machine gun or stuff a grenade in a tank hatch, well, that's closer to meaning something. But the picture in your imagination, Gentle Reader, may not bear much similarity to reality. I knew a guy who did just that—jumped up on a Tiger tank and dropped a grenade (or was it two?) down the hatch. Blew the hell out of it out too. But he'd just gotten a Dear John letter from his fiancée in the same batch of mail that informed him his brother had been killed. So I guess it was right on the line between heroism and suicide.

Don't take me for a cynic, though; I am not cynical

about bravery. There are some real heroes, some gold-plated heroes, here on this ward with me. There are still more lined up in rows beneath white crosses and Stars of David in Italy and France, Belgium, Holland . . . And some of them were friends of mine.

Oh boy, it's hard to type once I get teary. Goddammit, I'll just take a minute here. . . .

Anyway, my feeling bad doesn't raise any of those people from the grave.

They brought some wounded Krauts in today, four of them. They're in a separate ward of course, but I saw them through the window, saw the ambulance, dusty olive green with a big red cross on its roof. It wasn't easy to tell that they were Germans at first—they were more bandage than uniform—but even through the dingy window glass I could make out that one still had some medals pinned to his tunic. Not our medals. So I guess he was a hero too, just on the wrong side.

I hope the medals give that Kraut some comfort because he was missing both legs above the knee and his right hand was gone as well. I saw his face. He was a handsome fellow, movie star handsome, I thought, with a wide mouth and perfectly straight Aryan nose and dark, sunken eyes. I knew the eyes. I didn't know the Kraut, but yeah, I sure knew that look. I see it when I look in the mirror, even now. If you stay too long in the war, it's like your eyes try to get away, like they're sinking down, trying to hide, wary little animals crawling into the cave of your eye sockets.

No, not like animals, like GIs. There's nothing a soldier knows better than squatting in the bottom of a hole. Cat Preeling wrote a poem about it, which I'll probably mangle, but here's what I recall:

> *Dig it deep and in you creep,*
> *While all around there's the boom-boom sound.*
> *Mud to your knees while your buddy pees.*
> *Another hole, like the hole before . . .*

Yeah, that's all I remember. It goes on for a couple dozen verses.

Anyway, I still type away at this battered old typewriter, and some of the girls come by and take a few pages to read when they're tired of the magazines the USO gets us. They seldom talk to me about it; mostly they just read, and after a while they bring the pages back and maybe give me a nod. That's my proof that I'm writing the truth because sure as hell I'd hear about it if I started writing nonsense. We soldier girls—sorry, I mean Warrior Women or American Amazons or whatever the hell the newspapers are calling us now—we've had about enough of people lying about us. The folks who hate the idea of women soldiers tell one set of lies, the people who like the notion of women at war tell a different set of lies. If you believe the one side, we're nothing but a drag on the men, and the other side acts like we won the war all by ourselves.

We could probably get a pretty good debate going here on the women's ward over the question of which set of lies we hate more—the one denies what we've done; the other belittles what our brothers have done.

We won't have either.

We women are a red flag to the traditionalists—which is to say 90 percent of the military. But as much as we don't want to be, the truth is we're a symbol to people who think it's about time for women and coloreds too to stand equal. Woody Guthrie wrote that song about us. Count yourself lucky you can't hear me singing it under my breath as I type.

> *Our boys are all a-fightin' on land, sea, and air,*
> *But say, some of them boys ain't boys at all,*
> *Why, some of those boys got pretty long hair.*
> *It may surprise, but I can tell you all,*
> *When it comes killin' Nazis, our girls stand tall,*
> *And Fascist supermen die every bit as fast,*
> *From bullets fired by a tough little lass.*

For our part, we sure as hell did not want to be a symbol of anything, though we did sort of like Woody's

9

song. We wanted exactly what every soldier who has ever fought a war in foreign lands wants: we wanted to go home. And if we couldn't go home, then by God we wanted hot food, hot showers, cold beer, and to sleep in an actual bed for about a week solid.

But we're just GIs, and no one gives a damn what a GI wants, male or female.

Tunisia, Sicily, Italy, France, Belgium, Germany. Vicious little firefights you've never heard of and great battles whose names will echo down through history: Kasserine. Salerno. Monte Cassino. Anzio. D-Day. The Bulge. About all I missed was Anzio, and thank whatever mad god rules the lives of soldiers for keeping us out of that particular hell. There's a woman here, a patient on the ward, who was a nurse at Anzio. All she ever does is stare at her hands and cry. Though the funny thing is, she can still play a pretty good game of gin rummy. Go figure.

Whatever the newspapers tell you, we women are neither weak sisters nor invincible Amazons. We're just GIs doing our job, which after Kasserine we'd begun to figure out meant a single thing: killing Germans.

So, Gentle Reader, we come now to a period of time after Kasserine, when those truths were percolating inside us. We were coming to grips with what we were meant to do, what we were meant to be, what we had no choice but to become. We were girls, you see, not even women, just girls, most of us when we started. And the boys were just boys, not men, most of them. We'd only just begun to live life, we knew little and understood less. We were unformed, incomplete. It's funny how easy it is to see that now. If you'd called me a child three years ago when this started I'd have been furious. But looking back? We were children just getting ready to figure out what adulthood was all about.

It's a hell of a thing when a person in that wonderful, trembling moment of readiness is suddenly yanked sharply away from everything they've ever known and is handed over to drill sergeants and platoon sergeants and officers.

"Ah, good, the youngster is learning that her purpose is to kill."

Yeah, we figured that out, and we knew by then how to be good army privates. We could dig nice deep holes; we could follow orders. We knew how to unjam an M1, we knew to take care of our feet, we knew how to walk point on patrol. Mostly we knew what smart privates always figure out: stick close to your sergeant, because that's your mama, your daddy, and your big brother all rolled into one.

But here's one of the nasty little twists that come in war: if you don't manage to get wounded or dead, they'll promote you. And then, before you're even close to ready, you are the sergeant. You're the one the green kids are sticking to, and you're the only thing keeping those fools alive. Right when you start to get good at following, they want you to lead.

Some of us made that leap, some didn't. Not every good private makes a good sergeant.

But enough of all that; what about the war itself? Shall I remind you where we were in the narrative, Gentle Reader?

After Kasserine, the army in its wisdom got General Frendendall the hell away from the shooting war, and it turned the mess over to General George Patton, "Old Blood-and-Guts." He and his British counterpart, General Montgomery, finished off the exhausted remains of the German Afrika Korps and their Italian buddies and sent General Rommel back to Hitler to explain his failure.

Everyone knew North Africa had just been the first round; we knew we were moving on, but we didn't know where to. Back to Britain to prepare for the final invasion? To Sardinia? Greece? The South of France? Being soldiers, we lived on scuttlebutt, none of it accurate.

Turned out the first answer was Sicily.

Sicily is a big, hot, dusty, stony, hard-hearted island that's been conquered by just about every empire in the history of the Mediterranean: Athenians, Carthaginians, Phoenicians, Romans, Normans, you name it, and now it was our turn to conquer it. And damned if we didn't just do it.

This is the story of three young women who fought in the greatest war in human history: Frangie Marr, an undersized colored girl from Tulsa, Oklahoma who loved animals; time after time she ran into the thick of the fight, not to kill but to save lives. Rainy Schulterman, a Jewish girl from New York City with a gift for languages and a ruthless determination to destroy Nazis. And Rio Richlin, an underage white farm girl from Northern California who could not manage her love life and never was quite sure why she was in this war, not until we reached the camps anyway, but she could sure kill the hell out of Krauts.

They didn't win the war alone, those three, nor did the rest of us, but we all did our part and we didn't disgrace ourselves or let our brothers and sisters down, which is all any soldier can aspire to.

That and getting home alive.

PART I

1

RIO RICHLIN—CAMP ZIGZAG, TUNISIA, NORTH AFRICA

"What was it like?" Jenou asks. "That first time? What did you feel?"

Rio Richlin sighs wearily.

Rio and Jenou Castain, best friends for almost their entire lives, lie face up on a moth-eaten green blanket spread over the hood of a burned-out German half-track, heads propped up against the slit windows, legs dangling down in front of the armor-covered radiator. The track is sleeker than the American version, lower in profile, normally a very useful vehicle. But this particular German half-track had been hit by a passing Spitfire some weeks earlier, so it is riddled with holes you could stick a thumb into. The bogie wheels driving the track are splayed out, and both tracks have been dragged off and are now in use as a relatively clean "sidewalk" leading to the HQ administrative tent.

The road might once have been indifferently paved

but has now been chewed to gravel by passing tanks, the ubiquitous deuce-and-a-half trucks, jeeps, half-tracks, bulldozers, and tanker trucks. It runs beside a vast field of reddish sand and loose gravel that now seems to have become something like a farm field with olive drab tents as its crop. The tents extend in long, neat rows made untidy by the way the tent sides have all been rolled up, revealing cots and sprawled GIs in sweat-soaked T-shirts and boxer shorts. Here and there are extinguished camp-fires, oil drums filled with debris, other oil drums shot full of holes and mounted on rickety platforms to make field showers, stacks of jerry cans, wooden crates, and pallets—some broken up to feed the fires.

The air smells of sweat, oil, smoke, cordite, and cig-arettes, with just a hint of fried Spam. There are the constant rumbles and coughing roars of passing vehicles, and the multitude of sounds made by any large group of people, plus the outraged shouts of NCOs, curses and blasphemies, and more laughter than one might expect.

At the edge of the camp some men and one or two women are playing softball with bats, balls, and gloves assembled from family care packages. It's possible that the rules of this game are not quite those of games played at Yankee Stadium, since there is some tripping and tack-ling going on.

Both Rio and Jenou wear their uniform trousers rolled

up to above the knee, and sleeveless olive drab T-shirts. Cat Preeling, fifty feet away and playing a game of horse-shoes with Tilo Suarez, is the only female GI with the nerve to strip down to bra and boxers. She's a beefy girl with a cigarette hanging from her downturned mouth. Tilo, like many of the off-duty men, wears only his box-ers and boots, showing off a taut, olive-complected body that Jenou would be watching much more closely if only Tilo were six inches taller.

The bra and boxers look is a bit too daring for Rio and Jenou, but Cat seems to have a way of deflecting unwanted male attention, like she's wearing a sign that reads: Don't bother. Even the ever-amorous Tilo is content to toss horseshoes with her, though the shoes in question are actually brass rings roughly cut from discarded 155 brass and the peg is a bayonet.

Rio and Jenou both have brown-tanned faces, necks, and forearms, but the rest of them blazes a lurid white with just a tinge of pink where the skin is beginning to burn.

"What was what like?" Rio repeats the question slowly. She has a wet sock laid over her eyes to afford some shade. There is a half-empty bottle of Coca-Cola beside her. It was almost cold once and now is the temperature of hot tea. Jenou has a book held up to block the sun, *The Heart Is a Lonely Hunter*, in a paperback edition.

It is the summer of 1943 in Tunisia, and it is hot. Desert hot. Completely immobile—except when they swat at a fly—both young women are still sweating.

"You know," Jenou insists. "The first time. I'm just trying to get an idea."

"What are you, writing a book?" Rio says sharply. "Suddenly you're reading books and now you're trying to plumb the depths of my soul?"

"My usual appetite for fashion and Hollywood gossip isn't being satisfied," Jenou says, adopting a light, bantering lilt before restating her question in a more serious tone.

Rio sighs. "I don't know, Jen." She pronounces the name with a soft *j*, like *zh*. Jenou's name is inspired by the word *ingenue*, a perfectly inappropriate reference point for Jenou, who is far from being the innocent the name suggests.

Jenou is blond, with hair cut short to just below the ear. General Patton has decreed that all female soldiers will have hair cut to above the bottom of their earlobe. The general is improvising—army regulations have not quite caught up with the realities of female soldiers. In addition to being blond, Jenou is quite pretty, just shy of beautiful, and has a pinup's body.

Jenou remains silent, knowing the pressure will build on Rio to say something. And of course she's right.

"It was . . ." Rio searches for a word picture, a metaphor, something that will convey enough meaning that Jenou will not feel the need to ask anymore. Thinking about it takes her back to that moment. To the sound of Sergeant Cole's voice yelling, *Shoot!*

Richlin! Suarez! lay down some fugging fire!

Rio remembers it in detail. It had been as cold then as it is hot now. Her breathing had become irregular: a panicky burst followed by a leaden *thud-thud-thud.*

She remembers lining up the sights of her M1 Garand. She remembers the Italian soldier. And the pressure of her finger on the trigger. And the way she slowed her breathing, the way she shut out everything, every extraneous sound, every irrelevant emotion. The way she saw the target, a man in a tan uniform lined up perfectly on the sights.

The way her lungs and heart seemed to freeze along with time itself.

The moment when her right index finger applied the necessary seven-point-five pounds of pressure and the stock kicked back against her shoulder.

Bang.

The way she had first thought that he had just tripped. The way the Italian had seemed to be frozen in time, on his knees, maybe just tripped, maybe just caught his toe on a rock and . . . And then the way the man fell back.

From the *New York Times* bestselling author of the Gone series

 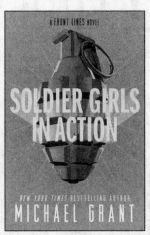 

"A magnificent alternate history."

—Elizabeth Wein, *New York Times* bestselling author
of *Code Name Verity*

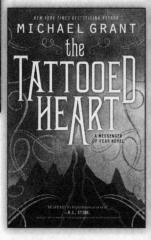

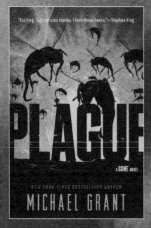

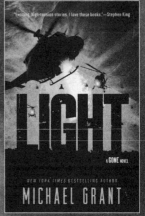

Confessions d'Amour
Anne-Marie Villefranche

Confessions d'Amour is the culmination of Villefranche's comically indecent stories about her friends in 1920s' Paris.

Anne-Marie Villefranche invites you to enter an intoxicating world where men and women arrange their love affairs with skill and style. This is a world where illicit encounters are as smooth as a silk stocking, and where sexual secrets are kept in confidence only until a betrayal can be turned to advantage. Here we follow the adventures of Gabrielle de Michoux, the beautiful young widow who contrives to be maintained in luxury by a succession of well-to-do men, Marcel Chalon, ready for any adventure so long as he can go home to Mama afterwards, Armand Budin, who plunges into a passionate love affair with his cousin's estranged wife, Madelein Beauvais, and Yvonne Hiver who is married with two children while still embracing other, younger lovers.

"An erotic tribute to the Paris of yesteryear that will delight modern readers."—*The Observer*

Ironwood
by Don Winslow

The harsh reality of disinheritance and poverty vanish from the world of our young narrator, James, when he discovers he's in line for a choice position at an exclusive and very strict school for girls. Ironwood becomes for him a fantastic dream world where discipline knows few boundaries, and where his role as master affords him free reign with the willing, well-trained and submissive young beauties in his charge. As overseer of Ironwood, Cora Blasingdale is well-equipped to keep her charges in line. Under her guidance the saucy girls are put through their paces and tamed. And for James, it seems, life has just begun.

Girl's Reformatory
by Anonymous

From behind the locked doors of a girl's reformatory in Victorian England, scandalous escapades of zealous reformers and their wards are revealed. In this most unusual institution, the wanton beauties Elaine, Sally, Michele, Jane, and others atone for their sins under the supervision of worthy gentlemen of the upper classes.

66 Chapters About 33 Women
Michael Hemmingson

An erotic tour de force, 66 Chapters About 33 Women weaves a complicated web of erotic connections between 33 women and their lovers. Granting each woman 2 vignettes, Hemmingson examines their sexual peccadilloes, and creates a veritable survey course on the possibilities of erotic fiction.

The Man of Her Dream
Briony Shilton

Spun from her subconscious's submissive nature, a woman dreams of a man like no other, one who will subject her to pain and pressure, passion and lust. She searches the waking world, combing her personal history and exploring fantasy and fact, until she finds this master. It is he, through an initiation like no other, who takes her to the limits of her submissive nature and on to the extremes of pure sexual joy.

Shadow Lane VI
by Eve Howard

In this enticing volume, a young girl discovers her sophisticated uncle publishes a spanking magazine; a stubborn beauty proves a challenge for a bookstore manager; and a wife's latent interest in spanking is instantly awakened while she and her husband are on vacation.

Order These Selected Blue Moon Titles

Souvenirs From a Boarding School . .$7.95
The Captive $7.95
Ironwood Revisited $7.95
The She-Slaves of Cinta Vincente . . .$7.95
The Architecture of Desire $7.95
The Captive II $7.95
Shadow Lane $7.95
Services Rendered $7.95
Shadow Lane III $7.95
My Secret Life $9.95
The Eye of the Intruder $7.95
Net of Sex $7.95
Captive V $7.95
Cocktails $7.95
Girl School $7.95
The New Story of O $7.95
Shadow Lane IV $7.95
Beauty in the Birch $7.95
The Blue Train $7.95
Wild Tattoo $7.95
Ironwood Continued $7.95
Transfer Point Nice $7.95
Souvenirs From a Boarding School . .$7.95
Secret Talents $7.95
Shadow Lane V $7.95
Bizarre Voyage $7.95

Red Hot $7.95
Images of Ironwood $7.95
Tokyo Story $7.95
The Comfort of Women $7.95
Disciplining Jane $7.95
The Passionate Prisoners $7.95
Doctor Sex $7.95
Shadow Lane VI $7.95
Girl's Reformatory $7.95
The City of One-Night Stands $7.95
A Hunger in Her Flesh $7.95
Flesh On Fire $7.95
Hard Drive $7.95
Secret Talents $7.95
The Captive's Journey $7.95
Elena Raw $7.95
La Vie Parisienne $7.95
Fetish Girl $7.95
Road Babe $7.95
Violetta $7.95
Story of O $5.95
Dark Matter $7.95
Ironwood $7.95
Body Job $7.95
Arousal $7.95
The Blue Moon Erotic Reader II . . .$15.95

ORDER FORM
Attach a separate sheet for additional titles.

Title   Quantity   Price

_____ ____ _____
_____ ____ _____
_____ ____ _____
_____ ____ _____

Shipping and Handling (see charges below)   _____
Sales tax (in CA and NY)   _____
Total   _____

Name _____
Address _____
City _____ State _____ Zip _____
Daytime telephone number _____

❑ Check   ❑ Money Order   (US dollars only. No COD orders accepted.)

Credit Card # _____ Exp. Date _____

❑ MC   ❑ VISA   ❑ AMEX

Signature _____
(if paying with a credit card you must sign this form.)

Shipping and Handling charges:*

Domestic: $4 for 1st book, $.75 each additional book. International: $5 for 1st book, $1 each additional book
*rates in effect at time of publication. Subject to Change.

Mail order to Publishers Group West, Attention: Order Dept., 1700 Fourth St., Berkeley, CA 94710, or fax to (510) 528-3444.

PLEASE ALLOW 4-6 WEEKS FOR DELIVERY. ALL ORDERS SHIP VIA 4TH CLASS MAIL.

Look for Blue Moon Books at your favorite local bookseller
or from your favorite online bookseller.